DENNISON'S WAR

We are fighting a new war. Around the globe, the terrorists, the exploiters, the hatemongers are infesting the corpus of society like cancerous cells.

This enemy recognizes no Geneva Conventions, no rules or legalities. They observe no law but the law of the jungle. They walk roughshod over humanity, smug in their brutality.

Until that moment when they look into the bottomless black hole of their own mortality, and see the true meaning of terror.

My people know that order and law will not stop the lawless. Total victory is our sole objective. We return terror to the terrorist; we fling savagery into the face of the savage. To keep the cancer from spreading throughout the body of the world, we cut out the infected patches like rotten spots on an apple. We are the surgeons of freedom.

We are Dennison's Warriors.

DENNISON'S WAR

Adam Lassiter

BANTAM BOOKS

TORONTO · NEW YORK · LONDON · SYDNEY · AUCKLAND

DENNISON'S WAR
A Bantam Book / December 1984

ISBN 0-553-24493-0

Published simultaneously in the United States and Canada

Bantam Books are published by Bantam Books, Inc. Its trademark,
consisting of the words "Bantam Books" and the portrayal of a rooster,
is Registered in U.S. Patent and Trademark Office and in other
countries. Marca Registrada. Bantam Books, Inc., 666 Fifth Avenue,
New York, New York 10103.

PRINTED IN THE UNITED STATES OF AMERICA

H   0 9 8 7 6 5 4 3 2 1

For Terry Webster
who shared the first adventure
and
thanks to Jim Nisbet
for several editorial suggestions and one very funny line

In war there is no second prize for runner-up.

—OMAR BRADLEY

Rome, Italy
The 23rd of March

George Dial stroked the butt of the Beretta and thought about killing the woman.

She looked like hell. Her cotton nightgown had been canary yellow sixty hours earlier, but now it was smeared with dirt and blood and the woman's own eliminations. The limp, befouled cloth was rucked up to the woman's waist so she sat with her bare bottom on the varnished seat of the straight-backed kitchen chair, and there was more blood on the insides of her thighs. The front of the garment was ripped open and one breast peeked out, the nipple rigid with the woman's terror even in her semiconsciousness.

The woman's hair, naturally pale blond, was now the dirty brownish shade of flat beer. It hung over her shoulders in limp, matted ropes, and nervous sweat pasted one thick strand to her cheek. Her face was purple and green and yellow with bruises; a livid reddish lump over her left eye had swollen it completely shut. Her nose was so badly broken that it was pushed over to one side of her disfigured face, a gelid lump of pulverized cartilage with an oversized stain of black-red dried blood beneath it, all over one corner of her mouth and down her chin. Her lips were bruised and bloodied and puffed up fat.

George Dial smiled thinly. The woman was the work of the Wops; that was the term Dial and his partner had years before adopted to refer to their Italian sometime employers. The slur had a certain dull, plodding sound to it that perfectly characterized the witless Italians. Their atavistic pleasures were not his. Dial recognized and acknowledged the occasion-

1

al utility of torture, but he always claimed to be above taking pleasure in abuse for its own sake. Only the cleanliness of the kill held attraction for George Dial.

He moved to the sliding glass door on the other side of the bedroom, pushed it open far enough to slip out on the balcony, and quickly shut it behind him. At the railing he rolled his head around on his neck, stretching the cramped muscles, then took several deep breaths. The air tasted of exhaust fumes. Below, on the Via del Gladiatoro, cars inched along bumper to bumper to a perpetual chorus of impatient horns. Italian drivers seemed genetically unable to sit behind the wheel without one hand continually pressed on the horn. It occurred to Dial that an instantaneous solution to Rome's traffic congestion and pollution would be legislation banning the installation of horns in automobiles—because without one, no Italian would leave his driveway.

Dial went back into the apartment, latching the door behind him. The Wops looked up expectantly, and one of them said, "Che ora è?" for the third time in twenty minutes. Dial glanced at his watch: a few minutes after noon. He did not bother answering the Wop.

The woman had not moved, but the man—her husband—was conscious again. His chair was positioned with its back to hers, and the noose of rope around his neck was strung taut to the coils around his wrists so that his head was pulled back and he could not rotate it more than a few degrees in either direction. He wore sky blue pajamas and stank of sweat and urine. A gash in his forehead was surrounded with the livid redness of infection, and the blood below was caked thickly enough to glue his right eye shut.

One of the Wops muttered something to his partner, and the other man snickered.

"Shut up," Dial snapped, mostly to be exercising his authority.

Nominally they—or at least their organization—were his employers, but when Dial and his partner took a job they were in charge right down the line, and no arguments. Jesus, Dial thought, imagine depending for logistics and planning—or common sense, for that matter—on the Wops.

"Che ora è?" the Italian said again.

Dial looked elaborately at his watch, smiled pleasantly at the Italian, and said in English, "Fuck you."

The Italian started to reply and then thought better of it. His name was Guillermo, and Dial could tell him from his buddy only by the old half-moon knife scar carved into his left cheek. Guillermo had watched through wide dark eyes, his face flushed with excitement, while his buddy—Pietro, he called himself—had beaten the crap out of the woman and then fucked her limp body. But Guillermo's pleasure came from the violence of the act, not whatever perverse sexuality it might have held. When Guillermo's turn came, he chose the husband, panting like a dog as he stripped down the blue pajama bottoms and parted the coarse, hairy cheeks of the guy's ass.

In the front room the buzzer sounded.

"Stay here," Dial said to the Wops. He went through a pantry into a small living room. Near the door was an intercom. He pressed its button and said, "Yeah?"

"I have your order." The voice was thin, electromechanical, distorted by the cheap intercom speaker, but Dial recognized it as Helena Frome. Still, he went through the password ritual. Taking care that way was what separated the pros from the deceased.

"The laundry?"

"No," Helena said. "This is from the grocer."

Dial pushed the button that unlocked the lobby door below, held it for a few seconds, then unlocked the apartment's door and went back into the bedroom. The Wops looked at him with eager anticipation. Dial ignored them.

The eyes of the bound man in the chair were dark and dull as coal. Dial met his gaze, and after a moment the man looked away. In a few minutes Dial would get to kill the man, and the woman as well—or he would be twenty-five thousand dollars richer. Either way would be fine. Still, when he thought about killing them—the clean finality of the bullet that sliced through muscle and organ and bone the way lightning cleaves a giant oak—when he pictured it, Dial felt a cool finger of delicious shudder tracing along the ridge of his spine, its tingle as tantalizing as a lover's caress.

In the other room the door opened, and a moment later

Helena Frome came into the bedroom. She wore her usual hard frown, which meant nothing in particular. Everything about her was hard-edged. She was skinny, sharp-boned, as angular as a Cubist painting, though her shoulders were disproportionately broad, nearly as broad as a man's. She had high cheekbones, and her eyes were dark and depthless, opaque as drapery. Her hair was the shade of dried grass and cut in a pageboy.

She was carrying a shopping bag with the stylized "Venuto's" logo on the side. She gestured with it at the Wops. "They paid up," she said crossly. "No need for anyone to piss his pants." She upended the bag over one of the narrow twin beds. American currency cascaded out.

"I took our cut," she told the Wops. "This is the rest —two hundred thousand dollars. Up the revolution," she added unpleasantly.

Dial knew what she was thinking: it was like pissing down a rat hole. Twenty-five grand to each of them, and four times that much to the Italians. Ah well, Dial thought philosophically, that was free enterprise. The Wops would take their cut down to their friendly neighborhood gunrunner, who as everyone including the Wops knew was one step removed from the resident KGB chief of station. The gunrunner would cheerfully supply whatever the Wops were into this month— AK-47 Russian submachine guns, C-4 plastic explosive, perhaps a SAM-7 shoulder-launched heat-seeking missile for taking out the odd passenger plane—and the Wops would go merrily on their way to grease a few more capitalists, politicians, Americans, or other citizens. But if it weren't for these dudes, and their buddies in the Red Brigades, the Organization, and all the rest of the terrorist hotshots operating in Europe, where would a couple of good old American folks like Dial and Helena Frome find honest labor?

Dial looked at the money and felt the slightest bit of disappointment. He touched again at the butt of the Beretta holstered under his left arm. Well, there went the real fun.

The Wops were pawing through the money and muttering to each other, talking too fast for Dial to follow. Probably Guillermo was telling Pietro about all the boys the money would buy for him, and what he planned to do to them. At times like this, the Wops never failed to turn Dial's stomach.

"Don't think we haven't had a good time," Helena said, "but let's get this wrapped up." The Wops did not look up. "Come on, George. The sooner we get out of here, the better. The smell of garlic and hair oil always did make me gag."

The man in the chair whitened when Dial pressed the release button and the six-inch blade of his knife snapped into view. As he sawed at the rope around the man's wrists, Dial let the knife slip, so the razor-sharp tempered steel gouged into the side of the man's hand. Blood wormed down and dripped from the tips of his fingers, dappling the rust-colored carpet. Helena was untying the insensate woman.

Dial pulled the noose roughly over the man's head and ripped the compress off his mouth. The man twisted around in his chair and nearly lost his balance.

He looked at his wife and let out an anguished moan.

"Uh-uh," Dial cautioned softly.

The guy twisted back to glare hate at him. He was in his late twenties and had been handsome before the Wops went to work on him. It would be a while before he was handsome again.

"Be cool," Dial said. "Ten minutes from now you'll be on the street again, and by this time tomorrow all of this will only be a bad dream."

The woman's head rolled on her shoulders, and she began to whimper. The man looked desperately to her and tried to stand, but his legs would not support his weight. He sank back into the chair. "You goddamned bastard," he muttered.

Dial shrugged. Guillermo and Pietro were pawing through the cash on the bed like bag ladies going through a trash can.

"Watch it, George," Helena said.

The guy had made it to his feet this time. He wiped at the crusted blood over his right eye, then turned and bent, moving stiff as a robot. It took him four tries to lift the chair over his head. Dial watched him with abstract fascination, like a scientist monitoring a white rat in a maze.

The man took a step toward him.

"George," Helena said, in a low warning voice.

The man took another painful step. Behind him the woman tried to say something, but her broken mouth would not work, and the words came out as garbled as child's gibberish.

The man stopped and stared down at her. Her legs were splayed, and there was a seep of fresh blood between them.

The man let out a pitiful agonized cry and lunged at George Dial. Dial sidestepped, and the man went down on one knee, dropping the chair.

"That's about enough," Dial said.

The man tried to grab Dial's leg, missed, raised himself to try again.

Dial took one step backward and shot him in the face.

At a range of about two feet the 9mm slug made a crater in the guy's skull as big as a fist. The guy dropped prone to the carpet, and for a few seconds his heart continued to pump spurts of glistening blood from the exit wound in the back of his head.

The woman in the chair opened her mouth to scream, and Helena punched her below the ear, close-fisted. The woman's eyes went glassy, and her head dropped on her bare chest.

Helena straightened and said, "You jerk. You goddamned stupid jerk."

"He was trying to—"

"You did not have to kill him, George. As you goddamned well know."

"What the hell?"

Helena advanced on him, and he took an involuntary step backwards. The Wops were watching; this was more fun than the money. Kicking the shit out of the man and the woman, raping them—that was old news. But this—Dial getting put down by the woman—this sort of humiliation gave the Wops a grand kick.

Dial turned the Beretta on them and said, "What the fuck are you staring at?"

Guillermo laughed and Dial's finger whitened on the trigger.

Helena grabbed Dial's arm and whipped him around to face her. "You did not have to kill him, George." Her voice was as cold as December.

"What's the difference?" Dial snapped.

"The difference, George, is that you have just put us out

of business. They *paid*, George: try to get that through your goddamned skull. We've got the money—but now we can't deliver the goods, thanks to you. Which means next time they won't pay at all. They won't pay because we'll have a rep as the kind who put people away, payment or no payment. Is that simple enough for you, George? Does any of this penetrate?"

Dial swallowed and nodded at the woman and said, "What about her?"

"She doesn't matter now, does she, George? We might as well let the Wops have her."

"All right, all right. But let's get her out of here."

"Now there's an intelligent idea, George. What a surprise."

"That's enough, Helena." There was a limit. But Dial sounded like a petulant child, even to himself.

Helena turned her back on him and started a quick cleanup check of the apartment. Dial went into the closet-sized bathroom and splashed cold water on his face. When he came out, Guillermo and Pietro were standing over the woman. The filthy nightgown was lying in tattered pieces on the carpet around her chair. Guillermo lit a cigarette. Pietro undid his pants, pulled them down to his knees. He slapped the woman twice, not too hard. Her eyelids fluttered.

"Let's go, George," Helena said from the other room.

Pietro grabbed a fistful of the woman's ratty hair and pushed her mottled face into his crotch.

"George!"

Reluctantly, Dial left the bedroom. Helena was waiting impatiently by the apartment's door, her fists on her hips. He hoped she would not make a big stink over him killing the guy. He always hated it when she came down on him. With other people he felt strong, secure, in control; other people were too weak to pose a threat. Only Helena could make him doubt himself. She knew all the ways to get to him, to make him feel stupid. He hated that worst of all. When women made him feel stupid it depressed the hell out of him.

Fisk, North Dakota
The 1st of April

In the Stockman Bar two men were grappling on the floor, beer-dampened sawdust clotting on their oil-stained coveralls. One of them got his mitt around a thick-bottomed beer mug and slammed it against the side of his opponent's head, so hard the glass shattered, leaving only a handle in his fist. The guy he hit went stiff as a plank. That ended the show; men clustered two-deep at the bar turned away and went back to their drinking.

Three doors down, two teenaged girls were stationed in front of what fifty years ago had been the finest—and only—hotel in town. One wore a blond wig, satin jogging shorts, a halter top, and green eye shadow. There were goose bumps on her bare stomach. The other wore a strapless dress with an elastic top that ended just north of her nipples and a hem that rode just south of her crotch and teetery spike heels that she did not seem accustomed to. A guy in coveralls came up to the second girl, said something, and showed her a greenback. The teenager smiled vacantly and wobbled up the stairs ahead of him. Across the street a guy was puking in the gutter. It was a few minutes before nine in the morning.

Three years earlier the population of Fisk, on the western edge of the North Dakota plains, was three hundred fifty-three, most of whom knew each other by first name. There was an International Harvester tractor dealership, three grain elevators, two bars, the Fisk Mercantile, a Thrif-T-Buy supermarket, and one bank, the First Fisk Trust. In those days there was nothing twenty-five miles in any direction but gently rolling rangeland, dotted here and there by herds of grazing cattle.

But that was before the big oil companies decided the Williston Basin might be worth a wildcat hole or two. As it turned out, the gamble paid off—in spades. There was an ocean of crude petroleum down there between the rock strata, and Fisk was sitting on top of it.

The current population of Fisk was better than three thousand, most of whom came from Texas or Oklahoma and would be going back when the basin ran dry. Twenty-five miles in any direction the rangeland was dotted with haphazardly laid out clusters of seedy, secondhand house trailers and copses of stark drilling rigs. The drills were manned continuously; the average roughneck worked a ninety-hour week and took home around two thousand dollars for his labors. There were now fourteen saloons, twelve basement gambling dens, and six whorehouses, all of them open for business twenty-four hours a day, seven days a week. The new Chevy dealership was selling an average of two pickup trucks daily. Seven motels, nine cafes, a jewelry store, an X-rated movie theater, and a McDonalds were doing a brisk business. The First Fisk Trust was still the only bank, but its assets had increased tenfold.

On the first and fifteenth of each month, when the roughnecks came in to cash their paychecks, the vaults of the First Fisk Trust held approximately three million dollars in currency.

The clock atop the new county building began to sound nine o'clock. The man who had been puking got unsteadily to his feet, and the head cashier of the First Fisk Trust unlocked the bank's front door.

Ninety seconds later six men entered. Each was dressed identically in black: turtleneck sweater, slacks, sneakers, wool cap, and dime-store mask. Five carried M16A1 automatic carbines. The sixth had an Ingram MAC-11 machine pistol hanging from a lanyard around his neck; this man was a good half-foot taller than any of the others. A suppressor was threaded on the muzzle of his weapon.

Two roughnecks in greasy Big Smith overalls were standing at one of the four teller windows. One of them turned and started to say, "What the hell . . . ?" There was a wad of currency in his fist.

The man with the Ingram swung it up, and the gun belched discreetly. The roughneck stumbled back and went down, his head striking the edge of the teller counter with a sickening thud. A dark crimson stain began to spread over the bib of his coveralls. Greenbacks were scattered like autumn leaves all around him.

There were three tellers—two young women and a man in horn-rimmed glasses—and a hatchet-faced woman sat at a desk in the space behind them. One of the tellers opened her mouth to scream. The leader swung the Ingram's black snout on her.

The woman shut her mouth.

"No one moves." The leader's voice was flat, toneless. "Hands in sight at all times. No talk, no arguments, no silent alarms, no funny business." The other five men flanked him, sweeping the room with their M16s.

Behind the hatchet-faced woman a door opened and a middle-aged man in a three-piece suit came into the area behind the tellers. He looked at the six men in black and shook his head in denial, as if he had encountered a long-dead relative.

"Hold it right there," the leader barked.

The banker hesitated for a heartbeat; he was a man whose daily profession involved shrewd human judgment and critical decisions. This time he made the wrong one.

The banker spun and plunged for the sanctuary of his office. The Ingram burped again, and the banker's head snapped forward, blood smearing the back of it as his face plowed a furrow in the carpet.

"Jesus, Greaves," one of the other men said. "Creed didn't say to—"

The leader turned and shot the speaker in the middle of the chest.

Almost before the dead raider hit the floor, another of the men in black had dropped to one knee. He pulled a Fairbairn commando knife from a belt sheath. The blade was nine inches long, serrated near the haft, and honed so finely that a single hard chop separated the dead man's hands from the wrists.

Cutting off the corpse's head took only slightly longer.

The three other men vaulted the teller counter. The hatchet-faced woman shrank into her desk chair as if trying to make herself invisible, but they ignored her. The door of the walk-in vault was slightly ajar. The men spent exactly fifty seconds inside, and each exited toting a green plastic garbage sack.

By then the fourth man had finished stuffing the two hands and the dripping head into a similar bag. Blood an inch deep was pooled on the marble floor around the corpse. One of the women tellers had passed out, and the oilfield roughneck had vomited all over the front of his coveralls.

"Let's move," the leader snapped.

Across the street from the bank, a deputy sheriff named Webster came out of the Stockman Bar and Cafe with a styrofoam cup of black coffee. He got into his double-parked patrol car and was prying off the plastic lid when a half-ton pickup truck with the tailgate down and swinging loose pulled into the loading zone in front of the First Fisk Trust.

A moment later, five men dressed in black and carrying military automatic weapons came out of the bank and piled into the back of the pickup.

Deputy Webster spewed a mouthful of coffee into his windshield, dropped the rest of the hot liquid in his lap, yowled with frustration and pain, and swore as he jerked the patrol car into gear. The pickup pulled out of the loading zone. Deputy Webster slewed around in a tire-squealing U-turn, clipped the rear fender of a parked Ford Bronco, then gunned after the pickup.

It was making no effort to escape, and Webster was able to catch it just beyond the city limits. The hell with them, Webster thought; he was county. He hit the siren and flashers.

A full thirty-two-round clip of 5.56mm slugs exploded through the windshield and separated Deputy Webster's head from his shoulders.

The patrol car swerved across the oncoming lane onto the shoulder, straightened of its own accord to cling to the edge of the pavement for another fifty yards, then cut hard left and plunged into the barrow pit. Its momentum flipped it out again, and the car rolled twice more before coming to rest on its roof. The siren continued to wail like a lost soul.

A half mile further on, the paved road turned to gravel. The pickup hit it, and a spume of dust rose up and swallowed it whole.

BOOK
ONE

Dennison's People

Chapter One

"I want them dead." The man's voice was fervent but steady. He leaned forward and placed both palms flat on Dennison's desk. "I want them to know that they are going to die, and I want them to know why."

"Would you like them to suffer first?"

The man looked up sharply, unsure if he were being needled, and if so what should he do about it. "I have been given to understand that if I pay you enough money you will see that they are killed. If that's not correct, let me know right now and we won't waste any more of each other's time."

The man sitting across the desk from Dennison was a fit-looking sixty. He had a full head of salt-and-pepper hair trimmed a little too short to be stylish, and he wore a dark suit with discreet pinstriping and a rep tie in three tones of gray. The suit fit him well; it was expensive, and cut to look it.

But there was something about the man that did not sit easily with the manicure and the cream silk shirt. The elegant clothing did not comfortably suit him, as if he had started out years before selling whole life insurance policies or late model one-owner cars and had never completely overcome his roots.

His name, Samuel Stanhope, was one Dennison knew. Until three weeks before he had been the United States' ambassador to Italy. But by profession Stanhope was a businessman, not a diplomat. During the past twenty-five years, Stanhope Export had become the largest broker of American trade and technology in Europe, with offices in fourteen major cities and headquarters in Rome, where Stanhope had made his home.

Dennison fingered a manila folder on the desk before him

but did not open it. He had already studied the four pages of computer printout inside.

On his appointment as ambassador, Stanhope had relinquished control of Stanhope Export to his son Peter, twenty-eight. Five weeks earlier, Peter Stanhope and his wife Janet were kidnapped and held for ransom of two hundred fifty thousand dollars. Three days after the ransom was paid, their bodies were found in an apartment in the Esposizione Universale district of Rome.

"If you are wondering if I can afford—" Stanhope began.

"I'm not," Dennison said.

"Then you will do what I want."

"That depends."

"On what?"

"On what you want."

For a moment Stanhope looked about to protest. Then he stood abruptly. The only window in the room ran from the floor to within a few feet of the ceiling and was twice as wide as a door. Stanhope stood at it, his hands clasped behind his back.

"They mutilated her before they let her die. Did you know that?"

"Yes," Dennison said to Stanhope's back. "I'm sorry."

"I've spent half a lifetime in Rome. I know my way around, and I've got friends. I know who to talk to, how to find things out. My people asked around." Stanhope turned. "Have you ever heard of George Dial and Helena Frome?"

"Yes."

Stanhope frowned, as if that were the wrong answer. "What do you know about them?"

"Are you testing me?"

"Maybe."

Dennison was a master of the smile, and he gave one to Stanhope now. In the smile was diffidence, compassion, warmth, empathy. Stanhope visibly relaxed. He moved around to stand behind the armchair in which he had been sitting.

"George Dial and Helena Frome surfaced in 1969," Dennison began. Stanhope nodded, unconscious of his own supportive gesture. "On April ninth of that year, radical Harvard students, including Dial and Frome, occupied University Hall. They were rousted the next morning, but it was the beginning of a period of intense student activism. Most of it took the form of pamphleteering, picketing, demonstrations, and so on, but that was too tame for Dial and Frome. Later that month they formed a spinoff from the mainstream radical organization. They called it the Progressive Democratic Front."

"Is this all germane?"

"That's up to you, Mr. Stanhope. The PDF didn't attract much attention until September of the same year, when Dial and Frome bombed a Selective Service office in Somerville. The explosion killed two draft board members, a secretary, and a pregnant fifteen-year-old who was apparently asking directions to the County Health Department office. Dial and Frome claimed responsibility and then disappeared, and so did their PDF.

"In 1975," Dennison said, "Dial and Frome were spotted in Dublin. In subsequent years they are alleged to have worked with the Provisional IRA, the Baader-Meinhof gang in West Germany, the Red Brigades, and the Popular Front for the Liberation of Palestine. In 1978 they seem to have attended a course of instruction at one of Wadi Haddad's training camps outside Aden in South Yemen, under the tutelage of agents of Cuba's DGI and the Soviet KGB. The specific reports of their activities range from eyewitness to hearsay, but their number and consistency confirms the general outline."

Dennison toyed with the manila folder. "Dial and the Frome woman specialize in violent terrorist actions, with particular expertise in urban guerilla tactics. They no longer profess any personal ideology, and they'll work for whoever pays their price."

"Something like you," Stanhope said unpleasantly.

Dennison stopped smiling.

Stanhope looked away. "How do you know all this?" he asked the window.

"It's my business."

"Exactly what is your business, Dennison?"

Dennison came around his desk. In the chair he seemed sluggish, perhaps somewhat overweight, but he moved with economy and grace. He closed the drapes, and the room went dim as twilight.

"You came here to tell me a story, Mr. Stanhope," Dennison said. "Why don't you get on with it."

Stanhope followed Dennison with his eyes as Dennison took his seat again. Dennison's chair had thick cushions upholstered in dark leather worked soft as a nun's skin. Dennison slumped slightly and clasped his hands over his stomach. His eyes were half shut, and he did not move as Samuel Stanhope paced the office and told his tale.

George Dial and Helena Frome, Stanhope told Dennison, were working for an outfit that called itself the Feltrinelli Front, after Giangiacomo Feltrinelli, who was considered a martyr among the loosely knit confederation of Italian terrorist outfits that called itself the Organization. A book publisher and scion of one of Milan's most wealthy families, Feltrinelli was an active supporter of terrorist causes both financially and physically. In March of 1972, he blew himself into several hundred pieces while attempting to dynamite a high-tension pylon in the suburb of Segrate, north of Milan.

"A traitor to his class," Dennison said.

"The pylon wasn't even damaged." But then Stanhope looked at him more closely and said, "Huh?"

"Nothing."

Stanhope shook his head impatiently. "I spent money," he said. "I learned things."

According to his sources, Stanhope went on, Dial and Frome got nervous after murdering Peter and Janet Stanhope. Maybe they realized they'd compromised their credibility, or maybe they got word Stanhope was on their tail, and spending money. One source told Stanhope that the Organization itself had put out a contract on the two mercenaries, for fear the killing after the ransom was paid would damage the credibility of all terrorist groups. Stanhope laughed bitterly at that notion.

"I did confirm this," Stanhope said. "Within sixty hours of the murders, Dial and Frome had left Rome, heading south. To Sicily."

"And a rendezvous with the Mafia."

"How did you know that?"

"A lucky guess," Dennison murmured.

Stanhope frowned and went on: according to his Sicilian contacts, Dial and Frome arrived in Palermo on March 29, six days after the murders. Two days after that, the two hired killers disappeared, and Stanhope's people lost a definite trail. But there was talk—talk that the two were smuggled to New York, and into the care of the American branch of the Mob.

"What I don't understand," Stanhope said, "is why they would come here? Why not Libya or Cuba or somewhere in the Middle East, where they could burrow in with the rest of their kind?"

"Two reasons," Dennison said. "This country may have been the only place available to them. They broke the rules, and they might be on the outs with their terrorist support network. The Mafia is a different story; they'll work for whoever pays, and Dial and Frome would be able to pay plenty—with your money."

Stanhope nodded. "What's the second reason?"

"You tell me, Mr. Stanhope."

"They could operate here," he said slowly, considering the idea. "The U.S. would be the perfect playground for scum like Dial and Frome, because here we play by the rules. We call it democracy and due process; they call it a license to do what they damned well please." Stanhope's voice was rising. "Some fourteen-year-old street punk beats up an elderly lady and he gets his rights read to him, a lawyer we pay for, and a free ticket back to the streets, so he can do it again. A drug pusher taking down ten thousand a week never sees the inside of a jail because he can afford a slick mouthpiece who gets him off when a word is spelled wrong in the warrant. Whores and pimps are all over the street every hour of the day, and everyone knows what they are, including the cops, but we can't touch them. Because we play by the rules.

"The only rules for the Dials and Fromes of the world," Stanhope said, "are greed and violence. So in this country they could employ the same tactics they used in Europe, and while the Justice Department lawyers are paging through the statutes trying to figure out which one applies, Dial and Frome will be cutting a wide bloody track to wherever they please."

Stanhope looked narrowly at Dennison, slumped comfortably in his chair. "They tell me you make up your own rules, too, Dennison. Is that correct?"

"I do what I have to."

"Let me tell you how the system has dealt with Dial and Frome so far. When I got back I went to the State Department. I had been a United States ambassador a week earlier, but suddenly I was nobody. They were real sorry that someone had killed my kids, but I had to understand how it was. There were procedures and channels and the delicate world balance and the potential for international incidents. I got out of there quickly. I would have gone for someone's throat with my bare hands if I hadn't."

There was a fine sheen of sweat on Stanhope's forehead, although the room was cool. "Two days later I got a call from one of the men I'd talked to at State. He told me off the record that nothing would ever come of the official investigation. If I wanted results and was willing to pay for them, he told me to contact you."

"I see," Dennison said.

"You don't see." Stanhope's voice almost broke. "They shot my son in the face, from so close there was nothing left that looked human. When the bullet came out the back of his head it punched a hole as big as a saucer. They used a knife on Janet. First they used it on her face, enough to put her in an eternity of agony but not so much that she would pass out. They kept her conscious all the time. Then they used it on her body. They put it up inside her and watched the blood flow. They had the money; there was nothing to it beyond their pleasure. They thrill to torture like others thrill to love."

"Sit down, Mr. Stanhope," Dennison said.

Stanhope looked up at him. The older man was breathing a little hard, and there was a sudden blank look on his face, as if he'd forgotten for a moment where he was. He nodded and dropped into the plush armchair, as if suddenly weary beyond strength.

"My fee is five hundred thousand dollars," Dennison said in the same soft tone, "payable in advance. Once you hand over the money, you are out of the picture. I choose the methods, I choose the people, and I decide when the job is over. After you leave this office, the operation will not be aborted for any reason, even if you change your mind." Dennison's hooded eyes opened slightly wider. "Especially if you change your mind. I've got my people and my interests to protect, too."

"What assurances do I get?"

"None."

"I suppose you're going to tell me that you've never had a dissatisfied client."

"You could be the first, Stanhope." Dennison's reserves of patience were extensive but not infinite.

Stanhope stared hard, and Dennison met the gaze easily and with no further hint of annoyance. He had made his point, and it did not particularly matter to him if Stanhope walked out. He didn't particularly like the man, and there were plenty of other matters he could turn his attention to. There always would be.

Stanhope dipped a hand under his suitcoat and brought out a leather-covered checkbook.

"I want to see those two butchers dead." Stanhope began to write. "That's all there is to it."

Dennison smiled his faint smile. Stanhope was wrong. There was a great deal more to it, and Dennison meant to find out exactly what.

Chapter Two

To the west, on the other side of the deeply cut valley, the sun hovered a few degrees above the ridge line. For a time nothing moved except the snow melt–swollen water of the river in the valley's crease, barely visible a half mile below. Then two birds rose up from among the quaking aspen and ponderosa pine, wings out stiff and motionless, riding the invisible spiraling thermals, circling each other like adagio dancers.

Hawks? Dennison wondered. On the mantelpiece of the big stone fireplace that dominated the wall opposite the window, he found a pair of 7X binoculars in a scuffed leather case. He set rough focus, scanned the sky until the birds came into frame, and readjusted to bring them into sharp relief.

They were bald eagles, a male and a female. Dennison could make out the white feather skullcap and the matching bands near the tips of the majestically spread wings. As he watched, the larger male wheeled out of the thermal's draft, graceful as a spirit, and plummeted toward the valley floor, wings rigid, great beak thrust proudly forward. A few seconds later both eagles soared up from the trees again, beating at the air, then gliding away toward the ridge. Dennison did not try to catch them in the field of the binocs again. Before, the two great birds had been performing, but now the show was over and they were heading home for the evening. Dennison replaced the glasses in the leather case and was putting it back on the mantel when the door of his office opened.

Her name was Miss Paradise, and she stood six feet tall stark naked, six-two in heels. She carried her height with grace and aggressive pride; her poise was leonine. Her waist was breathlessly slim, and her legs seemed to go on forever. She carried two legal-sized folders crushed against breasts, which were full and high and not especially large.

Dennison showed her his faint smile. Miss Paradise enjoyed dressing-up games, so he never knew what to expect when she came into his office. On this day she wore one of her Efficient Secretary costumes, in deference to the client who had left not long before. Her straight-line dark wool skirt was cut a few inches below the knee and topped with an unruffled shirtwaist so purely white it seemed luminous. Her hair, pale and as brilliantly radiant as electrum, was tucked into a bun wrapped in a snood; a yellow No. 2½ pencil stuck out of it. She gave Dennison a businesslike, at-your-service look over the tops of her severely styled wire-rimmed eyeglasses. The image of the spinsterish executive aide was nearly perfect, marred only by the fact—apparent to any normal-sighted person—that she wore no bra.

"Eagles are monogamous," Dennison said. He sat and pulled his chair up to the desk. "When they reach sexual maturity—about three years after birth—they pick a mate for life, and they use the same nest each year to incubate the female's clutch of eggs. Did you know that?"

"No." Miss Paradise dropped into one of the armchairs opposite Dennison. She used her toes to pry off plain black high heels, then drew her legs up under her. She was wearing silk hosiery with seams up the back. "When they're ready to settle down," she said, "does the male pick the female, or vice versa?"

Dennison blinked. "I don't know."

"You should find out," Miss Paradise said solemnly.

Dennison watched her take a flat gold case from the pocket of her wool skirt. She clicked it open, removed a filtered cigarette, and tapped it firm on her fingernail. There was a heavy brass lighter on Dennison's desk, shaped like the lamp from which Aladdin summoned the genie, and she used it. Her face was as classically beautiful as a Ming vase. On this day she wore no makeup beyond a minimal touch of lip gloss. Her cheekbones were high but not angular, and the delicate curve of her jawline and long neck were as fragilely perfect as ice sculpture. Her eyes were dark blue, the color of the ocean where it meets the sky on a late summer afternoon, wide and limitlessly deep.

"Did you monitor my interview with Stanhope?" Dennison asked.

"Of course, boss." She blew out smoke.

Under a spine-up copy of Jaeger's *The North American Deserts*, Dennison found a heavy ashtray fashioned from cut green-tinted glass. He placed it on Miss Paradise's side of the desk. "Ideally," Dennison said, "we need someone with bona fide Mafia connections. But we need some way to assure his loyalty to us."

"I know your methods, boss dear."

"An insider," Dennison said, "but not a Company man."

"That's a tall order."

Dennison nodded. "An alternative would be an entree to George Dial and Helena Frome, someone who knows them, or who did at one time and could reestablish the relationship." Dennison sighed. "Dial and Frome bother me. What's your take on them?"

"Trouble." Miss Paradise stubbed out her cigarette and sat up straighter in the chair. She held up her index finger. "First, Dial and Frome have a confirmed history of involvement in a lot of very dirty dealings. They've survived ten years in a highly hazardous profession, and as far as we know they haven't made a serious mistake, until they killed the Stanhopes."

Miss Paradise counted off another finger. "Second, if they *have* come to this country, they've got a reason. You were woofing Stanhope a little; even if they did screw up, they still could have bought sanctuary in plenty of other places. They deliberately chose the Silician Mafia over the terrorist support network. They wanted to come here and nowhere else."

"Why?"

"Because someone made them an offer. They were invited here."

"By whom?" Dennison wondered aloud.

"By someone who could use them."

Oblique rays of the last of the day's sunshine stabbed through the big window, suspending motes of dust in their shafts. Dennison furrowed his brows. "I think you're close to the mark, my dear."

"If I am," Miss Paradise said, "it means this business goes beyond Stanhope's revenge. We're going to have to get past Dial and the Frome woman to find out who's pulling their strings, and to what end." She tossed the two folders on top of the jumble on Dennison's desk. "So I accessed the file of potential recruits. These look like the top candidates."

Dennison opened the top folder and scanned the printout inside. Miss Paradise reached up and removed the pencil from her hair and undid the snood. Her hair came loose all at once, the buttery waves falling free over the immaculate white shoulders of her blouse. She undid the top two buttons and stood, stretching like a Manx. Dennison looked up and studied her for a moment before opening the second folder.

Atop the mantel were several crystal decanters and matching glasses. Miss Paradise poured a generous dose of Scotch, then stood behind Dennison. As she read over his shoulder, she began absently to caress the nape of his neck.

Dennison closed the folder. He stretched his head back, and Miss Paradise began to knead his shoulder muscles. Dennison closed his eyes and his smile broadened.

"Good work, my dear," he said dreamily. "These two should do just fine."

Chapter Three

The waiter was at least sixty. He was tall and skinny, with an Adam's apple the size of a golf ball, and it bobbed when he frowned at the remains of the spaghetti with clam sauce on the plate he was removing. "Il cibo non le è piaciuto?" He sounded personally offended, as if he had cooked the dinner himself.

"Scusi," Matthew Conte said. "È stato buonissimo. It was very good. Lo dica a Mario, per favore."

The waiter looked mollified. "Espresso, Signor Conte?"

"Si, grazie."

The food *was* good, but it had neither brightened Conte's mood nor stimulated his appetite. The elderly waiter returned with the little cup of thick coffee and the check. "Mario says grazie," he said as he set it down. "I did not tell him you did not finish," he added, like an accusation.

"Grazie, Arturo. Buona séra."

In New York City's Little Italy there were dozens of restaurants that were virtually indistinguishable. They featured red-checkered tablecloths, fat-bellied green wine bottles with candles in their mouths and ripples of multicolored wax congealed around the necks, waiters in tight vests, and Cinzano ashtrays. Everything on the menu came smothered in the same bland, clotted tomato sauce, too acidic and bright as fresh blood.

Mario's Restaurant was not one of them. Few tourists discovered it, so most of the customers were regulars from the neighborhood. The tablecloths were white linen and the walls paneled hardwood; that was the extent of the decoration. There was a menu, but most diners ignored it in favor of whatever Mario was preparing specially that evening.

Matthew Conte drained the dregs of his espresso and tamped out his cigarette. He removed the napkin from his lap and whisked imaginary crumbs from his spotless brushed cotton slacks. When he stood he shot the cuffs of his sport jacket and adjusted the lapels. The jacket's middle button was fastened. In his billfold he found four one-dollar bills. He dropped three of them on the table, paused, then shrugged and added the fourth.

When he crossed the dining room a few people met his eye, murmured a low greeting, and looked quickly away. The rest paid close attention to their plates. Conte knew most of them by name and the rest by sight. The only stranger was a slight Oriental man in a jumpsuit that zipped up the front. He was sitting alone at a table in the back and did not look up as Conte went past and pushed through the stainless steel kitchen door.

The kitchen was a bedlam of steam and noise and rich insistent aromas, and instantly Conte was carried back twenty-five years. He remembered coming here each day after school, taking down the apron that was always spotless as a saint's soul and stiff with starch, wrapping the ties twice around his waist, and knotting them in front in a bow. For the next six hours he would be up to his elbows in hot soapy water, but when the last diner had gone home and the front door was locked, there was supper. Mario's good cooking was the first luxury the young Matt Conte experienced, a taste of the sort of life he was determined to live someday.

Mario was in front of a twelve-burner gas range, stirring two kettles at once. He wiped sweat from his forehead with the back of his sleeve and shot Conte a quick, tight grin.

Conte held up the dinner check. "Can you help me out, Mario?"

"Ha," Mario said happily. "Can I help you out?" He plucked the check from Conte's fingers and ripped it in half, then again. "You need money, Mattie?"

"No, Mario. Grazie."

"You're good for it, Mattie. You got prospects."

"Yeah," Conte said. "I got prospects." He made a fist, thumb extended toward the ceiling. "Buona séra, Mario," he said, and went out the back door.

It was raining again, a light spring drizzle. Across the alley a cat squawked, leaped from the top of an ashcan, and slinked into the shadows, its fur spiky with the rain. Oily, stagnant puddles reflected the streetlight on Mulberry Street, and niches of black shadow hugged the walls. Passing through them was like swimming underwater.

Ten yards to Conte's left, two pairs of dark shoes appeared at the edge of the streetlight's elongated oval spot. Conte flattened himself against the restaurant's brick wall.

"Take it easy." The man's tone was supposed to be casual, but Conte heard the tremolo of tension in it. "He only wants to talk to you, smoke the peace pipe. You know how it is."

Yeah, Conte knew. He unbuttoned his jacket as he edged away from the voice. The restaurant was out; he would not involve Mario in what was about to come down.

"Don't be an asshole, Conte."

Headlights swept in from the Mulberry end of the alley, the car's width nearly plugging it. Conte presssed back into the shadow. From under his left arm he uncrated a .45 caliber Colt automatic pistol and held it close against his right thigh. The car stopped, its motor idling throatily.

Conte stepped into the headlights, turned his back to them, and moved toward the two men.

"That's the boy, Matt." Tension had turned to relief. "That's the smart way to play—"

"Watch it!" someone hollered from the car. "The son of a bitch is heeled!"

Conte worked the slide of the .45 and brought it up in both hands, arms out straight in front of him. Within the alley's narrow canyon the big handgun sounded loud as a cannon. The range was less than five yards, and the first guy threw out both his arms and slammed over on his back. Rainwater splashed up as he hit broken pavement.

The second guy got off a shot and missed, the bullet thwacking into the metal of the car behind him. Conte shot him in the base of his neck, and blood black as night spurted over his front as he pirouetted and fell face down. More blood swelled the rivulets of rainwater washing down the alley's ruts.

The car leaped at Conte's back.

Conte whirled, held his firing-range stance. He put three slugs into the car's windshield, and the glass starred but did not shatter. The car swerved; paneling buckled and bent, and sparks lit the alley as brick abraded body metal. Then the wheelman regained control, and the car was bearing down on Conte once more.

He spun away at the last possible moment, graceful as a bullfighter. The big black sedan passed so closely that the outside mirror clipped Conte's elbow. Its right side bucked and settled again as the tires ran over the body of one of the gunpunks. Conte put his last two rounds through the car's rear window. Glass crackled.

Conte went in the other direction at a dead run. Behind him the black sedan skidded out of the alley and around in a four-wheel-drift U-turn, tires whining on the wet pavement. Conte was maybe twenty-five steps from the alley's Mulberry Street end.

He wasn't going to make it.

Ahead of him a man stepped into the streetlight's illumination and dropped to one knee. His arms cradled an automatic rifle. Conte dove out of the firing line and into covering shadow a microsecond before the guy opened up.

The submachine gun ratcheted, and lead sprayed the front of the charging sedan.

One headlight blinked out, then the other. Someone gave a ragged cry of pain. The gunner loosed off the rest of the autorifle's clip. Conte, to one side, climbed to his feet.

The sedan scraped into the wall again. Its wheels were cranked hard left, as if the driver were trying to climb out of the alley's confines. The rear end tried to drift with the momentum but had nowhere to go.

The sedan rolled almost gracefully onto its side, skidding along on the passenger doors for perhaps twenty feet before toppling over on its roof. A single tongue of flame glowed red-orange somewhere near the dashboard.

Conte was up and running when the gas tank went. The shock staggered him, and he almost went down on one knee. Heat and oily fumes billowed around him. Fire embraced the belly-up vehicle, and tongues of flame licked two stories high.

A late model Buick was parked at the Mulberry Street curb; both back doors hung open. It looked a lot like the car that Conte had just eluded.

"Get in, please."

The man with the automatic rifle had materialized on the other side of the car. Conte recognized him as the slight Oriental from Mario's.

He gestured toward the open car door. Behind Conte in the alley, superheated metal groaned and twisted. Sirens sounded, not far away.

Conte got in.

The Oriental man slid in the other side, and the big car eased almost silently away from the curb.

The man beside Conte was about five-six, built spare and compact. His hair was dark, straight, and fine as floss, cut moderately long and parted in the middle. Conte guessed his age at forty, but he could have been ten years older or younger. His waist and shoulders were narrow, almost boyish, but Conte's instinct told him there was nothing frail about the man.

"Thanks," Conte said.

The Oriental looked at Conte with no apparent expression, nodded politely but meaninglessly, and looked straight ahead again.

Okay, Conte got the idea. The guy hadn't broken up the gunplay out of regard for Conte's ass. He was doing a job, and there was nothing personal about it.

Conte lit a cigarette and rolled down the window a few inches. Glass tinted so dark it was opaque hid the driver. The car turned right on Delancey, toward the Williamsburg Bridge. Conte settled back against the seat cushions and blew out smoke.

He asked no questions because he figured he'd get no answers. That was all right; at least no one was shooting at him.

Given the last month, that was a change for the better, and answer enough for the time being.

Chapter Four

Outside in the yard, the heavy woman spit into the hard-packed dirt and barked, "Cabron mugre! No tiene cojones! Tu madre es una puta grande!" She wore a loose gray cotton dress that hung over her massive body like a tent. There were dark stains under each arm and a long rip down the front, so both of her breasts swung free, big as melons.

The guard held an automatic rifle at port arms. He snorted and advanced on her, and the woman danced away with unlikely grace. The guard wore a khaki uniform that was not much cleaner than the woman's dress, and his teeth were stained yellow-brown by strong tobacco. He showed them in a lupine grin and said, "Si, y tu madre es una cochilla." He waved at her breasts, to make sure she understood the crude comparison.

The woman screamed out a string of curses and charged him, her fists up beside her face.

The guard caught her with the butt of his weapon, full at the point of her jaw below the left ear. The heavy woman's eyes went glassy. She staggered back a step, then sat down hard in the dirt. She opened her mouth and swallowed air, and then her eyes closed and she flopped onto her back, her arms outspread.

The guard's twisted smile broadened. He bent and grabbed a fistful of what was left of the gray dress and tore it off in one hard yank. The woman wore nothing underneath, and her skin was a uniform bronze color. She was not so much fat as big and hard and thickly built, and her breasts and the mound of her stomach heaved with her labored, unconscious breathing.

The guard slung his rifle over his shoulder by its web belt and unbuttoned the front of his pants, then stood straddling the woman's supine figure, waiting for his water to come.

Chris Amado let go of the bars that cross-hatched the one-foot-square aperture that served as her window. Her cell was six feet high and wide, eight long. Three walls and the floor were dingy concrete; the fourth wall was barred and faced out on a narrow corridor that bisected blocks of similar cells. There was a filthy, bare straw mattress, a wash basin, and a slop bucket. A yellowish bulb burned in a ceiling fixture twenty-four hours a day. It was oven-hot, and the air was stale and close. It smelled of sweat and human waste, ripening in the thick torpor. As Chris turned, a rat the size of a kitten scurried out under the bars.

In the yard, the heavy woman began to scream. Chris did not return to the window.

She wore the same kind of cotton dress, and she was as filthy as everything around her. Her dark hair was a greasy tangled nest, and her face and legs were streaked with sweat-washed grime. Around her she could hear the voices of other women, calling to each other in Mexicano Spanish.

It was springtime, late March or maybe early April. Chris wished for the hundredth time she had kept a calendar from the beginning. It was something to do, and keeping occupied and keeping sane had a lot in common. It had been about nine months; she knew that.

It seemed like a lifetime.

She lowered herself to the stinking mattress, and roaches scurried for new shelter. She would have cried; she did not fear tears. But she did not, and had not since they brought her to this place.

"Amado!"

Her head snapped up. It was the female warder, the one they called El Mostacho. Still, she was the best of the lot. Chris stared past the Mustache at the two men with her.

These men wore khaki uniforms, too, but unlike the guard in the yard theirs were spotlessly clean and pressed crisp as iceberg lettuce. Each wore a pistol in a holster with a flap that snapped over the gun's butt. The taller one had a two-inch worm of scar running along the line of his jaw, shocking white against his swarthy complexion. His name was Mauricio, and his partner, who had thick hands with rugs of fur over their backs, was Llosa. Chris knew these men; they had come to her cell from the first.

The Mustache unlocked the door and stepped to one side.

She did not bother to conceal the disdain in the look she gave the two men. "Vamos, chica," Mauricio said. When he smiled the white dappled scar twitched.

Chris did not move.

"Viene, chiquita," Llosa put in. "He wants you, pero yo no se que." He wrinkled his nose to indicate how much she disgusted him. "Pero le necesita la gringa puta."

"Media," Mauricio put in.

"Si," Llosa agreed. "Pero half a gringa is better than none." Both men laughed.

Chris smiled with them and said, "Chinga tu madre."

Llosa grunted, but Mauricio's face went dark. He came into the cell, bent, and locked his fingers around Chris's upper arm, digging his thumb into the muscle below the armpit. Mauricio knew the places where a body could be most easily hurt.

She let him pull her up and out into the corridor. When he was off balance, she twisted and brought her knee up between Mauricio's legs.

Mauricio squealed like a ewe and doubled over, staggering away from her. From the other cells up and down the corridor, women shouted their approval and encouragement in Spanish.

Mauricio gasped for breath. He balled his fist, but Llosa grabbed his arm and jerked him around.

"Don't be estupido," he hissed. "He will not want her marked. He will see to us if she is. But afterwards, when we bring the puta back . . . then there will be time for the bruises to heal before he calls for her again."

Mauricio pulled roughly away from his partner. He stared with loathing at Chris through dead dark eyes. "Si," he said. "Then we will see to the cono."

It was at that moment she determined to kill Enrico.

She had been considering the idea in the abstract for months. Now she saw she could no longer put it off and still hope for any chance of success. Her strength was waning daily, and so were her looks. Nine months ago she had been a beautiful young woman; by the time a year was out, she would no longer be desirable to anyone, even Enrico.

And when he was finished with her she would be

dispensable. They would give her to the guards to do whatever they wished, like the poor woman in the yard. Tonight might be her last chance.

The odds of killing Enrico were minimal; the odds of survival afterward, nil. But she had reached the point where to try and to die was preferable to the alternatives.

"Vamos." Mauricio planted a dark hand in the small of her back and pushed her along in front of him. A chorus of obscene catcalls accompanied them from either side. Women in prison grays were pressed to the bars of every cell, laughing and shouting and pointing at the two men. As they reached the end of the corridor the prisoner in the last cell reared back her head, hawked, and let fly a glob of spittle.

It hit Mauricio in the cheek. He lurched toward the woman, his face black with rage. The woman danced away from the bars, laughing madly. Mauricio cursed, then wiped off the sputum with the back of his sleeve and gave Chris a vicious shove.

Llosa led the way through a maze of corridors, up a double flight of stairs enclosed in barren cinder-block walls, then through another cell block, this one populated with male prisoners. Instantly Chris was the object of every filthy proposition she had ever heard, along with several that were original. She kept her eyes straight ahead. They came out into a dayroom, passed a guard who was reading a Spanish-language edition of an Uncle Scrooge comic book, and exited into a yard, the ground packed hard as stone by thousands of prisoners' bare feet.

On the other side of the yard was a barred gate, wide enough to admit a single vehicle and topped by a guard tower. The tower housed two warders and a heavy-caliber machine gun mounted on a tripod. The wall was stone and mortar topped with double coils of rolled razor-wire. Every few inches along each coil there was a tempered steel barb, no bigger than a thumbnail, shaped like a medieval battle-ax. A couple of months ago, one of the male prisoners had somehow made it to the top of the wall. The guards did not try to stop him when he began to climb over the wire, and they left him where he lay when he didn't make it. He sprawled spread-eagled across the coils, the barbs embedded in his flesh in a hundred places from his face to his feet. The man's screams echoed into every corner of the prison for the twenty minutes it took him to bleed to death.

An unmarked, dark blue panel truck was parked a few steps from the door, its back open. Chris had a moment to breathe the fresh outside air; it was nearing twilight. Then Llosa pushed her toward the truck, and she stumbled inside. There were no windows, but the dome cargo light was on. Mauricio dug a packet of American cigarettes from the pocket of his uniform blouse and got one lit. He coughed out the first draw of smoke, then bent and winced, still tender from Chris's kick.

He would hurt her for that, badly as he knew how—if he got the chance. But Chris was thinking about Enrico. . . .

That was the only name by which she knew him. From his fine house she assumed he was some kind of Mexican bigshot. He wore a uniform with a lot of gold braid and colored ribbons over the heart, like the heir to a Ruritanian throne.

A month or so after she had been thrown in the jail, Mauricio and Llosa came for the first time. They moved down the cell block, eyeing each woman like dry goods. They stopped in front of Chris's cell, told the Mustache to unlock the jail, then ordered Chris to strip. They took their time appraising her body and laboring to come up with coarse remarks. A week later they returned and took her to Enrico for the first time. Since then they had come back on five occasions. Sometimes almost two months passed between his summons; sometimes less than two weeks. There was never a warning, but that was a blessing.

It spared her the dread.

She had never been touched by a human being as grotesque as Enrico. He was about fifty, shorter than her five-six, and shaped like a keg. His skin was swarthy and pitted with the permanent scars of a violent losing bout with acne, and his face was always greasy with sweat, despite the air conditioning in his villa. His hair was as close-cropped as a pig's bristles, his lips thick and too red, his eyes bulging, dark orbs floating in viscous yellow.

The panel truck swerved, and Chris was thrown against Llosa. He grabbed one of her breasts and squeezed, not very hard, the gesture mechanical, automatic. Mauricio glowered at both of them. The truck went up a grade and around a long gentle curve, then lurched to a stop.

Though it was full dark, the night was no cooler than the day. Chris saw a long, sloping lawn cut by a gravel drive, a high fence mostly hidden by hedge, and beyond, the lights of Mexico City, Mauricio grabbed her arm and hustled her past a garbage bin toward the villa's back door. He feinted for the knob, then in the same motion slapped her open-handed across the breasts, hard enough to take her breath away.

Mauricio darted back out of range. "Do not think that makes us even. There will be much pain for you this night, puta."

Chris concentrated on keeping the hurt out of her face. She stared at Mauricio, then cupped her hand over her own crotch and laughed. Mauricio darkened.

"That is enough," Llosa snapped.

After the thick night air, the artificial chill of the villa's interior was as shocking as a dive into a spring. The carpet under Chris's bare feet was soft and plush, but dyed a garish red. The paintings hanging on the walls were crudely fashioned nudes framed in ornately carved wood that only emphasized their crudeness. The walls were papered in red, velvetlike material that would have been right at home in a whorehouse.

Chris pushed past Llosa and went on down the corridor. She knew the way. She turned up a double-wide staircase, went down the upstairs hall to the last room at the back. Mauricio and Llosa followed her inside.

"Buenas noches, senorita." The maid was middle-aged and darker skinned than the guards. She was Honduran, and Chris knew from the brief snatches of conversation they had managed that she was somehow indentured to Enrico. In six more years she would be allowed to apply for citizenship and leave his household—or so he had promised her. In the meantime she was his slave.

"Buenas noches, Manuela," Chris said. "Como esta usted?"

The older woman managed a wan smile. "Ah si ah si."

"He is waiting," Mauricio snapped. "Date prisa!"

They followed her into the bedroom opening off the main dressing room and watched while Manuela stripped off the prison dress. Chris let her eyelids droop as she began to scrub the dirt out of her pores, and within a few minutes the guards, the room, even Manuela's hands on her body—all ceased to exist. Chris made her mind blank, until there was nothing but the warm water enclosing her.

When she opened her eyes ten minutes later and rose from the soapy bath, she felt calm. There were things to be done on this evening; she would do her best to see to them. The path to Enrico's death stretched before her, as clearly marked as a freeway. Beyond that was a void.

It took another hour to make her ready. Manuela worked on her fingernails and her face, brushed her dark hair until it shone, perfumed her neck and body, made her up. Enrico liked her in a lot of paint. Lastly Manuela dressed her: the gown hung off one shoulder and was slit up one thigh, and it was covered with red sequins. But even the garish cosmetics and the absurd costume could not obscure the fact that Chris Amado was an extremely beautiful young woman.

Enrico did not rise when Mauricio walked her into the downstairs dining room, but his pig eyes glowed dully.

"Come here." Enrico always spoke English to her. He grabbed her arm and pulled her down, kissing her hard on the lips. He had begun without her; his mouth was greasy with food. It was like kissing fish entrails.

"Eat," he ordered. "Drink wine."

Chris tried to straighten, and Enrico's grip on her arm tightened. His rodent eyes challenged her.

"Yes, Enrico," she murmured. "Gracias."

"In English," he snapped.

"Thank you, Enrico."

The soft fat man laughed and swatted her on the ass, hard enough to make her stumble. From the far corner Mauricio watched, careful to keep his expression neutral.

She took no pleasure in the food. She ate because survival required nourishment.

And the will to kill.

"They are treating you well?" Enrico slobbered down a goblet of wine and snapped his fingers, and instantly a man in service livery appeared to refill it. Enrico was already drunk. "The other girls, I mean, they see to you? The Latin woman is hot in the blood like you, no? Just because she is in prison she does not let the itch go without scratching. You are part the gringa, so you are the popular one, no?"

Enrico picked up the steak bone from his plate and gnawed at a piece of gristle. "Next time," he said with his mouth full, "we will bring two of them here, and I will watch. I would like to see their faces shoved into your cunt, both of them at the same time, and their faces wet with your juice."

Chris pushed her plate away.

"What do you say to that?"

Chris stared.

"What do you say?" He was suddenly shouting. Mau-

~~straightened in his corner.~~

Enrico," Chris said.

fucking wine."

" Chris tilted up her goblet. When she

ablecloth the level of wine had not gone

his face, scrubbing as if it were a

at and food behind anyway.

stood he swayed.

them into an

alone. He

like the

king-size

side were

estick, two

wo candles,

light.

ing; gauzy

ed in a

Enrico climbed up on the bed and lay back in a nest of pillows. "Begin," he ordered.

Chris came around the other side. "I have something special for you." The words were meaningless, part of the ritual Enrico demanded.

From the drawer of one of the end tables Enrico took a marijuana joint the size of a cigar. He lit up, drew in deeply, then patted the bedsheet beside him. Chris sat and took the joint. They blew out great clouds of smoke together, though only Enrico inhaled.

The close room was thick with the fumes when Enrico stubbed out the roach. "Proceed," he murmured dreamily.

It took Chris almost ten minutes to undress him. He mad no effort to help; that was part of the game. She had to tu the uniform trousers with all her strength to get them over his fat ass. When she finished he still had no naked body was a quivering mound of fla suet. His flabby breasts were big as a stomach was so massive it nearly hid hi small and thin as a boy's. On other over an hour to get it hard.

It would never get hard

Chris stood and we framed by the twin spl her, slowly unzip breasts for panties, a Enrico ha told her

Enric around the

She t with her l

B

Chris got both hands around it, brought it up over her head, and hammered it down in the middle of Enrico's gargoyle face.

But the fat man was more agile and less stoned than he appeared. He twisted away, and the thick metal staff caught his shoulder instead.

Chris heard the sharp crack as his clavicle shattered. Enrico yowled with pain and fear. Chris raised the club again.

Enrico tried to sit up, and Chris swung the candlestick with every ounce of her strength.

It caught the fat man in the middle of his face at the bridge of his nose. There was a nauseating thump, and cartilage and teeth and face bone shattered under the metal's weight.

Something slammed into the locked bedroom door.

Enrico flopped back into the pillows. There was no shape where his nose had been. Blood bubbled out of his mouth, floating bits of teeth over his chin and womanish chest.

Chris bashed the candlestick into his face again. Now it was a red mask, a Halloween horror.

A bullet whined into the door lock.

The candlestick made a mushy sound the fourth time Chris used it. She left it embedded in Enrico's skull. Flames were licking up the far side of the bed, feeding on the red sheets.

The bedroom door slammed back against the wall, and for one long moment Mauricio and Llosa were framed within its jamb. They took in the curtain of flame climbing one side of the bed, the gore-smeared mess that had been Enrico, and Chris, breasts shiny with the fire's heat, the blood-washed candlestick still in her hands.

Llosa came into the room, Mauricio on his heels. Llosa fumbled at the flap of his holster, but Mauricio had already drawn. He barked, "No. Ella es por yo." He drew a bead on Chris's bare chest.

A gun went off, but it was not Mauricio's.

The scar along Mauricio's jawline came unstitched, and bits of his jawbone splintered out of the gap as he plummeted forward.

Llosa turned to see where the bullet came from and took its brother in the side of his neck. His jugular parted, and as he went down his heart pumped one last great gush of blood in a three-foot arc.

The Oriental man who came into the room wore blousy fatigues with no insignia. He was about Chris's height and had an open, unlined face that wore no expression. Her nearly nude body seemed to excite him as much as a five-pound lump of ground chuck.

"How many others in the house?" His tone was neutral, as if he were asking the time. He carried a Beretta 9mm automatic pistol.

"Two servants," Chris said, "but they're okay. Two, maybe three other armed guards."

"One is dead," the Oriental man informed her. "Would you put something on, please?"

Chris grabbed up Enrico's voluminous shirt from the pile of clothing and underclothing on the carpet. Its touch made her skin pucker, but it covered her. She kicked off the spike heels. Flames were edging across the bed like a forest fire in a high wind.

"Come, please," the Oriental said.

"Where?"

The Oriental sighed.

Chris skirted the fire and stooped to grab Mauricio's pistol. "Sorry. Let's go."

Manuela was bustling down the corridor toward them. "Vamos," Chris snapped. "Fuego! Di Carlos!" The maid and butler were as much victims of Enrico as she.

Chris followed the Oriental man down the wide staircase. Smoke billowed after them; the fire was spreading more quickly now. The adrenaline rush that had come with the killing of Enrico was peaking, strong as a narcotic. A guard with a submachine gun trotted down the first-floor corridor, and the Oriental shot him from the third stair riser, a single bullet in the forehead.

The front door opened on another sloping lawn and a wider paved drive that ran down to an open gate.

"Stay here, please." The Oriental man disappeared.

Behind Chris a man cried, "Madre de dios!"

She flattened against the front of the house, then edged

around until she could see past the lip of the open door. One of the guards was in the corridor, buttoning his trousers with fumbling fingers as he stared down in horror at his dead buddy slumped at the foot of the stairs. Clouds of smoke pierced by tongues of flame lapped down from the second floor. The guard had an autorifle clutched under his arm.

The guard shook his head and came out of his shock. He jerked back the charging lever of his rifle and headed for the open door.

Chris flattened back, holding the pistol in both hands. She drew a breath, let half of it out, and held the rest.

She whipped around into the doorway and dropped to a crouch. The charging guard snarled at her and tried to take aim.

He was four steps away when she fired.

She squeezed the trigger twice and saw holes appear like conjuring in the middle of his chest, the second a few inches from the first. The guard stumbled and went down on his face, his momentum carrying him to Chris's feet.

Behind her, headlights raked the lawn.

Chris spun back into shadow, the pistol at the ready and tracking the car that was sweeping up the drive toward her. But when it slid to a stop in front of her and the passenger door swung open, the dome light illuminated the Oriental man behind the wheel.

He gave her a clinical once-over as she slid in beside him, then slewed the car around in an effortless one-eighty. At the gate he waited for a pickup truck to pass, then pulled smoothly and without haste into the stream of traffic heading toward Mexico City.

"You're not injured?"

Chris looked at the Oriental man. He stared into the oncoming headlights. Chris pulled the tails of Enrico's shirt over her bare thighs. "No," she said. "Not like you mean."

The answer seemed to satisfy him.

Chris closed her eyes and let her head fall back against the seat's headrest. The pistol in her hand was part of another time. She sat up and worked the magazine release; there were four cartridges left, plus one in the breech.

"You will not need that." The Oriental man kept his eyes on the road.

"Maybe not," Chris Amado said into the darkness. "But it's a comfort having it near."

Chapter Five

Where Dennison's office was cozy, cluttered, studiously old-fashioned, the living room of his quarters was the opposite: cheerfully bright, stylish, understatedly modern. The cream-colored walls were blank except for three subdued black-and-white photographic landscapes keyed by track lighting near the line of the ceiling. The furnishing was minimal: a wide, three-cushion sofa covered in a light fabric, two low-slung matching chairs, a coffee table in front of the couch, and a smoking stand beside a recliner. This armchair was Dennison's proprietary reserve; Miss Paradise called it his daddy chair. Behind it was a wet bar with two stools and a real brass rail, and facing the sofa was a color television set and video cassette recorder on a wheeled stand.

Dennison was reading Nevins's description of Lee's victory at Second Manassas, in the second volume of *The War for the Union*. He wore corduroy slacks and an open-necked shirt, and he was sipping from a highball glass of Martel Five Star Brandy with soda over cracked ice. Miss Paradise was curled up on the couch, watching a cassette of an old episode of M*A*S*H. Her glistening pale hair was down and parted on one side, so it half fell across one eye. She wore billowing lounging pajamas and tortoise-shell cheaters, and every once in a while she took them off and nibbled at the earpiece.

Dennison lowered his book and said, "Carole Lombard?"

Miss Paradise smiled brightly; she had been waiting for him to guess. "Nope." She put the specs on again. She was drinking from a stemmed glass of white wine. "Give up?"

"Um," Dennison said.

"Veronica Lake," Miss Paradise chirped triumphantly.

"Veronica Lake." Dennison shook his head ruefully in a moderately successful imitation of a man who should have known better. "I was going to guess Veronica Lake."

"Sure you were, boss dear."

On the television screen a red dot began to blink above Colonel Henry Blake's head. Miss Paradise put down her glass and went out of the room.

Dennison watched her leave and thought what an incredibly handsome woman she was.

He had read another three pages of Nevins by the time she returned. She retrieved her glass and topped it off at the bar, adding a half handful of crushed ice to Dennison's highball before returning to the sofa. She used the remote control to click off the television's audio. On the screen, Hawkeye Pierce was mouthing a wisecrack over his shoulder to Trapper John McIntyre, while both dug blithely into the mangled entrails of wounded infantrymen. The fronts of their white operating smocks were as bloody as butcher's aprons.

"Vang," Miss Paradise said. "He's got them both."

Dennison marked the page with his thumb and folded the book closed. "Any problems?"

"Nothing that Vang couldn't handle, and nothing that can kick back. You know Vang."

Dennison knew Vang all right. The Hmong warrior worked without rancor, pleasure, or any emotion in between. He did what had to be done, with ruthless efficiency; the most dangerous job seemed to have no more impact on him than buttering a slice of whole wheat toast. Vang had been trained by the best in the world, and then he had turned his back on his trainers. But Dennison knew what was behind that decision, and respected it, as much as he respected the man.

Dennison reopened Nevins and had read another paragraph when Miss Paradise said, "Can we trust this Conte?"

"I don't know," Dennison said. "I hope so."

Miss Paradise fiddled with the VCR's remote control. On the screen Hawkeye Pierce raised a foam-flecked glass and said, "Beer today, gone tomorrow." She turned the sound off again. Dennison waited patiently.

"Okay," Miss Paradise said firmly, as if they had been debating. "I see how he fits. He's on the outs with the Mob, but he must still have contacts. If his people sponsored Dial and Frome at this end, he might be able to learn where they've gone to ground."

"He might."

"I don't trust dark-haired men."

"My dear," Dennison said patiently. "I have dark hair."

Miss Paradise unfolded herself from the sofa, picking up Dennison's glass on her way to the bar. She dumped out the dregs of his drink and built a fresh one. She set it on the smoking stand beside his chair and ran her hand through his crop of hair. "It used to be dark, boss honey. Haven't you noticed the touch of gray at the temples?"

"I hadn't," Dennison murmured.

Miss Paradise went back to the couch. "It looks distinguished." She gestured with the tortoise-shell glasses. "What about Chris Amado?"

"Do you distrust dark-haired women, too?"

"Better safe than sorry."

Dennison smiled. "To begin with, she can handle herself in a fight. She's had her share, and she's come out looking pretty damned tough."

"For a woman."

Dennison pretended not to hear. "She's proven her courage several times over, and I think she can be persuaded to share our . . . ah, world view."

"I can show you the files of a dozen others whose credentials are just as strong. And we could have recruited most of them without going to the trouble—and the expense, boss—of cracking a Mexican prison."

Dennison sipped at his drink. "You're testing me, my dear."

"I'm helping you stay sharp. At your age the memory starts to go."

"I appreciate your concern," Dennison said dryly.

Miss Paradise came around behind his chair. She put her drink down beside his and began to work on his shoulders and neck.

"George Dial and Christina Amado were lovers," Dennison said, like a schoolboy reciting a lesson. "My guess is that Chris Amado can exploit that relationship, even ten years later.

I think she can get close to Dial and whatever he and Frome are mixed up in." He stretched his head back and smiled upside down at her sculpted face. "Here's something that wasn't in the file, my dear: Dial is still carrying Chris Amado's scars."

"What's that supposed to mean?" Miss Paradise said warily.

"When she told him it was over, Dial took a razor blade to both of his wrists."

Miss Paradise's hands froze for a moment, then continued to knead at the hard knot of muscle at the top of Dennison's spine.

"It was a lot more than a grandstand play. He was unconscious when he was found, within a few minutes of bleeding to death. It's possible that the blood loss did cause oxygen deprivation to the cerebrum."

"Brain damage?"

Dennison shrugged.

"So he's doing Camille," Miss Paradise said thoughtfully, "and someone breaks up his act just before the final curtain."

Dennison rolled his head in a lazy arc. "Helena Frome."

Miss Paradise gave a low whistle. "She saved his life."

"And they've been together ever since. But every time he sees those scars on his wrists, he must think of Christina Amado."

"Even if that's true, there's no way of predicting how he'll react to her now. The guy's been a hired killer for a decade, and aside from any possible brain damage, there's a good chance he's a certifiable psychotic."

"Most terrorists are."

"And Helena Frome definitely isn't going to be happy to see Chris Amado. There are dangerous holes in it, boss."

"I know that." Dennison felt a little weary. He drained half his highball and made a sour face. Miss Paradise let her fingernails trail along the nape of his neck.

"It will be up to her," Dennison said, half to himself. "No one is going to twist her arm." But then he straightened and looked over his shoulder at Miss Paradise. "Stanhope was right, even if he is a jerk. Dial and Frome loose in this country would be like two kids locked in a candy store after hours."

"And if we sit around waiting for the Feds to put the lid on them, we might be waiting a long time."

Dennison nodded. "The cops have to play by the rules."

"And the crooks make up the rules as they go along."

Dennison smiled wanly. "You know what they say, my dear: Rules are made to be broken." But then he thought again of Chris Amado, of the danger in which he would be placing her, and the smile faded.

Miss Paradise sensed his concern; she always did. "Don't worry about her," she said softly. "She sounds like a woman who can take care of herself. Worry about what would happen if we didn't send her out. Worry about the Dials and Fromes of the world running loose." Her fingers grazed over his skin. "If you've got to worry, worry about what would happen if we did nothing at all."

Dennison rarely got melancholy, mostly because she would not allow it. She bent and kissed the top of his head and said, "Worry about how you're going to pay my salary, boss dear." Dennison reached around and held her forearm, and she knew he was coming out of it.

"Speaking of money," Miss Paradise said in his ear, "we've got another customer coming in tomorrow. Her name is Elaine Hammond, and she sent along a roll of 8mm film that you'll want to screen first thing in the morning."

"I'm not very tired," Dennison said. "Maybe I'll take a look at it now."

"Uh-uh," Miss Paradise murmured. "Take my advice. I took a look already. You'll have nightmares."

"I never have nightmares."

Miss Paradise reached across his chest and took his hand in both of hers. The soft silk of her lounging pajamas was cool against his skin, and he felt the featherweight of her breast on his shoulder. "Come on," she whispered. "I'll make sure you don't start tonight."

Chapter Six

On the luminescent surface of the folding screen, men in black carrying large plastic bags and M16s moved jerkily from left to right. On the soundtrack, voices barked orders against a background of moans and sobs. The camera looked down on the scene from an odd angle and moved back and forth over a limited range. Dennison guessed it was mounted near a corner of the ceiling on a motorized gimbal.

The camera reached one end of its scan. There was a gunshot, but at that moment no one was captured in the camera's frame. Then, as the camera began to pan back, men crossed, too quickly to distinguish individually. A body was sprawled on the floor, and a woman was screaming hysterically. The body was headless and handless and surrounded by a great dark wash of blood.

The film ran out. Dennison clicked off the projector motor and stared thoughtfully at the blank screen. The drapes were drawn, and his eyes had become adjusted to the room's dimness when Miss Paradise entered and flicked on a lamp.

Dennison blinked. On this morning Miss Paradise's blond hair was done up in a lacquered permanent, with a spit curl pasted to her forehead. She wore a flower-print dress, a double rope of fake pearls, and boxy heels with ankle straps. She was vigorously chewing a wad of gum.

Dennison studied her and said, "Lee Patrick as Effie Perrine?"

Miss Paradise nodded solemnly, in character. "There's a girl wants to see you," she said around the gum. "Her name's Hammond."

"A customer?" Dennison recited.

"I guess so. You'll want to see her anyway—she's a knockout."

"Shoo her in, Angel," Dennison deadpanned. "Shoo her in."

Elaine Hammond was in her early thirties. She wore a light turtleneck, a skirt and blazer, and low shoes, and her auburn hair was cut short. She had a pretty smile, and she showed it to Dennison when she shook his hand with a firm, dry grip. He sat her in one of the armchairs and said, "Would you like coffee?"

She shook her head. A single shaft of sunshine slipped through the space where the curtains came together and stabbed into the surface of Dennison's desk.

"How did you get this film?" Dennison asked.

"I bought it."

Dennison nodded and waited for the rest.

"I bought it from a man named Robert Franey," she went on. "They call him Big Bob. He's the sheriff of Fisk County, North Dakota."

"You bribed him?"

"Not personally," Mrs. Hammond said. "But yes. He came cheap."

Dennison watched her cross her legs. He thought he liked her.

"Soon after my husband disappeared," she said, "I hired a private investigator. He made a deal with Sheriff Franey: five hundred dollars for a copy of the film and no questions."

"Do you have a lot of money to spend on this?"

"I suppose that's important to you," she said with a trace of annoyance. Dennison did not react. "No," she said finally. "We had some savings when Albert disappeared. Very little is left. I work, but . . ." Her voice trailed off.

Dennison began to rewind the projector. "Would you mind if I—?"

"I've seen it, Mr. Dennison," Elaine Hammond said sharply. "I'm not going to vomit on the carpet."

Dennison threaded the film, turned on the projector lamp, and rolled it. The camera panned the dead oilfield roughneck. There was a gunshot, the thump of a body, a woman's choked sob. A man's voice croaked, "Jesus, Greaves, Creed didn't say to—" The camera caught up with the speaker as the bullet slammed into his chest. When he went down, the camera had a clearer view of the gang member who had been standing behind him. This man's face was contorted with fear and revulsion.

"That's him," Elaine Hammond said. "That's my husband."

On the screen, the man with the commando knife was dropping to one knee. He raised the knife over his head and brought it down in a vicious chop.

Dennison flicked off the reel motor and the knifeman's arm froze, the blade an inch above the dead man's wrist. Dennison turned off the lamp, and the image faded from the screen.

"Are you sure?" Dennison asked.

"He's masked, Mr. Dennison. I'm not a fool; I'll admit I could be wrong." She uncrossed her legs and leaned toward him. "I don't think I am."

Dennison rose. He unhooked the screen from the top of its tripod and rerolled it into the cylindrical container. He set it to one side and threw open the heavy drapes. Sunshine splashed into the room. At the edge of the clearing, a yearling deer, startled by a sudden, instinctual sense of being observed, bounded into the woods.

"What are you asking me to do, Mrs. Hammond?"

"Find him. Bring him to me."

"And then?"

"I want to talk to him. If . . . if he left with free will, I want to try to understand."

"And then?" Dennison persisted.

Behind him she drew breath. "I don't know," she said softly.

The deer was nosing out of the edge of the woods again, curiosity conquering fear. It stared up at Dennison, sniffing the air like a Chesapeake retriever. Dennison returned to his chair. He slumped a little, clasped his hands over his stomach, and said, "Tell me about your husband, Elaine." He smiled encouragement and said nothing else after she began. Occasionally when she made a point and looked up for his reaction Dennison opened his hooded eyes a little wider and nodded sympathy or understanding or reassurance.

She and Albert Hammond were married nearly twelve years ago, she said. Both of them were nineteen, and six months later Albert was drafted. Neither was pleased, but they were young and very much in love, and they knew their marriage would survive the separation.

"He went from basic training to Vietnam," Elaine Hammond said. "He was in the infantry. Afterwards he didn't talk about it, but I had to know. I had to understand how it had been, so I talked to other men who had gone through the same thing. He was in the jungle twenty days out of thirty for most of a year, and men were trying to kill him. Albert wasn't political or antiwar, but he didn't want to die. So he fought, and he came back with a satchel of decorations and a body full of scars to prove he wasn't a coward.

"He was two weeks away from rotation," she went on, "when he was captured. He spent the next twenty months in a prison camp near Hoa Binh. There were sixty of them, and they waited for someone to come for them, and no one ever did. So he escaped. I don't know how. I don't want to know. Sometimes I think I know too much already."

Her voice broke. Dennison waited while she rummaged in her bag and found a cigarette and a disposable lighter. She took a deep breath, so when she lit the cigarette her hands were steady.

"Understand, Mr. Dennison: for almost three years my husband lived in an absolutely insane world, one that could not possibly be comprehended in terms of rational experience. He was beaten and starved and tortured—and then he was sent home to pick up where he left off and live a normal life."

Elaine Hammond laughed. "Do you know what the most insane thing is, Mr. Dennison? The fact that he made it work. He returned and we all pretended it wasn't any more real than a nightmare, and after a time maybe we believed it."

Dennison spoke for the first time since she had begun her story: "Except for your husband."

Elaine Hammond shook her head helplessly. "I don't know. I thought he was okay. I wanted to believe . . ." She took a deep drag on her cigarette and blew out smoke before going on. While Albert was serving, she had lived with her mother in Prescott, Arizona. Albert joined her there when he was discharged and took a job managing a 7–11 store. Four years later her mother died and left enough of an inheritance for a down payment on the store and on a home in the wooded hills north of the city. They had a good life, Elaine Hammond told Dennison.

"At first the fact that Albert wouldn't talk about it worried me," she said. "I was afraid he was keeping it stoppered up inside him, and that someday it would burst free. But as time passed, I convinced myself that he had adjusted. When people started arguing about the war at a party or something, Albert was likely to wander off, as if he were bored. He didn't seem depressed or frightened by what had happened in Vietnam; it was more like he had lost interest in the whole business."

She cut herself off too sharply. Dennison murmured, "But there was something."

"We have no children. Albert refused. There was no point, he said."

"What do you think that meant?"

"I . . . I don't know. That he was afraid something would happen to them—like what he suffered. He . . . he said there would be no more wars like Vietnam, dragging on for ten years. The next war would take ten minutes, and there would be no such thing as a civilian. The losers would be dead, and so would the winners; that's what he told me. Then he smiled and said, 'Now that's my idea of a sensible war.'"

"Did he talk about it often?"

"He was not obsessed, Mr. Dennison, if that's what you're suggesting. He was afraid of nuclear war. A lot of people are."

"Not so afraid that they refuse to have children."

"I didn't say that was the reason. I never understood completely. I thought . . ."

She leaned forward and stubbed out her cigarette in the heavy green-glass ashtray. "He left three months ago. Three months and six days, to be exact. He went to the store to work on the books, and around noon he went to lunch at a restaurant a block down the street. He ate with three other men who worked in the neighborhood; they were regular lunch buddies. Albert usually walked to the restaurant, but that day he drove. As they were leaving, he told one of the men he was going to the bank."

Her cigarette butt was still smoldering. There was a faint pink stain around the filter. Dennison watched the smoke spiral toward the ceiling.

"That was the last time he was seen," Elaine Hammond said. "He left no signs he had been planning to leave. The store's ledger books were open on his desk. He didn't take any money from the store or from our personal account. I found our car in the bank parking lot the next morning."

"You went to the police?"

"Of course. They investigated, found no sign of foul play, and told me there was no law against a husband leaving his wife. So I engaged the private detective. He spent almost a month on the case without developing any leads and finally advised me that retaining him any longer would be a waste of my money."

"What do *you* think happened to him, Elaine?"

"I don't know." Dennison heard despair in her voice. "One day everything is normal, and the next your husband disappears, and nobody—*nobody*—has any idea of how to help you. Try to imagine that, Mr. Dennison. Try to imagine how I felt. The world had been tipped on its ear once before, when they told me Albert had been captured in Vietnam. Now it had happened again, the same kind of insanity and again not a thing I could do—until this film."

"You were upset," Dennison suggested. "You were desperate for news of your husband, and when you saw—"

"No," Elaine Hammond interrupted. "I was resigned. I had given him up in my mind, and I was only trying to make some kind of normal life out of whatever was left to me. Then a week ago I was making supper and watching Dan Rather, and he showed part of that film, and I said to myself, That's him. I felt relieved and a little numb. You don't jump for joy, Mr. Dennison, when your husband shows up among a gang of bank robbers and murderers."

"So you went back to the private investigator."

"I couldn't very well return to the police. I went to Mr. Shanks and sent him to get a copy of the film. As I told you, that wasn't difficult. After Mr. Shanks watched the whole thing, he recommended I contact you and told me how to go about it."

"Ron Shanks?"

Elaine Hammond nodded. "He said you'd know his name."

Dennison had not seen Shanks for six years, since before the investigator had opened his own agency, but he remembered the man with fondness. That was *two* favors Dennison owed him now. . . .

"Do you have a picture of your husband?"

Elaine Hammond rifled through her bag again. From a plastic sleeve in her wallet she removed a snapshot and passed it to Dennison. "This was taken at Mormon Lake last summer." The photo showed a medium-sized, sandy-haired man in bathing trunks, posing in an exaggerated muscle-man posture, bicep flexed, wrist cocked. Dennison found a geographer's loup in the desk drawer and skidded it over the photo. Four roughly parallel scars, each about six inches long, were etched diagonally across Hammond's pectorals. There was a more pronounced ridge of white raised tissue along his right side, just above the waistband of his trunks, and opposite it, a few inches to the right of his navel, a dime-size pucker, like a vaccination mark. Aside from the scars, Hammond looked tanned and healthy, his grin natural and genuine. He appeared to be what he was: a moderately successful man on the threshold of middle age, enjoying himself on his vacation.

"May I keep this?"

"Does that mean . . . ?" Elaine Hammond bit at her lip. "Mr. Shanks told me your fee was high, but he said you sometimes took factors into consideration . . . made adjustments."

Dennison smiled a smile that might have been apologetic. "My fee begins at two hundred and fifty thousand dollars."

Elaine Hammond paled. "I don't . . . there is no way I could raise that kind of money."

"I'm sorry," Dennison said, and his smile did not change.

Elaine Hammond stood, a little unsteadily. Dennison got quickly to his feet. She took a deep breath, as if steeling herself, and Dennison thought she was going to protest or plead. Instead she said, "I'm sorry, too, Mr. Dennison. Thank you for your time." Her voice was cold but civil. Dennison liked her for that.

He held the office door. "If your husband makes contact, would you let me know?"

"Why?"

"Because I need your cooperation, Elaine," Dennison murmured.

"Why should I—?" She cut herself off. "Do you . . . can you help me after all?"

"I have no idea," Dennison said blandly.

Elaine Hammond stared at him. "I'll tell you if I hear anything," she said finally.

A few minutes later Dennison heard the growl of twin turbines revving up to speed. The big helicopter rose past his window, close enough so he could see Mrs. Hammond in the passenger seat. She did not look in his direction. The rotors dipped, and the copter skated off down toward the valley far below. Dennison watched until it was out of sight. It would be a day or two before the deer returned now. Each spring when the high-strung animals came back to the high country it took weeks for them to become reaccustomed to the human comings and goings. By autumn they would be at ease around the clearing again, and Miss Paradise would have her usual successful hunting season. Dennison had no interest in stalking game, but he liked venison.

Miss Paradise came into the office and stood with fists on hips. "You know something, boss?" she said crossly. "Sometimes you can be a real heel. Have I mentioned that to you?"

"Yes, my dear. Often."

"I liked her," Miss Paradise declared. "I think we're going to have to help her."

"Are we?" Dennison said vaguely. He was redrawing the drapes.

When he ran the film this time he stopped it several times. One frame showed four of the raiders together; he studied it for several minutes. Miss Paradise stared stoically at the footage of the mutilated corpse and waited for Dennison to finish.

When the film had run out, Dennison put his elbows on his desk and steepled his fingers. "Six men," he said to himself. "Seven, if you count the driver. Military weapons and something like military discipline. A man speaks out of turn and is executed on the spot. There is nothing clumsier to carry than a fresh corpse, so they take only the identifiable parts. Everything is planned."

"Why didn't they shoot out the camera?"

"I was wondering the same thing, so I made a call this morning before you were up. The camera was encased in Kevlar. Apparently they knew that too; if they had fired on it they would have sent random lead flying around the room."

Dennison pursed his lips and said, "Nevins."

"How's that?"

"The Civil War history I was reading last night. There hasn't been a military assault on a bank in this country since 1864."

"That was no unit of the U.S. Army, boss."

"No, but it was paramilitary. That bothers me."

"You're trying to figure a tie-in between this bank job and George Dial and Helena Frome."

"Do you see one?"

"No," she said firmly. "First, the time frame is no good. Dial and Frome would have to get to Sicily, arrange passage to this country, and recruit accomplices—in one week. Not to mention promoting a half dozen automatic rifles, a pickup truck, intelligence on the timing of the cash flow at the First Fisk Trust, and a dozen other items." Miss Paradise smiled sweetly. "Besides, if you were back in this country after a ten-year exile, would you pick North Dakota for your first stop?"

She showed Dennison two manicured fingers. "Second, none of the bank gang was a woman, and none looked anything like our file pictures of George Dial. I checked." She shook her head. "Sorry, boss."

"Maybe we should look into this business anyway," Dennison said casually. "What do you think, my dear?"

Miss Paradise perched her rump on the edge of the desk, leaned down, and kissed him on the lips. "I think you're not such a heel after all, boss."

"This doesn't have anything to do with Hammond," Dennison snapped. "I sympathize with the woman, but—"

"But a rule is a rule, right, boss sweetie?"

"Somewhere in this country," Dennison said gruffly, "there is a criminal outfit with the discipline and resources to carry off a bank job using terrorist and paramilitary techniques. I don't know about you, but I find that distressing."

"Okay, boss, okay." It was almost impossible to ruffle Dennison, so each time she did Miss Paradise considered it a victory. She liked games as much as costumes, and she was having too good a time to let it drop. "I'll call Colonel Price right away."

Dennison glared at her back. At the office door she turned to face the look without flinching. She did not mean to lose this one in the late rounds. "Well gee, boss," she said innocently, "what with those desperados coming on like soldier boys, I thought, it takes one to know one, and so I said to myself: Who would the boss call in a situation like this?"

Dennison sighed dramatically, to indicate his vast forbearance.

"He'd call Colonel Price, I answered myself," Miss Paradise said. "So why don't I save him the trouble of telling me and go ahead and get Price on the phone ipso-pronto?" She batted big eyes at him. "Did I do good, boss?"

"The business at the end with the eyes was a little much."

"You know what I mean."

"You have a lot of initiative, my dear," Dennison said.

"I know. When I grow up, I want to be just like you."

"Call Colonel Price, would you please?"

"Coming right up," Miss Paradise said, and waltzed out of the office.

Chapter Seven

Taste, elegance, and wealth were commonplace on Saint Simons, across the Intracoastal Waterway from south Georgia's shore, but even by the island's rigorous standards the seaside estate was remarkable.

The house had two stories, and people seeing it from the air or sea usually described it as "rambling." Actually its lines were classical; similar homes had dotted the South for over one hundred fifty years. The main section was square-cut, with green-shuttered windows contrasting the brilliant white siding; symmetrical one-story wings were appended at either end. Dormers peered out of a mansard roof, and a vast porticoed porch ran the length of the front. Purple bougainvillea twined up the columns.

Spikes of palmetto fanned the corners of the house, and at one end, by a stand of pecan trees, there was a formal flower garden. Beds of roses, tulips, grape hyacinth, poppies, iris, snapdragons, and flowering kale were separated by walkways of crushed oyster shells bordered by old handmade bricks. A boxwood hedge trimmed as flat as a tabletop framed the garden.

In the rear a carriage house had been converted into a four-stall garage, and from it a paved drive ran under a canopy of live oak, ancient gnarled roots exposed above the rich soil. To one side was a guest cottage fronted by rows of hibiscus bushes and azaleas; to the other was a twenty-five-meter swimming pool and a dozen cabanas shaded by the thick, glossy leaves of a magnolia.

The porticoed facade of the big house faced a lawn the size of three football fields, the Bermuda grass groomed as uniform as carpeting. It was roughly triangular, with the house forming the base and the two legs represented by sea walls topped by concrete walkways. Twenty feet below, the Atlantic surf pounded on a jumble of jagged granite boulders. Dried seaweed, green as jade, was plastered to the rocks.

This close to the ocean the weather did not vary too much over a year's course, with the exception of an occasional autumn hurricane. But now it was spring, and the day was warm and bright. The sky was cloudless, and the offshore breeze tasted fresh and slightly saline.

At the foot of the lawn, a yard from the sea wall's edge, a man drew a knife and lunged at William Sterling Price.

Price sidestepped and darted out a booted foot, catching his attacker hard in the shins. The man grunted and went down, but dropped his shoulder and rolled back to his feet in the same seamless motion.

He bent to a crouch on the edge of the concrete walkway, circling warily away from the dead drop. The knife had an all-in-one steel haft with three finger holes and a grip molded to the shape of the palm. The blade was eight inches long, with a double edge as thin as membrane. The man holding this pig-sticker was somewhere in his thirties, perhaps ten years younger than Price.

He feinted, and Price seemed at first to go with the move. But then he twisted in the other direction, and his leg snapped out in a mule-kick. Price's foot missed the knifeman's wrist by a half inch. Price was in position before the guy could recover from his surprise, weight forward on the balls of his feet, hands up and palms out, the textbook defensive stance of the unarmed man against blade attack.

Price stood two inches over six feet, and his broad shoulders tapered to a slab-flat stomach. There were traces of gray at the temples of his crewcut, the only hint he had passed his fortieth birthday a few years back. He wore tan slacks, a black T-shirt, and black boots that laced up the front and had been shined that morning.

The knifeman faked again, and Price dodged left. The younger guy circled, holding his crouch. He was trying to get Price's back against the sea wall's plunge.

Price let him.

The guy jabbed again, and Price stepped back. The other man pressed the advantage, slashing at Price's mid-section and missing by millimeters, following with an upthrust that passed under Price's chin. Price shuffle-stepped onto the concrete walk. The crash of the ocean on the sharp rocks roared in his ears.

Price felt behind with one boot, came up against the lip of the sea wall. The concrete was slick with spray.

The knifeman faked to the side and charged, the flesh-parting steel outthrust before him.

Price shifted his weight in the other direction, then sidestepped toward the guy's feint. His right hand shot out as fast as a rattlesnake's strike, locking around the wrist of the knife arm. Price twisted it hard, and the guy yowled with pain. The pig-sticker flew out of numbed fingers and clattered over the edge.

Price had leverage on the guy now. He used it. The guy went down on one knee on the concrete walk, his arm wrenched up behind him. Price put the sole of his boot against the small of the guy's neck.

Price pulled, and the guy's neck arched back so Price

could see the shiny film of sweat on his forehead. A good yank and the guy's wrist and elbow would snap like kindling, but that was the least of his peril. All Price had to do was release the wrist and lean forward, and the guy would go hurtling into space. About the same effort it would take to open a swinging door, for a one-way ticket to eternity.

For long moments neither man moved, neither man spoke. It was the knifeman who broke.

"Goddamn it, Colonel." The words edged out between clenched teeth. "That was a good knife you just fed to the fishes."

"Trying to walk me off the sea wall was your idea, Al." A smile was forming at the corners of Price's grim mouth.

"Aw right, aw right," Al said. "Now how about giving me back my arm?"

"Sure," Price said, and let go of the wrist.

For one awful beat the knifeman teetered on the edge of the wall, his fingers clawing concrete in a vain search for purchase.

Price grabbed his wrist again and pulled him away from the drop and to his feet.

Al tried to rub circulation into his right arm. "If you don't mind me saying it, Colonel, sometimes you've got a real shitty sense of humor."

"Watch yourself, sergeant."

"Right, sorry," Al said briskly. "You've got a real shitty sense of humor, *sir.*" He snapped a crisp salute that employed only one finger.

Price laughed. "That's better."

Al snorted, but then he grinned, too. "Anyway, Colonel, I guess you still got it."

"Yeah," Price said, "and I'm planning on keeping it. How about a beer?"

A woman came out on the porch as they neared the house. She wore white slacks, a white linen blouse with rolled sleeves, and white open-toed pumps. She was maturely pretty, with dark hair touched with gray and cut stylishly short, and leathery tanned skin that spoke of a lifetime's acquaintance with the golf course and the tennis court.

"Telephone, dear," she trilled.

"Who is it?" Price asked.

"It's Mister Dennison, dear. I suppose this means we'll miss the flower show and the Silberfelds's brunch." She turned to the younger man. "Did you enjoy your stroll, Alan?"

Al glanced at Price. "It was educational."

"Could you fetch Al a beer, hon? I'll take the call in the den." Price could hear her quizzing Al on the latest details of his love-life as he went on down the hall. He shut the door of his den and her voice became an indistinct murmur.

One wall of the room was floor-to-ceiling shelves filled with leather-bound volumes; on another hung six framed portraits of men in military uniforms. Price picked up the phone and said, "Go ahead." He was staring at an oil of a chin-whiskered, middle-aged man in Confederate gray and general's stripes. The old soldier stared dourly back.

Price listened, then said, "Spell it, would you please?" On a leaf of a desk pad embossed in gold leaf with his name, Price wrote in block letters, "CREED," and below it, "GREAVES." He repeated the names aloud, then said, "Not off hand, but I'll ask around." He listened, shook his head at the general's portrait, and said, "Make it thirteen hundred hours. Right, I'll be there."

Price grinned at the general, who stared stonily back. "Don't mention it, Dennison," he said. "My pleasure." He cradled the phone and said softly to the general, "Battle stations, sir."

In the kitchen, his wife was smiling slyly and making Al squirm under her questions, but she cut herself off as Price came in. From the earliest days of their marriage, nearly twenty-five years earlier while he was still at the Point, she understood his commitment as a professional soldier, and accepted what that would cost her in concern, uncertainty, and occasionally, dread. Now, though out of the military, he was hardly retired; she sensed well enough what the calls from Dennison meant, and what sort of work engaged her husband in the absences that followed. Beyond that, there was nothing gained in pointless questions.

Now she studied his face briefly. "We will miss that brunch, won't we?" she said, half to herself.

Al shot Price a questioning look. Price shook his head. "This one is solo."

Al glanced at Mrs. Price. "I'll wait for you out front." He picked up his beer and went out.

Outside the kitchen window, the garden was blooming into a riot of color. Price came up behind her. He put both arms around her waist and his chin on her shoulder. "I'll be back soon."

She faced him, smiling and dry-eyed. "Of course you will," she said softly.

Chapter Eight

Dennison watched from his front porch as Chris Amado came running up the deer trail and into the clearing. She wore a red-white-and-blue headband, a sleeveless T-shirt, red satin jogging shorts, and Nikes. The muscles in her legs were sharply defined, and her naturally dark skin was beginning to tan. She slowed to a cool-down walk, stretching her arms out behind her, then swinging them in loosening circles. On the porch, Dennison beamed with satisfaction, like a trainer whose filly has just clocked a 2:03 mile.

The clearing in front of Dennison's headquarters complex was level and roughly square, about fifty yards to a side. It was sodded with grass, which Dennison noted would soon have to be mowed for the first time that spring. At the far edge, a ten-foot pole supported a bright orange windsock, which now hung limp in the still mountain air. The helicopter was parked beside it: a Bell Model 222 Executive, white with blue and red trim. There was no insignia except the aircraft ID number on the fuselage, just behind the stubby stabilizer wings.

The clearing was surrounded by heavy timber, mostly lodgepole pine and blue spruce with some quaking aspen, virgin growth that had never been logged or even thinned, except for the space carved out for Dennison's needs. Beyond it the forest sloped away, gently at first and then more sharply, into a valley that bottomed nearly two thousand feet below, where a creek flowed between steep rock walls. At this time of the year it was swollen by snow-melt runoff, and its rapids coursed over three-foot drops and rushed between boulders big as cars. The thin, high-country air was so still that if Dennison concentrated he could hear the susurrus of the faraway stream from where he stood.

To Dennison's back, the slope of the mountain steepened precipitously. The forest ended five hundred feet above, and the remaining thousand feet to the summit was a friable granite face, nearly vertical. Atop the narrow pinnacle was a twenty-foot steelwork tower anchored by guy wires strung from eye-bolts drilled into solid rock. The tower supported two antennas and a microwave dish mounted on a remote-controlled direc-tional rotor. To one side of it, with an unobstructed line on the southern sky, was a satellite dish receiver; although Dennison was not much of a television watcher, Miss Paradise enjoyed a few shows, and Dennison enjoyed pleasing her.

An observer who took the trouble to climb to the pinnacle would have a view of at least ten miles in any direction. In that expanse of territory there was no sign of civilization or habitation beyond Dennison's compound, and even that could be overlooked in a casual scrutiny. There was no obvious or easy way up the mountain; with the exception of a logging trail on the far ridge, there were no roads within view. The logging road had not been used for a decade, and its access was beyond the ridge and three thousand feet below, almost forty land miles from Dennison's compound. A ditch had been bulldozed across it, six feet wide and deep, according to the terms of an easement Dennison held under the name of a cousin who had been dead for seventeen years.

The mountain was steep enough, and its forest cover thick enough, to effectively bar trail-bike or horseback traffic. In the summer it was possible to reach Dennison's compound on foot, if a person were in good enough physical condition to undertake a four-day uphill walk carrying a fifty-pound pack. In winter an expert Nordic skier might be able to get in. Dennison preferred the helicopter.

Dennison came down the three steps from the porch and took an appreciative breath. The spring afternoon was mild, and the breezeless air tasted sweet as mint candy. A bank of old snow nestled against the rocky pinnacle above, reddish with lichen and pocked and dirty.

Chris Amado lay on her back on the lawn doing leg lifts. Dennison crouched on his haunches beside her. "How do you feel?"

"Better." She raised one fine leg and held it a few inches above the grass, her stomach sucked in hard.

Dennison smiled politely. "Your time in prison," he said, almost delicately. "It must have been tough."

Chris laughed mirthlessly. She put down her leg, drew up her knees, and began to do sit-ups.

"A drug bust?" Dennison asked.

"That's what they said."

"What do *you* say?" Dennison inquired, in the same neutral tone.

Chris sat up, twisting her torso to touch her right elbow to the outside of her left knee. She looked extraordinarily fit considering where she had spent the last year or so. That pleased Dennison; it told him she had the discipline to take care of herself—particularly when things got tough.

She would need that kind of discipline. If she bought his proposition, things would get a lot tougher.

Her sleeveless T-shirt rode up to reveal ripples of defined muscle across her stomach. She was small-breasted, her nipples outlined under the thin material, and her long, lean arms ended in fingers that were almost delicate, tapered as the fingers of a pianist or an Old West gunslinger. Her face was strikingly beautiful, the *café au lait* skin smooth and unlined. Her hair was dark and shiny like patent leather.

Chris did one last sit-up and held, her arms hugging her knees. "I didn't want to return to the U.S.," she said, "but there was nowhere else to go—at least nowhere I could do any good. The idea was to raise money and raise public awareness of what's happening to the people—to *my* people," she corrected. "But my involvement was over." She smiled with her mouth only. "Four different countries were offering a bounty to anyone who brought me in."

She straightened her legs, then bent and grasped her toes, holding the muscle-loosening stretch. "I almost didn't make it to Mexico City," she said. "Once I did, I thought I was safe. It turned out I was wrong." She looked at him for the first time. "Why am I telling you this? Can I trust you?"

Dennison was still crouched, forearms on his thighs, looking as at ease as if he were in his desk chair. "What do you think?"

She studied him for a long moment. "I made it to the airport," she said finally. "They called my flight, and I was almost to the gate when three men in dark suits grabbed me. They all had mustaches; I remember that, for some reason. Nobody bothered to show me any identification, and there didn't seem any point in asking. They strong-armed me into a back room, where some fat pig in a comic opera uniform was waiting. He turned out to be Enrico. He dismissed the matron and took care of the strip-search himself. He didn't find anything, but he seemed to have a good time. Then they brought in my suitcase. There was a half kilo of uncut cocaine in it."

"They set you up," Dennison suggested.

Chris shook her head. "The coke was just a prop, something to show the three guys with mustaches, who turned out to be legitimate airport cops. Enrico pulled rank on them and said he'd personally deliver me to the customs authorities. I never saw them—or the inside of a courtroom."

"Of course not," Dennison said.

Chris climbed to her feet and gazed around the compound. She pushed her dark hair out of her face, then shook her head so it fell naturally into place. Dennison was reminded again of a fine thoroughbred. The best of them—the ones born to run—anticipated the race with the impatience of a birthday boy. They thrilled to competition, to the chance to extend themselves to the limits of skill and speed and endurance.

"I think it's time you told me why I'm here," Chris Amado said.

"I think you're right," Dennison said.

Chapter Nine

Matthew Conte was not by nature a patient man. He was too quick-tempered for judicious deliberation and too full of energy to enjoy sitting still for long periods of time. But years before, when he was learning the only job he had ever held, he decided to acquire patience through discipline and application, as another might learn touch-typing. He had no alternative; patience was a necessity in the profession Matt Conte had chosen.

Matt Conte was an assassin.

So although he had been at this place for almost a week, Conte had not pushed for explanations, or asked any but the most inconsequential questions. Instinct told him that this man Dennison did not pose a threat, and for now that was enough.

Here at least there were no alleys concealing men with guns.

Conte thought he liked Dennison, though Conte had few casual acquaintances and no intimate friends. Yet in Dennison he recognized something special—a quiet confidence coupled with the feeling that Dennison had seen his share of dangerous action at some time—and could still handle it if he had to. Conte was curious about the man, but curiosity could wait.

Answers would come in time.

Conte was sitting on the bottom of the three steps leading up to Dennison's front porch. It had become his favorite spot in the week he'd been here, in part because he had found he did not like getting too far from the house. He had fought in his share of jungles and against his share of animals of both the four- and two-legged variety, but the vast serene woods surrounding the compound made him uneasy. Too much time lately in the city, he decided.

The building at his back was angular and multifaceted, as if a dozen or so prismatically shaped boxes had been glued together at random. The exterior was finished with redwood shakes, stained pine trim, and tinted glass, in a design that concealed the interior layout like magician's misdirection. Conte had been there a couple of days before he realized that there had to be entire sections he had not been in.

To someone overflying the place, it would have looked like a modern, expensive, somewhat oversized, but unimaginative forest retreat. It could have been the shared private hunting lodge for a group of city-bound executives; for such a crew it would probably represent a showcase specimen of contemporary rustic architecture. There was a cedar-shingled canopy over the porch behind Conte, with several pieces of cane-and-canvas lawn furniture. Conte had not seen anyone use them, but they reinforced the vacation cabin ambience.

Conte fished a crumpled pack of cigarettes from his shirt pocket, extracted the last one, straightened a crimp in it, and was lighting it with a gold Zippo when a voice behind him said, "Conte!"

He rose and turned, blowing out smoke. Miss Paradise was on the porch, hands on hips, looking down at him with what Conte supposed was meant to be faint disapproval. He got a kick out of this woman. Like him, she was quick with a wisecrack, and what relationship they had established was based on verbal jousting. Conte didn't put any special stock in that kind of flirting; for starters, he had already figured out she was off limits. But that didn't mean he couldn't enjoy looking at her. Only a dead man would not, and Conte suspected that even a corpse might open one eye for a quick peek at the majestic Miss P.

"Enjoying your stay?" she asked.

"No," Conte said. "There's not enough people, it's too quiet, and the air is too clean. I miss the city. I want to get jostled on the sidewalks and see crime in the streets."

"You *are* crime in the streets, Conte."

"Not anymore."

"He's ready to see you," Miss Paradise said.

On this day she was wearing white knee socks, saddle shoes, and a pleated skirt that ended at mid-thigh. From where Conte stood at the foot of the three steps, the view of her legs was heart-stopping. Over a white blouse with a Buster Brown collar she wore a bulky blue crewneck sweater with a white felt "Y" over her left breast.

"Yale?" Conte asked.

"Ypsilanti," Miss Paradise said. "Come on, hotshot." She nodded over her shoulder. Her blond hair was in a ponytail held in place by a double elastic band. There were circles of rouge on her cheeks, like the blush of a crisp autumn day.

At the top of the steps Conte said, "Didn't you forget your pom-poms?"

"I don't use pom-poms. I get them to cheer with my bare hands."

Conte sidled past. He had to look up to meet her eyes. "What are you doing after work?"

"Practicing some new routines," Miss Paradise said. "You ought to do the same." But she smiled.

The front door opened into her office. Conte was quartered in one of several apartments in the back of the complex, and he had not been inside this part of the building yet. In addition to patience, Conte had learned the art of observation and the habit of casing any new place. He took in a picture window to his left, looking out over the valley, and a plain rectangular mirror on the wall to the right. His image in it was slightly distorted, and he guessed that it concealed a one-way window. He made a mental note to get a rough idea of the configuration of the hidden room when he got back outside.

The walls of Miss Paradise's office were white. There were several modern prints in plain metal frames; Conte recognized Mondrian's "Broadway Boogie Woogie" and de Kooning's "Mailbox." A contemporary sofa, all stainless steel and white vinyl-covered cushions, faced a long, low coffee table on top of which an immaculate ceramic ashtray was framed by four rows of *People* magazine overlapped in date order. The headline on the most recent issue read, "Liz— Diets, Diamonds, and a Mid-Life Dilemma," beside a photograph of a woman who appeared to be stuffed with kapok. Near the foot of the sofa was a matching chair, and between was a four-foot potted avocado plant, its stalk emerging from between the split halves of a fat seed.

The floor of the reception office was waxed and polished hardwood. There was no carpet. Miss Paradise's desk was an eight-by-three butcher block slab on gleaming stainless steel legs, with a sculpted swivel chair covered in the same white

vinyl as the sofa. Atop the desk was a vinyl-edged blotter, a
legal-sized folder covered in the same material, a pen set with
a split-quartz base, a digital clock/calendar with a green LED
display, and a white telephone with three pushbuttons. Set
against one end of the desk like the foot of an L was a smaller
matching stand holding the low-line keyboard and video
display of a computer terminal.

"Walk this way," Miss Paradise said.

Conte let the line lie and followed her through the door
behind her desk.

Dennison rose and offered his hand. "Matt," he said
warmly, "thanks for staying for this meeting. I appreciate it."
His handshake was firm.

Chris Amado was curled in one of the armchairs. Conte
nodded to her and said, " 'Lo, Chris." Although they had
shared the chopper to the compound, they had not spent much
time together since. Conte got the impression she disliked him,
but since he'd done nothing to put her off, he determined to
treat her civilly and leave it at that. He sensed some darkness in
her, some anger that she had nurtured for a long time and was
reluctant to give up.

Conte had renounced anger long ago. He had killed in
anger once—and had killed that emotion at the same time.
Discipline dissipated anger. He wondered how disciplined
Chris Amado was.

She shot him a look that said, "Hi," pleasantly enough.
She wore a clean T-shirt, hiking shorts, and sandals, and she
was drinking from a can of Miller beer.

Dennison gestured toward the chair next to Chris.
"Would you like a drink, Matt?"

"No. Thanks." Conte stubbed out his cigarette in the
heavy desk ashtray and took a seat.

Dennison's office was the antithesis of Miss Paradise's. It
reminded Conte of the library in a gentlemen's club, in the kind
of movie where Arthur Treacher played the major domo. In
contrast to the stark efficiency of the reception area, it seemed
measured, leisurely, comfortable—like Dennison.

The heavy, sober-colored drapes were pulled back from
the double-wide window that reached from the floor almost to
the ceiling, and sunlight brightened the room. The opposite

wall was dominated by a fireplace fashioned of river stones chinked with cement, topped by a heavy mantel worked from a single thick plank of mahogany. Its lined firebox was four feet wide, and three bark-covered logs were pyramided on andirons within it, awaiting winter.

Bookshelves ran chest-high along the other two walls. Above one was another distorting mirror. The tops of the shelves, like the mantelpiece, were covered with a jumble of papers, books, liquor decanters, glasses of various sizes, and a miscellany of knick-knacks. There was a one-eighth-scale model of a 1933 Rolls Royce Phaeton, with the open chauffeur's seat and enclosed passenger compartment; a conch shell; a fishbowl containing a plaster castle, a plastic plant, a handful of crushed coral, and three guppies; and an original-year-issue presentation model Colt .45 Peacemaker revolver with a ten-inch barrel in a glass-covered sandalwood case. There were no plants. In two of the corners were brass floor lamps, with curled toes on their stands and beige satin shades. The carpet was an earth-brown Kerman.

Dennison's desk was oak, stained and polished to the deep, rich color of a Brazil nut. The edges of the surface and the legs were baroquely carved, and the whole thing looked to weigh maybe a ton and a half. Almost none of the surface was visible; it was cluttered with a jumble of books lying spine up or sprouting multiple bookmarks, along with newspapers, clippings, letters, memos, and files, arranged without any concession to order. Scattered among this mess was a goose-neck lamp with a green skullcap shade; a mechanical clock shaped like an old cathedral radio, with a glass front that revealed the works; and a coiled cord that presumably was attached to a telephone buried somewhere under the pile.

The four chairs that faced the desk were upholstered in navy blue velvet into which a pattern of whorls and curlicues had been worked. They were arranged in a neat semicircle, as if awaiting the heirs of Uncle Morris, come to hear the first reading of the old geezer's will.

"I'll be frank," Dennison began disarmingly. He held up two file folders. "You've both been checked out. I'd like to go over the details."

Chris shrugged. "I've got nothing to hide."

"That makes you one in a million," Conte said.

Dennison smiled and opened the top folder. His glance lingered almost fondly on the contents before he spoke. "Christina Maria Amado: born Ithaca, New York, to Rafael Aguilar Amado, citizen of Santa Cruz, and Judith Bingham Amado, of Old Lyme, Connecticut. Educated—"

"Mr. Dennison," Chris interrupted.

Dennison looked up.

"My father—" Chris began, and as abruptly stopped.

Dennison waited.

"My father's family were farmers." Chris plunged on. "He went to work in the fields almost as soon as he could walk. He was educated at home."

"He still managed to win a scholarship to Cornell."

"The College of Agriculture."

"Santa Cruz?" Conte put in. "I don't think I've ever heard of it."

"It's located in the northeastern corner of South America," Dennison said. "Surinam shares its border. It's a small country, about ten thousand square miles, but it's on the coastal plain and has a temperate climate and a long growing season."

"Except that ninety percent of the land is in the hands of five percent of the population," Chris said. "My father's family were sharecroppers, like nearly all the farmers. He wanted to see changes made. That was why he worked so hard to get into Cornell."

"Your mother . . ."

"He met her there." She seemed in a hurry to get this storytelling over with. "They were married in his third year of college, and I was born a month before they both graduated."

"So you're an American citizen?" Conte said.

"That's right," Chris snapped with unwarranted heat. "Are you?"

"After college," Dennison put in smoothly, "your father returned to Santa Cruz."

"With my mother and me. He took a job as an agronomist with the Santa Cruz Ministry of Agriculture—he thought he could change the system by working from within. He was wrong," she added bitterly.

"My father sent me to a private school in the capital,"

Chris said, "and when I got into Harvard he pushed me to go. By then he was deputy minister of agriculture. He'd spent most of his career drawing up a comprehensive plan for redistributing the arable land in Santa Cruz. Up to then the argicultural system had been feudal: peasants worked for pennies an hour and a hut to live in, with no hope of ever owning land on their own. Under the system my father devised, that would have changed, and no one would have suffered from government appropriation. Any landholder compelled to give up part of his acreage got a package of financial considerations, tax breaks, and so on. Soon after I left for college, my father introduced the plan publicly.

"Ninety-five percent of the people hailed it as the most equitable land reform ever introduced in a Third World country. Five percent called it a Communist plot—but they were the ones who controlled Santa Cruz's government, military, and wealth. The debate went on for years, and during that time the minister of argiculture died of natural causes. My father succeeded him. He was a powerful and charismatic speaker, and he had the support of the people."

Chris stopped abruptly. Conte could feel the heat of the anger he had previously sensed, but its source was still a mystery to him.

"In the spring of my junior year at Harvard," Chris said, "my father was assassinated."

"Sorry," Conte said softly. "Do you know who killed him?"

"A pig named Ricardo Fulgencio," Chris spat. "A lieutenant in the army, working for the big landowners."

"Did you . . . ?" Conte let the question trail off.

"Kill him?" She barked a humorless laugh. "No."

Conte waited for the rest.

"But I watched him die," Chris Amado said.

"Okay," Conte said mildly. Her gaze drilled into him.

"My mother fled to the States, about the same time I returned to Santa Cruz."

Chris turned to Dennison. "My father dedicated his life— the years he lived, and the years they stole from him—to an idea. He did it for one reason: he believed it was right."

She flashed a look at Conte, and again the heat in her gaze was palpable. "I believed the same thing. I still do."

Conte was thinking of his own father and the way he had died. They were not so much different, he and this dark, smoldering young woman. He wondered if he would be able to find a way to tell her.

Chris leaned forward, placed her palms on the edge of Dennison's desk. "My father's death pushed the farmers over the edge. They didn't have money or guns, but they gathered whatever weapons and supplies they could find and went into the jungle. A few days later, I got to Santa Cruz and joined them. They called themselves Amadistas. I was with the squad that ambushed Ricardo Fulgencio.

"They wanted to please me," Chris said. "They wanted to show their respect for my father. Later, when the generals found Fulgencio, there was a note pinned to his chest"—she looked at Conte and added—"his bare chest. It read: 'Fulgencio: Muerte a Asesinos.'"

"'Death to Murderers,'" Dennison muttered.

Chris was still staring at Conte. "They had to put his name on the note. After what they did, no one could have recognized his face."

"You became a rebel," Conte said slowly. "A guerilla."

"I've done my fighting."

"And killing?"

"That's right," Chris said levelly. She looked at Dennison. "I'm Rafael Amado's daughter. I have propaganda value, to both sides. After a while I spent most of my time establishing liaison between the Amadistas and other reform groups in Guatemala, El Salvador, and Honduras. The established governments in those countries, along with the ruling generals in Santa Cruz, were offering a ten-thousand-dollar reward to whoever delivered me to any of the capitals."

"Or your corpse," Miss Paradise guessed.

"No," Chris corrected. "They wanted me alive so they could use me. They'd interrogate me first, and then I'd publicly denounce the Amadistas as terrorists. Outside funding and popular support would dry up, and the Amadistas would be broken. They're operating on the edge already."

"So you left?" Conte asked.

"That's right. I had no choice. If I were captured, I'd do everything they asked sooner or later. I've stood some pain in my time, but everyone's got a limit, and these bastards are pros. I left Santa Cruz through the same underground channels I had established for moving around Latin America. I made Mexico City, and you know the rest."

"Why did Enrico hold on to you?" Miss Paradise asked. "Why didn't he turn you in for the reward?"

Chris shrugged. "My guess is that he was haggling over price, trying to up the ante. Maybe he thought he could work out some way of using me himself. The generals in Santa Cruz weren't in a big hurry, as long as I was locked up and unable to raise money for the movement." Chris ran her tongue over her lips, as if she had just tasted something unpleasant. "Maybe he didn't want to give up his monthly rape."

Conte felt vaguely embarrassed, partly for Chris and partly from the vestiges of the Catholic upbringing he'd never been able to transcend completely.

"What about your mother?" Dennison asked.

"She's back in Old Lyme. She thinks I died in the jungle years ago, and that's for the best, I think. Nothing in the way she's lived has equipped her to deal with the path I chose."

"The question is," Dennison said, "what are you going to do now?"

Chris looked at him narrowly. "I have the feeling you've got a suggestion about that."

"You need money."

Chris shook her head. "The Amadistas need money," she emended. "Are you pledging a donation to the cause?"

"In a way," Dennison said.

Conte was looking at her with renewed interest. "Listen," he said. "I didn't—"

"That's right," Chris snapped, and the nameless, suppressed fury seemed to burst to the surface. "And what have you been doing lately, Mr. Conte? Why are you here now?"

He had done nothing to provoke this. "I killed people," he said.

"For some noble cause, I suppose."

"For money."

She drained the last of her beer and crushed the can in her fist. "I don't think I like that," she said in a tight, hard voice.

"I don't think you know what you're talking about, lady."

"I'm listening."

Dennison rubbed his palms together briskly. "Matt, do you want to fill us in?"

"Let's hear your version."

Dennison smiled. "Being cautious?"

Conte returned the smile. "Put it this way: I like you, Mr. Dennison, and I probably owe you a favor. But I'm not real sure what this is about. So why don't you start the verse, and maybe I'll jump in on the chorus."

Dennison opened the second file. "Matt was born and educated in the Little Italy neighborhood of New York City." He was talking at Chris, and there was a conciliatory note in his voice. "He enlisted in the army when he was seventeen and served four years, including two one-year tours in Vietnam."

"You volunteered?" Chris asked.

"It's a long story," Conte said.

"When Matt was discharged," Dennison went on, "he joined the staff of Carlo DeChristi, the *capo* of the Mafia family that controlled lower Manhattan."

"Wait a minute," Chris said. "You mean you walked into the local Mafia branch office and applied for a job?"

"It's a long story."

"The details don't matter," Dennison said. But Conte had the feeling that Dennison knew the whole story. That was an idea he did not like. "Matt began as DeChristi's bodyguard," Dennison continued. "Within a year he was . . . how would you describe it, Matt?" Dennison asked disingenuously.

Conte sighed. "I was nominally under Carlo's control, but I really worked for the Old Men, the ruling council. I kept the peace. Sometimes that meant that people had to die." He turned to Chris. "Is that what you're waiting to hear?"

The connecting door opened, and Miss Paradise came in with two cans of Miller. She handed one to Chris and popped the tab on the other one, then chugged a healthy gulp.

"You sure you don't want something, Conte?" she asked, perching on the edge of the desk near him.

"No thanks. I don't drink."

"Why not?"

Conte looked up at her. "My father's example."

"He didn't drink either?"

"He drank enough for both of us."

"Thank you, my dear," Dennison murmured. Miss Paradise looked miffed as she left, but it occurred to Conte that her timing with the fresh beer was too good. He was pretty damned sure that her role around here was not as a waitress and that a lot of this business was for his benefit, and Chris's. He hadn't forgotten the one-way glass mirrors.

"You did your job," Dennison said to Conte, "and you were respected. When you were growing up, your family didn't have a lot of money. After you got a taste, you decided you appreciated the good life."

"I like to dress well," Conte said. "I like to bet money on the turn of a wheel or the turn of a card." He shot a sidelong glance at Chris. "I like women."

"How much does a woman cost these days?"

Conte stared at her for a few moments. "Here's some free advice, Chris: you keep on dealing in snap judgments, and someday your ass is going to be in one hell of a sling. You piss on everyone you meet, and you're liable to come up short of friends just when you need one." To Dennison he said, "Sorry. Go on." But from the corner of his eye Conte saw that Chris was looking at him with something like thoughtfulness.

"Matt's problems began six months ago," Dennison said, "when a man named Frank Bressio moved into New York. Bressio wasn't Mafia, and he got on the wrong side of Carlo DeChristi and the Old Men from the start. He was horning in on what they considered to be their territory, and he was making a lot of the wrong kind of noise. He was involved in the kind of crime the Old Men would never touch—armed robbery, hijacking, kidnapping, extortion."

"You mean there's supposed to be clean crime and dirty crime?"

Dennison gave Conte a chance to answer. When he didn't, Dennison said, "In a way, yes. The Mafia tries to avoid the kind of flashy violent crime that attracts the attention of cops and reporters. The St. Valentine's Day Massacre was fifty years ago, and the stereotype of the mobster with a Tommy gun is legend now. The Mafia deals in status quo crime these days: drugs, loan sharking, gambling, prostitution—"

"The service industries," Chris said dryly.

"The point is," Conte cut in, "Bressio was making waves. The Old Men called him in and warned him to cut the shit, but it didn't take. A week later, some of his thugs picked up a top executive of an oil company and held him for a half million bucks. When the money didn't arrive within six hours, they shot the guy three times in the head. A gunhand named Prince ran the operation for Bressio. The Old Men told me to hit him."

"And?"

"I hit him."

Conte pinched wearily at the bridge of his nose. "For a couple of weeks things were quiet. The Old Men were beginning to figure Bressio had left New York. Then Carlo DeChristi was found in his bed. His brains were all over the pillow, and his dick was in his mouth. That last touch made it more than revenge for Prince. It was a taunt, a slap in the face of the Old Men."

"Did . . . were you close to him?" Chris asked.

"I don't believe in vengeance," Conte said instead of answering. "I tried it once and it turned out lousy."

"So you quit," Dennison said.

"It wasn't that simple. With the Mafia, it never is. The Old Men wanted Bressio, but it was starting to look like the son of a bitch was too strong to stop with anything short of an all-out street war. Nobody wanted that. At the same time, I figured it was over for me. With Carlo dead I'd lost my job security. From then on I'd never know for sure where I stood with the Old Men. I told them I wanted out."

"They acted like they were relieved to see me go," Conte said. "By then Bressio had gone underground again, so as long as I didn't run off half-cocked after the guy—which I didn't plan to do anyway—it looked like things might settle back to normal. So the Old Men told me to keep my mouth shut and my nose clean, and I was on the street.''

Conte sighed. "Which still left me with plenty of trouble. First, I was mostly broke with no idea of what to do next. Second, I didn't completely trust the Old Men; they know where the bodies are buried—figuratively and literally—and I'm always going to have to keep an eye over my shoulder, in case they change their mind and decide I'm less of an annoyance dead. Third, there was already a gun on my back.''

"Bressio?"

"That's right. I could smell the son of a bitch from the beginning, and there was nothing wrong with my nose. For the past month, guys keep trying to kill me.''

"Why does Bressio want you dead?"

"I'm a loose end. Maybe he thinks I'm mad about what he did to Carlo. Maybe *he's* mad at what *I* did to Prince. His reason doesn't matter—it never does.''

Dennison closed the folder and tossed it on top of the desk's jumble. "The two of you are caught in the same squeeze.''

"I don't think so," Chris said darkly.

"Neither of you has money or a place to go. You're on the run, and there are substantial rewards offered for your deaths. You're effectively cut off from the Amadistas, Chris, and you've slammed the door on the Mafia, Matt.'' Dennison folded his hands on the desk blotter. "I have a proposition.''

He stood and came around the desk to lean on its edge in front of them. Conte was struck again by how eerily mutable Dennison was. When he was behind his desk the man seemed sedentary, almost passive—a medium-sized man going a little soft around the gut as he settled without protest into middle age. But he came out of the cushy chair with feline grace, and with Dennison in front of him Conte was reminded the man was no shorter than his own five-eleven. The pot belly suggested by Dennison's seated posture was myth; in reality Dennison was broad-shouldered, barrel-chested, and nowhere near fat.

He spoke firmly and with assurance. "Some time ago I established an organization," Dennison said. "It has no official name, but it's been called Dennison's People. Miss Paradise and I run the day-to-day operation; there are no hidden partners.

"My organization provides skilled professionals to do difficult jobs," Dennison said. "I've developed a pool of freelance warriors, people who know how to handle themselves. Miss Paradise and I provide client contact, intelligence, logistical support, and certain necessary equipment."

"Are you offering us jobs?" Conte asked.

"Yes."

"What kind of jobs?"

"Jobs that no one else is willing or able to tackle. Jobs that need doing."

"Dangerous jobs?"

"Invariably," Dennison said.

"Killing jobs?" Conte pressed.

"Sometimes."

"The trouble is," Conte said thoughtfully, "there are people who frown on that sort of business. The law, for example."

Chris sat up straighter. "Of course," she said slowly. "I should have figured it out right away. You *are* the law, aren't you? Which is it: CIA, FBI—or did they invent some new kind of cop while I was locked up?"

"I'm not a cop," Dennison said, "and I don't play by cop rules. Neither will you, and you'd better be comfortable with that idea before you hire on. If you work for me and break the law—and you will, because you're going to find out damned quickly that law and justice are two different things—if you commit a criminal act, you'll be at the same risk as anyone else."

Dennison held up a warning finger. "I won't mislead you or withhold any information you should have. In turn, you'll play it straight with me. For starters, get used to the idea that you'll have to cover your own butts at all times."

Dennison's voice softened. "At one time," he admitted,

"I had certain . . . official affiliations, and I maintain contact with a variety of people in positions of knowledge and power. Some of my activities are known to certain law enforcement and espionage agencies. On occasion, they ask for my help. Miss Paradise doesn't like waiving our fee, but I figure we get paid in good will and fast accurate intelligence when we need it. It promotes what you might call a spirit of cooperation."

"And they give you free rein?"

"Let's say they choose not to interfere. They are forced to operate according to rules and procedures; they're half-hobbled by technicalities. I'm not, and I get results—results they happen to support—at least philosophically."

Dennison looked hard at each of them in turn. "My People make up their own rules. They don't deal in technicalities or legal loopholes or due process—they deal in action. They do what they have to, and *they get the job done*."

Dennison straightened abruptly. "Questions?"

Chris gestured with her beer can. "I can guess why you need Machine Gun Kelly here, but why me?"

"I need to get close to a man—someone you know."

"A friend of mine?"

"No."

Conte felt eyes on the nape of his neck. He peered around his chair and saw Miss Paradise next to the door. He wondered how long she had been standing there.

"I pay my operatives one hundred thousand dollars per assignment."

That got Conte's attention back. "Just what is the assignment?"

"What does it matter to you?" Chris snapped. "Blood money is blood money."

"That's unfair." Miss Paradise came around and dropped into Dennison's chair. "There's plenty you don't know about Conte here, Chris. He didn't wake up one morning and decide to go into the killing business. It was a little more complex than that. Real life usually is."

So she knew the story, too, Conte thought. Unbidden, the image of his dead father came full-blown into Conte's mind.

He saw the old man lying face up on the sawdust-covered plank flooring, both hands over his navel in the pose in which he'd died, trying to hold his guts in. The front of his white shirt was stiff as crinoline where the blood had dried.

"Both of you know how to handle yourselves," Dennison said. "You've seen some violence in your days, and you've fought back—as violently as you had to. You've been hurt, but you haven't been victims—not like most people have. That's why my organization exists—for the victims, the ones without the skills and power to fight back on their own.

"I'm no crusader," Dennison said. "I'm not under any illusion that I can eradicate injustice or wipe evil from the face of the earth. I just like to see the good guys win once in a while."

"He's not offering you a job," Miss Paradise cut in. "He's offering you a chance. Chris, you know what it means to fight for something you believe in. So do you, Matt—at least you did once."

Conte saw himself kneeling over his father's body, and the promise he had made.

"I don't have much choice," he said. "You've bought yourself a gun, Mr. Dennison."

"I want more than your gun, Matt."

"You'll get it—everything you pay for." But Conte felt vaguely uncomfortable. He looked past Dennison and saw Miss Paradise studying him, as if he were an experiment in which she had devoted a good deal of time and research. "You'll have to give the rest of it some time," Conte finished lamely. "Maybe it will come."

"It will," Dennison said. "You wouldn't be here if I didn't believe that."

"I need some time to think this over," Chris Amado said.

"You can't have it," Dennison said. "The clock is running down right now. People have already died." He looked at Conte. "The wrong kind of people. I need you both, and I need you now."

Chris nodded. "Let's hear the rest."

"Excellent," Dennison said. Miss Paradise nodded encouragement at Chris. It occurred to Conte that the tall woman's wisecracks screened a commitment as total as Dennison's. Chris wasn't the only one who had jumped to conclusions.

Dennison clapped his hands together as a prelude to serious business. "Okay," he said to Chris Amado. "Tell me all you can about George Dial."

Chapter Ten

The sun was still a few degrees above the distant ridge to the west, but within the forest it was already twilight. This early in spring the high-country air became crisp and sharp not long after sundown, and the night sky would be clear and star-flecked. Chris Amado rose from where she had been sitting with her back against the trunk of a lodgepole pine. A warm-up jacket was tied by its arms around her waist, and she undid it and draped it over her shoulders before starting back.

In the brutal months of her internment in the Mexican scumhole prison she had had plenty of time to think—and had been careful not to. She had feared descending into maudlin regret, or self-recrimination, or despair. She had survived through suspicion and cynicism and by nurturing hate, and if she had not let those feelings fester and ferment until they could no longer be contained, she may never have escaped.

But now she was free, and it was time to take stock. The hard shell she had built up around her had been necessary for survival, but now it was time to crack out of it. The first step was to get word back to the Amadista rebel forces that she was alive and free, so they would not falter in their fight. Dennison had volunteered to use his contacts to take care of that.

She could not go back herself. She was a target of the generals and their allies in neighboring countries, and not only would she be committing virtual suicide, but she would also draw unrelenting heat on the other Amadistas. It would be a long time—perhaps years—before she could fight for *la causa* again.

In the meantime, Dennison had given her an opportunity. There was the money, of course, a great deal of it. The money would do as much—perhaps more—than she possibly could now for the Amadistas. But beyond that, she had come to realize as she sat meditating in the thick piney woods, Dennison was providing a chance to pick up where she had left off. She was a warrior; all she had known in her adult years was the fight.

With Dennison she could fight again—and on the right side.

She found Matt Conte at his favorite spot at the bottom of the porch steps. By now the trailing edge of the sun was visible above the ridge, and the sky behind it was a brilliant wash of red and violet, divided by a plume of cumulus cloud sun-burnished to the sheen of molten gold. Conte flicked away a cigarette butt and said, " 'Lo, Chris," in his soft neutral voice.

"Interested in some company?"

Conte looked at her quizzically.

"Would you like to come by for a beer?" She was still not comfortable with him and the idea of what he had been, but if Dennison were willing to accept the man, she owed it to both of them to give him a chance.

"I don't drink," Conte reminded her.

"Look," she said. "I need someone to talk to, and I'd like it to be you."

"Okay," Conte said mildly. Neither said anything else as they went around to the upslope side of the building. Dennison had installed them in a pair of studio apartments; Chris was to the left. The furniture was new and nondescript: a convertible sofa-bed, a couple of chairs and a table, a television, and off the main room a lavatory with shower to one side and a narrow pantry to the other.

Conte stopped inside the door and stood, arms folded.

"What would you like?" Chris asked.

"Ginger ale. And an ashtray."

When she came back with his glass and a can of beer for

herself, he had not moved. "You're not making this easy for me," Chris said.

Conte had nothing to say to that.

"Well, sit down," she said, more irritably than she'd meant. She plopped down on the sofa, and Conte took the chair opposite. Chris felt suddenly shy and saw herself in her college dormitory room, facing a boy she did not know very well, wondering who was going to make the first move and how awkwardly it would come out.

"You don't like the idea of working with a woman, do you?" Chris said, and immediately wished she hadn't.

"I've always worked alone," Conte said, as if that were an answer.

Chris took a pull on her beer, to be doing something.

"I get the idea," Conte said mildly. "You don't think much of me."

"I don't know what I think," Chris blurted. "I don't understand you. I think you frighten me, and I don't like being frightened."

"Because I've killed for money?"

"That's part of it," Chris admitted. "That's most of it."

Conte unfolded his legs and leaned forward. "Let me explain a few things. The Mafia isn't like in the movie or TV, a bunch of fat Guineas with greasy hair and spaghetti sauce stains on their white silk ties, talking with Chico Marx accents and carrying chatterguns with drum magazines. They're businessmen."

"Now wait a minute—"

"It's an illegal business," Conte pressed. "Sometimes it's a dirty business. But the problem is, the public—all those law-abiding citizens—are the best customers. If you've ever smoked a joint or watched a dirty movie or bought a brand-name stereo at sixty percent off in Times Square, the odds are you were dealing indirectly with some branch of the Mob. Without customers, the Mafia would have been bankrupt years ago—but it has plenty of customers, and they are just about everyone you know.

"Okay, so the Mafia doesn't deal in terms of price control or monopoly capitalism or fair trade or any of that crap—those are rules for the legitimate crooks, the big business, ways they keep an eye on each other. But the Mafia has its rules, too. And I was part of the mechanism for enforcing those rules."

"By killing?"

Conte took out a cigarette and rolled it between his fingers without lighting it. "Look," he said, "when you're driving down the highway at seventy and you see a cop car going the other way, you slow down. He can't bust you from over there, but you slow down anyway, because seeing the cruiser reminds you that you could get busted, somewhere down the line.

"I worked for Carlo DeChristi and the Old Men for nine years," Conte said. "People knew about me—I was always right over the next hill, like that cop car. But in all that time I hit a total of five targets, and that includes Prince, the Bressio lieutenant who got trigger-crazy.

"The first was cutting in on the porno racket—except that in the flicks he was financing, half the stars were kids. One of them was a five-year-old girl. They grabbed her out of a playground in Queens, and they put her in a closet for a week to soften her up, and then they brought her to a room in a hotel on Fortieth Street where they had cameras set up. They used ropes on her, belts, a Coke bottle. After three days of it she managed to slip out of the room somehow. She was naked and she couldn't understand why she was being punished, why she was being hurt—but she must have thought she'd done something very bad, because she found a maid's cart and drank a bottle of cleaning fluid."

Chris's beer tasted flat, bitter. She put it down; her hand was shaking a little.

"The second was a *caporegime*—a sub-boss—who wanted to kill a guy who was screwing his wife. But he didn't want to hire a pro, because then the word might get around and everyone would know he was wearing the horns. So he found a drunk in a bar on Second Avenue and gave him a hundred bucks to deliver a package to the guy he wanted bumped. It worked, all right. The package blew up as the guy opened the door and tore him into a dozen pieces. It also killed the drunk, the *caporegime's* two-timing wife, and a young couple and their baby in the apartment above."

Chris stared at him whitely.

"The third was an interrogation specialist," Conte went on relentlessly. "A black dude who worked for the folks uptown. He was an expert in getting answers with a Black and Decker half-inch electric drill—you guess how he used it. Only thing was, he liked his work too much. He started to pick up strangers on the street, in bars, whatever—mostly women—and take them someplace where no one would hear the screams."

"Okay," Chris said thinly.

"The fourth one figured there was money in organizing the freelance hookers, the street trade. When a few of the girls argued, they got their faces slashed up so badly no man would ever look at them again.

"That one," Conte said, "was a woman."

Chris got up and went into the bathroom. She shut the door, then turned on the tap and let the water run a few moments before splashing a double handful into her face. She stood there with water dripping off her chin and took three deep breaths. After she dried off she found she had unconsciously locked the door, and she felt vaguely foolish.

Matt Conte had not moved. She took his glass into the pantry, rinsed it and refilled it with ice and ginger ale, and got a fresh beer from the half-sized refrigerator. This one tasted a little better.

"Listen," she said, not looking at Conte. "Maybe I've been a little quick on the trigger."

"Okay," Conte said, "but I'll tell you something, Chris: sooner or later it will get you in trouble, and trouble is something we're going to see our share of anyway. Between us we've already got plenty of real enemies to keep us busy, and after we go to work for Dennison we'll have more. So you might as well start realizing that I'm *not* an enemy, Chris—not now, not ever."

"Are you my friend?"

"That depends."

"On what?"

"On you."

Chris nibbled on a knuckle, while Conte used the Zippo on the cigarette he had been toying with. He smoked in silence, watching her. When the cigarette was finished and stubbed out, he said, "Are you all right?"

"I think I will be," she said. "Now."

Conte nodded and smiled and raised his tumbler. "What will we drink to?"

Chris clinked her beer can against his glass. "To us," she said. "Welcome back to real life."

Chapter Eleven

The front gate of the hillside ranch commanded a striking view of the California town of Santa Barbara, and beyond it the great expanse of the Pacific, rich azure in the bright spring sunshine. But the two men standing in front of the barrier evinced no interest in the view. Both wore suits, wing-tip shoes, narrow rep ties, and gray fedoras; there were sweat stains under their arms, dust on the cuffs of their trousers, and sour expressions on their faces.

They were CIA agents. The taller one, whose name was Fishman, had been posted to this assignment for over a year. The other one, Berger, was new on the job.

"We're gonna be stuck here together for God knows how long," Fishman said dourly. "We might as well let our hair down. What'd you do?"

"Nothing," Berger said defensively.

The road up to the gate was rutted gravel. Fishman spit expertly into the exact center of one of the ruts. "Okay," he said, "be that way."

Berger dug a finger inside his shirt collar. "There was, uh, this one thing. It wasn't any big deal."

Fishman examined his fingernails.

"It was one lousy Bulgarian," Berger said.

"Uh-huh."

"He was only a tobacco broker," Berger said. "He swore he was only a tobacco broker. But I knew he was KGB right down the line. I'd checked him out, I knew the score. He was ready to turn double and come over to us. I offered him fifty thousand dollars. He said he'd love the fifty thousand dollars, but he was only a tobacco broker. Finally I got him to take the fifty thousand dollars."

"So?"

"So," Berger said glumly, "he was only a tobacco broker."

"Fucking Bulgarians," Fishman said sympathetically.

They could see the ranch house from where they stood, a four-bedroom, one-story home that had been built especially for its occupant, with all the modern American comforts, including an electronic surveillance system that bugged every room and the immediate yard. Behind the house, rolling foothills sloped up toward the distant peaks of the Sierra Madres.

"What about you?" Berger demanded.

"Huh?"

"What'd you do to draw a wonderful posting like this?"

Fishman looked at his new partner. "I shot the Spanish ambassador's son."

"Jesus," Berger breathed.

"Well hell," Fishman said disgustedly, "all those Spics look alike in the dark. Anyway, I only winged him."

The pocket of Fishman's suitcoat began to hiss and sputter. From it Fishman took a radio transceiver and extended a whip antenna. The sputters turned into the voice of Rabinowitz. "You assholes still alive?"

Above the house a bunker had been dug into the hill and meticulously camouflaged. In its dimness, Rabinowitz lived like a mole, headphones growing out of his ears, a control console blinking and buzzing before him. Fishman shuddered to think what Rabinowitz must have done. He'd never had the heart to ask the guy.

"Yeah," Fishman said into the radio. "What's happening?"

Rabinowitz's voice was replaced by the tinny sound of a cheering crowd, and Vin Scully's voice saying, "It's going, it's going, it's . . . gone!" Rabinowitz came back on. "Dodgers six, Giants two, bottom of the seventh, none down."

"Great," Fishman said. "What about Vang?"

"Oh," Rabinowitz said with studied nonchalance. "You want to know about *Vang*."

On the radio there was a cacophonous clatter, like Fibber McGee's closet being opened. "What the hell is that?" Berger said with alarm.

"Son of a bitch," Fishman muttered. Into the radio, he said, "Hey, Rabinowitz."

"Yeah?" Rabinowitz's nasal whine came back.

"Get fucked." Fishman turned off the radio. "*That*," he said to the bewildered Berger, "is the sound of Vang's basement freezer, along with his furnace, his washer, and the rattle of the subcode plumbing the agency was kind enough to install. Vang doesn't like us to get nervous about the silence, so he opens the basement microphone—"

"What?" Berger bleated.

"Oh yeah, I guess I forgot to tell you: he rewired the bugging system. Anyway, he opens the basement mike and turns on all the stuff downstairs, to keep us company while he's gone. Sweet guy, that Vang," Fishman added sardonically.

"Gone? Gone? He can't be gone. He's not supposed to leave here. That's why we're posted."

"Yeah," Fishman said. "Ain't we doing a hell of a job?"

"Oh my God. The agency'll crucify us. They'll send us to the moon."

Fishman nodded solemnly. "Son," he said, "you ain't lived 'till you've seen the Aleutian Islands in February."

As Berger was contemplating whale blubber and mukluks, Vang was a thousand miles away, in Dennison's office. But the Central Intelligence Agency's solicitous interest in Vang's well-being—and more importantly, in his whereabouts and activities, went back a lot further—nearly twenty years and half a globe.

The French who annexed Laos at the turn of the century called Vang's people Montagnards, "mountain people." The government in Vientiane called them Lao-Soung, or Meo. They preferred to be called Hmong, and to be left alone.

When they were not, they went to war.

The Hmong homeland was high country above the Plain of Jars, that vast eerie plateau where the urns stand sentinel like some alien form of vegetation. In the forested mountains near the panhandle of eastern Laos that juts into Vietnam like a hitchhiker's thumb, the Hmong raised subsistence crops and opium poppies. Each village was an extension of a clan, and the family unit was of paramount importance. The elderly were respected, and ancestors revered. But by the time Vang was growing into manhood, the war that was at first a disruption had become a commonplace.

It began in 1950, when the Pathet Lao's insurrection against French rule spread into Hmong country. Villages were razed, people driven from their homes and fields, dray animals slaughtered. Still, the family must be supported—and so the Hmong men learned a new profession.

They became warriors, and because by tradition and temperament they didn't trade in half measures, they became as fitly vicious fighters as the world had seen.

When the war was over, the United States, China, Russia, and eleven other major powers met in Geneva to decide the future of Laos. Vang went back to his home and kin.

Although a young man, Vang became village headman. He had already established a reputation for honesty, compassion, fierce loyalty—and a tenacious will to survive. He would need all these qualities, because the civil war was the prelude to decades of violence.

By the early sixties the fate of Laos was inextricably tied to Vietnam. The Viet Nam Doc Lap Dong Minh Hoi, or Viet Minh, was allied with the Pathet Lao from the beginning, and the thickly overgrown river valleys carving through Hmong country became vital segments of the Communist supply line known as the Ho Chi Minh Trail.

At about the same time, the Americans began to arrive.

Vang was by then a regional leader, a figure of respect, influence, and responsibility. The lives of his people depended daily on his decisions. Vang had no special regard for the United States or its forces, but he hated the Communists. Besides, his people had to eat, and the United States offered top dollar.

The Americans were savvy enough to recognize Vang's suasion among his people and realized they could use him—for the time being. His recruiting officer, the CIA's Vientiane chief of station, approached him with respect and made him a decent offer. Vang's induction rank was major.

The furious jungle fighting lasted for the next six years, but long before it was over Vang knew the Americans were disorganized, unfocused, and doomed to defeat. That was not his concern. His focus was, and had been all along, to save his people's blood, tears, and homeland.

At the time of his recruitment, the CIA had promised that, if and when necessary, Vang would be resettled in the United States. Vang did not particularly distrust the agency's word, but he was a cautious man. He knew the CIA was actively involved in the opium trade because he had brokered several major deals. The agency called it an agricultural stabilization program, but Vang knew that several agents on station, in collaboration with high-ranking officers in the ARVN and the Royal Laotian Army, were using the CIA-financed Air America cargo line to run a multi-million-dollar drug operation.

By the height of the war, Vang was a brigadier general. He also had amassed documentary evidence of every link in the drug chain, from the warehoused bricks of raw opium passed in Saigon to the baggies of powder in the inventory of a New York street pusher. Two months before the fall of Saigon, Vang took his evidence to his CIA control, an agent named Peter Chamberlain. Chamberlain was humorless, straitlaced, and incorruptible. Vang explained to Chamberlain what he wanted.

Three weeks later, Vang and one hundred of the people of his village had been resettled in Santa Barbara. Vang was installed in the tricked up ranch house and put on retainer as a "consultant" at a generous monthly stipend. His only duty was to keep his mouth shut and stay put.

That wasn't possible. Despite the displacement, Vang was still headman.

The Central Committee of the Lao People's Revolutionary Party had a standing offer of one hundred thousand dollars for Vang, dead or alive. That hadn't stopped him from making three secret infiltrations since the end of the war, each resulting in the liberation of more of his people. There were nearly four hundred Hmong in his extended community now, and other large groups in Missoula, Montana, Denver, and other cities around the country. They suffered in the ways a transplanted culture invariably suffers despite the best intentions of its host—language barriers, unemployment, resentment, petty misunderstandings. For relief the people came to Vang; from patriarch he had evolved to demi-savior. The Hmong believed that if they ever returned to Laos, they would be led by Vang.

Vang was a practical man. Someday repatriation might be possible, but until then the people had to survive. And helping them took much more money than he received from the CIA.

That was where Dennison came in.

Dennison was different from most of the Americans Vang had known in Southeast Asia. He was not venal or dishonest, and he did not become wrapped up in means and methods and ideologies to the exclusion of results.

The only method that interested Dennison was the one that worked. The only result that interested him was unconditional success, total victory.

Which was fine with Vang. He'd had a bellyful of losers.

Now, in his office, Dennison was wrapping up the story of Albert Hammond. In the chair beside Vang, William Sterling Price shook his head.

"I'm with you, Bill," Dennison said. "It makes no sense. What do you think of the possibility that Hammond's trolley has jumped the tracks?"

"Delayed stress syndrome?"

"You're the expert."

Price nodded. "No one comes through combat—not to mention two years in a Cong prison camp—without picking up a few scars. Sometimes they take years to come to the surface."

Miss Paradise backed through the connecting door, carefully carrying a japanned tray holding a porcelain teapot and four small white cups, delicate as eggshell. Dennison hastily cleared a space amid the mess on his desk, and Miss Paradise set the tray down and poured. She wore a silk kimono, white as a bridal gown except for a sinuous representation of a dragon on the back, all bright primary colors. Her pale hair was rolled into a loaf held in place by a black-enameled comb. Either Anna May Wong in *Shanghai Express* or Lotus Long in *Think Fast, Mr. Moto*, Dennison decided absently. He'd ask later.

"Thank you, my dear," he murmured. Miss Paradise took her cup and curled up in the armchair next to Vang.

"What did you find out about Creed, Bill?" Dennison asked.

Price took a three-by-five dime-store scratchpad from his shirt pocket and flipped it open. "Benjamin Creed graduated from the Point and assumed his commission in '54. There were the usual career officer postings—West Germany, NATO headquarters, Fort Bennett, the Pentagon. Nothing particularly sensitive or noteworthy, but those were Cold War days and nobody was having that much fun anyway. Still, Creed pulled excellent marks for initiative, intelligence, integrity, and leadership ability, and in the early sixties he completed the course of study at the War College. That's a plum, of course. By the time he graduated he was a major, and they offered him a Pentagon slot with Tactical Services, a hell of a cushy spot for an officer of his age and grade."

"And a chance to settle down with his family."

"Right—except Creed had no family, and he turned down the Pentagon job cold. Instead he volunteered for Vietnam."

"Did you know him, by any chance?"

"It was a big army and a big war. I heard of him, and what I heard was impressive. Creed was the kind of officer who isn't afraid to soil his fatigues or duck bullets, and he had a powerfully charismatic personality to boot. Apparently the loyalty he commanded from his men in the field was almost fanatical. He was a model field commander, as perfect as a recruiting poster."

"What about Greaves?" Dennison asked. "Does his name come up anywhere along the line?"

"Greaves was one of Creed's aides in Nam. University of Michigan graduate in the sixties, ROTC commission, entered as a second looey, served with Creed, mustered out as a captain in '73. No black marks, no distinctions. Just another officer."

"That's it?"

Price nodded.

"Where's Greaves now?"

"I don't know. I can try to find out."

"Don't waste the time," Dennison decided. "If he's with

Creed again—as the film seems to indicate—we'll find him where we find Creed. What happened to him after the war?"

"When it ended," Price said, "Creed had a Silver Star with two clusters, a chestful of lesser decorations including three Purple Hearts, and the rank of full bird colonel." Price looked up and half-shrugged. "But the end of the war must have been a letdown for the guy. He went back to the War College for two years, this time as an instructor, and then he gave in and took the Pentagon desk job. He retired four years ago, at age forty-eight."

"A credit to the uniform of the United States Armed Forces," Vang murmured.

"Yes," Price said, "and no. There are two blots on his record—or there would be if the papers hadn't been removed from his official file. Luckily, the army is like my wife: they never throw anything away. A buddy of mine dug the info out of a back file."

"In which," Miss Paradise said, "the army files the files removed from other files."

"Right." Price flashed her a faint grin. "The first incident is dated '69, and was never fully investigated. An enlisted man in Creed's battalion filed a report claiming that in April of that year, in a village southwest of Danang called Quang Hoi, two squads under Creed's personal command killed fourteen women, three children under age ten, and six elderly men, then dumped the bodies in a hut and torched it."

"Why did the army drop it?"

Price pursed his lips. "The grunt who made the claim had been disciplined by Creed a couple of times and could have been holding a grudge. And no one else who was supposed to have been there would substantiate."

"Could all of them have been covering for Creed?" Dennison asked.

"For Creed, and for themselves—yeah, it's possible. From what I heard back then, Creed's men were so loyal they would have stuck both hands in hot coals on his order. Circumstantially, you can take your pick—atrocity or fabrication."

"Would you say Creed had the predisposition, that he was capable of the act?"

"I'd say Benjamin Creed was a dangerous man. You all know I was never happy with the half-assed, no-win way Nixon and the Joint Chiefs ran the war, but Creed was something else. He hated Communists with pure, irrational bigotry, like Hitler hated Jews. A Communist was someone to be eradicated from the face of the earth; Creed was a political-cartoon hawk. He had preached escalation in Vietnam, and he preached first-strike nuclear capability when he got back to Washington. At the War College he once presented a paper advocating a secret nuclear arms buildup to the point of overwhelming advantage, and then bombing the living hell out of the USSR. The idea was: no more Russians, no more arms race."

"Interesting notion," Miss Paradise said.

"But it still doesn't make him another Lieutenant Calley," Dennison pointed out. "It doesn't look like there's any way we'll find out the truth about what happened at Quang Hoi at this point."

"Nope," Price agreed. "But I said there were two black marks on Creed's record, and the second one isn't nearly as ambiguous. In fact, it's damned solid—and damned trouble-some, too."

Price flipped a page of his notebook. "Six months before he retired, Creed was seen in the company of what the newspapers like to call 'a reputed underworld figure.' Apparently Creed was playing it extra safe, but he got unlucky. It was almost funny, the way MI got wind of him. An FBI man named Acker was staking out a joint on Illinois called Magnolia's, and he saw Creed go inside. Creed should have been safe—what would anyone who knew him be doing in that neighbor-hood?—except that Acker *did* know him, from Nam. Acker wasn't suspicious, he just thought Creed was drunk or his car had broken down or something, and he figured he could maybe score points by riding shotgun for his old commanding officer. So Acker follows Creed into the joint and finds him sitting at a corner table with a guy named Frank Castelli—the mobster who's the reason Acker is staking out the joint in the first place.

"Acker faded before Creed spotted him," Price said. "After he filed his report, a tail was put on Creed. In the next month he was observed meeting with Castelli four more times.

At the end of that time, Castelli was nailed in the FBI sting operation that Acker had been part of from the first. The sting shut down a pipeline that was smuggling U.S.-made military armament to European underground weapons supermarkets."

"Which sell mostly to the terrorist community."

"That's right," Price said.

Dennison steepled his fingers. "The problem is that nearly every one of the established terrorist groups are Russian-backed and supported. That doesn't jibe with Creed's rabid and anti-Communist stand."

"That's a mystery we'll have to deal with," Price said doggedly, "because Creed *was* directly involved with the weapons pipeline. There's plenty of evidence—coincidentally timed bank deposits, weapons shortages from stockpiles under his direct control, even a couple of recordings of some really nasty calls he made from pay phones."

"But he was never charged," Vang guessed.

Price shot him a look. "I'm afraid you're right, friend. He should have been, but he wasn't. Part of it was the army's way of looking at life—they figured that the guy had been a hell of a soldier for twenty-five years, and they didn't want to come down on him hard for one mistake—I know, I know," Price added hastily, "it was a hell of a mistake. But the army can be like that, and besides, they'd end up with egg on their face as well. The deciding factor was that all their evidence was circumstantial, and no one was willing to testify against Creed."

"What about Castelli, the Mafioso?"

"Castelli committed suicide in his cell three days after he was nabbed." Price smiled humorlessly. "As near as I can figure from the investigator's report, Castelli put cyanide in his own meatloaf."

"De gustibus non disputandum est," Miss Paradise pointed out.

"What did happen to Creed, Bill?" Dennison asked.

"The big brass called him in and told him it was time to retire. He didn't argue, which was surprising—until it turned out that he had been expecting the move for some time. When he left, he gave the same personal address he'd maintained since returning from Nam in '75, a P.O. box in Arlington. But the first three pension checks sent to it came back, and when MI investigated they found out that Creed hadn't emptied the box since the day he took off his uniform. The guy had disappeared into thin air, and as far as I can find out, no one has seen him since—at least not in person."

Price closed the notebook and slipped it in the breast pocket of the khaki shirt he wore. "You remember Luke Kane, don't you?"

"You used him in that Malawi operation last year," Dennison said.

"Lately Luke has been biding his time as weapons and tactics advisor to a survivalist group in northern New Mexico. Three years ago he accompanied a member of the group to a sales presentation for a condo survivalist community in the southeastern Utah desert. The presentation included a five-minute videotaped endorsement by Colonel Benjamin Creed, U.S.A. Retired, explaining that when the bomb dropped, only those who prepared would survive."

"A condo survivalist community?" Miss Paradise echoed. "That's a new one on me."

"Survivalists believe nuclear war is inevitable," Price explained, "but that you can survive if you're ready—which means building shelters, stocking several years' supply of chow, water, medication, and so forth, in anticipation of going underground when it hits."

"There are many survivalists in Southern California," Vang said. "I have suggested to them that they go underground immediately, from the neck up."

"Since the mid-seventies," Price went on, "a number of survivalist organizations have established condominium communities in isolated areas, mostly in the West. They usually provide individual housing units, along with a community-owned and stocked shelter. The one in Utah seemed typical, from Luke's report, but apparently Creed had no direct involvement. He was paid for his endorsement, and that was the end of it for him."

"Maybe," Dennison said slowly. "There's a paramilitary flavor to the survivalist movement, isn't there?"

"Usually. Uniforms, chain-of-command discipline, military-style armamen, that kind of thing. The AR-15 and the

Ruger Mini-14 are popular—anyone with a few tools can modify either to fire full-auto. The idea is that after they survive the holocaust, they'll need firepower against attacks by raiders who were less well prepared."

"All right," Miss Paradise said. "Line that up against a paramilitary-style bank robbery in which the name Creed is mentioned, and what do you have?"

"A lot more questions," Dennison answered. "Bill, can you find out if Albert Hammond served under Creed?"

"I think so."

"Vang?" Dennison said. "Any ideas?"

"Yes. Is it possible that Creed is running a sanctioned deep-cover operation? His involvement with this mobster Castelli could have been part of a set-up."

"A deep-cover operation involving bank robbery and the murder of several citizens and a cop?" Miss Paradise asked incredulously.

Vang shrugged. "Perhaps Creed has turned renegade. Perhaps one of your agencies has a grand plan. I never second-guess the CIA."

"Can you look into it?"

"Certainly. I always enjoy Washington when the cherry trees are in blossom."

Price stood. "I'd like to get started. I can run down some leads from here."

"Use the back room," Dennison offered.

"I'll come along," Vang said.

"Creed is too dangerous to leave on the loose," Dennison said suddenly, as the two men reached the office door. "From here on, he's guilty until proven innocent. Even if Vang's idea turns out to be right—if he *is* sanctioned—that doesn't clear the guy. The agency has made its share of deadly blunders."

Dennison's voice was hard. "I want him."

"You'll get him," Price promised.

Chapter Twelve

The Bell lifted from the front lawn as gentle as a kiss. Its long, dolphin snout bobbed once in farewell, and through the blue-tinted glass of the oversized, sloping windshield Chris Amado could see Vang in the pilot's seat, his right hand on the T-bar. Beside him, William Sterling Price raised a hand in salute, and Chris waved back. The chopper pivoted one hundred eighty degrees on its rotors and lifted up out of the clearing, then sheared off toward the river valley, away from the lowering sun. The day was edging toward twilight, and a breeze had come up. Chris listened for a moment to the rustle of the leaves in the quaking aspens.

"Has Matt made contact?" she asked.

Beside her, Dennison said, "We don't expect to hear from him until he has something to report. He didn't get out until after midnight last night." Dennison stared down into the tranquil valley. "There's a small commercial airport about forty air miles south. I have a part interest in a Gates Learjet Longhorn run by the charter service based there. Combined with the chopper, it's the fastest way to get where we want, or at least to the nearest major air terminal."

That was more answer than she'd asked for, and Chris wondered if he were trying to change the subject. But then he said, "There isn't much point in worrying about him. It won't accomplish anything, and besides, he can handle himself."

"I know that," Chris said. "I'm beginning to think he might be human. The next thing you know, I'll be liking him." But then she added seriously, "You're right, but I can't help it. I'm worried about him, sure. I'm worried about all of us."

Dennison looked at her, and there was something in his eyes she had not seen before, something dark and lethal. "We're in a deadly business," he said coldly. "Get that straight, Chris, and never forget it. You'll risk your tail every time you go out there."

"I know that," Chris said, "and I can accept it."

"We're in a war," Dennison went on. "We didn't start it, and we probably won't finish it, but we're the ones who have to fight the battles. The world is changing—and I'm doing what I can to change it for the better."

"So far—"

"So far the world is going straight to hell. In Europe, Latin America, and half of Africa, terrorist attacks are part of everyday life. Now they're trying to export that kind of terror to this country, on a wholesale basis."

"In the form of George Dial and Helena Frome."

"They're the tip of the iceberg. We're already up to our ears in the kind of corruption that their type of jackal thrives on. In Florida, drug smugglers are financing big business and taking over banks to launder their profits. In places like Detroit and Chicago and New York, elderly people are prisoners in their own homes, afraid to walk to the corner store in broad daylight. In Washington the FBI can get jail-time convictions of congressmen, but you can bet ten times as many corrupt officials will never be exposed. It goes on and on—turn over any rock and they'll come crawling out leaving a trail of slime behind them."

Dennison drew breath. "We can't do it all, Chris, so we do what we have to. I call in my People for the tough ones, the ones the ordinary agencies of law enforcement can't handle. Most law officers are dedicated men and women, but they can't begin to get the job done, because the system won't let them. Their bosses are the bureaucrats, and the bureaucracy has become as ponderous as a circus fat lady. The cops are wearing the handcuffs now."

The twilight was deepening. Chris thought she could hear the last faint echo of the chopper motor. It might have been the wind.

"The rules used to work, in the days when everyone agreed to play by them," Dennison said. "We called it democracy, and we designed it to protect the rights of the people. Well, lately it hasn't been doing its job.

"That doesn't mean the system is wrong," Dennison said. "But it needs some help. The Creeds and Bressios and

Dials and Fromes of the world no use for systems or democracy or human rights. They laugh at the rules."

"So we fight fire with fire."

"That's right, Chris." For several moments he stared toward the ridge where the chopper disappeared. "It takes money to run my kind of operation," he said more softly. "I also happen to believe that professionals should be paid for their work; I'm a realist, and I want my People to be realists. If you think that makes us mercenaries, you and I, you're right—but don't get too concerned or carried away with the idea. Maybe it's convenient for me to represent myself as a hired gun, because the sort of people who come to me—people like Samuel Stanhope—understand money as a motivation. I don't give a damn what Stanhope or anyone else thinks, and if he figures he knows what makes me tick, that's fine. It saves me the trouble of speeches or explanations."

"But isn't money the reason your People work for you?"

"Is it?"

"It is for me," Chris said. "At least part of the reason. I need the money to support the Amadistas."

In the thickening darkness Chris could still make out the shine in Dennison's eyes. "Vang has his 'Amadistas,' too," he said. "Four hundred displaced Hmong who depend on him. Then there's Bill Price. In seven cities across the country a nonprofit corporation called VetNet has local offices. VetNet helps American service veterans obtain benefits, jobs, medical treatment, even loans—at no charge. VetNet is financed by something called the VetNet Foundation—established by William Sterling Price and financed by him and a few others who happen to believe that the men and women who fought for this country deserve some support."

"What about Matt?"

"We'll see about Matt—but already he isn't the man who arrived here a week ago." Dennison put his hand on Chris's shoulder. "Are you frightened?"

Chris shook her head. "I know what I'm buying into. I think I hate the idea of dying, and I know I'm angry. But no, I'm not frightened."

"I'm here if you need me."

"A lot of people need you, Mr. Dennison."

He offered his arm, and she took it. It was full dark now, but there was a light on the front porch. As they approached, Chris made out Miss Paradise waiting for them at the foot of the steps, and she wondered how long the beautiful tall woman had been standing there, how much she had heard. Chris half-expected some kind of wisecrack.

Instead, she found herself suddenly enveloped in her embrace. "Welcome aboard," Miss Paradise said warmly.

When she pulled free, Chris's eyes were moist. "Let's get to work," she said, and her voice cracked with emotion and anticipation.

Near Baynesville, Maine
The 19th of April

Helena Frome duckwalked silently up behind a thicket of huckleberry bushes. Through the bristly branches, leafless this early in spring, she had a clear view of the entire clearing, carved years ago out of the dense pine woods. The night was overcast; the cover of the brush was adequate for the few minutes of surveillance that was a necessary precaution before they went in.

A dirt track, rutted by spring runoff, cut in on her left. It was the only access to the clearing and ended in a locked gate two miles away; they would not be bothered by unexpected guests. The log cabin was about the size of a two-stall garage, with a sloping, pine-shaked roof painted green and a low porch elevated a half foot above the hard-beaten dirt yard. The canopy over the porch was as swaybacked as a plow horse.

George Dial moved up beside Helena, and she put a warning finger to her lips, nodding toward the cabin. On the rickety porch, a kerosene lamp atop a shaky deal table attracted mosquitos and illuminated two men in folding chairs, sipping from cans of Narragansett beer. They could have been tourists, in jeans, hiking boots, nylon windbreakers over bright flannel shirts, and snap-backed one-size-fits-all billed caps with "CAT" logos on the crowns.

Actually, they were off-duty officers of the Massachusetts State Police. Helena could make out the bulge of handguns in shoulder leather under the half-zipped jackets, and she knew a third armed guard was staked out at the cabin's rear.

One of the men lumbered lazily out of his chair, which

creaked with relief. He went to the far end of the porch and turned his back to them, and Helena heard the splash of his stream on the dirt.

George Dial reached under his jacket and took out a Beretta 92S-2 compact 9mm automatic pistol with a fat black silencer threaded to the muzzle. He raised the gun in both hands and sighted on the guy's neck.

Helena grabbed the Beretta's slide and shook her head violently. George gave her a blank look. He was unconsciously trying to raise the gun against the pressure of her hold.

Then comprehension dawned in his expression. He relaxed and grinned sheepishly. "Sorry," he whispered. "I spaced out."

That's for goddamned sure, Helena thought. George was spacing out a little too often since the killings in Rome. She did not need the added responsibility of playing nursemaid to him. There were other things to worry about. The United States had seemed like a smart idea four weeks ago. Now she was not as confident about the move. Helena Frome was a suspicious person by nature, and now she sensed they were somehow being manipulated. The idea enraged her.

She and George had been met in New York as promised, by two dark silent men waiting on the lower West Side pier where the freighter on which they had been smuggled was docked. The dark men took them to a loft building not far away, a stark brick structure in a neighborhood of narrow streets, deep shadows, and faceless warehouses unmarred by decoration or identifying signs.

There they had cooled their heels. George had been edgy to begin with, but this time Helena shared his concern. She had the uncomfortable feeling they were prisoners, and she did not even know who was holding them. She was beginning to work on ways of busting herself and George out when the bossman called them into his barren little office. He had a job for them, he said. They could help themselves by helping him.

Helena listened and decided, why not? It was better than being cooped up in the loft, and there was nothing to the job, providing George kept his head.

Whoever their sponsor was, he had contacts. His intelligence on the layout at this cabin was correct down the line.

He'd even known about the three moonlighting state cops. He was a pro—that was some reassurance.

The guard on the porch zipped up his pants and hitched at his belt. Helena tapped George's shoulder, and when he turned she held up one hand, palm out, fingers spread. She gestured six times and George nodded understanding: thirty seconds. Counting beats in her head, Helena melted back into the forest's underbrush thicket and circled toward the back of the cabin.

The third guard was leaning against the wall, enveloped in shadow. As the beats ticked toward zero in Helena's mind, the guy struck a kitchen match on the seat of his pants. When he fired his cigarette, the flame revealed two days of stubble on his chin.

The match winked out, and the ember on the tip of the smoke glowed more brightly as the guard drew on it. Helena framed the pinpoint of light over the Beretta's open sights. It brightened again as the thirty seconds ran out.

Helena stroked the trigger, and the silenced Beretta snorted and bucked in her hand. The cigarette glow fell away, and a moment later limp, dead weight thumped to the hard ground.

By then Helena was sprinting across the open yard toward the porch. As she rounded the corner, one of the guards whirled around like a dancer *en pointe*. His arm caught the lantern, and it rolled from the table and shattered and went out.

The other guard got his hand inside his jacket before Helena fired. She had to rush the shot, and instead of hitting him in the temple, the jacketed slug shattered the guy's jaw. In shocked reaction the cop pulled the trigger of his own gun, still seated in its shoulder holster. His eyes bulged with pain as the bullet furrowed down through his side, shredding organs before coming to a ragged stop in several pieces around his groin, while hot muzzle gas and uncombusted flecks of smokeless powder seared his skin.

George came out of the cover of the huckleberry bush as the cabin's door swung open. The man framed in it was around fifty and wore only a pair of jeans. He had a ruggedly handsome face, but his thick wavy hair was too dark to be naturally colored, and his skin was soft and pasty. A roll of stomach hung over the waistband of his levis: he was the type who would always look better in clothes, Helena thought. As far as she was concerned, all men did.

The guy on the porch stared down at the two corpses bleeding into the planking and took a startled step back. Helena snapped, "Hold it right there, McDonough."

The guy's head whipped around and took in her angular figure and the compact Beretta in her fist.

George Dial moved into the rectangle of light streaming from the open door, and Helena eased around to flank him. There were only supposed to be three guards—but taking that kind of information on faith was a good way to die.

"What . . . what do you want?" McDonough said. "Who do you think you . . . ?" He took a ragged breath, and it steadied him. "This man is still alive," he said.

Technically, McDonough was right. Helena's bullet had amputated the lower half of the guard's face. Blood from the wound in his side had filled the inside of the waterproof windbreaker and was leaking out the bottom hem. The guy lay face up, the back of his head soaking in the puddle of kerosene.

"For God's sake do something," McDonough pleaded.

"Okay," George Dial said, and shot the dying man in the face.

McDonough gasped.

"Inside," Helena ordered. "lead the way, Congressman." She gestured with the Beretta.

The interior of the cabin was a single room, with a cast iron stove in one corner, a basin-mounted hand-pump, some cupboards fashioned of unplaned pine, and the usual assortment of cast-off cups and dishes and furniture with which cabins of this sort were always furnished. A blanket strung over a rope partitioned off a back corner.

Helena Frome yanked the blanket to the dirty floor.

In the alcove it had formed, two bare mattresses were laid out on a double-bed-size frame-and-plank platform. Two down sleeping bags had been unzipped and spread over the mattresses in place of bedclothes. A young man was sprawled on top of them, dressed in white jockey shorts. He was about twenty and had blond hair and skin pale as flax. His face was open, guileless, as fine-featured as an adolescent girl's.

"Please," he whimpered.

Helena felt a wave of physical nausea. "All right, McDonough. Get on with it."

"I don't know what you mean."

From under her jacket Helena produced a Nikon camera with a built-in flash. "You know the routine, Congressman," she said wearily. "Don't make me tell you twice."

George held his gun steady on the young man's cringing figure.

"Do it and live," Helena said, "or don't, and watch my friend blow your sweetie's guts out his asshole. Your choice."

For a long moment no one moved. Then McDonough turned his back on them and went to the bed. He sat on the edge and began to caress the young man's stomach.

"The pants, congressman," Helena ordered. "We want the voters to see you in all your glory."

McDonough slipped off his jeans, then skinned down the young man's jockey shorts. He murmured something in a comforting tone. The young man stared up at him through doe eyes, then came into his arms.

The explosion of a flashbulb splashed lurid illumination over the scene on the bed.

Helena Frome was halfway through the first roll of film when she noticed George. He had lowered his gun, and he was staring at the two men on the bed with a rapt expression.

"George!" Helena said sharply. He turned to her slowly, looking puzzled, like a preoccupied child unsure why he is being reprimanded.

On the bed the two men were a tangle of white hairy arms and legs and buttocks, and cocks shriveled with fear. McDonough's slack torso was oily with the sweat of his terror.

The nausea tried to rise into Helena's throat. They were disgusting, she thought as shot the last picture of the roll. All of them were disgusting.

Nevada
The 22nd of April

Albert Hammond was concerned, and he was confused, but that didn't make him crazy.

He remembered what happened in the bank, which was a good sign. But he wondered: What had they done with Bates's head and his hands?

Another thing: Why were they going to kill him?

He'd done everything they'd asked, and yet he was certain they would do him as they'd done Bates. He'd heard the two of them talking, Colonel Creed and Captain Greaves. He remembered Captain Greaves from the days in Nam, and Greaves was the one who had led them during the bank job.

"I'll admit the error," Creed had said. "In Vietnam they'd do whatever I ordered, without question. I neglected the fact that this is not Vietnam—for which we may be thankful in some ways."

"I know a way to correct that problem," Greaves said.

"There's no hurry. Bates is out of the picture. Dickson and Hammond aren't going to cause any trouble, and we might find some future use for them."

"Sure—like for target practice."

Hammond understood what that meant—but he wasn't too concerned yet. He'd have to stay alert, but hell, the Cong had almost two years to break him, and they couldn't do it. Compared to the Cong, Greaves was an amateur.

Compared to the Cong, everyone was an amateur.

But why had the colonel abandoned him again? It had to be part of a secret plan. For now he would go along. . . .

111

Hammond had not meant to sleep, but suddenly a hand on his shoulder was shaking him free of uneasy and undecipherable dreams. Hammond opened his eyes and looked up into Dickson's face. The other man's hand was clamped over his mouth.

"Easy, Al, it's me. You gonna be okay?"

Hammond nodded against the pressure of the hand, and Dickson slowly removed it.

"Get dressed," Dickson said. "We're getting out of here."

"I told you, Don. I'm not going."

"Why the hell not?"

"It's hostile territory out there, Don. We'd be on foot, and who knows how far to food or water or friendlies?" Hammond smiled. That was logical thinking. There was nothing crazy about his powers of reasoning.

"Listen to me, Al." Dickson's voice was low and urgent. "You're not feeling so good, are you? I know how it goes. But you've got to realize: they killed Bates, and they're gonna be after us. Those other men out there, they're different from us. We're the only ones who served under Creed in Nam, right. We took his money then, but that was another story. We should have never taken it this time. We're in over our head, Al."

"Fuck 'em."

Dickson sighed. "I'm making a break for it, Al, tonight. We got no business here. I've been checking things out. When they change guard shifts at midnight, sometimes they don't bother to pull up the ladder, and I figure those guys on the cliff are half asleep anyway. It's the last shot, Al, and I'm taking it."

Hammond shook his head. "Good luck, Don."

Dickson looked like he was going to say something else, then changed his mind. He went out like he'd come in, silent as a wraith.

Hammond fetched the straight-backed wooden chair and dragged it to the window. He turned off the room light, then cautiously raised the window shade. He sat patiently, hands on knees, like a playgoer awaiting the overture.

He had a view of maybe ten degrees of the arc of the enclosing cliff. It rose two hundred feet, beginning at an easy slope at the bottom but steepening rapidly, so by the top it was ninety percent of vertical. The rope ladder, anchored to a boulder beyond the rim, draped down along the segment Hammond could see, access for rotating the four guards posted up there twenty-four hours a day.

Don Dickson appeared at the corner of the building. He was unarmed except for a pistol in a hip holster. He scanned the compound, then darted across the open space to the base of the cliff. He went hands and knees up the first twenty feet and made the foot of the ladder.

Hammond watched, fascinated.

Dickson was halfway up.

Maybe Don was right—but then if it were that easy to get out, Hammond could do it on his own the next night. He *would* do it, he decided. Then he would not be confused and concerned anymore.

Hammond counted down from the rim: Dickson had fifteen rungs to go. Hammond's pulse began to race, as if it were he up there on the ladder.

Dickson was five rungs from the rim when the guard spotted him.

The guard aimed an automatic rifle down at Dickson and said something, because Dickson looked up and stopped climbing. An arrow of flame flared at the rifle's muzzle, and Dickson let go of the rope ladder. His head raced back and his whole body bent like a bow, and then he tumbled backward in a slow flip, graceful as a high dive.

Dickson hit the slope at the bottom head first and tumbled down its incline. When his body came to rest, his head was bent way over at a right angle to his torso.

Albert Hammond carefully drew the window shade, moved the chair back to where it had been, got back in bed, and began to holler.

Twenty seconds passed before the door burst open and a fully dressed, armed man came in. "What the hell is your problem?"

Hammond sat up in bed and made a show of rubbing at his eyes. "Geez, sorry, Pete. I must have had a bad dream."

"Next time drink some warm milk before bed," Pete growled. "Meanwhile, put a sock in it."

"Sure, Pete. Sorry."

But when the door shut, Hammond grinned broadly. His plan had worked.

It had struck him that he might have been turned over to the gooks again, and he had screamed to get Pete into the room so he could look the guy over.

But Pete was as American as he was. That was fine. That's how it was supposed to be.

Oh, maybe he was a little crazy, sure. But if you knew you were crazy, you couldn't really be crazy after all. Wasn't that right?

Albert Hammond allowed himself a low laugh. It went on for some time, and he did not notice when it turned into sobbing.

BOOK
TWO

Dennison's War

Chapter Thirteen

As soon as Matt Conte entered the Stage Door Delicatessen, the bald guy in the penguin suit came bustling over with the menu. Conte waved him away and the guy shrugged. To Conte's right was the takeout counter, a shoulder-high glass case filled with a jumble of cheeses, toad-green pickles, potato salad, knishes, and smoked herring. Bread and rolls of various sizes, colors, shapes, and flavors sat in baskets on its stainless steel top. In the narrow space between the case and the cutting board-topped counter against the wall, four men in white shirts, aprons, and caps were waving long-bladed knives and shouting. Every so often a sandwich appeared atop the case, flanked by two wedges of dill pickle. The four sandwich makers' shouting was indiscriminate: they shouted at the waiters, the customers, and if no one else was available, each other. One of them looked at Conte and shouted, "Waddaya want? Waddaya want? Waddaya want?" meaningless as a mantra.

A long banquette separated the counter area from the dining room. In the trench along its top, plastic flowers grew from styrofoam. To its left were maybe a dozen and a half tables, jammed together in an ingenious asymmetrical pattern that exploited every square inch of floor space. It was midmorning, and half the tables were unoccupied. The room smelled of fresh baked goods, spiced meat, and strong coffee.

Benny Batista was sitting by himself at a table for two in the far corner, reading the *Daily News*. He turned a page and reached around the paper to grope for his plate, which contained most of a prune Danish.

Conte threaded his way between the tables. Benny's

117

fingers were still waving futilely, wondering where the pastry had gone, while his brain was involved with the prospects of this year's Mets in general and that afternoon's point spread in particular. Conte pushed the plate toward him, and as fingers found the Danish, Conte said, "'Lo, Benny."

Benny Batista looked up and paled. He was a short man, mostly bald, and he wore a brown suit that did not fit very well. There were crumbs on his chin.

"How ya been, Mattie?" He did not ask Conte to sit down.

A waitress came over with a Pyrex coffeepot. She had dark hair cut in bangs that had been tightly curled, so they rolled inward. Conte turned the second cup upright and sat down anyway, while the waitress poured. Benny did not protest. The waitress set down the pot, dug a pencil from the pocket in the front of her white skirt, wet the business end on the tip of her tongue, and poised it over her pad, as if ready to preserve for all time Conte's next words.

"You got any more of those prune Danish?" Conte asked.

The waitress peered over her pad at Benny's plate. "That's apricot." She pronounced it "eh-pricot."

"Okay," Conte said. "You got any prune Danish?"

"All out."

"How about apricot?"

"All out of apricot, too. How about cheese?"

"How about," Conte said, "we go out back to the kitchen and do more gags and see who breaks up first?"

The waitress laughed. Her voice was brassy, but she had a gay laugh, light as a soufflé. "You win," she said. "Now waddaya want to eat?"

"Surprise me."

When she had gone, Conte said, "I've been fine, Benny. Thanks for asking."

"Hey, Mattie, I heard about that trouble out back of Mario's." Benny Batista talked in the rapidfire bursts of the eternally nervous. "I heard you were dead. Then I heard you left town."

"I wasn't dead. I left. I'm back."

"That's good, Mattie, that's real good." Benny picked up his coffee cup and put it down again. "Actually, it ain't that good. There's paper on you, Mattie."

"How much?"

"Fifty grand." Benny tried on a wan smile. "You shoot yourself, you die rich." The smile hurt his face, and he gave it up. "Listen, Mattie, you know none of the boys would try cashing you in. The Old Men, they put out the word: you show up back in town, no one touches you. Anyone does has to answer to them. That's the word from the Old Men."

"You sure, Benny? You sure the Old Men don't want me as badly as anyone else?"

"I only know what I heard, Mattie. Shit, gimme a break."

The waitress came back and set a thick white plate in front of Conte. She stood back with arms folded, like a sommelier awaiting the verdict of a picky oenophile.

"What is it?" Conte asked.

"Apricot."

"I thought you were out of apricot."

"You said surprise you. The surprise is we're not out of apricot."

"Thanks," Conte said.

"Money talks," the waitress said, and left them alone.

Conte looked at the Danish. "Who?" he said.

"Huh?"

"If it wasn't the Old Men, who hung the paper on me?"

"You know."

"Bressio."

"Sure," Bennie said. "Fifty grand, your head, no questions asked. Only he ain't been heard from so much lately. Since he scragged DeChristi—sorry, Mattie—and the Old Men called him in and said bygones are bygones but to shut it the fuck off or else, he's made himself missing. Except for this paper on you—and hell, lots of the boys aren't even sure it's good anymore. Not that they'd do anything if it was," Bennie added, pizzicato.

"Where is he, Benny?"

Instead of answering, Benny said, "You're a stand-up guy, Mattie. The Old Men know you're a stand-up guy. They say lay off, the boys know that if any of them greases you and is tabbed, the Old Men will cut his nuts off and serve them in white sauce over fettuccine." Benny looked confidentially to either side. "Still, fifty grand is a lot of kale, maybe enough so some shithead figures he is maybe good enough to take a chance. You watch yourself, Mattie."

"Where's Bressio?"

"I dunno, Mattie. No one does."

Conte thought about that. "You still with Agricola, Benny?"

Benny shook his head no and said, "Sure. But you know me, Mattie. I'm a kind of guy who just hangs out—open car doors, fetch the coffee, work a few collections if the other boys are busy. I don't have any—"

"Let's you and me go look him up, Benny."

Conte finished his coffee and put a five-dollar bill beside the saucer. They were nearly at the door when the waitress brayed across the room, "You didn't touch your Danish."

"It's yours."

"I don't like apricot." She shrugged and stuffed the money in her skirt pocket and was nibbling on the edge of the pastry when they left.

They turned south on Seventh, then east on Fifty-fifth. Benny led the way into the third door down, which opened into the high-ceilinged, ground-floor lobby of an office building that was not shabby yet but was gathering steam in that direction. In the elevator Bennie punched "10." On the way up the car stopped twice: once to let a mailman on at the sixth floor, and once to let him off at the seventh. In between the mailman looked at the two of them and said, "Hot enough for you guys?"

On the tenth floor they went down a corridor to another elevator. This one was fronted by a heavy guy in a dark suit. He needed a shave. He had the kind of face that would always need a shave.

"Is he in?" Benny rapped out.

The man sneered. He was ugly to start with, and the sneer was no improvement.

"We got to see him."

"You, I don't think so. Him"—he stuck a fat dirty thumb in Conte's direction—"definitely not."

Conte looked behind him down the corridor. It was empty. Benny started to say, "Listen, pal . . ." and the ugly guy put a palm the size of a catcher's mitt on Benny's chest and pushed him up against the wall.

Conte's right hand came out of his jacket pocket. There was a neat little leather sap in it, filled with maybe a couple of pounds of lead shot. Conte laid it against the guy's temple and was rewarded with a glassy-eyed stare. The guy's legs went rubbery and wobbled and gave out.

"Well, shit," Benny said, and stepped over the guy into the elevator. As it began to rise, Conte took the .45 from under his left arm and held it loosely at his side.

Benny shot a look at the gun. "This isn't going to look good for me."

"I could sap you down, too," Conte offered. "That way you'd still look like a stand-up guy."

"Thanks," Benny said. "Never mind."

The elevator opened into a reception office. A guy was sitting with his feet up on the desk, reading a *Hustler* magazine. He lowered it at the sound of the elevator door, took in Conte's gun, and said, "Well, fuck me."

Conte waved the barrel of the automatic. The guy swung his legs to the floor, moving carefully, as if they were fragile. He reached inside his coat and brought out a snub-nosed .38 revolver, holding it by the butt with two fingers. He placed it on the desktop, then stood and edged away.

"Nice work so far," Conte said. "If you get any ideas, reconsider."

Benny Batista was still in the elevator. "You first," Conte told him. "Grab the heater on the way in."

"Geez, Mattie," Benny whined. "You're putting me in a hell of a spot."

"Move."

Benny went past him. The little man picked up the gun as if it were a turd, then pushed through the connecting door, Conte on his heels.

Philip Agricola was a handsome, graying man with strongly Latin features, a face that was all angles and planes. His skin was unwrinkled except for a few laugh creases at the corners of his eyes. He reminded Conte of the sisters who had been his first teachers, their ageless, smooth visages a testimony to the benign influence of God and a life free of worldly worries.

"Hello, Matthew." Agricola nodded at Conte's gun, as if it confirmed some long-held suspicion. "Benny. How can I help you?"

The bodyman behind Agricola's chair glared at them.

"Put the gun on his desk, Benny," Conte said. To the bodyman: "Do the same with yours. Then take a walk."

The bodyman's eyes never left Conte's as he took out his gun and laid it softly on Agricola's desk blotter, within easy reach of the older man. "Take a walk," he repeated, as if he wanted to be certain he had it correct. "There's an idea. Maybe I'll walk around the block and pick up about a dozen of the boys and bring 'em back with me. Then we can spend until lunch jumping up and down on your fucking face."

"None of that," Agricola said sharply. "It's all right. Wait outside with Ralph, and don't make any noise." Agricola's tone was sternly paternal, and the bodyman went out as sullen as a child.

"Sit down, Benny," Conte said. "You're doing fine."

Agricola's office was too good for the building. It was airy and modern, with an excellent north view toward the park. There was a long, low sofa to one side, parked under a row of portraits in gilt frames. Benny Batista sat at one end, barely half of his buttocks perched on the edge of the cushion, as if he were afraid the furniture was mined.

"Sit down, Matthew," Agricola said pleasantly.

Conte holstered the .45 but did not otherwise move. Benny got out a cigarette and gave all his attention to getting it lit.

"He doesn't have to hear this," Agricola said.

Bennie looked relieved. He started to get up.

"Sit down," Conte said without looking at him. Benny sat. "I like having people around me these days. I don't want to get too wrapped up in myself. You know how it is, Mr. Agricola: you never know when you'll need a witness."

Agricola removed a ballpoint pen shaped like a stylized plume from a desk set. He poked at the little .38 on the blotter in front of him, careful not to touch it with his hand. "I understand, Matthew. Carlo, may he abide with God, he meant a lot to you. Like your own blood kin. Like a father, right?"

No, not right. Matt Conte's father was as different from men like Carlo DeChristi and Philip Agricola as piss and pineapple juice. Maybe that was why he had died. . . .

"When he was killed," Agricola said, "you wanted to do something about it."

Conte stared at him, startled. Agricola had no right to talk about his father. Then he realized the *capo* was referring to Carlo.

"Maybe you don't think the Old Men did right by Carlo," Agricola said. "Maybe you still want to handle it yourself."

"What do I want to do?"

Agricola shrugged, too elaborately. "One man is killed, another must die. An eye for an eye."

There had been a time when Conte might have agreed, but that was in another life. But it seemed like a lot of people thought—or wanted to believe—that he was gunning for Bressio's ass.

"Now I will give you advice," Agricola said. "Leave it lie."

"So there isn't any question in anyone's mind," Conte said. "It was Bressio who put the hit on Carlo, wasn't it?"

"That is how the talk goes."

Conte took out a cigarette and examined it. "Benny says no one is sure where Bressio is."

"Benny is wise."

Benny smiled, too quickly, too brightly.

"But is he telling the truth?" Conte asked Agricola.

"Who knows? Bressio is gone, disappeared. Who can say where?"

"You can, Mr. Agricola." Conte flicked the Zippo and drew flame into the cigarette. "You've got an idea how to find him."

Agricola showed Conte the palms of both his hands. "Matthew, listen to the advice of a man of years."

"I didn't come for Bressio, Mr. Agricola. You might not believe me, but aside from the fact that he's supposed to have put money on my head, I've got nothing personal against the man. Carlo is dead, and nothing I do to Bressio will bring him back."

Agricola smiled. "That is the truth, and I am glad to hear you speak it, Matthew."

Agricola started to stand. Conte reached under his jacket and Agricola sat down again. His expression did not change when Conte's hand came out holding an envelope, but on the couch Benny Batista sighed relief. Conte took two snapshots from the envelope and dropped them in front of Agricola, next to the .38. "This is who I want," Conte said.

Agricola picked up first one picture, then the other, using a thumb and forefinger. He tilted each toward the natural light of the oversized window and frowned at it, all of his movements stylized as mime.

Finally he looked up. "Who are these people supposed to be?"

Conte sighed elaborately. "Don't kid me please, Mr. Agricola. These people are supposed to be assholes, and I think you know that, because there's been talk about these people. The talk is that they bumped two Americans in Roma, then stole a lot of money from the poppa of one of the Americans. When the heat came down—as the heat will when you operate that way—they went south. They looked up our brother Matthews in Palermo—probably because they'd had dealings with them in the past—and they asked to buy help. They had money to pay, so our brother Matthews in Palermo agreed to ship them over here.

"Once they arrived, Mr. Agricola, someone took delivery. I want to know who."

"All right, Matthew, I will tell you the truth." Agricola squared the two photos like a blackjack hand. "I do not know what you are talking about."

Conte slammed a fist down on the desk, so hard the .38 jumped and spun around. "The fuck you don't!" Conte shouted, his face two feet from Agricola's. "You listen to me, *vecchio*. I want some fucking answers, and I want them now!"

The door of Agricola's office slammed back on its hinges, and Ralph and the other bodyguard came barreling in. Somewhere along the line they had found more guns. On the couch Benny said, "Oh shit."

Conte spun around and stabbed at the two men with a forefinger. "Get the fuck out of here!" he barked. He had gone beyond performance; he'd genuinely lost his temper, and he did not care.

"It is all right," Agricola said. He flapped fingers up and down as if he were shooing a cat. "Leave us for now. But don't go too far," he added pointedly, looking at Conte.

After the door shut again, Conte said, "All right, we've both got our rocks off. Now let's talk like men." His voice was tight.

"I can be of some help," Agricola admitted. He looked at Benny, who squirmed uncomfortably. He had forgotten the cigarette between his fingers, and an inch of ash hung crazily from its tip.

"It's good to have two guys listen to a story," Conte insisted. "That way there's less chance it'll change later."

"Where is your respect, Matthew?" Agricola said with dignity.

To his discomfort, Conte felt slightly abashed. The old attitudes died hard. He *had* respected this man once—but now, he realized, he had only despite for Philip Agricola. There was nothing dignified or romantic about the man; he was a mobster, and not one whit more.

"All right," Conte said. He looked at the rumpled man in the brown suit. "Get out, Benny. Forget you were ever here."

"Already my mind is a blank," Benny chattered, and darted for the door.

"Benny," Conte said.

Benny turned.

"Grazie," Conte said. "Buona fortuna."

Benny frowned, as if unsure if he were being kidded. "Yeah, thanks, Mattie," he said quickly. "Same to you." He scuttled out the door.

"Matthew," Agricola said. He worried the two snapshots apart again with the blunt end of his pen. "What do you want with these two?"

Conte smiled and shook his head.

"You are going to kill them?"

"Probably."

Abruptly, Agricola stood. He wore a charcoal gray suit, cut so well he looked trim as a teenager. He went to the window that looked out on the park.

"Tell it please, Mr. Agricola."

"It is true," Agricola said to the window. "Our brother Matthews in Palermo did contact the Old Men for assistance in moving these two. They wanted someone to accept delivery and arrange . . . sanctuary for a while."

"And?"

"And the Old Men turned them down."

Shit, Conte thought. He had been afraid of that.

"Our Sicilian brothers do not have vision or a sense of history," Agricola said. "Sometimes they seem to think it is still the fifteenth century, and they are protecting the peasants from the Ottoman invader. Other times they behave like gangsters in a bad movie, selling themselves to any trash who comes along with money. Okay, maybe this is all right for our brothers in Sicily; it is anarchy there. But here in America we have a system." Agricola turned to look at Conte. "It is a good system, Matthew, a fair system. One does not fight it, or try to undermine it. One works within this system."

Agricola gestured at the pictures on the blotter. "The Old Men want nothing to do with such trash as these. They are Communists, traitors, with no more regard for their country than a pig for its sty. They do not want to fit into the system but to destroy it. The Old Men are good Americans. They do not give aid to terrorists."

There was no irony in Agricola's tone, and Conte knew the old hypocrite believed every word. Every one of the Old Men had emigrated from Italy before they were through their teens—as had Conte's own father. Now the Old Men were wealthy and powerful; among their acquaintances they numbered politicians, businessmen, famous entertainers. People sought their approval and counsel. The Old Men believed in the American dream because they lived a version—or more accurately, a *per*version—of it. Success had blinded them to their own corruption.

"Mr. Agricola," Conte said, with as much patience as he could manage. "Do you know where these two are?"

Agricola stared back. Just as Conte was beginning to despair of an answer, Agricola said, "It goes back to Bressio. That is why I am reluctant to talk. He is a powerful man, Matthew, and I don't want you hurt."

"Are the Old Men afraid?" Conte needled.

"Only for you," Agricola said mournfully.

Conte let that pass.

"You know that after Carlo was killed," Agricola said slowly, "it became quiet in the streets once more. But still this Bressio was a concern to the Old Men. We determined to keep track of his activities, so we placed one of our own among his organization. Do you know Eddie Turin?"

"He was head cock in your family, wasn't he?"

"Caporegime," Agricola corrected. "He was ordered to join Bressio and to report to the Old Men from time to time. What we know is from Eddie Turin."

Conte knew Turin only slightly, and liked him about as much. Turin was smart enough to be dangerous, but he lacked imagination. He was like a chess player who usually makes the right move but still loses because he can't see three moves ahead.

Conte took a stab in the dark. "Turin never came back, did he, Mr. Agricola."

It hit the target. "It seems he has joined up with Bressio," Agricola said carefully. "He is not the first. Nearly two dozen of the men—those with rank as well as street soldiers—have quit us for this man. *Omerta* means little these days. Anyway, they will not be missed that much—thugs, rough trade. Good riddance to bad rubbish, and the same goes for Eddie Turin." Agricola shot Conte a shrewd look. "All the same, Matthew, if you were to find Turin and it is true he has given his allegiance to Bressio, maybe you could see to him. A man who breaks *omerta* must not be allowed to live; it is not right, and besides, it gives others bad ideas. The Old Men would be grateful if they were to learn you had hit Eddie Turin."

There was something to that: whether Conte liked it or not, it never hurt to have the Old Men on your side. Especially now, when he was still not convinced they weren't after his skin.

Agricola sat down and impatiently pushed the revolver out of the way. "We know some things from Eddie, before he stopped reporting. It seems that somehow Bressio learned that these terrorists were seeking asylum and a sponsor—"

"Maybe Bressio learned it from Eddie."

"Maybe," Agricola agreed. "Anyway, it appears Bressio made contact with them through our brother Matthews in Palermo—who, as I said, will trade with anyone—and gave them some sort of offer."

"What sort?"

Agricola shrugged, and Conte let it go. "We also know," Agricola went on, "that Bressio rented three floors of a loft building on Houston Street and was using it as a warehouse."

"Guns?"

"Among other items. Food—canned, preserved, whatever—and drugs, not for the street but medication. Clothing, flashlights, radios, all kinds of garbage."

"What for?"

"Who knows?"

"Where is this warehouse exactly?"

"They cleaned it out. The goods are gone and Bressio with them, as far as anyone knows. Turin, too, and all the others who went over to Bressio's side."

"Where did they go, Mr. Agricola?"

"No one knows."

Conte swore and started to turn away.

"There is one thing," Agricola said to his back. "Three days ago one of our people in Reno thought he saw Eddie Turin in a casino. By the time he could get close enough to be certain, the man had left. This person thought he should contact the Old Men anyway. We have let our . . . interest in Bressio and Turin become known. That is another thing for you to remember."

Conte nodded. "Thanks for the help, Mr. Agricola."

Agricola spread his hands, to indicate it was nothing. "Maybe next time you come in here, Matthew," he said with mild reproach, "you mind your manner a little better, show some respect."

Conte should have let it lie. He had spent enough years around Agricola's kind to learn to tolerate their posturing and their supreme arrogance, or at least to ignore. Maybe it was the influence of Dennison—whatever, he could no longer stand to listen to Agricola's puerile bullshit.

"I don't think so, Agricola," he snapped. "I don't owe you politeness or respect or anything else. You and the other

Old Men are just some people I used to work for. As employers you were fairly decent, but as human beings you stink."

For a long moment Agricola stared at him in surprise, and then surprise became rage. Agricola began to sputter, and his carefully assembled creaseless face contorted and seemed to come apart. He began to curse in a low, hard voice. "You had your chance, you fucking son of a bitch," he said. "Now you are dead meat, you bastard." But it was just noise, and Agricola was just another hood and always had been.

Conte turned his back on the blustering old man and left the office.

Ralph was leaning against the wall next to the elevator, one foot crossed over the other. He gave Conte a steely, mirthless grin. "Come around again soon," Ralph said. "Next time we'll play by my rules."

"Sure," Conte said. "Meanwhile, don't lose your gun." Ralph was getting out an obscene reply when the elevator doors shushed shut, but Conte wasn't listening. He'd had enough little men with big mouths for one day, and it was still an hour to lunchtime.

Chapter Fourteen

Miss Paradise leaned over the chattering teletype to scan the printout as it advanced jerkily from the top of the machine. When two pages of accordion-fold computer paper had been ejected, the machine went silent. Miss Paradise ripped them off along the perforation, handed them to Dennison, and said, "You were right, boss. As always."

"Thank you, my dear." Dennison looked her over more closely, as if he had just noticed she was in the room. Miss Paradise wore a divided leather riding skirt with a rawhide-fringed hem, pointy-toed boots with whorls of gold thread worked into the uppers, a shirt that looked like it had been made out of a tablecloth from an Italian restaurant, and a white silk neckerchief.

"Well, howdy, Miz Dale," Dennison said brightly. "How's Roy and Trigger?"

"They ran off to Bimini together," Miss Paradise said solemnly. "I found out they'd been seeing each other behind my back for years."

"You mean," Dennison said, "they were horsing around?"

"Boss," Miss Paradise said, "I'm going to pretend you never said that."

They were in the Back Room, the nerve center of Dennison's compound. It was adjacent to the two offices and the size of both of them together, so the perimeter of the three rooms formed a rough square. On the long wall was a bank of standard twenty-two-inch mounting racks holding several radio receivers, an antenna rotor slaved to the installation atop the mountain peak behind the compound, four reel-to-reel audio tape decks, and two video recorders, along with a variety of power supplies, amplifiers, tuners, and switchers. At the end of the rack was a control console and two swivel chairs.

One end of the room was fronted by four wall-to-ceiling cabinets; they contained Dennison's on-site armory. Next to each was a digital display and a standard ten-digit keypad, for input of electronic lock combinations. At the opposite end was the computer system: two terminals, a processor/memory unit, video monitor, printer, and modem phone link. A third terminal at Miss Paradise's desk was ganged to this unit, as was a fourth in the study of her living quarters in the back of the building. Beside the terminals was the communications system, a series of transceivers as well as several land-line telephones.

Dennison skimmed the printout that had just come in, then looked up and said, "Have Chris meet me in my office."

"Yippee-yi-kiyo," Miss Paradise said by way of assent.

Set into the fourth wall of the back room were two windows; the other side of their glass were the mirrors in the offices. Between them were two doors, and Dennison entered the one on the right. That put him in a closet. He pushed aside a half-dozen coats and stepped over a pair of galoshes, then put his thumb against a two-by-two glass panel next to the inner door. A second passed while the computer read his fingerprint, then a light above the panel flashed green and Dennison heard the snick of the doorlock. He opened it and stepped into his office.

His desk was the usual disorganized potpourri, but it only took him a few seconds to find the newspaper article he had been going over earlier that day. It had been clipped from the front page of the Boston *Globe* of two days earlier.

NO LEADS IN SLAYINGS OF MCDONOUGH AIDES

BANGOR, ME.—Law enforcement agencies have reported no new leads in the slaying of three off-duty Massachusetts State policemen yesterday at a cabin near Baynesville. The cabin is owned by Congressman Richard "Sonny" McDonough, D-Massachusetts.

Mason Thom, Deputy State Attorney in charge of coordinating the investigative efforts of the Baynesville town constable, the Peterson County sheriff's office, and the Maine State Police, said that at this stage the inquiry into the killings is "at a standstill. All we have are several 9mm shell casings, and a blank wall," Thom said.

The three Massachusetts officers were on off-duty rotation and were working under a private arrangement with Congressman McDonough. A spokeswoman for the State Police said off-duty work was not unusual for officers and is permitted under department rules. The three officers had worked for McDonough several times in the past.

McDonough described their duties as driving and general assistance. When asked if it would be accurate to call the officers "bodyguards," McDonough commented that "in these times all public officials are at peril. It is a fact of life," McDonough continued. "This shocking incident speaks for itself."

McDonough said he often goes to the cabin to work undisturbed. Congress is in recess for the Easter holiday.

McDonough gave this account of the killings:

At approximately ten o'clock on the night of April 19, McDonough was working on constituent correspondence when he heard a "dull thud." When he investigated, he found two of the patrolmen on the front porch, and the third at the rear of the cabin. All had been shot at close range. Police surmise the killer's gun was equipped with a silencer.

McDonough offered no possible motive, nor did he speculate on why the killers fled without attempting to enter the cabin itself.

The slain officers were identified as . . .

Dennison stuck the clipping between two pages of the *World Almanac* and set it aside. When he'd read it for the first time two days earlier, he'd been suspicious; now he knew it was mostly nonsense.

The printout told Dennison the real story. Congressman "Sonny" McDonough turned out to be a patriot, and he had immediately gone to the Justice Department with the truth, even though it could have—might still—cost him his political career and personal reputation. But in coming clean to the Feds, McDonough had served his country more faithfully than he would probably ever realize.

As a homosexual, McDonough had long been aware that he was susceptible to extortion attempts, and judging by the photos that had been taken of him and his young lover, he guessed this was one. Dennison agreed. But the fact that McDonough's description of the killers fit Dial and the Frome woman beyond the possibility of coincidence meant this was no ordinary blackmail attempt.

It also put the mission on priority-one status. Dial and Frome had to be found and neutralized before they killed again.

What bothered Dennison was the missing element: so far McDonough had received no demand for payment in exchange for suppression of the pictures showing him engaged in homosexual acts. So what were Dial and Frome—or their employers—waiting for, and what were they expecting to accomplish?

Dennison responded to a knock on the office door, and

Chris Amado came in. He gestured her to one of the armchairs, and as she sat he said, "It's coming down."

She listened without comment to the story of McDonough and the three dead cops. "Add in what Matt reported a few hours ago from New York," Dennison finished, "and it is not a pretty picture. George Dial and Helena Frome are definitely tied to Bressio, who in turn is tied to several dozen experiencd Mafia butchers. Bressio has already pulled enough jobs and made enough from them to fill a warehouse with equipment—which has already left New York, along with Bressio and his boys—hopefully destined for Reno, since it's the only clue we have."

"But before he left, he recruited George and Helena."

"Right. He got word they were on the run and figured he could use them, so he took them in. For now we're working on the assumption that if we find Bressio, we find Dial and Frome."

"What do we know about Bressio?" Chris asked.

"Very little. Miss Paradise has tried a half-dozen angles of approach to the guy's background, and every one ends in a brick wall. He appeared on the organized crime scene a couple of years ago; before that he's a man without a history. In an amazingly short time after he popped up, he was able to build an organization so powerful even the Old Men were reluctant to go head to head with him."

"How do George and Helena fit into his plans?"

"My guess," Dennison said, "is that he's going to adopt their methods to whatever he's up to."

"Imported terrorism," Chris said slowly.

"That's right." Dennison closed his eyes for a moment and worked the bridge of his nose between thumb and forefinger. "Terrorist activity is extremely difficult to stop and essentially impossible to prevent—especially in a democracy based on freedoms and civil liberties. Have you ever noticed that terrorist acts do not occur in the Soviet Union?" Dennison opened his eyes. "The individual becomes extremely powerful if he or she is willing to use terrorist methods. One person with a SAM-7 heat-seeking rocket in a shoulder-launch tube can bring down a loaded commercial airliner and be miles away before all the pieces fall to earth. One person can wire an automobile, or poison a restaurant meal, or boobytrap a phone. It only takes a single gunman to shoot a Kennedy, a Martin Luther King, the Pope.''

Dennison placed both palms on his desk. ''Imagine what a team made up of Bressio, Frome, and Dial could do.''

''What about the authorities? Have you informed them?''

Dennison shook his head. ''They do their best, but dammit, it's not good enough. Their way can take weeks, even months, to show results. How many people would die in the meantime? We don't have weeks; we may not even have days.

''Bressio has to be stopped,'' Dennison said flatly. ''He's got to be crushed so there's nothing left but a greasy stain, and then that stain has to be mopped up. It has to happen quickly— so quickly that the public doesn't learn the threat even existed. There are enough lunatics out there who would stumble all over themselves trying to copy the idea.''

''Where do I start, Mr. Dennison?''

Dennison looked at her and saw one young vulnerable woman. He shook the doubt from his mind; they were all vulnerable, dammit, as long as the vultures roamed the country.

''In Reno,'' he said firmly. ''I wanted to wait until Matt had something definite from there, but we can't hold off any longer. Assuming that the two of you find Bressio there, your assignment is to get inside his organization, using your old relationship with George.''

''And then?''

''And then,'' Dennison sighed, ''you're on your own.''

''All right,'' Chris said calmly. ''How do I find Bressio?''

''You ask for him. Don't bother to be loud or obvious— Reno is a small town, and word will get around fast. Start in the casinos, with the pit bosses, floormen, cocktail waitresses, and so on. Try to give them the idea that Bressio will want to hear what you have to say.''

''Before he has me killed, you mean.''

''First he'll want answers. It's up to you to make them sound convincing. Getting Dial on your side may be the key.''

''How do I contact Matt?''

''You don't. Once you're in with Bressio, don't do

anything that violates your cover story. You and Matt will have to play your own hands, and no kibitzing."

Chris stood. "Is there any reason I can't leave now?"

Yeah, Dennison wanted to say, there are dozens of reasons, and they have to do with living and dying. He wished there was a way to run his People from behind a screen, so he would never know them or come to care for them. Maybe that would keep him from waking at three in the morning in response to the phantom ring of the communications link. When would that ring be real, he wondered; when would he pick up the line to hear a report that one of his People had been fished from a river or dug from a dump or pulled from the wreckage of a blown-up auto?

"Are you all right, Mr. Dennison?"

Dennison blinked. "Sorry." He conjured up a smile and donned it like a mummer's mask.

"Wish me luck, Mr. Dennison."

Dennison offered his hand. Chris snorted. She came around the big oak desk, pushed the hand aside, and threw both arms around the big man before her.

Her face was buried in his chest, and she did not see the mist that clouded Dennison's vision as he held her.

Chapter Fifteen

Weepy Moyers had the eyes of a cocker spaniel, soft and melancholy and perpetually moist. Matt Conte did not know whether Weepy Moyers was a particularly sensitive man or suffered from endocrinal pathology.

When Weepy looked up and saw Conte coming across the floor of the Golden Lady casino, his eyes went more moist, and their melancholy deepened into the purest sorrow.

There were a dozen crap tables on this side of the gambling floor, arranged in an elongated oval like wagons under Comanche attack. They were connected end to end by velvet-covered rope, which kept the customers from straying into the pit area, Weepy's domain. Conte glanced up; the ceiling was an array of semi-mirror panels set at odd angles to each other, so it took him a moment to spot the few that were darker than the rest. These were the "eyes in the sky," from which the casino management could monitor the action. The bosses were not worried about customers winning as much as their own employees cheating. Reno was that kind of town.

Conte went up to the nearest table. The shooter was a fat man in a Hawaiian shirt and pork-pie hat, with a button pinned to the crown that said, "Have a Nice Day, Asshole." He cupped the dice in both hands and blew on them.

Conte put a yellow five-dollar chip on the pass line, and the stickman said, "Coming out." The fat man reared back on one leg like a pitcher with no men on and chucked the dice the length of the table. The red cubes bounced off the sidewall and stopped in front of Conte, coming up seven. The croupier set a second yellow chip next to the first, and Conte said, "Let it ride." The shooter went through his ritual and shot a four. He made it the hard way two rolls later.

Without looking up, Conte said, " 'Lo, Weepy. How's the boy?"

On the other side of the table Weepy Moyers said, "How they running for you, Mattie?"

Conte moved the twenty dollars worth of chips to the Back Line. The fat man had two black hundred-dollar chips on the pass line and dark circles under the arms of his Hawaiian shirt. He let fly, and Conte looked down at double threes. The fat man crapped out on the next roll, and the croupier placed a duplicate stack beside Conte's chips. The fat man looked at the croupier and said, "Thanks for nothing, motherfucker," without much heat, and went away.

"Not bad, Weepy," Conte answered. The stickman hooked the dice and passed them down, along with three fresh ones. Conte moved his stake back to the pass line, picked out two of the dice, and rolled.

"Let's you and me have a drink, Weepy." Conte watched the dice come up eleven, and the chips pile up in front of him. He let all of it ride.

"Thanks, Mattie. Maybe later."

Conte rolled two more naturals, hit a straight-ways eight,

then another natural. By now the yellow chips had been replaced by black, and there was about thirteen hundred dollars in front of him. The croupier looked nervously over his shoulder at Weepy, his boss. Conte flipped him a black chip; the croupier tapped it on the rail to show the men upstairs it was a tip, then dropped it in his lockbox. He still looked like he wished Conte would do his gambling at someone else's table.

"Let it ride," Conte said, and flipped the dice the length of the table. Snake eyes stared back him.

"There's the thing about Lady Luck," Weepy Moyers said blandly. "Sometimes she makes love to you, and sometimes she just fucks you."

A young woman came up to the railing in time to hear him. She wore a strapless sheath made of something that stuck very close to the skin. Her shoulders were deeply tanned and showed no strap marks.

She smiled at Conte and said, "You had the dice for a long time." She had a French accent. "You did well?"

Conte looked her over. "I was ahead for a while," he said, "but I ended up five bucks down."

"Tant pis."

"I'm no gambler."

"You are what?" Somewhere along the line the woman had moved closer to him.

"I forget," Conte said. "I'll ask my wife."

"You are not fun," the woman said, and wandered off.

"Let's get that drink, Weepy."

Weepy was watching the woman's exit. "Huh?"

"Drink. You and me. Now."

Weepy blinked. "I can't, Mattie. I'm working."

Conte pursed his lips and shook his head, as if that were the most ineffably dopey thing he had heard in a week.

"Awright, awright," Weepy said, looking like he was on the verge of tears. "Let's get it over with."

Weepy called a pit man at the other end of the enclosure, then ducked under the velvet rope. Conte steered him across the room to one of the small cocktail bars. The decor of the Golden Lady was Old West Saloon, so the bar had a brass rail, lamps with fringed shades, and a bedsheet-sized painting of a naked dancing girl over the cash register. The bartender was a hardbitten woman of around forty, dressed in boots, denim hot pants, matching push-up bra, neckerchief, and Stetson. She scowled when Conte led Weepy to seats at the far end of the bar.

When she came over, Conte put a five-dollar chip on the bar and said, "I'll bet your dogs are killing you."

"Yours would too, you were on your feet all day in these goddamned boots." But she stopped scowling.

"I don't care why you're in Reno," Weepy Moyers said when she had gone to fix the drinks. "You know there's paper on you, and you know the Old Men can't protect you here, but you come skipping in anyway, big as a bull's-eye. That's your business. I don't care why you're in Reno."

"I get it," Conte said. "You don't care why I'm in Reno."

The bartender came back and leaned over to place drinks in front of them. Stretch marks showed above the low-cut waistband of her shorts. Conte added a second yellow chip to the first. That bought him a smile before she glided away.

"Bressio's here," Conte said into his ginger ale.

"That's how the talk goes. No one's so happy about it neither. The boys have got their own way of doing things in Nevada. They got to have a system and everyone's got to stick to it if the gaming business is gonna run smooth."

The gaming business. Conte had always gotten a kick out of the euphemism.

"Bressio, on the other hand, has got a reputation for stirring up trouble," Weepy Moyers went on. "But that isn't your problem." Weepy turned his sad eyes on Conte. "Which is not to say you don't have a problem."

"What's my problem, Weepy?"

"Bressio thinks you're gunning for him because you think he had Carlo DeChristi iced, which the smart money says is odds-on correct. So Bressio is afraid you'll get lucky and screw things up for him. Like you might kill him, which would be a real drag for the guy. So he wants you dead first and puts out the word: keep an eye out for Matt Conte, and if you run into him and have the legs to do him, bring his head to Frank Bressio. Only Bressio is not Family, so why should anyone do anything for him? I'll tell you why: the paper. It's up to a hundred grand now, by the way. Money don't go so far here as it does in New York." Weepy said all of this in a low monotone, like a child reciting by rote a poem he does not really comprehend.

"Where is he?"

Weepy shook his head.

"Don't hold out on me, Weepy."

"I'm telling you, Mattie, I don't know. Someone does, probably, but it ain't me. I don't like knowing things like that. I like to be dumb."

"So far," Conte said, "you're doing a hell of a job at it." He pushed away the mostly full glass of ginger ale and slid off the stool. "Give my love to all the little Moyers," he said, "if you know who they are."

Weepy Moyers said, "Wait a minute."

Conte waited.

"Never mind," Weepy said.

"Cut the shit, Weepy."

"I was just gonna ask: you're not working with someone else, are you?"

Conte felt a prickle at the back of his neck. "What's that mean?"

"Someone else came around asking about Bressio, some dame. About three o'clock, I heard. That was before I came on shift."

"What'd they tell her?"

"Same as I told you. The truth."

"Finish it, Weepy."

"Well, I heard she was in other places, asking around, more or less making a pest of herself. But she's not so bad looking—young, dark hair, good figure if you like a lot of leg, which some guys do—so she more or less gets away with it so far."

Damn it, Conte thought. It had to be Chris, and already she was operating over her head. What the hell could Dennison be thinking of? The plan had been to hold her back until Conte was able to get a firm make on Bressio's whereabouts. She sure as hell was looking for deadly trouble by careening around town making loud noises. Chris Amado had no idea what Bressio's kind was like, or by what rules they played.

Conte knew they were like savages and played by no rules whatsoever.

Bressio had a good head start, but Conte had to find her first, and double quick.

Chapter Sixteen

Conte almost won the race.

As he came out of the Golden Lady onto South Virginia, Chris Amado was three blocks away, near the bridge where Virginia crossed the Truckee River.

There was a grassy verge along the bank, a twenty-yard width of open space between the slow-moving water and the rush of traffic on Second Street. For the next four blocks north, Virginia was a garish, neon-splashed canyon of casinos, but this was a tiny island of serenity, and Chris sat down to watch the night reflections in the sluggish river water. She kicked off her shoes and flexed her toes. She wore a pantsuit, and beside her on the grass was a small leather handbag.

The afternoon had gone well, she thought, and she was excited with the anticipation of the payoff. She had spent nearly six hours making the rounds of the casinos. The gambling fraternity was a tight-knit, in-bred, shadowy group, suspicious of everything and everybody, including its customers. It was the only service industry in which the consumer was invariably treated with rudeness and contempt. It preferred to mind its own business and police its own members, and in front of outsiders it kept its mouth shut. Yet within itself, the gambling infrastructure had no secrets. It was made up of perpetually nervous people, and the nervous love to talk.

Gambling was a business, based on the purest of mathematical principles. For every dollar wagered at the roulette table, the house kept ninety-four cents. From every savvy crapshooter who took the odds, the house exacted a two percent levy. Of every ten coins a slot machine swallowed, it spit back nine. Of course, odds were accurate only over what mathematicians called "a statistically significant number of trials," and what gamblers called "the long run"—but the long run was the only run there was. A single moderately busy crap table could turn a hundred thousand dollars in an evening. During a typical shift, a pit boss like Weepy Moyers might see a million dollars' worth of chips pass back and forth across the green felt layout.

Yet even though the inexorable realities of probability were always in their favor, most casino employees were as superstitious as druids. Empirically, they knew the house always won. They had watched day in and day out for years and had *never* seen a cash-out in which management had not come out a winner. Yet they worried constantly that the next day or the next their "luck" would run out. In their perception of the arcane mysteries of wagering, most dealers and pit bosses were as naive as the farmer from Ames, Iowa, whose idea of a big time was a whirling slot machine and a Dixie cup of nickels.

Because they totally distrusted the "marks" whom they routinely fleeced, the casino people talked among themselves endlessly, incessantly. The briefest informal get-together was as voluble as a barbers' convention.

So an hour after Chris Amado hit Virginia Street, the word was out about the chick asking for Frank Bressio.

Chris could tell it from the looks she began to get, the monosyllabic negative answers. That was okay. She had not expected anyone to cheerfully volunteer Bressio's whereabouts. As long as they were talking, Bressio would hear the noise soon enough.

It was about ten o'clock, a cool, clear spring night. Ten miles out into the desert, the sky would be a star-spackled bowl, the Milky Way a dense opalescent band overhead. Here in Reno, the natural light show was subsumed by the candlepower of the casino marquees, washing out the starlight's brilliant purity. The rush of passing cars at Chris's back was constant and uniform, so she did not know what instinct moved her to look over her shoulder in time to see the long dark sedan pull to the curb and stop, its motor idling.

Chris slipped on her shoes and stood. Two men got out of the back of the car. Chris gawked at them. Even in Reno, they stood out like circus freaks.

Both wore dark suits, and that's where any similarity ended. One of them was hugely fat. His torso was a perfect sphere, out of which arms and legs stuck like the limbs of Mister Potato Head. His head was as big and round as a basketball, and his eyes and even his nose had settled deep into his flesh, as if it were quicksand. When he crossed the sidewalk he seemed to roll instead of walk, bobbing gently from side to side like a child's pull-toy.

His partner was so skinny he was almost skeletal; he looked like something brought back to life in the far parapet of a ruined castle, by a mad doctor played by Basil Rathbone. He stood maybe three inches under seven feet tall, and his jacket hung on him like he was a coat hanger. His fingers were as long and brittle as breadsticks, and his cheeks were so concave you could spoon soup from them. He looked like his pituitary gland had been on a twenty-year binge.

Chris Amado put her hand in her leather bag and around the butt of the Colt Python .357 Magnum it contained. She thumbed back the hammer and stepped out of the backlight of a nearby stanchion.

The two men flanked her, standing too close on either side. The fat one stank.

"What is this?" Chris demanded. Twenty yards away traffic streamed by. "What do you want?"

"We was gonna ask you the same thing," the fat man said. "Why've you been shooting your mouth off?"

Chris tried to move away, and the skinny guy's hand darted out, quick as a lizard's tongue. His long fingers went all the way around her bicep. He had a surprisingly strong grip.

"Let's go."

"Get your hands off me."

"Listen, babe," the skinny guy said, "I'm easygoing. But Chubb here, he likes to play rough. He don't get so many girls—you can figure out why, probably—so when he does, he likes his money's worth."

"Shut up," Chubb grunted.

The skinny guy laughed. "Come on. The night ain't getting any younger."

"You can't—"

"Yeah," Chubb said, "we can."

He grabbed a fistful of Chris's hair in fingers fat as knockwursts and yanked.

Chris let the leather bag fall away from the Colt and jabbed the barrel into Chubb's pudding of a gut. The fat man grunted fetid breath into her face. His pig eyes widened as far as the suet in which they were embedded would allow before narrowing with pain.

Chris stroked the trigger.

All of the Colt's four-inch barrel, and a good part of the cylinder, were buried in Chubb's pillow-soft stomach, so the report of the big handgun was only a soft splat, like someone had dropped a phone book on the carpet. Chubb's eyelids flew open like window shades. When he sat down on the grass, Chris could feel the ground shake. Chubb stretched his arms to get both hands over the hole in his stomach. He raised a palm to his face, looking curiously at the blood smeared across it, then lay down on his side and closed his eyes. He smelled just as bad dead.

Chris pointed the Python at the skinny guy. His hand was frozen in position under the lapel of his coat, and his eyes were blinking like a stroboscope.

"Bring it out very carefully and drop it by Chubb," Chris said. "It's got prints on it," the skinny guy whined.

"Don't fuck around!"

The skinny guy used two fingers to dig out a small automatic. He let it fall to the grass. Blood was oozing between Chubb's swollen fingers and soaking into the dirt.

"All right," Chris said. "Let's go."

"Huh?"

"You wanted to take me to see someone. Now's your chance."

"You gotta be nuts," the skinny guy said with something like admiration.

"Maybe we should kick it around," Chris snapped, "until someone gets curious about the Incredible Bulk here." She nudged Chubb's body with one foot.

The skinny guy turned abruptly and started toward the idling sedan. "Let's always see those hands," Chris said, following. At the car she said, "You first," and slid in behind the skinny guy.

The driver was very young, no more than twenty, and had a badly pitted face, like his mother had force-fed him with a slingshot. He flicked a glance at Chris in the rear-view mirror.

She leaned forward and tapped his shoulder with the barrel of the Colt. "Both hands on the wheel from here on." The driver's eyes were as expressionless as buttons. He turned them on the skinny guy and said, "What gives?"

"It's her play," the skinny guy answered. "For now."

"Okey-doke," the driver said. "Where to, lady?"

Chris moved into the corner where she could cover both men. "You're the driver."

The young guy shrugged and pulled away from the curb, glided across two lanes of traffic, and turned north on Virginia into the lights of the casino facades. At the first signal he popped the shift lever into park, turned, and studied Chris. "What happened to Chubb?" he inquired casually, like who won the third at Del Mar.

"Stomach trouble," Chris said. "He bit off more than he could chew."

Chapter Seventeen

As he waited to cross Fourth Street at North Virginia, Matt Conte saw Chris Amado in the back of the black sedan.

He was on the wrong side of the street, and at the same moment that he recognized her the light changed and the car pulled forward. Conte stepped off the curb, and brakes squealed as a bumper came to a quivering stop a few feet from his legs. A florid-faced man stuck his head out the window and hollered, "What the fuck . . ." Conte didn't hear the rest.

He looked around frantically for a cab—and spotted one at the light, four cars back and blocked in on either side. A block in the other direction, the dark sedan ran a yellow light and cruised on, heading north toward the interstate. Conte watched helplessly as its taillights blended into the traffic's stream and became indistinct.

"Goddamnit," Conte muttered. His shoulder muscles were tense with frustration. He'd gotten a good look at the dark sedan and the two thugs in it, and he had no doubt that Chris was in deep trouble.

Across the street a guy came out of the Golden Lady, and suddenly Conte was in trouble of his own.

Conte melted back under the marquee of a porno theater on the corner. The man looking up and down the street from in front of the Golden Lady was named Rudy Marcoux. Conte had met him only once, years before, when they were nominally in the same business. At that time Marcoux was attached to the Anatolli family in Brooklyn, but Reno was a hell of a way from home for the guy. That meant he was on his own—or working for Bressio.

It took Conte maybe thirty seconds to make the other two. One was a long-haired guy in a denim jacket, standing in the doorway of the casino next to the Golden Lady. The other was a small, dapper man who looked vaguely familiar. He was staked out three doors up from Conte, to complete the three-way box. They were supposed to blend into the milling crowd, but to Conte's instincts they stood out like whores at a debutante party.

Marcoux was still pretending to take in the sights, but Conte knew he'd been made. That pressed the issue; he'd have to take them out right now, and he'd need one alive—preferably Marcoux—to lead him to Chris. All of this ran through Conte's mind, instinctual as breathing. He did not think of what was about to happen in terms of danger and violence and killing and living. It was simply a step to accomplish before he could get on with the main business at hand.

The throngs on the sidewalks gave an edge to Marcoux and his crew. A crowd was excellent cover for hitting one man. You walked up, stuck the gun between a couple of ribs, and squeezed the trigger. Soft-nosed bullets that shattered into a dozen pieces on impact assured death by scrambling the victim's insides and eliminated the possibility of slugs exiting the other side and picking off some guy from Boise who was taking in the sights. The noise of the gun's report, along with the suddenly bleeding body on the sidewalk, invariably scared the hell out of the people in the near vicinity. While they were shitting themselves, you walked away.

No one ever followed.

Van Dyne, Conte thought. That was the name of the dapper man three doors up. A street soldier in Anatolli's mob.

The light changed, and the long-haired guy crossed Virginia Street. Van Dyne edged in Conte's direction. Marcoux was watching him openly now.

That was fine with Conte. The sooner the curtain came down on this show, the sooner he could get to Chris.

Conte wheeled and walked directly at Van Dyne. The dapper man began to study a display of discount stereos in a store window. Conte bore down on him. Van Dyne twitched.

Conte veered left into a casino called the Argent.

He went down two steps to the gambling floor and weaved past a line of blackjack tables. It was still early by Reno standards, and there were no players at the last table, the deck fanned out face up in a flawless crescent in front of the woman dealer. She gave Conte what was supposed to be an encouraging smile as he went up the steps on the other side, toward a door that said "Gentlemen."

Ten seconds later the long-haired guy in the denim jacket came in the street door. Conte waited until he was certain the guy had spotted him, then strolled into the restroom.

He went through a closet-sized vestibule and another door. One wall of the lavatory was three sinks set into a marble countertop below a three-paneled mirror. Around each of the basins, in identical neat arrangements, were razors, shaving cream, bottles of cologne, hair dressing and hand lotion, vials of aspirin and antacids, and stacks of perfectly folded, snow-white hand towels. In front of each assortment was a polished glass ashtray salted with a single silver dollar.

The attendant was a middle-aged black man. He wore a white mess jacket, black slacks, and black brogans buffed to an incandescent shine. He nodded at Conte and said, "Yes sir," automatically and to no point.

"Can you whistle?" Conte said.

The attendant stared at him.

Conte took out a neat roll of currency. He peeled off a ten-dollar bill and stuffed it in the breast pocket of the attendant's mess jacket.

"I do a right mean 'Old Man River,'" the attendant said. He looked at the bill peeking out of his pocket. "For a C-note I do all four movements of Mozart's Fortieth."

"Very soon now," Conte said, "a man is coming in here. He's got long brownish hair, and he's wearing a denim jacket. Very hard around the eyes."

"Like you?"

"That's right." Conte skinned another ten from the roll and gave it the same home as its brother. "He'll ask if anyone is in here. You'll tell him no. He'll call you a liar. You'll tell him to see for himself."

Conte gave the attendant another ten and pointed a thumb over his shoulders. "He'll check out those stalls, one at a time. When he gets in front of the one I'm in, or if he pulls a gun before that, you'll whistle."

"Did you say 'gun'?"

Conte gave the man a twenty.

"When I whistle, he'll guess why," the attendant said.

"Right."

"I'm not so young anymore. I've lost some of my speed."

"I haven't," Conte said.

There were five stalls. Conte went into the one farthest from the door. He grabbed the lip of the side wall with both hands, flexed his knees, and boosted himself up so he was draped over the wall on his stomach. From there he could reach the slide latch of the door. Conte locked the fourth stall, then dropped back inside the fifth. He left the latch of that stall open and the door slightly ajar.

He took a seat on the toilet tank, his feet on either side of the bowl. He took out and charged the .45, and then he waited.

It was a standoff for the moment. The lavatory was a cul-de-sac, but that worked two ways. Sure, if Conte tried to leave he'd be walking into a three-man squeeze, but with triple odds against him they'd box him sooner or later anyway. Besides, he wasn't planning on leaving. He meant to wait out Marcoux and his two boys, which is why he let himself get "trapped." Maybe his back was to the wall, but he'd had time to dig in.

He heard the pneumatic wheeze of the lavatory door, and then the black attendant's noncommittal, "Yes, sir." A toilet flushed, water rang in the sink, and a chip clacked into a glass ashtray. Someone else came in, tried the door of the stall next to Conte, then moved down to do his business in the next one. The attendant said, "Thank you, sir," as the man went out.

Twelve others came and went; Conte counted. Twenty-five minutes passed.

Conte silently stretched his right leg to work out an incipient cramp. His ankle joint softly popped—and the attendant began to whistle.

"Where is he?" The long-haired guy had a faint Slavic accent.

"Ain't no one here but me, boss."

"Conte!"

Conte held the gun at fire ready, the barrel pointed at the ceiling, and waited. A stall door slammed back on its hinges, followed by stillness. Conte heard footsteps, then the second slam open, and seconds later, the third.

"What you doing, boss?" the attendant said, with genuine alarm.

The locked door of the fourth stall rattled. The long-haired guy swore under his breath, and a foot slammed into the door and metal bent and tore.

Conte came silently off the toilet and tank and eased out the door. The attendant was in the far corner, trying to make himself small.

Conte whirled into the open door of the fourth stall behind the long-haired guy.

The killer was trying to recover his balance and bring up his gun at the same time. In his expression there was frustration and hate, and regret at having been as careful as he could and still making the wrong play.

Conte shot him in the forehead, and the guy crashed backward, the edge of the toilet bowl catching the back of his knees. His legs folded and he sat down, toilet water slopping out around him. Blobs of pulpy red quivered like jellyfish on the gleaming porcelain of the toilet tank.

The attendant looked over Conte's shoulder, gasped, and plunged into the adjacent stall. Conte went to the door, flattening himself against the wall beside it. When the attendant had finished his retching, Conte said softly, "Lock that stall door and stay where you are." The attendant did not have to be told a second time.

Soundproofing was standard in casino construction— marks tended to gamble more when they were not distracted by the noises of traffic and flushing toilets and the other sounds of real life. But Conte was betting that Van Dyne had planted himself just outside the bathroom and had heard at least the concussion of the shot.

Perhaps three minutes passed. The door opened a crack, and Van Dyne said in a low voice, "Hey, Slaski."

The door eased open a few more inches.

Conte reached through the crack, got his fist around Van Dyne's wrist, and yanked him into the small room. Van Dyne tried to pull free, and Conte twisted his arm around and up behind him. He jerked hard and was rewarded with the sound of snapping bone.

"Oh Christ," Van Dyne moaned. The gun dropped to the tiled floor.

Conte used more leverage, and Van Dyne stumbled to one knee. He tried to reach the gun with his good arm. It was awkward work.

Before he could finish it, Conte had the little shot-filled sap out. He hit Van Dyne hard at the point of the sharp bone on the right side of the back of his skull.

Van Dyne flopped over on his back. His muscles spasmed as his brain tried frantically to unscramble itself, so for a moment he was bent like a torsion bar and only his heels and head contacted the floor. Blood streamed out of his right ear, and Van Dyne went limp and still.

The attendant came unsteadily out of the stall. There was vomit on the front of his mess jacket. He looked down at Van Dyne, gulped, and dove back into the stall. Nothing came out this time, but he stayed there on his knees, his head hanging limply over the splattered bowl.

Conte ruffled through the roll of bills, separated two one-hundreds, folded them twice, and dropped the little wedge in one of the ashtrays. "Sorry," he mumbled to the attendant's back, and went out.

* * *

When Rudy Marcoux saw Matt Conte come out of the men's room alone, he had a pretty good idea what Conte had left behind. He wasn't much bothered: he hadn't thought much of Van Dyne and the Polack, but little men with big guns came cheap in Reno and there was nothing lost in giving them a try. He'd promised them a one-third cut, but that didn't mean anything. Especially now.

A hundred grand was not bad money for a few seconds' work. Conte was good, sure, but no one was good enough to dodge a bullet in the back from a gun he never saw. However, for now the hit would have to wait, Marcoux decided. The rhythm of the night had gone wrong, and there'd be other times, other chances.

Marcoux nodded and smiled across the room at Conte and went out the side door onto Fourth.

He crossed in the middle of the block, and a kid in a candy-apple red pickup blasted his air horn and swerved around him. Marcoux caught a glimpse of Conte coming out of the Argent. Marcoux went down two doors and into a bar whose only identity came from a neon "Coors" sign in a filthy window.

The joint was a long slot of a room just wide enough for the bar, some stools, and the space to walk behind them. A black whore wearing a couple of pounds of paint gave Marcoux one second of a professional smile and clicked it back off. The only other customer was asleep, his cheek pressed into the burn-scarred bartop, his arms dangling like bunting. As Marcoux shut the door, a great gurgling snore came out of his mouth and nose. The bartender had one cauliflower ear, a dirty apron, and heavy ridges of scar tissue above both eyes.

Marcoux went past the row of stools, a rattling ice machine, two doors marked "Pointers" and "Setters," and out into the alley. Across it was another unmarked door with a bare fifteen-watt bulb burning yellowly above it. Inside was a kitchen. A Chinese man was scooping handfuls of bean sprouts into a wok. He gave Marcoux a machine-gun burst of Chinese that might have been a question or a curse. Marcoux ignored him and went back into the alley. He went in the direction of Virginia Street and into the third door. That put him in an all-night drugstore. At the counter he bought a pack of Winstons, then went out the front. The double-back put him two doors down from the dismal bar. A cab was idling at the curb, its "for hire" light shining. The driver was slumped behind the wheel with the bill of his cap pulled over his eyes.

Marcoux tapped on the window with his knuckles, and the driver started and sat up straighter. Marcoux opened the back door and got in, and the driver said "Where to, bud?"

Rudy Marcoux did not answer. He stared across the seat at Matt Conte, and into the gaping barrel of his .45. The bore of the automatic looked big enough to crawl into.

"The Fairgrounds," Conte said, watching Marcoux. "Around back of the racetrack, at the stables."

"There ain't nobody out there this time of year, bud," the driver complained into the rear-view mirror. He gave the gun the same look of disgust he might have given someone who'd littered his floor.

"I know," Conte said, staring icily at Marcoux. "That's what I'm counting on."

Chapter Eighteen

"Who let you in?" Peter Chamberlain said peevishly.

"It wasn't Freda's fault. She said you were out."

"I am," Chamberlain said. "I'm out of sorts."

"You look well, Peter," Vang said courteously. It was the truth. Chamberlain was invariably immaculate. He was in his mid-forties, tall and lean with perfect posture. His blond hair might have been trimmed that morning, and his tailored suit and white shirt were as unwrinkled as a catalog model's. Even in Laos at the height of the war, his fatigues were always precisely fitted and spotless as a wedding gown. Chamberlain was the only man Vang knew who could come through an all-night firefight with clean hands.

Vang smiled pleasantly and looked over the black-enameled wooden captain's chair facing Chamberlain's desk, a new addition to the decor. "A gift?" Vang asked.

"From an old classmate," Chamberlain said. "I . . . uh, did him a favor."

A Yale College seal was decaled on the back of the chair. Vang looked at it and laughed.

"What's so funny?" Chamberlain snapped.

"'Lux et Veritas,'" Vang read. "Your old classmate has a sense of humor."

"What are you talking about?" Chamberlain was the most literal man Vang knew. To him, verbal communication was absolutely linear, and irony, ellipses, and double-entendres were meaningless.

"'Light and Truth,'" Vang translated. "What a fine ironic slogan to find in the office of a CIA senior agent."

"I am not a CIA senior agent."

"Of course not. How could I forget?"

Strictly speaking—which was the only way Chamberlain spoke—he was right. The D.C. office in which they sat was attached to the Department of State, in which Chamberlain was a deputy assistant secretary. His name did not appear in any list of CIA personnel in either the so-called open files or the "eyes-only" lists. Chamberlain's name never appeared in the newspapers either, mostly because no reporter had ever considered him newsworthy. However, when a Cabinet member, a high-ranking member of Congress, or the president needed a sensitive—and confidential—contact with the agency, it was Chamberlain who got the call. Even these officials were unaware of Chamberlain's real position and mandate. They believed Chamberlain's job was to act as liaison and expediter; actually, he was on order from the agency to keep meddlesome civilians out of its hair, politely but firmly.

The technical details of the song and dance that was Chamberlain's day-to-day routine did not interest Vang. For him Chamberlain was simply a source.

"Why can't you stay put, Vang?" Chamberlain said plaintively. "We give you this wonderful house overlooking the Pacific. Don't you like it? Movie stars don't live that well, or businessmen. Even some crooks don't live that well." Chamberlain, as always, was serious. "Why don't you take it easy and live off the fat of your adopted land?" Then his face clouded. "You're working again, right?"

Vang smiled pleasantly. He had known Chamberlain for

almost twenty years, since American "advisors" first became involved in the Vietnam conflict. In addition to being chief of Vientiane station, Chamberlain was an agency "headhunter"; he had recruited Vang. Chamberlain had also fought at his side more than once, and Vang knew he could be a courageous and resourceful warrior.

They might have become friends if either man could have afforded the friendship. But for Chamberlain the maintenance of professional distance between recruiter and recruit was basic tradecraft, as automatic as survival. For Vang, friendship was inexpedient, because he'd had a hunch from the first that Chamberlain was destined to be used. He was Vang's contact when he presented the evidence of Air America involvement in the opium trade, his people's ticket to safety. That had been a bitter pill for Chamberlain to swallow because of all the agents he was the most honest and incorruptible—but then that was why Vang had picked him. Chamberlain went to his superiors, and Vang's demands were met.

Vang understood Chamberlain's lingering resentment— but that was part of the game they all played. There were times when Vang needed what Chamberlain could provide, and Chamberlain was leverageable; those were the facts of life.

"I wish to know," Vang said, "if a retired U.S. Army general named Benjamin Creed is associated in any way with the agency at this time, or if he has ever been."

"Go to hell, Vang."

"Peter . . ."

"Listen, pal. You don't walk in here and ask me questions. It does not work that way. You've got nothing to do with the agency anymore."

"Then why does the agency pay my rent?"

Around his perfectly starched collar, Chamberlain's neck reddened.

"I have written a story, Peter," Vang said evenly. "You can guess what it is about. I made copies. Do you know where they are?"

Despite himself, Chamberlain shook his head.

"One is in a safe deposit box in the Santa Barbara branch of the Bank of America. Isn't that where Americans put their valuables? Another is in the First National Bank of Green River, Wyoming."

"Why Wyoming?"

"I beg your pardon. Why what?"

Chamberlain sighed. "Why did you pick a bank in Wyoming?"

"For the same reason I picked banks in Mississippi, Rhode Island, and Kansas. Also Bangkok—and I think I also left a copy of my story in the safe of the Hotel Continental in Saigon—pardon me, Ho Chi Minh City."

Chamberlain's eyes went wide as medallions. "Jesus, Vang, if the fucking Commies find—"

"I was joking about Saigon," Vang said. "Where is your sense of humor, Peter?"

"It got shot off in the war."

"I wasn't joking about the other locations. You know I am a cautious man. Now, please: answer my question about Benjamin Creed."

"You want information, try the Library of Congress. Turn left on Constitution, go down about two dozen blocks, and take a right on First. Tell 'em I sent you."

"Peter," Vang said patiently.

"What's the job?" Chamberlain said. "I need to at least know that."

Chamberlain gave Vang a pugnacious stare. Vang met it for perhaps ten seconds, then rose. "Good day, Peter."

Vang had his hand on the doorknob when Chamberlain snorted and said, "Son of a bitch." He punched an intercom button on his desk and said, "Freda, come in here, please." He released the button and said, "Sit down, Vang, goddamn you."

The woman who came into the office was around fifty, a big, bony, horse-faced woman, plain as a governess. She was tall and broad and wore a dress with old-fashioned padded shoulders that made her look as wide as a boxcar.

"Watch out he doesn't steal any paper clips," Chamberlain said. "I'll be in the basement."

After he left, Freda sat in Chamberlain's chair and fixed a stern glare on Vang. "Are you well?" Vang inquired.

Freda snorted, as if Vang had said something so frivolously lewd it did not merit reaction. Neither of them spoke again. Ten minutes passed.

When Chamberlain returned, he waited until Freda had returned to her reception office before dropping into his chair. "What's Creed involved in?"

"I don't know."

"Where is he right now?"

"I don't know. Can you tell me?"

"No," Chamberlain snapped. Then less harshly: "If you find him, will you let me know?"

"Possibly. You have asked three questions, but you have not answered the one I asked you."

"All right, all right. Creed is not now nor has he ever been sanctioned. Of course, he had contact with the agency in Nam, like any other ranking officer. But it was strictly routine."

Chamberlain tapped manicured fingernails on the polished surface of his desk. "However, the agency does have an open file on him. There was some trouble several years back—"

"You mean the guns."

"How did you know that? Never mind," Chamberlain added quickly. "If you do turn up Creed, we'd like to talk to him."

"I expect to turn him up," Vang said, "but he may not be in condition to talk."

"Shit." Chamberlain suddenly wrenched open his shirt collar and loosened his tie. Coming from the eternally groomed man, the gesture was as startling as if he had exposed himself on a bus. "All right," he snapped, "here's the rest. I'm telling you this for one reason only: I want you to know how potentially dangerous Creed may be and why we want very much to get him in the hot seat and sweat out some answers. Except you didn't get it from me. You weren't here. I don't even know you. Right?"

"Go on, Peter."

Chamberlain sighed mightily. "When the FBI told the army about Creed's contacts with that mobster Castelli, they should have tossed him in a cage and thrown away the key. Instead they gave him a pension and told him to run along."

"Why?"

Chamberlain shot him a narrow look. "You've been

dealing with the U.S. long enough to know the answer to that, Vang. They were covering their asses. If Creed were prosecuted, the whole story would come out and the army would have egg on its face. If he quietly disappeared, no harm would be done—to anyone."

"Has he?"

"How's that?"

"Has Creed quietly disappeared?"

"Obviously he has not," Chamberlain said, "or you wouldn't be here asking about him."

"Why do *you* wish to speak with Creed?"

Chamberlain hesitated. "The FBI and the agency don't necessarily agree with the army's action in this matter," he said carefully. "It has to do with Creed's last psychological evaluation, done two months before he was eased out. The results could be interpreted as disturbing." Chamberlain picked up a letter opener from his desk blotter and unconsciously ran his thumb along its dull edge. "The examining physician described Creed as intelligent, socially facile, a strong, confident, even charismatic personality with excellent leadership quality, high self-esteem, with a strong adherence to a personal code and his own notion of integrity."

"Should I be impressed?"

"Not yet." Chamberlain examined the point of the letter opener. "The psychiatrist also described Creed as exhibiting the classic symptoms of the paranoid schizophrenic—and given his background, experience, and personality, Creed may have the potential to attempt to act out his delusions."

"Then the man is insane."

"No," Chamberlain said firmly. "That's what makes him dangerous. By what we consider the usual manifestations of insanity—irrational behavior, incoherent pronouncements, inappropriate social intercourse—Creed is absolutely normal. His military career is proof of that."

"Then we have nothing to worry about."

Chamberlain ignored the sarcasm, if he recognized it at all. "What we have to worry about is Creed's capacity to lose it, to break loose into full-blown mania. Creed could be like a malaria carrier, who may never show symptoms, or who may become deathly ill years after exposure. Given the way he disappeared as soon as he left the army, and the fact that neither the agency nor the FBI has been able to find any sign of him since, I'd say we've got at least a legitimate concern."

"Then you have been looking for him."

"Yeah, Vang, we have been looking for him," Chamberlain said wearily. "And no, we haven't found him. If you want to wisecrack about that, go ahead. I'm a big guy. I can take it. Otherwise, get the hell out of here."

"One last question: what about a man named Greaves?"

Chamberlain showed his surprise for a moment before covering. "You know, Vang, you've already got so much information I'd figure coming to me was a waste of precious time."

"Coming to you, Peter, is invariably a pleasure."

"Cut the shit, friend. Greaves was Creed's righthand boy in Nam. He was discharged a captain, he's missing, too, and we wouldn't mind a word with him also. Now, have you got everything you came for?"

"Yes," Vang said, "I do." He stood. "Thank you, Peter. I'll look forward to seeing you again."

"Sorry I can't say the same." But as Vang reached the door, Chamberlain added, "How's Dennison?"

"Well."

"Tell him I asked for him."

Vang smiled. "He'll be pleased to know he is in your thoughts."

The tourist season was getting underway and the long canopied boardwalk across the street from the plaza in Sante Fe, New Mexico, was lined with vendors. Arranged on blankets smoothed over the planks were bracelets, earrings, necklaces, beadwork, belts, charms, a vast wealth of turquoise and silver presided over by somber-faced, dark-skinned Pueblo Indians, watching the browsers through intensely stoic kohl eyes.

William Sterling Price moved slowly down the line, admiring the workmanship of the jewelry. There were several pieces he liked, but he knew his wife would find them flashy for her taste, and he couldn't really picture himself in a silver bracelet. He nodded pleasantly at the plump Indian woman and moved on. He wore slacks, a black T-shirt, dark aviator glasses with gold frames.

He was near the end of the line of blankets when a voice behind him said, "I knew a woman who never went out of the house without putting on about forty pounds of that stuff."

Price turned. The man was perhaps ten years younger than he, dressed in jeans, a nacre-buttoned shirt, scuffed cowboy boots, and a sweat-stained buff Stetson with a rattlesnake-skin band around the crown.

"Four bracelets on each arm," the man said. "Two around each wrist, two above the elbow." They waited for a car with California plates to pass, then started across the street toward the plaza. "Earrings and earclips, with tiny silver spurs at the end of them. A hand-worked silver belt buckle with a chunk of turquoise the size of your hand, and enough necklace to ruin her posture. One of her pussy-lips was pierced, too; she wore a silver star in it. Swear to God," the man said, as if Price had expressed doubt.

They sat on a bench near the center of the grassy square. Two young women in dresses were eating sandwiches on another bench a little way down the walk, but there was no one close by.

"So we got drunk one night," the man said. "You know how it is: you get drunk, things happen. I talked her into getting it on. Except I figured unclipping all her hardware would take maybe an hour and a half, and I was too shitfaced to deal with that, so I said the hell with it." The man spit between his boots. "Shit. When I got off her, I looked like I'd been bucked into a barbed wire fence."

"Maybe you ought to slow down a little," Price suggested.

"Nope," the man said. "I just can't sit still." He pulled a magazine, folded lengthwise, from the back pocket of his jeans.

Price straightened the crease. The magazine was called *The Survivalist*. The cover showed a pudgy man in a green beret peering over the sight of an automatic rifle, above the legend: "Post-Nuclear Poaching—See Page 37 Now!!"

"In the back," the man said.

The corner of the third-to-the-last page was dog-eared.

There were three columns of classified ads, set in agate. One was bracketed in black·felt pen:

> Ready to die?—or willing to kill. If you want to survive to fight you must fight to survive. Contact BC, Box 46, Winnemucca, NV.

Price glanced at the bottom of the page. The issue was dated the previous September, over six months back.

"The ad ran only this one time," Price's companion said. "I answered it—purely for the sake of information. In my line it's good to keep an eye on who's doing what."

"Are you still consulting with the survivalist groups?"

"Consulting . . . and other stuff. Training. Procurement. You know how it is." The man looked at Price for the first time. "I'd rather be working with you again, Colonel."

"You're still on the duty roster, Luke," Price said. "You're the only armorer I've ever used, and you know it. But I have to go this one alone."

"Like I said, Old Son, I get restless. I've got nothing against survivalists, but they're pretty much play soldiers. I miss the real thing."

"The war is a long way from over, Luke. Depend on being a part of it."

"How's Al?" Luke said.

"Just as anxious to get back in harness." Price gestured with the magazine and cocked a questioning eyebrow.

"There was talk of a new survivalist compound," Luke said. "This was about six months back, same as that ad, and the place was supposed to be somewhere up in the desert— southeastern Oregon, southern Idaho, Nevada, in around there. That's high country, isolated as you'd ever want. Winnemucca is the only place like a city for two hundred miles in any direction, and it ain't got but twenty thousand people. All in all it's a nice lonely spot for waiting out the holocaust.

"Anyway," Luke said, "all I ever heard were rumors. One said Benjamin Creed was involved, but I got no second-source corroboration. They didn't say whether he was supposed to be part of the day-to-day operation or only lending his name, like he did with that Utah project."

"You said you answered the ad."

"All I got was a preliminary screening application. It asked a lot of questions and didn't give any answers."

"What's your take on it?"

Luke shrugged. "Whoever placed the ad changed his mind," he suggested. "His deal on the property fell through, he got into some other scam, the ad was a front for something else he abandoned—whatever."

"Maybe he found a better use for the site."

"Like what?"

"Beats me," Price said. "What else have you got?"

"That's the ball of wax, Colonel. The ad might have to do with Creed, or not, and there is or isn't something going on in that desert country. Sorry."

"Don't be," Price said. "Thanks for the help, Luke."

"It'll be a bitch to find," Luke said. "You might be able to spot something from the air, but not without tipping them off. That's figuring there's something to spot."

"I'm going to have to find out—with my hand close to my vest."

"The only way to play cards," Luke agreed.

At the next bench the two young women had finished their lunches. They crumpled wrappings and dropped them in a trash bin, then came down the walk toward Price and Luke. One of the women smiled and said, "Hi," but the other kept eyes rigidly ahead until they were past. She leaned and whispered something in her friend's ear.

"I think I was talking to her in a bar the other night," Luke said, watching their backs. "I must have done something to put her off her feed." He stretched his legs. "Wonder what it was."

They stood and shook hands. "If you need me," Luke said, "you know where to find me."

"Yeah. Probably where you don't belong."

Luke nodded solemnly. "If you have to wake me up, Old Son," he said, "do it quiet. And remind me not to leave my boots under the bed."

Chapter Nineteen

"Where's Bressio, Rudy?"

Matthew Conte's tone was patient as a schoolteacher's, though he had already asked the question eleven times. He had counted; it was a way to track your technique.

He held an aluminum five-cell flashlight, and now he clicked it on and off three times, aiming the beam full in Rudy Marcoux's face. The hitman was slumped in the corner of a vacant horse stall, the plank-enclosed space not much longer or wider than the animal it was designed to house. The dirt floor was covered with straw and dried horseshit. The straw was fermented and gave off a sickly sweet smell, but the horseshit was odorless with age.

"We're making progress, Rudy," Conte said. "We know that since Bressio came to Reno he's stepped up the recruiting. Boys have been coming in from Vegas, Oakland, even L.A. He's gearing up for something. We've got that straight now. That's fine. That's moving in the right direction. But I've got to know more, Rudy. You know how it is."

Marcoux squinted into the flashlight's probing glare. Dried blood was smeared below his nose like a charcoal mustache. There was more blood on the front of his jacket, along with a darker smudge of filth. His hands were hidden behind his back, tied at the wrists with a bridle rein. His lips were puffy and cracked.

"What's Bressio gearing up for, Rudy?"

Marcoux had said nothing for thirty minutes. Conte clicked the flashlight off, listened to the darkness for a moment, then shined the beam toward the ceiling. He brought it down slowly, like the sword of a monarch knighting a loyal subject, until it was focused in Marcoux's frightened eyes again.

"Talk to me, Rudy."

Conte rose from his haunches and moved closer, keeping

away from Marcoux's legs. He clubbed the flashlight, bent and tapped Marcoux on the top of the head with the butt, not very hard. Wetness in Marcoux's eyes reflected starry flashes of the light.

"You know Augie Franklin, Rudy?" Conte asked. "Little Pink from Pittsburgh, they called him. You hear what happened to Little Pink, Rudy?"

Conte tapped Marcoux's head with the flashlight again. "Little Pink got his hand caught where it should not have been, couple years back. The boys checked under the mattress and so forth, and what do you know? Money was missing. They asked Little Pink where it had gone to. They asked real nicely, but Little Pink wouldn't say.

"What they did," Conte said, "was start in hitting him on the top of the head. Like this." Conte demonstrated. "Not very hard, not very often—but they kept it up all night long. I'm no doctor, Rudy, but the way I understand it, after a while it starts to screw things up, the kind of damage you can't undo. Bruises the brain or something, I don't know."

Conte stepped back. "Jesus, Rudy, you ought to see Little Pink Franklin now. The poor fucker can't even feed himself. His idea of a good time is sitting around drooling and shitting his pants. Just because some guys hit him on top of the head a few times."

Conte turned the flashlight butt-end-to again and said for the thirteenth time, "Where's Bressio, Rudy?"

Marcoux licked his dry lips. "I'm dead if I tell you." His voice was dry, scratchy.

"What are your chances if you don't?" Conte took out the automatic, hefted it lightly on the palm of his hand. "Where's Bressio, Rudy?"

Marcoux shook his head helplessly, as if he'd swallowed his tongue.

Conte worked the slide of the gun. "I'm not going to kill you, Rudy," he said. He thumbed back the hammer of the automatic. "I'm going to shoot you in the foot."

Conte took his time aiming. Marcoux tried to pull back his leg, and Conte said, "Uh-uh. You move that foot and I'm liable to get so nervous I fire before I'm ready."

Conte bent and lay the muzzle of the .45 against the tongue of Marcoux's shoe.

"First off," Conte said, "you won't feel anything except the impact. There won't be any pain for maybe ten seconds."

Marcoux stared at the gun.

"But when the pain comes," Conte said, "it'll be just awful, Rudy. It will hurt like nothing ever hurt before."

"Oh Christ," Marcoux whimpered.

"You'll never walk right again, Rudy, and that's the best you can hope for. If we stick around afterwards, it'll get infected—because I'll rub some of this horseshit into it to make sure. That means blood poisoning, and if a few hours passes after it sets in, they'll have to take off the whole leg. Beyond that it won't matter; you'll be dead."

Conte moved the gun ever so slightly. "Last chance, Rudy."

Marcoux moaned, and Conte pulled the trigger.

The hammer dropped on an empty chamber.

Conte rose and smiled. He dropped the magazine out and began to replace the cartridges from the handful in his pocket. When he was done he recharged the handgun and aimed it at Marcoux again. "Where's Bressio, Rudy?"

Marcoux's face was yellow in the flashlight's relentless glare. His forehead was feverish with sweat. He closed his eyes and shook his head hopelessly.

Conte sighed. "Okay, Rudy, if that's the way you want it," he said. "We've got a whole night of fun ahead of us, at your expense."

Chapter Twenty

The Happy Bungalow Saloon was outside the Winnemucca city limits on Route 49, about a mile and a half west of where the Little Humboldt flowed into the main fork. It was far enough from the interstate and the half dozen downtown casinos to be off the beaten tourist track, so the customers were mostly regulars, with regular drinking habits. If you visited the Happy Bungalow at the same time on two successive days, the chances were the faces would be nearly identical.

The interior looked shabby; it had probably looked shabby the day it was built. Most of the light came from signs provided by beer distributors. There was an eternally flowing waterfall courtesy of Olympia, a molded plastic lampshade fringed with molded plastic billiard balls over the pool table from Budweiser, a Michelob clock, a Hamm's bear with a Rudolph-red nose, neon tubing fashioned into the logos of Dos Equis, Coors, Ranier, Pabst Blue Ribbon. There were Lucky Lager napkins, Miller High Life matches, Lite beer ashtrays, and no windows; within the Happy Bungalow twilight was forever.

Along the wall next to the front door was a row of three slot machines and an electronic keno game. Their front panels were covered with an irregular layer of dust adhering to the oil of overlapping fingerprints. Opposite was the bar and its dozen stools, with four round tables on the floor between. At one end were restrooms, at the other a back door. Conway and Loretta were harmonizing on the jukebox.

Vang stood alone at the bar. On the back shelf there was a jack rabbit, stuffed and mounted in a two-legged stance on a stained plank. A four-point deer rack had been wired to the jack's head, and a hand-lettered cardboard placard taped to the plank identified it as "The Seldom Seen Western Jackalope." Vang sipped at iced soda water and looked over the rest of the back bar. Among the rows of bottles and the pyramid stacks of clean glasses was a plastic model of a man in an open-doored privy with the legend, "Best Seat in the House," a framed two-dollar bill, a dice cup, a pair of mechanical teeth that chattered when wound up, and a card of thirty-nine-cent unbreakable rubber pocket combs. There were cartons of individual packets of aspirin, Rolaids, Smokehouse almonds, beef jerky, and Cornnuts, and a couple of two-gallon Mason jars, one of pickled eggs and another of turkey gizzards.

The bartender came over. Although Vang's glass was half full, the bartender pointed at it and said, " 'Nother?" His big hands were red and chapped from too much time in dishwater, and he had the pale, washed-out face and quick eyes of the one-time alcoholic who has been on the wagon for years and who can now be around other drinkers and stand it, even if he is miserable all the while.

Vang put a five-dollar bill on the bar. "Yes, please." He pushed his glass forward.

The bartender ignored it. He was looking over Vang's shoulder. The door banged shut behind a barrel-chested, gutty man in his mid-twenties. His long hair was dirty and matted, and there was dried egg yolk on the ends of his droopy mustache and motor oil on the thighs of his denims. His T-shirt was white except where it was smeared with black dirt, the sleeves cut off to show his arms ropey with muscle. He outweighed Vang maybe two to one.

He came up to the bar, and the bartender said, "Hey there, Billy Roy."

Billy Roy put one hand on Vang's shoulder and said, "You been asking questions."

Vang put down his glass.

"You been asking about Creed."

"Can you tell me where he is?"

"I can give you some advice."

"Please."

"Get out of town tonight."

"Thank you," Vang said.

The bartender put a shotglass on the bar in front of the big man and filled it to the brim with Sagebrush bourbon. Billy Roy put the whiskey down in one gulp. Between his big fingers the glass looked small as a thimble. He wiped his mouth on the back of his wrist.

"Did you hear what I said?" Billy Roy grunted.

"Yes."

"Maybe you don't understand American so good. You sure you get my drift?"

Vang stepped back from the bar, so he was facing the towering hulk of Billy Roy. "Certainly," he said. "As long as you stand upwind, I can smell it."

William Sterling Price came through the door and stepped to one side. He looked at Billy Roy and Vang and shook his head with vague disappointment, like he'd accidentally walked into a theater showing a movie he'd seen before.

Billy Roy grabbed Vang's arm at the bicep and started to say, "You little gook son of a b—" Before he could finish, Vang was going backward—but somehow the huge, awkward, flailing body of Billy Roy was flying over Vang in a high arc. He landed very hard, the whole length of his body crashing into the floorboards simultaneously, leaden as a sash weight.

Vang was on his feet. No one in the bar could have said how he'd gotten up; one moment he was on the floor, an eye blink later he was standing.

Billy Roy stirred and moaned and lay still.

At the nearest table another man stood, so quickly that his chair toppled over backward. Others were moving away from the center of the room. The second man could have been the twin of the first; instead of a T-shirt he wore a denim jacket with "Born to Fuck" embroidered on the back.

Near the door, Price's look of disappointment turned to disgust. Some people would not believe their own eyes.

Vang turned toward the second man, his face a mask of indifference.

"Kung fu, huh?" the man said. He bent at the knees and reached around behind him, got a hand around one leg of the fallen chair. "Well, kung fu this, asshole."

The big man took a step forward and swung the chair down on Vang, using both hands and all his weight, as if he were trying to ring the gong at the carnival.

But Vang was no longer there. The back of the chair splintered into kindling on the bartop.

Vang was a step further down the bar, motionless. Price eased toward the bar. *Now would be a good time to grab your buddy and haul ass, pal,* Price thought.

Instead the big slob cocked a fist and brought it back next to his ear. Price closed his hand over it and levered the guy around. "Having fun?" he asked.

"I'll show you fun, fuckhead," the guy said, and wrenched his fist free.

Price stepped inside the long roundhouse right and blocked it with his left forearm. He hit the big guy once, using the upper edge of his right hand, the four fingers out stiff, the thumb tucked down against the palm so the impact would not fracture it. Price laid the blow along the guy's jawline, just below the ear.

The guy stepped back on legs that wobbled like a drunk's in a cartoon. He tried futilely to focus the double image of Price his brain was receiving, then pitched forward on his face, stiff as a sequoia.

Behind Vang, the bartender said, "There now, that's enough," more reproachful than angry. He held a stubby-barreled, nickel-plated revolver, not pointed at anyone but ready for action if action were required. The other half dozen patrons shifted around, making sure they were well out of any line of fire.

Price stepped over the lump on the floor and came up beside Vang, but the bartender said, "Sorry boys, you have just wore out your welcome."

Price put the hand he had used on the big guy on the bartop beside Vang's glass. The green of a banknote, folded several times, peeked out from between thumb and palm. Price shifted it slightly so the bartender could see the "50" in the corner.

The bartender's hand danced over Price's, and the money was gone. "Don't be running off so quickly," he said with no evident irony.

"Who are they?"

"Name's Rankin," the bartender said in a low voice. "Billy Roy and Jake. Truth is, no one has got a whole lot of time or regard for them two. What they mostly do is drink around, gamble, drive their pickup up and down Main, and shoot holes in highway signs. When they get broke they do a little carpentry or auto work, and usually make a shitty job of it. They are a bucketful of trouble and no use to anyone.

"But then," the bartender said, "they live around here and so do I. Can't say the same for you two."

"You sure take the long way to make a point," Price said.

"I'm a bartender. I got to like to talk."

On the floor behind them, Billy Roy Rankin's eyes opened, then went wider with panic. "Oh Jesus God," he whined. "I can't move my arms or legs. My goddamned back is broken." He tried to swear at Vang, but talk cost him too much pain, and the curse ended in a pitiful half-scream. "Someone help me," he moaned.

No one did. Price imagined enough of them had been bullied by the Rankin boys to take silent satisfaction in all this.

"Thank you," Vang said to the bartender.

He and Price bent to the inert form of Jake Rankin and got him under the arms. Lifting him seemed no more of a strain to Vang than to Price. Walking backward they pulled him through the door at the end of the bar, his heels making furrows in the sawdust on the barroom floor.

Out back there was an unpaved parking lot and a trash dumpster. Price flipped back its lid and hung Rankin's arms over the lip of the bin. He began to slap Rankin's face, rhythmically and not very hard. On the fourth slap the guy's eyes opened. Price waited until they focused, and hate returned to Rankin's expression.

"Where's Creed?"

"Get fucked."

Price jabbed him in the stomach with stiffened fingers. Rankin gasped.

Price repeated, "Where's Creed?"

"Get f—"

Vang reached up to Jake Rankin, his hand moving so quickly that Price could not follow it. There was no sound of a blow landing, but whatever Vang did produced a moan of pain and an agonized contortion of Rankin's features. His eyes screwed up tight.

"Don't," he begged. "I'll talk. Just tell me what the fuck you want to know." He opened his eyes slowly, tentative as a child at a horror movie.

"Where's Creed?" Price asked for the third time.

"I don't know. Don't hit me! It's the truth."

"Then why," Vang asked, "did you cause such trouble?"

"Doing my job."

"You work for the local Welcome Wagon?"

Rankin didn't get it, but he figured the truth was the safest way to play it. "A couple months back, this guy comes to town. He tells me and Billy Roy, he says he heard we were guys who know how to take care of ourselves, that we get lots of respect around here."

"He was wrong," Price said. "What did he look like?"

"Medium height, maybe a couple inches under six feet, kind of stocky. Dark hair and eyes, maybe a little older than me."

Vang shot a look at Price. The description did not fit Creed.

"What did he want?"

"He gives us two hundred bucks. Each. He says he works for a guy who doesn't like to be bothered, people nosing around, that kind of thing. He says if any suspicious strangers come around, especially if they're asking about someone named Creed, we're supposed to let him know. If we can keep 'em on ice until then, that's even better."

"How do you make contact?"

"Write 'em. There's a post office box here in town."

"Shit," Price said under his breath. That told them nothing they didn't know. "Have a lot of people been asking about Creed?"

"You guys are the first ones. Up to now we been getting the two hundred every month for doing nothing. That's a good deal."

"Up to now," Vang said.

His right hand flashed through starlight, and Jake Rankin's eyes closed again. Price caught him under the arms, and Vang grabbed an ankle and flipped it upward. Rankin's form made a mushy splat as it settled into the ripe-smelling contents of the trash dumpster. Price flipped the cover closed.

"A waste of time," he said, dusting his hands together.

"Not entirely," Vang said. "Time spent in exercise is never wasted."

Chapter Twenty-one

The dormitory cubicle contained a metal-framed cot with a thin mattress and two khaki blankets, a three-drawer dresser that also served as night table, a gooseneck lamp, and a narrow wardrobe. George Dial sat on the edge of the bed and turned on the lamp, adjusting it so it shined down into his lap. He unbuttoned the cuffs of his fatigue blouse and rolled the sleeves up to the elbows. Moving slowly, almost ritualistically, he held his hands in the lamp's splash of light, palms up like a mendicant.

On each wrist, where the pulse beat could be felt just to the outside of the two ridges of tendon, was a ridge of scar tissue no more than a half-inch long, running lengthwise.

George Dial ran his fingertips over the scars and thought: *She's here.*

He hunched forward on the edge of the bed, his forearms laid out along his thighs, and stared at the faded marks, still as shocking as the relic of some barbaric puberty-rite mutilation. He did not move for perhaps five minutes, but his eyes softened and gradually lost focus as the memories flooded back.

George Dial had grown up in Poughkeepsie, New York. He achieved two distinctions in high school: he was the only student in his class with a perfect grade-point average, and the only one to almost do time. He remembered the girl's name: Cheryl Scott. She turned him down for the sophomore semiformal so he broke her nose. Her father made such a big stink that it took a glib lawyer and a lot of sincere lying to get Dial off with a suspended sentence.

All right, so he got angry sometimes; that was simply a facet of his complex personality. Some people got depressed; some people got pimples. George Dial got angry.

At Harvard he found new ways to channel his anger.

Those were the days when both the Vietnam War and public condemnation of it were reaching peaks. The hotbeds of protest were the college campuses across the nation, and no hotbed was hotter than Harvard.

Watching those days replayed in his mind's eye, George Dial saw as clear as sunrise the day of his blood initiation into the dark brotherhood of those who devoted their lives to violence.

It was the morning of April 10, 1969, and the smell of tension in the air was as pungent as ozone. He was one of three hundred students who had occupied University Hall on the quadrangle the morning before; they would not leave, they said, until the administration booted ROTC off of campus. Warmongering was no subject to be taught for credit at a liberal institution of higher learning.

At dawn, the war came home.

Sunup was breaking when the four hundred helmeted cops broke through the barricaded doors of U Hall, nightsticks flailing and insane pandemonium descended on Dial and the others. The cops had removed their badges, and as far as Dial was concerned, that made it no holds barred.

Cops were charging up the stairs shouting obscenities. Dial ducked behind a desk; when he came up a girl was sprawled across it, blood flowing from her forehead. He crawled away, found a back staircase and an unlocked window. When he was outside, he circled around to the Yard.

It looked like a battlefield. Cops charged across the spring-green lawn, running down the panicked students like slaughterhouse cattle. Through drifting clouds of tear gas, Dial saw a state trooper club his baton in both hands like a Louisville slugger and slam it into the back of a long-haired guy's head. A girl jumped on a cop's back to stop him from beating on her boyfriend, and the cop jabbed a vicious elbow into her side. The girl dropped off and curled into a fetal position, and the cop stopped working on her pal long enough to give her two booted kicks in the ribs.

Near the edge of the melee, two hippies had wrestled a cop to the ground and looked like they had the better of him. His nightstick lay a few feet from the writhing pile of arms and legs.

Dial sidled up and grabbed the stick. He straightened in time to see another cop charging toward them. Without thinking, Dial slammed the three-foot stick into the cop's gut. The cop grunted with pain and doubled over, hands to his stomach. He was wearing a riot helmet, so Dial brought the stick down across his shoulders. When the cop went down and rolled over, Dial jabbed him hard in the testicles.

Across the Yard the battle was winding down, and the cops had won. Bloodied students were being dragged toward the Square; those who could were running. That seemed the right move to George, and he slipped away.

All that day he floated on a sea of euphoria. In his mind he could see the cop, hurt and helpless at his feet, and in his viscera he felt only the incredible ecstatic thrill of the nightstick in his hands slamming into flesh and fracturing rib bone.

Two weeks later, Chris Amado came into his life.

He noticed her at a meeting of the Students for a Democratic Society. These gatherings always bordered on anarchy: masses of sincerely idealistic kids jammed into a poorly ventilated room in Burr or Lowell, all rabid with commitment, swept by the group's solidarity into a collective high as joltingly intense as a snort of pure methedrine. To get the floor you had to outshout everyone else, and you held it only as long as the fire of your rhetoric burned at a white-heat level.

On the edge of this barely suppressed mass hysteria, across the room from Dial, sat Chris Amado. She seemed at that moment the most beautiful woman he'd ever seen, and he knew he had to have her.

It was a warm spring, and she wore denim cutoffs, huarache sandals, and a "Sisterhood Is Powerful" T-shirt with the tails knotted above a sweep of flat stomach. Her hair in those days was long and perfectly straight, a cascade of shiny black silk reaching in a great lush flow to her waist. She said nothing, but she seemed to be listening to everything at once, her dark eyes darting around the room. To George she was beguilingly romantic: her dark skin and high cheekbones were those of a Spanish noblewoman in an eighteenth-century romance.

George Dial was on a roll in those days, filled with fervor and power and potency. He accomplished anything he attempted, and got whatever he wanted.

He wanted Chris Amado.

That first weekend they spent thirty-six hours in the narrow single bed in Dial's room on the third floor of Leverett, entryway H. They made love and argued politics and occasionally dozed and did not leave the bed except to go to the refrigerator for bread and cheese and cheap Chablis. When they finally got up, the sheets were stained with wine and sweat and semen and littered with crumbs and greasy napkins and abandoned underclothes.

They began to quarrel that same week. Sometimes days would go by when Chris refused to see him and would not answer his calls, a torture that George found almost unbearable. With the addition of Chris Amado to his life, it had become rarified and pure. He felt constantly high; reality had been redefined and made flawlessly linear. It consisted of two components only: the Movement, and Chris's lush body.

Nine weeks to the day after they met, she told him it was over. He had lost touch, she told him. For all his bombast about the capitalist pigs and the necessity for the people to overrule the warmakers, the goals of the Movement were no longer what counted for him. The demonstrations and the violence had become ends in themselves. Especially the violence.

His first response was to slap her face.

Chris stared back at him for the longest time, her mouth a hard line beside the vivid blush his palm had raised on her cheek. Then she punched him in the stomach, hard as she could. While he was trying to cough breath back into his searing lungs, she drove her knee into his face.

He screamed in pain and frustration. She could not leave, he sobbed. Without her he would be dead. Blood bubbled out of his nose and mixed with his tears. He would kill himself, he swore. She would have to live with the guilty knowledge for the rest of her life: she had murdered him, as surely as if she had put a gun to his head and pulled the trigger.

She stood in the open door of his room. "Goodbye, George," she said tonelessly. On her face was a look of infinite pity, a look that told him he was pathetic beyond words.

Suddenly the narrow path that Dial had invented as his life ended in a cliff edge. He could turn back, or he could dive off.

After a time he went to the bureau next to the closet. In the top drawer, under a pile of socks was a baggie of marijuana, a cheap corn-cob pipe whose bowl was covered with pin-punctured aluminum foil, and a dispenser of single-edged razor blades. The blades were for cutting lines of crystal meth; Dial had been doing a lot of speed those days.

It did not hurt when he drew the sharp blade along the flesh of his left wrist. Skin and tissue and vein-wall parted cleanly, and sticky blood welled out. He shifted the blade and opened his right wrist. He felt the blood flow out and over his arms, warm as a baby's bath water. It oozed steadily out and ran down into his cupped hands, and he bent his head and tasted it. It was as rich and thick as beef broth. He straightened his fingers and watched the blood drip off their tips and beat a muffled tattoo on the floorboards.

He lay back on his bed and closed his eyes, and then he was somewhere else. It was like going to sleep in the intimate warmth of your childhood bed. For the first time in memory, he felt peace . . .

The door of George Dial's cubicle kicked back against the wall, and Helena Frome stalked into the room.

Dial blinked and shook his head, as if an invisible hypnotist had snapped his fingers. He felt unmoored, and it took him several seconds to leap the ten-year gap to the present.

"So you know," Helena Frome accused. "You should see yourself, George. You look like a little kid whose mommy caught him beating off." She wore blousy fatigues, and standing there, arms akimbo, she looked disconcertingly mannish. She kicked the door shut behind her. "How did you find out she was here?"

"I saw them bring her in, walking her down the hall. I didn't talk to her. I think she was passed out; she looked like someone had been working on her."

Helena smiled. "You'd like to work on her, wouldn't you, George?"

Dial clamped his mouth shut. There was nothing to be gained by responding to that kind of baiting.

"You've become a concern to me, George. You might as well know it. That business in Rome made me wonder if I can depend on you anymore." Helena took a step toward him. "What's she doing here, George?"

"How should I know?" But in the back of his mind was the thought: Chris had come for him.

It was during the weeks of recovery from his nearly-successful suicide attempt that he and Helena had come together as lovers. They had known each other casually for some time from the Movement, but they had not been close. It was purely chance that she was the one to find and save him: she had come to his room to borrow a back issue of the *Real Paper* that she thought he might have. But afterward she came to the hospital, and then to the infirmary when he was transferred there, and after a time they became a couple.

Helena had never liked Chris; George knew that. First because Helena blamed her for hurting George, later because George would not stop talking about her, even after Helena and George became lovers.

Now she bent and put her face very close to his, and hissed, "Did you send for that bitch?"

Dial shook his head, too quickly, like a child denying cookie jar larceny. "How would I know where she was?"

"Then what's she doing here?"

"Maybe she's looking for me," Dial snapped defiantly.

Helena Frome straightened and laughed. The sound had as much to do with mirth as hotdogs have to do with horseshit.

"Listen to me, George. Right now we've got a chance to make a fresh start—as long as your trolley stays on the tracks." She lowered her voice. "These people—Bressio and his creeps—we can use them for a while. When they're no longer useful and we're on our feet again, we ditch them—however we have to. Just like always, George: you and me—as long as you don't fuck up."

"Since when are you the boss, Helena?"

"Since you started going off the deep end, George. You straighten up, or . . ."

"Or what?"

"Try me, George. If you want to find out, you try me."

Dial finally looked away, and hated himself for it.

"Chris Amado means trouble," Helena pressed. "Her coming here stinks, and if you got your head out of your ass you'd know it as well as I. There's no such thing as coincidence, George. She's here for a reason.

"So if you want to fantasize like a fourteen-year-old," Helena said, "you go ahead. Just don't get any stupid ideas about her." She laughed again.

At the door she looked at him once more, and shook her head. "Sometimes, George, you are truly wretched."

He stared at the door's blank surface for a long time after she left, as if answers would appear on it. But he could not concentrate; images of Chris Amado keep getting in the way.

Helena could become a problem; he was beginning to see

that. But for any problem there was a solution—the same solution he had always used. It was simple and it had not failed him yet.

Dial pulled open the top drawer of the little dresser. The compact Beretta lay atop a sheet of oil-stained newspaper. Dial ran his fingers over the cool metal of the barrel.

Then he lay back on the bed and saw Chris Amado as she had been when she was his: the wonderous expanses of her bare brown skin, the swell of her breasts, the lush sweep of her buttocks, perfect as nature. He felt her cool hands stroking his chest, her tongue on his nipples and moving lower, tracing a moist line with its tip, gentle and then more insistent, until she held him in the warmth of her mouth and he felt every muscle in his body stiffen with tension, and then release so intense it was transcendent.

George Dial pulled down the zipper of his pants and began to stroke himself. He felt the thickening, but when he closed his eyes the picture of Chris distorted, began to fade. It was replaced by the angular form of Helena. She was naked, too, but she was frowning and shaking her head in disapproval, and her scrawny body was as arousing as a dead mackerel. He began to soften.

Helena would not leave his mind or even look away, and in a few seconds he was completely limp. From long experience he knew nothing would help now, and after a moment he gave it up as a bad job.

Chapter Twenty-two

Chris Amado opened her eyes to impenetrable blackness and felt the panic rise in her like vomit.

She stood, steadying herself against bare wall. Fighting down the fear, she edged three steps and came up against a corner. She continued around the perimeter without encountering obstructions or windows, until her hand found a doorknob. It was locked.

She moved on to where she started, then crossed through the thick darkness. Nothing impeded her. The room was about eight feet to a side. The only sound was a faint mechanical whirr above her head, a ceiling ventilation fan, she decided.

She sat again, facing the door, her back against the wall and her legs drawn up, and fought down the anxious sense of *déjà vu*. She had spent too much time too recently locked in a room about this size. She closed her eyes and concentrated on the fan's monotonic hum. When she reopened them a few minutes later she was calm, and ready to consider possibilities.

There was a dull ache in her head, and she felt dried blood caked in her hair, but she did not think she had a concussion. She needed to urinate, but not badly enough to piss in the corner.

In the long dark sedan, with her gun covering the scarecrow and the kid, everything had gone fine. The pock-marked driver went north on Virginia to the eastbound I-80 on-ramp and accelerated to an even fifty-five. Ten miles later he pulled off at the Sparks exit, turning south on a road that immediately became gravel. On either side were two of the whorehouses that were the only possible attractions of the forlorn desert town. Each consisted of an unmatched collection of ramshackle trailer houses set amid the barren scrub sagebrush and gnarled juniper. Most of the buildings listed at odd angles, and they were surrounded by junked cars, long-abandoned privies, and packs of lethargic, gaunt dogs, as if somebody had decided to build a theme park called Hillbilly-land.

The dirt road ended a couple of miles farther on at a gate in a chain-link fence. It surrounded a long squat warehouse, about half the size of an airline hangar, with concrete block walls, no windows, and a corrugated tin roof. A sullen man in a windbreaker under which gunmetal bulged peered inside the car. "We got her," the kid told him, following Chris's orders. Her gun was hidden under her bag. The sullen guy nodded and passed them in.

The straw-thin man and the kid walked in front of her to the side of the building and through an unmarked door with a light bulb in a wire cage above it. That put them in a long corridor. They passed three doors and turned into the fourth, and another tall guy stood up behind a desk and stared at her.

Chris showed the guy the Colt Python and opened her mouth to order him to sit down. Before she could, someone set off a depth charge in the side of her head, and the lights blinked out like dying stars.

She wondered now how long she'd been out. Instinct and her bladder told her several hours at least. They had kept her alive, which meant they had questions. Her life would depend on good answers.

Time crawled by.

When the door opened she involuntarily screwed up her dilated eyes against the glare. Through slitted lids she recognized the silhouette of the bony, tall man. He worked a switch on the outside wall, and an overhead light fixture flared. Along with the effort of standing up, it made Chris's head hurt again.

"Time to go," the guy said.

"Where to?"

"Come on," the guy ordered. He grabbed her arm and walked her into the corridor.

"What do they call you?" Chris said.

"What's it to you?"

"Don't be that way," Chris said. "We might turn out to be working together."

"Don't hold your breath." But then the guy said, "Skelton."

"Huh?"

"The name is Skelton."

Chris laughed. "Imagine that." Laughing hurt too.

At the end of the corridor they went through an open door, which put them in the same office where she had been cold-cocked. The same tall guy was behind the desk.

"Here she is, Eddie," Skelton said, almost eagerly. Chris imagined he'd taken some heat for letting her get the drop on him.

"Let's start with a name," Eddie said.

"I want to go to the bathroom."

Eddie studied her. "Take her," he said finally. "Keep an eye on her."

Skelton put another vise-lock grip on her arm and half-towed her two doors down. When she tried to shut the stall door, Skelton held it open with one hand and grinned nastily. "Keep an eye on you is what he said, sugar." He watched while she dropped her pants and did her business. His lips were slightly parted, but his eyes were as dead as sand dollars at low tide.

"Hell of a kick, isn't it?" Chris stood and pulled up her pants. "Beats whacking off, anyway."

Skelton slapped her across the face, and the dull ache in the side of her head spasmed. Her eyes went moist.

"That's for Chubb," Skelton said. "You killed a buddy of mine."

"You could be next, Freakshow," Chris said in a hard, tight voice.

"Don't fuck with me, lady. There's nothing but pain down that road."

"You're reading the wrong map." She pushed past him before he could come back. The guy behind the desk was waiting.

"A name," he said, as if she had never left.

"Eddie Turin."

That got minimal reaction. "Cute," Turin said. "We both know who I am. Let's both know who you are."

"The name is Chris Amado."

"Chris Amado," Turin repeated. He looked at Skelton. "What the fuck is a Chris Amado?"

Skelton shrugged.

"What do you want with Frank Bressio?"

"I'll tell that to him."

"Tell it to me."

Chris pretended to consider. "I'll talk to George Dial."

"Who's George Dial?"

He asked in the same flat, bored tone, and it shook her. If Conte were wrong—if George and Helena had not hooked up with Bressio—she was swimming in deep water with no shore in sight.

"You get George Dial in here," Chris said, "and you'll get straight answers. If you'd rather fuck around, that's up to you."

Turin bobbed his head. Skelton grabbed Chris's wrist and cranked it up behind her back. The thin guy looked like his bones were as brittle as uncooked spaghetti, but he was amazingly strong—and a few millimeters from breaking her arm.

"What are you doing here?" Turin said.

"I'll talk to George Dial," she said through teeth clenched against pain, "or I won't talk at all."

Eddie Turin opened the desk's middle drawer and took out a small automatic. He took his time charging the slide and cocking the hammer, before fixing the sights on a point between Chris's breasts.

"Then you won't talk at all," he said, his finger whitening on the trigger.

Chapter Twenty-three

For six generations the male members of the Price family had made the military their profession. A sense of duty, patriotism, and dedication to responsibility were Price traditions. If a person wished to enjoy the benefits of the American way of life, that person was duty bound to do whatever was necessary to preserve that system against those who would destroy it.

William Sterling Price had accepted the mantle of duty without reservation when it was passed to him. He had no love of warfare, but he recognized its inevitability. When the cause was just and the battle engaged, a warrior did whatever was necessary to carry it to a decisive victory.

Unfortunately, it seemed that some people involved in the command of the U.S. armed services did not agree. Price had never compromised his own principles, but it was a constant uphill fight, and one he was destined to lose. Finally the frustration became untenable; with reluctance Price resigned his commission, a few years after the half-assed conclusion of the Vietnam War.

There was nothing complicated or metaphysical about it. Price believed that when forced to fight, you fought to win. Now that belief was frustrating his sleep at three in the morning.

Price lay open-eyed on one of the twin beds in the Winnemucca hotel room he and Vang were sharing. He had been dozing on and off for hours, but he seemed unable to fall into any satisfactory slumber. The darkness of the room was cut by the intrusion of neon light that managed to penetrate whatever arrangement of curtains he devised, but that wasn't the primary problem. Each time he awakened his thoughts returned to the frustrating search for Benjamin Creed. So far it was a meandering path to a dead end.

As near as he and Vang could determine, Jake Rankin had told them all he knew, which was very little. His brother Billy Roy had clammed up altogether, and there wasn't much they could do to make him talk since he was already in a body cast and a hospital bed. No one else in Winnemucca was talking either, from ignorance or from fear of the Rankin boys.

Price had partnered with Vang before. He knew the Hmong habitually slept very little, and he suspected that the formless lump on the bed next to him was just blankets and sheets. Price didn't give it much thought; he figured that Vang's whereabouts and activities were his own business.

All they had learned so far was that every Saturday someone emptied Box 46 at the Winnemucca Post Office. This was Thursday night—or more precisely Friday morning—and there was nothing more to do but wait.

Across the room a key snicked in the door lock.

Price lay still. Thirty seconds passed. In the neon's wash Price saw the doorknob slowly turn. More silence, and then the door eased open, quiet as flowers blooming. Someone slipped inside, and the door noiselessly closed.

The silhouette of the intruder was a half-foot taller than Vang and twice as broad. Price froze.

An arm came up and Price caught the gleam of gunmetal in the diffuse light. Price rolled to one side and dove for the carpet. As he hit and gathered his feet under him he heard a soft *pffut* and a gutteral "Goddamn."

A heartbeat later there was another *pffut*, from somewhere else in the room. A body fell leadenly.

Price cautiously raised his head over the level of the bed. Vang was next to the open bathroom door, wearing pajamas and a silk robe.

"I thought you were out," Price said hoarsely.

"I am back."

"Like the U.S. Cavalry." Price picked himself up and turned on the wall switch. The bulk on the floor lay facedown. Price squatted and flopped it over on its back, grunting with the effort. The corpse was big, fat-gutted, and bemuscled and had a droopy mustache, long greasy hair, and a leaking hole in the middle of its bare chest. Jake Rankin wasn't any better looking dead.

Price picked up the gun lying beside him. "Look at this piece of shit," he said. The idea of Rankin trying to bushwhack them had not helped his mood. Rankin's weapon was a cheap, Spanish-made .38 automatic. The threading on the barrel was uneven, as if it had been done in someone's garage workshop, and the silencer that went on it was two concentric lengths of iron pipe, perforated and separated by wads of the kind of glass filament kids used in aquarium filters. "This shouldn't have lasted for one shot," Price said. "He's lucky he didn't blow his hand off."

"Not lucky enough," Vang said.

Price tossed the gun on the bed. "Was he trying to even up the score for his brother, or was he working for Creed?"

"It's a little late to ask."

"That's right," Price said, a little shortly. "Did you have to kill him?"

"I beg your pardon," Vang said dryly. "The idea that he was trying to kill me must have warped my judgment." Vang gave the slightest of bows, a barely perceptible nod of the head.

"Sorry," Price mumbled.

"At any rate, he could not have told us anything more, unless Creed for some odd reason opened his heart to him in the last day."

Vang was right—which meant they were still stuck on square one. It came down to that damned post office box.

"It will be daylight in an hour," Vang pointed out. "We'd better get rid of him before then."

Price sighed. "Right." He contemplated the body. "But we're going to have a hell of a job getting those stains out of the carpet."

Chapter Twenty-four

Chris Amado squinted through her pain at the pistol Eddie Turin held leveled on her chest from four feet away. Skelton wrenched harder on her arm, and she remembered the dull look he had given her when she had her pants down. He reminded her of Mauricio, Enrico's lieutenant, whose pleasure in women depended on their pain and degradation.

Turin straightened his arm so the muzzle of the pistol was three feet from her face.

"You're about to make a big mistake," Chris said, trying to keep her voice steady. "You're not the boss, Eddie; we both know that. Whoever is the boss ordered Mutt and Jeff to pick me up—and to deliver me alive because the boss wants to know where I picked up his trail, and how much I know. If you kill me he'll never find out, and he might not like that."

"You might not like dying," Eddie Turin said. "If you're not going to talk, it doesn't matter if you're cold as a polar bear's dick."

Skelton laughed.

"I'll talk," Chris said. "To George Dial."

For one heart-thumping moment she thought she had pushed too hard. Turin's trigger finger was tense against the mainspring.

Then he raised the muzzle and gently let down the hammer. The trigger made a dry click, like the snap of a wishbone.

"Let her go."

The stickman did as he was told, but he looked disappointed.

"Watch her," Turin said, and went out. He locked them in from the corridor.

Chris perched on the edge of the desk and stared defiantly at Skelton. Her head and arm hurt, and she was tired. The idea was not to show it.

"So," she said blithely, "how do you like working for a swell guy like Eddie?"

One of Skelton's sunken eyes twitched.

"Does he treat you right? Does he let you go down to the whorehouse once in a while and beat up on the girls?"

"I don't need them, lady. Pretty soon now, I'll get to play with you."

Chris laughed. Winning the poker game with Eddie Turin put her on firmer ground. He had shown his hole card: Dial and Frome had to be there.

Chris Amado had played tense games for most of her adult life; the struggle of the Amadistas was an endless teeth-grinding showdown. She was dealt out of that war for the time being, but she was beginning to understand that Dennison's War was just as important—and just as deadly.

Five minutes drifted past. Skelton kept his deep-socketed eyes on her all that time. When Eddie Turin came back he did not looked pleased. Chris liked seeing that.

"Let's go," Turin said. Like a robot, Skelton grabbed her arm in his favorite painful grip. It was starting to annoy her.

As they went through the door, Chris threw her weight away from him. Skelton did not let go, but he had to take a step with her to keep his balance.

"I can walk by myself, bonebag," Chris rapped. "I've been doing it for years."

"Keep moving, babe."

"Sure," Chris said. "Let go of my goddamned arm."

Skelton yanked her along. Chris went with the momentum and drove the point of her shoe into Skelton's reed-thin shin.

His tibia should have snapped like a pencil, but Skelton just grunted and grabbed at her. The guy had to be strung together with piano wire.

As Skelton clutched a fistful of her hair, Turin snapped, "That's enough."

Skelton looked startled, as if in his pleasure at hurting her he had forgotten they were not alone.

"Let her be for now." Turin looked at Chris. "But if she acts up again, break her arm."

"It'll be a pleasure," Skelton said.

The corridor turned left, and one wall became a row of large-view windows opening on the warehouse's open storage area, an arena-sized cavern under a cantilevered ceiling fifty yards to a side. Crates and cartons were stacked on pallets in neat rows, with aisles wide enough for the two forklifts Chris could see.

On the far side two semitrailers were backed up to a dock, their double doors yawning open. The forklifts were in the process of loading them. One truck was almost full, and the other was waiting its turn. Chris counted eleven men dressed in unmarked khaki fatigues.

Farther down the corridor they passed a pallet stacked with a cross-hatch arrangement of long wooden boxes, like dogs' coffins. Chris had seen crates like them in Santa Cruz on the few occasions the Amadistas could scrape up enough hard currency to make international black market purchases. The stencil read, "Prop. U.S. Army Govt. Issue"; each contained six new M16A1 automatic rifles.

It was beginning to look like Bressio was one hell of a lot more than a renegade crime boss. His operation had to be well financed, well established, and well organized, with far-reaching contacts. Everything about it was big.

For Chris Amado, it could be big trouble. In the next few minutes she would have to be very, very convincing.

At the far end of the view corridor Turin led them into another office. Skelton planted a spidery palm on Chris's back and shoved her through the door.

The gooseneck lamp on the battered desk was bent down as far as it would go so most of the room was in concealing shadow. Within the penumbra of the oval of light splashing on the desktop Chris made out Helena Frome. Chris had not seen her for a decade, since they were students together in

Cambridge. The years had not done much for Helena: she was still scrawny and plain-faced.

Behind her was the lower half of a man; Chris guessed it was George. As her eyes became accustomed to the dimness she made out the vague shape of another figure standing in the corner in the most opaque part of the shadow.

Turin sat on the corner of the desk, folded his arms, and said, "Her name is supposed to be Chris Amado."

"So far, so good," Helena said nastily. She turned the lamp up so it was in Chris's face, then came around the desk. Helena Frome made a big production out of circling Chris, studying her as if she were the ambassador from an alien planet. She fingered a strand of hair clotted with dried blood, brushed ostentatiously at a smear of dirt across the front of Chris's pantsuit.

"You're a mess, aren't you?" Helena said.

Behind Helena, George Dial had come around the desk into the light's beam. The years had not been kind of him; in fact, he looked like shit. He had lost a lot of weight since Chris had seen him last, and the skin of his face was slack. He held himself stiffly; he looked like at any moment his whole nervous system was going to let go in a single spasmodic tic. His eyes were bright as a wounded animal's. He was stroking the insides of his wrists.

"Hello, George." Chris forced warmth into her tone. "It's nice to see you again."

"Hello, Chris." His voice broke, and his eyes brightened.

"We were all in college together for a while." Helena Frome stared at Chris. "Little Sister here went through a radical stage, and she and George played house for a while. When she got bored she dumped him. You took it pretty hard, didn't you, George," she added cruelly.

Dial pulled his gaze away from Chris, slow as a sleepwalker.

"You're still a little stuck on her, right George?" Helena needled.

"What are you doing here?" The cold voice came from the man in the shadows.

"Looking for work."

Helena laughed. "What kind of work? Mimeographing leaflets? Making picket signs? Organizing antidraft rallies?"

"Actually," Chris said, "I was thinking of taking over for you, Helena. I hear the money is good, the hours are short, and I can see"—Chris returned the once-over Helena had given her—"I can see you don't have to dress your best."

"Tell your story, Little Sister," Helena Frome said. "Don't leave anything out, and tell it right. Around here you only get one chance."

"Wait a minute," George Dial protested. "Maybe we should—"

"Shut up, George, or get out. Start singing, Little Sister."

The first part was pure truth, but Helena Frome frowned anyway while Chris told them about the murder of her father, the people's rebellion in Santa Cruz, and her role in it. She told them about the rewards posted for her dead or alive, the flight to Mexico, and the eleventh-hour arrest. "I did nine months," she said in a level voice.

"And then?"

"I got away."

"How?"

"I killed some people." She sketched in the rest, leaving out Vang. "I'd just as soon forget it, except for the killing. That was all right. I owed them some pain."

"Very tough," Helena said cynically.

"Listen, Helena," Chris snapped, "if you think I spent the better part of a year in that Mexican shithole to set up a cover story that you yahoos would buy, you've got even less brains than tits."

George Dial smiled at Helena's back.

"I got back to the U.S.," Chris said. "I had no money and I was wanted. All I had were contacts."

"Names, please," the man in the corner said.

"Sorry," Chris said. "It doesn't work that way, as you know. I can tell you this: over the years, the Amadistas occasionally raised enough pesos to buy dollars, which they spent on guns, grenades, and other essentials of a good guerilla war. I'm an American citizen. I know the language and the customs. I did the shopping."

"And where did you shop?"

"Abercrombie and Fitch," Chris snapped. "Where the fuck do you think I shopped? There are people who deal in that kind of merchandise. You've got the money and they've got the goods and you tend to find each other sooner or later. They're very trustworthy; they deliver, because they know what will happen to them if they don't. Also, they know people who know other people who know people. Some of these people along the line heard stories of an operation, with a name attached to it. A guy named Frank Bressio was making big purchases, for one thing."

Chris stared at the figure in the corner. "These people gave me the idea that you could use someone with a few contacts and a working relationship with the business end of a gun. That's me."

No one said anything. Behind her Chris could hear Skelton breathing. Each time he inhaled, the bones of his chest rattled like dried beans in a gourd.

"If you're lying," the man in the corner said, "you are going to be killed. You may be killed anyway."

"That would be a waste."

"Maybe. I like your story to a point. What bothers me is your motivation. Why should I believe you're willing to give up a noble cause to join—I don't think I'm giving anything away here—a criminal organization?"

"For starters, I'm technically a criminal already, as I told you. Second, I have no place else to go and I need money—to stay alive and away from the cops, and to support the Amadistas."

"And you don't care where it comes from?"

Chris sighed. "I left out something. I told you my father was killed, but I didn't say who killed him." She stared into the shadow. "The military coup in Santa Cruz was CIA-sponsored. So you see, I don't have a lot of love for my country. In fact, you could say I'm holding a hell of a grudge." That part was a lie, but Chris figured it would rest easy on the foundation of truth she had laid down.

"I don't know exactly what you are up to, Mr. Bressio." She paused to give him a chance to deny his identity. When he didn't bother, she went on. "I do know you can use people and that I'm damned good. Believe in that."

"Possibly I do."

"As long as we're spilling our guts," Chris went on, "you might as well know the other reason. George and I were pretty close once, and it gets lonely on the run. I heard George was in on this, and I needed a friend." She flashed Dial a smile.

His eyes went puppy soft, as if she had suggested they run away together that minute. He was vulnerable; he could be played like a brook trout.

"I asked around. Maybe I asked too loudly, but I was scared that the wrong people would find me before you did. When the beanpole here and his butterball chum got rough, I had to shoot the butterball." She showed Bressio a sardonic smile. "Hope he wasn't a bosom buddy."

During the story, the storm clouds had been growing darker in Helena Frome's expression. Now she turned toward the dark corner. "So she's telling the truth—so what? Who needs her?"

Bressio did not answer.

"I say we get rid of her."

Chris laughed. "Any time you think you can handle the job, give it a try. But you'd better have a valid will first."

"I think we're finished here," Bressio cut in smoothly.

"Take her back," Turin told Skelton.

"Move her into a billet," Bressio ordered.

Helena Frome shot him a furious look. Turin saw it and told Skelton, "Put them next to each other. If they can't figure out how to make nice-nice, it'll at least make a hell of a cat fight."

Skelton liked that idea. "That'll be a kick." His chest rattled some more.

But in the corridor he grabbed her again and pulled her up short. "Don't think you're suddenly smelling like roses, babe. I still owe you for Chubb."

Chris didn't bother to answer. So far her head was above water, but she had a hunch there was a long swim ahead.

"I was involved with her once," George Dial said. "I'm not denying that." He saw Helena smile triumphantly, as if she had wrenched the confession from him. "But that's not the point. She's smart, she's experienced, she's got to be tough, and a lot of people are after her ass."

"Have her story checked out, Eddie," Bressio said.

"It'll hold up," Dial said. "She'd have to be a moron to pass a story like that if it were bullshit. Anyway, once she's in with us she has to play it straight, and she has to stick it out. She knows she's dead if she doesn't. I say we give her a chance."

"You know, George," Helena said laconically, "I'd accuse you of thinking with your prick—if you had a prick."

"You could push too hard, Helena." Chris Amado's arrival had germinated a seed of an idea in Dial's mind. Until now he had always taken for granted his need for Helena.

"Take it easy." Bressio moved into the light. He was a good-looking, silver-haired man, somewhere between forty-five and sixty; his carefully pressed fatigues fit his physique and his manner. "We can't afford to reject any talent out of hand, now or in the future. And as George says, she needs us. If she's planning a doublecross, she'll wait until she gets what she's after." Bressio looked at each of them in turn. "I think it's fair to say that applies to all of us."

"I hope she does try to pull something," Helena said.

"She gets her tryout," Bressio said. "First thing tomorrow."

"Now wait just one minute—" Helena said furiously.

"That's an order," Bressio cut in coldly. "She's going with you. The two of you will work together, or measures will be taken."

Measures. That was a good word. George Dial turned it over in his mind.

Helena stared coldly at him. He had been with her for so long. How was it that he had not come to truly know her until now?

He could see a time when he might have to take measures with her. He thought he would enjoy that.

Chapter Twenty-five

Chris Amado stripped off her jacket, pants, and blouse, wadded them up, and tossed them in a corner. She had been wearing them for almost thirty-six hours, and they were filthy beyond redemption. In panties and nothing else she crossed to the freestanding wardrobe. Inside were several sets of the same kind of fatigues Helena had been wearing. They'd do for now.

She had spent most of the day with Helena, going over her story again and again. She had tired of telling it long before Helena had tired of listening. George had not approached her; Chris was beginning to get the idea that a major aspect of the George–Helena relationship was based on fear on his part, and loathing on hers.

The billet contained a narrow cot, a table and lamp, and a window with a plain, spring-loaded shade. Chris heard the throaty rumble of a diesel motor and looked out in time to see one of the semis pull around the building toward the gate. It was a cloudless night, and she left the shade up. She had been in small rooms too long, and the stars at least provided the illusion of space and distance. She was not locked in, although Skelton was stationed outside her door the last time she looked.

Her head was beginning to pulse again, and she was sore all over with fatigue. She looped her thumbs inside the waistband and skinned off her panties, tossing them atop the pile. The sheets of the narrow bed were cool, almost sensual against her bare skin.

She was halfway to sleep when someone knocked on the door.

"Who is it?"

"George."

Chris closed her eyes wearily. She knew she should talk to him, but she knew also what it would lead toward, and she did not have the strength to deal with that.

Chris shook her head, angry at herself. She would have to find the strength. Sleep had to wait; one screw-up and she'd get an eternity of sleep.

"Come in." She sat up and flicked on the lamp, holding the blanket up across her bare breasts.

George Dial fairly radiated excitement. He was smiling tightly, and he looked awkward coming through the door, like a farm boy at a debutante party. He looked over Chris's bare shoulders and the tops of her breasts.

"How have you been, George?" Chris said softly.

He kicked the door shut and crossed tentatively to her. Chris took his hand and pulled him down to sit beside her, and Dial bent and kissed her, lightly at first, then more insistently. His hand crawled up the blanket, began to strip it down her nude body.

Chris held it. "We have to talk, George."

He sat up again, looking almost sheepish. Chris pulled the blanket back up. "What's going on, George?"

"It's going to be fine, Chris. Bressio is going to take you on—I talked him into it."

"Thanks, George. I owe you."

That lit up his eyes. "There's more. You're going out on a job with me and Helena, first thing in the morning."

She felt a little jolt in her chest. "What kind of job?"

"I . . . I can't tell you. Listen," he went on quickly, "you're not playing games with me, are you?"

"What do you think, George?"

He looked down at her. "I think there's always a chance—if you want something badly enough."

Chris took his hand, and felt it tremble. "Whatever we can rebuild between us has to be based on trust, George. I came here on my own, because I trusted you. I've told you the truth since. If you can't do the same—if you think you have to hold back—then it won't work. It's up to you."

As she spoke she traced a finger over the inside of his wrist. His whole body tensed, like she had jabbed him with a cattleprod.

"Talk to me," Chris whispered.

He swept his gaze over her body, and in his eyes Chris

saw the reflection of the image of her nakedness his mind was conjuring.

"It's a snatch," Dial breathed.

"Who, George?"

"It's big. It's bigger than hell."

"How big, George?"

Dial wet his lips with his tongue. "Charles Martin Stern."

Chris whistled, genuinely surprised. "That's pretty big, George. How are we going to do it?"

Dial stared at her, and emotions—pain and lust and fear—flickered over his face like the symbols of a whirling slot machine. He stood up and shook his head. "Tomorrow," he breathed. "I promise it will be all right. Trust me this once, Chris." He backed to the door and fumbled for the knob, unable to stay, unable to leave her. She sat up a little and let the blanket fall away from one breast. Dial looked at it with something akin to terror, and bolted out the door.

Chris flopped back, as tired as if she had run a marathon. She managed to raise enough strength to turn out the light, before sleep enveloped her like a shroud, dreamless and deep as death.

When she opened her eyes the darkness was heavy as wet wool. A hand was clamped over her mouth, the thumb and forefinger pinching her nostrils shut. She could not breathe, and her heart was hammering.

A nightmare face loomed in front of hers, deformed as a gargoyle. Moonlight reflected off bug-eyes on the end of three-inch stalks, popping out at her in a monstrous blank gaze. The face had no nose, and its mouth and chin were an unnatural black, the color of charcoal briquettes.

Chris kicked frantically, tossing the bedclothes to the floor. The horror fell on top of her naked body, pinning her under its weight, hands black as its face denying her voice or breath.

Then the bug-eyes disappeared, and underneath were normal features, flesh-colored amid the black, like a raccoon's mask.

"Are you okay now?"

Chris closed her eyes with relief and nodded against the

194   *Dennison's War*

hand's pressure. The hand went away. Chris gasped wracking half-sobbing breaths into her lungs.

"My God," she rasped. "I'll get you for this." She drew more breath. "What the hell—?"

"Night vision goggles," Matt Conte said. He held up what looked like a pair of mini-binoculars with a headstrap. "There are men out there with guns, and I wanted to spot them before they spotted me. Are you all right?"

"No," Chris said. "Your belt buckle just punctured my ovary."

Conte rolled off her. Chris gathered up the covers from the floor and wrapped herself in them. "How did you know which room I was in?"

"I saw you in the window, a couple of hours after sundown. I've had the place staked out since noon. Is there a guard in the hallway?"

"Yes."

"Then we'll go out the way I came in." He rummaged in the pockets of his black slacks and came up with what looked like a jar of cold cream. "Cosmetic goop. Blacken your face and hands, and I'll find something for you to wear." He began to rummage in the wardrobe.

"Conte," Chris whispered to his back, "come here."

He came back to the cot.

"I'm not going anywhere."

"What are you—?"

"Listen to me," she whispered urgently. "Something big is going down, and we've got to find out how far it reaches and then put it away. Bressio is trying—"

"I know what Bressio is trying to do," Conte said. "I just spent a long night making a guy tell me. Now let's move."

"No."

"Damn it, get your ass in gear."

"I'm in with them, Conte," Chris insisted. "I'm safe for now. I'm going on a job tomorrow."

"What kind of a job?"

Chris told him. Conte gave the same low whistle.

"I need your help, Conte. I've got to make it look good, or I'm blown. I may even have to go along with the kidnapping, if it will lead us to the heart of Bressio's scheme. But I'll be playing it by ear."

Conte shook his head. "Too dangerous."

"That's what we're paid for."

"Stern isn't. If one thing goes wrong, he's dead."

"If one thing goes wrong, so am I. Bressio's already suspicious; he'll know it was me. That's why you've got to figure out some way to safe Stern, a way that won't tip Bressio."

"Me?"

"Can you think of anyone else?"

Before Conte could answer, the doorlatch snicked back.

Conte hit the deck and rolled under the bed as the door flew open.

Skelton turned on the overhead light. "Someone's in here."

Chris stalked up to him, letting the blankets drop lower. "Yeah," she snapped. *"I'm* in here. And you're in here." She jabbed a finger in his chest. "Only you're getting out of here."

He stared down hungrily at her.

"They're called tits," Chris told him. "Now scram."

Skelton looked past her around the room. "If you're hiding someone . . ."

"The seven dwarfs are under the bed," Chris rapped. "Now would you please get the fuck out of here?"

She pulled the blanket back up. Skelton gave her a long look, but he'd lost the edge and he knew it.

Chris shut the door behind him and doused the light. Conte rolled into the open. She gave him a hand to his feet, so they were suddenly standing very close.

"You look good coming out from under a bed," Chris breathed. "I'll bet you've had a lot of practice."

"You look good, period."

"Later, Conte. Right now you've worn out your welcome."

"I'll try to reach Dennison."

"You do that. Now get."

Conte checked the window.

"Hey," Chris said behind him.

"What?"

"Thanks for worrying."

"Yeah," Conte mumbled. "Good luck."

She brushed her lips across his. "Cover my ass."

"Someone has to." Conte slipped through the window, and darkness swallowed him whole.

Chris rearranged the bedclothes and slid under them. This time she was smiling into the darkness, and the smile was still on her lips as she drifted away from there into sleep.

Chapter Twenty-six

Charles Martin Stern's swivel chair consisted of a fiberglass shell custom-designed to fit his body's contours precisely, and lightly padded in white leather for maximum comfort over long periods of sitting. An arm jutted out from its pedestal, then up at a right angle to support a small table on which there was a box of cigars, an ashtray, a Bic lighter, and two cans of Diet Pepsi in insulating foam sleeves.

To Charles Martin Stern, watching television was serious business.

He was about fifty, a slight, reedy man with thin, artistic fingers. Except for a wispy ring of floss around the crown of his head he was bald, but there was humor in his blue eyes and a confident, almost indulgent turn to his mouth. He would not have been unattractive except for the mass of livid scar tissue that covered his face and neck from jaw to Adam's apple, like a hideous beard of worms.

The only light in the room came from the screen. It was five feet wide, the images dancing across its surface almost life-sized, and Stern's special chair was no more than a yard from it. Stern puffed blue rings of cigar smoke into the darkness.

On the screen, Boss Hogg whined, "Them Duke boys is got more brass than a New Orleans cathouse." Sheriff Roscoe P. Coltrane twitched like a bitch in heat and brayed, "That's a big 10-4, little fat buddy." *The Dukes of Hazzard* was Stern's favorite show, and the Friday evening hour when it was on was inviolate.

Ironically, Stern himself was quite a bit more famous than either of the actors he was watching. A month rarely went by that he was not profiled in some magazine or interviewed by telephone for a radio or television program. Not long ago, a national pollster had conducted a random survey in which respondents were asked to identify ten names. Charles Martin Stern came in fourth, ahead of George Bush but behind E.T.

However, while hundreds of millions of people around the world knew his name, fewer than a dozen knew what Stern looked like. The articles about him were usually accompanied by "artist's conceptions." Each was a little different and none was accurate, although Stern was secretly pleased that he was always depicted with a full head of hair.

The last photograph of Stern had been published in 1957.

The room in which Charles Martin Stern sat was part of a luxurious apartment suite on the penthouse floor of a modern, five-story building in California's Berkeley hills, not far from the San Pablo Reservoir. The building was home to Stern Associates. Stern referred to his firm as a consultancy, but the media insisted on calling it a "think tank," whatever that meant. When Stern heard the term he invariably pictured a group of men and women around a conference table deep under water, with cartoon thought-balloons instead of bubbles coming out of their heads.

Stern Associates specialized in advanced theories of applied political science, with particular attention to sociological and macropsychological modeling and simulation on a national and global scale, as well as experimental defense applications. Its largest account was the U.S. government, primarily the Department of Defense. Other clients included seven of the top ten Fortune 500 companies, and a half dozen major Western allies of the United States.

It was a field of rarified skills and extreme sensitivity, and Stern's work in it had been consistently brilliant for three decades. A writer for *Time* had stated, "In the last twenty years, Charles Martin Stern has been responsible for averting two wars and aborting a third. He did so not by negotiation, nor by pressure nor leverage, but by devising a scenario that showed the antagonists beyond argument a more sensible and equitable method of settling their dispute. The wealthy recluse's favorite method? Point up the ineconomy of war. 'Hit 'em in the wallet,' says he." *People,* in an article sandwiched between profiles of James (*Centennial*) Michener and Charles (*Nicholas Nickleby*) Dickens, called Stern "the Greta Garbo of his generation, and the Svengali of international relations."

Stern was privy to the most secret details of national and international affairs. He had served as an advisor to the last six presidents, and each had come to Stern's quarters to listen to his advice.

Stern had been a recluse for twenty-five years because he was vain. Although his field was theoretical social science, his hobby since college had been applied chemistry. The scars that covered his neck like a garish ascot were the result of a long-ago lab accident.

Stern did not consider himself deformed, and he was married to a beautiful woman about half his age. Her name was Hilda. She was warm, witty, intelligent, and in love with him. If she had a flaw, it was that she refused to watch *The Dukes*.

So Stern's vanity did not stem from fear of being rejected or mocked. He simply did not want to disappoint his public. The world had spent twenty-five years inventing him as a superfigure, and they would be chagrined and disheartened to learn the great man was not flawless. At least he thought they would.

On the desk behind Stern, the telephone rang.

All of his incoming calls were screened; no one spoke with him without explaining themselves to at least two of his staff of Young Men. The Young Men were polite, soft-spoken, deferential, and impossible to con. If the phone were ringing during *The Dukes*, it had to be important.

Stern let it ring.

On the television, he watched every bit of the closing credits. Just as the station ID appeared, the phone rang again. Stern sighed, went to the desk, picked up the receiver, and said, "Yes?"

He was on the line about ninety seconds. He said "Yes," twice more, then "I see," and finally, "No, not at all. I appreciate your concern, old friend."

After he hung up, Stern did not move for several minutes.

He stared with unfocused eyes into the middle distance, brows knit. Finally a smile dawned on his face.

The most unflappable of Stern's unflappable Young Men was named Paul. For years Stern had been trying to rattle him, and for years Paul had accepted everything Stern dished up with unshakable sangfroid. Stern laughed aloud; this time he had Paul by the short hairs. He picked up the phone again and dialed two digits.

"Paul," he said when the cool voice on the other end responded, "could you see that my suitcase is packed? I'll be going away for a day or two."

Paul did not even hesitate. "You don't own a suitcase, Mr. Stern." Stern could picture Paul's blandly equanimitous expression. He was crestfallen.

"I'd be pleased to lend you one of mine," Paul said.

"Thank you, Paul." Stern could not keep the disappointment out of his voice.

But after he hung up the smile slowly returned. With any luck, this would be a grand adventure.

Besides, it was good to get out of the house once in a while.

Chapter Twenty-seven

"Kill me, God damn you!" Albert Hammond screamed. "For Christ's sake, get it done with!"

The echoes of his scream reverberated for a long time, but when they finally faded to silence Hammond realized he had never opened his mouth. The scream was in his head, crowded in with everything else. Where did his mind find the room to billet the army of thoughts marching through it?

They *were* going to kill him; he was certain of that. What he did not understand was why they had not done it already. Bates was gone, and now Dickson; his turn would come soon enough. Already Hammond could sense the change in the air. In the compound there was a hubbub of activity; they were bringing gear in, or moving it out—he didn't care which. But something was up; he had not spent a year in the jungle and all this time in camp without developing instincts.

It wasn't fair, Hammond thought, and immediately laughed. Of course it was fair. What did they say? All's fair in love and war?

Well, this sure as hell was not love.

Yet he could not stifle his resentment. Why had Colonel Creed abandoned him again? Hammond had followed the man blindly through the stinking jungle because he respected the officer like no man he had ever met, and the man had been good to him. But Creed responded by giving up his soul to the gooks for two hellish years.

And still, when the man needed him, Hammond had come, so great was his respect for the finest soldier he knew.

But now—*Why?* his mind screamed. *Why have you deserted me, my commander?*—now it had happened again. He had done as he was told; he had consecrated his love for Creed in the blood of other men—and he was abandoned to the heathen yellow bastards once more.

They didn't look like gooks, but that didn't mean shit. Dickson had only been dead a few minutes, or hours—anyway, that same night they busted into his room and dragged him out and into the compound, stabbing at him with the butts of their rifles when he stumbled or protested, and threw him in this cell. The bars were cold steel, not bamboo, but he wasn't fooled. He'd been here before; he knew what the fuck was coming down.

The gooks had him again, and they would toy with him until they got bored, and then they would kill him. Creed would not come, any more than he had the first time.

Riveting fear washed over him. He could feel his testicles shrink up against his body. He knew what was going on outside: they were moving the camp. "Oh my God." This time he did speak aloud, a low desperate despairing moan.

He remembered the first time. He pictured the forced march through the jungle, felt the rasp of his parched throat, the wet, oppressive heat, the pricks of pain all over his body as insects lunched on his dying flesh. A man collapsed into the undergrowth with exhaustion, and immediately the razor point of a bayonet cut through his sternum and heart muscle to momentarily pin him to the ground. The gook guard planted his bare foot on the guy's chest for the leverage to extract the blade, and when it came out blood geysered into the air before subsiding, like an ornamental fountain when its valve is closed at sundown.

This time he was the only one left, so they would not take him on the march. They would kill him right here in his hooch. He wanted to scream again, but he would not. Don't waste energy. Don't draw attention. Don't do anything—but God damn it, don't give up.

"I want to live," Albert Hammond murmured. "I want to live." He said it again, and a fourth time, and continued to repeat it in a quickening chant, the words jumbling together to become a hopeless prayer to whatever gods had not yet forsaken him.

The room Benjamin Creed had chosen for his billet and office was forty feet to a side and half as tall. It contained a cot, a desk and chair, a stand-alone metal wardrobe locker, an overhead light, a hot plate, a two-way radio transceiver, a hard-wired field telephone, and a small cabinet housing a few cooking utensils. A narrow ventilation shaft in the ceiling was covered by a grid that shielded an exhaust fan. There were two doors, one facing the desk, the other to its right. Both were a little less than five feet high and wide, fashioned of the same kind of laminated steel used for safes.

The field telephone rang, and Creed looked at it and frowned. He lay on the cot with his hands clasped behind his neck, fully clothed in khaki fatigues with no insignia beyond a single gold star on the flap of the breast pocket. The ringing died, then sounded again. Creed rose and pulled out the receiver just as the second ring stopped. He said his name, listened, then said, "Send him down. I'll meet him in the Big Room."

He went to the door to the right of the desk, worked a combination dial, levered back the latch, and pushed open the steel door. It took only a few pounds of pressure; it was perfectly balanced on well-lubricated hinges. It admitted him to a smaller, lower-ceilinged cubicle. To one side, food, water, medication, and other survival supplies were stored in crates; to the other was a lightweight, four-horsepower generator that ran off third-generation ni-cad batteries that were kept on constant trickle charge. A locked metal cabinet held an assortment of personal weapons, and from it Creed took a military-issue .45 automatic pistol and a web belt with a flapped leather holster, which he strapped on.

Like the other room, this one had walls of dark, seamless granite. Like the other, the temperature here was a dank sixty degrees.

Like the other room, this one was two hundred feet underground.

Between the stack of supply crates and the weapons cabinet, the rock wall was more regular, the planes more flat. In the dim light the difference was not apparent. It would take some time to find this section of the wall even if someone knew what they were looking for.

No one did—at least no one still alive.

This part of the "rock" was made of molded fiberglass. Behind it was a narrow rock chimney, partly a natural formation, the rest chiseled out by hand. The shaft was more or less vertical for about one hundred fifty feet, but hand and foot holds were chipped into its wall, and if a person knew where to look for them it was not a difficult climb. After that the passage continued up at a more gentle angle for a couple of hundred yards, before coming out at an adit heavily camouflaged with brush and rock rubble.

The existence of this escape shaft was known only to Benjamin Creed. Two men had helped him fashion it, but just as the job was completed, both had died in a timely cave-in—which Creed had engineered. It was necessary—Creed considered the men casualties of war. You did not share every detail of your strategy, and you sure as hell did not allow yourself to be backed into any corners. You didn't have to attend West Point to know that.

Creed went back into the main room, shutting and locking the door to the storage cubicle behind him. He bent and worked the combination of the main door, then pushed it open.

This door accessed a tunnel a little more than four feet high and wide; it ran fifty feet on an even pitch, then sloped up for the last twenty before coming out into more open space. The length and narrowness of the passage was deliberate and strategic, part of the overall defensive system. Aside from the natural claustrophobia any person feels while advancing into a narrow, dark, unexplored passage, it forced an aggressor to stoop, handicapping him physically and psychologically. Not only did he have to bend his neck at an unnatural angle to see ahead, but no matter how much he concentrated, one part of his mind would always be concerned with not bumping his head.

There were a couple of other surprises for anyone foolish enough to try to breech Creed's quarters. At three positions, fiberglass fake-rock ceiling panels hid deadfalls of a ton of rubble each. Set between them, other panels in the walls hid spring-loaded arrays of steel spikes, adjusted to swing out between chest and eye level. Sometimes the oldest tricks were as good as the most modern weaponry.

The booby traps could be used defensively from within Creed's quarters, or they could be enabled from a hidden switchbox near the tunnel's egress to trip if any unauthorized intruder tried to pass. Creed set them before he moved down the last ten feet; he never left his quarters without doing so.

He came out on the far rim of what he had dubbed the Big Room, a man-made cave that seemed to defy the laws of physics and geometry. It was fully one hundred feet in diameter and fifty tall at its peak, a dome that roughly approximated half of a sphere, carved from solid rock.

Halfway up the wall, a metal galley ringed the room, and from it two men in khaki fatigues were directing the operations below. Their names were Sturges and Preston, and Creed had made them foremen because they had once been members of a loaders' and handlers' union. That had been years ago, before they moved from the rank and file into union positions—primarily having to do with strongarm and extortion tactics on workers and bosses alike who didn't toe the union line. Now Creed had bought their guns and whatever passed for loyalty in their minds. They were vicious men, but they weren't particularly stupid, and they did remember some of what they had learned in their brief tenures in legitimate work.

The cavern was about half filled with boxes, crates, and

cartons of the supplies Creed had no doubt he would soon require, and he was pleased to see that more was coming in. There were also a dozen vehicles, ranging from the electric forklifts the men working on the floor were using, to 4WD rigs, ATVs, and one two-ton flatbed. Its hood was up, and a couple of men were elbow-deep in its engine. They were brothers named Pastori, and they were always together; Creed suspected that they were a little dull-witted and had learned to avoid the problem by facing the world as a team. They had served ten years in various U.S. Army motor pools before the army found out they had been selling spare parts and kicked them out. What the army didn't learn was that they had come back a few months later and killed the man who informed on them. Notwithstanding, the Pastori boys were excellent mechanics and wheelmen, and that was all Creed cared about—at least for the time being.

Across the Big Room were two arrays of a half dozen storage tanks each, one for fuel, the other for drinking water, each equipped with pumps. To one side, stacks of gray-painted wooden trunks contained cold-weather gear, and cross-country skis and snowshoes were racked nearby. But there were also boxes marked as containing insect repellant, sun-blocking cream, and salt tablets.

A dozen halide lights rigged to the metal catwalk cast garish artificial illumination on the already unnatural cavern and its contents.

A man on an electric forklift crossed in front of Creed and tossed him a casual, half-assed salute. Creed returned it. All of these men were exmilitary; Creed insisted on it, as well as the nod to military discipline, because like any discipline it gave them a common ground, a method of communication that, like the gold star Creed wore, codified their different stations and statuses. All of them were also thugs; Creed did not believe in deluding himself, nor did he flinch from calling a spade a spade. The people he had hired knew how to kill from personal experience and did not hesitate to do so if there was something to be gained by the act. Many had existed within the structure of organized crime, or at least on its fringes; a few were fugitives from other countries. All of them knew what they had bought into.

The two sets of storage tanks flanked the mouth of another tunnel cutting through the rock; this one was high and wide enough to admit a full-sized semi and trailer. Creed started across the flat rock floor of the cavern in its direction. As he neared the entrance he could hear the subtle hum of an electric motor, and as he reached it he was met by a surplus open-top Jeep that had been retrofitted for battery power so it could be used inside without necessitating venting the fumes. The driver, a slight, sallow-faced man named Parr, gave Creed a desultory salute and got out a cigarette, but did not light it.

The other man was compact, a few inches under six feet and stocky; he had dark hair cut short like Creed's, revealing a thin, two-inch line of scar behind his right ear that a longer style would have easily covered. He wore an identical uniform to Creed's, except the star on his pocket was silver. As Parr brought the Jeep around and to a stop in front of Creed, the stocky man saluted crisply.

"Well?" Creed said.

"It's coming down, sir. We should talk."

Creed jabbed a thumb into the air like an impatient hitchhiker, and Parr got out. The stocky man slid behind the wheel, and Creed took the passenger seat. The electric Jeep didn't have much acceleration, but the tall man managed to raise some dust and gravel as he slewed it around. Creed frowned but said nothing.

Two hundred yards ahead, up a three percent slope, sunlight was framed by the tunnel's entrance. Near the top end the Jeep jounced over a set of shallow, diagonal overflow ditches laid parallel before converging into a drainage sump. As far as the others knew, the tunnel was the only way in—or out—of the cavern.

At the top, the Jeep turned right, crossed the flat canyon floor, and stopped at the foot of a set of railed wooden steps that switchbacked once on the way to a small porch that fronted a frame building set above the rest of the compound. Creed paused for a moment there, but everything looked normal. He gestured curtly with his head, and the stocky man followed him inside.

Creed did not speak until he was seated behind his desk. "What is it, Captain Greaves?"

The stocky man hesitated.

"Is something wrong, Greaves?"

Greaves looked him in the eye. "I'd like to know what's going on."

"I think you know what's going on," Creed said coldly. He had expected something like this, and he was not surprised—but the timing could surely have been better.

Greaves had been with him on and off for almost twenty years, since the early days of Nam. In those days Greaves had fronted Creed's Saigon black market operations in drugs, choice rations, and currency, and Creed had bought both his protection and his loyalty by paying well. After the war, when the opportunity involving the arms shipments and the mobster Castelli arose, Creed had called in Greaves again; by that time Greaves had set up on his own in a deal involving off-season poaching expeditions for wealthy clients in the Colorado Rockies, but that was chickenshit compared to what Creed offered.

"There isn't much I won't do if you order it, sir," Greaves said. "I guess you know that."

Creed knew that all right; there wasn't much he had not already ordered Greaves to do—up to and including murder, beginning with those civilians at Quang Hoi. But there had been a reason for that, just as there was a reason for what was going down now.

"I only want to know where all this is leading," Greaves said.

"Where do *you* think it's leading, Captain Greaves?"

Greaves shook his head impatiently. "I don't know. When this business started, you were talking about survivalism, but . . ."

All Creed did was look at the man and shake his head, almost sadly, but Greaves's voice trailed off. He did not understand; none of them did.

Creed had begun to see the problem in Vietnam, when he looked around and saw how badly the war was being screwed up. Westmoreland and the rest of the generals—especially the ones sitting on their asses at conference tables in Washington, worrying about how the American effort would look to the world instead of how to fight—they were the ones responsible. Creed knew how to fight: you fought to win.

He had been involved in the black market, certainly, because it took money to fight properly. He used the money to make certain the men under him had the very best of weapons, supplies, medical treatment, and whatever else they needed in the field, and the best liquor, dope, and girls on R&R. He paid them off as well, because they deserved it. He made them professionals, and he made them fight like professionals—and they dedicated their lives to him for it.

That was the way to run a war.

But there was a limit to what one man could do, and long before the war was lost Creed knew defeat was inevitable. When they offered him the Washington desk job again, he took it. He had a new idea: this time he would be one of the boys at the conference table, working changes from inside the military establishment.

But that didn't work either, because the beast was simply too ponderous, too inertial to change. Yet the more Creed saw, the more he understood that change was vital.

Change was a matter of life or death.

The country was going to hell. The soldiers had become the politicians, and the politicians were in charge. They talked until they were red in the face about freedom and humanity and equal rights and the Constitution and did not do a damned thing to stop the real problems, the crime and immorality and godlessness that permeated the nation.

But that was nothing to what the politicians had done in the name of what they called foreign policy. Creed could see that the U.S.A. had become the big kid on the playground who could whip anyone but instead gets the crap kicked out of him because he's afraid to fight. The Communist movement already surrounded the country; it existed, it was real. Yet no one seemed to notice or care. In the Caribbean and Central America, countries like Cuba and Nicaragua were already Soviet satellites. Socialist movements were spreading like the plague in Mexico and Canada, even taking over national institutions in those places. The United States was caught in a Commie net, and the strings were being drawn.

At the same time, the United States was getting its face rubbed in the dirt around the world. The humiliation in Vietnam was only the beginning. As far as Creed was concerned, anyone who did not see a direct link from that failed war in Southeast Asia to the year-and-a-half nightmare of four dozen Americans in Iran had his head in the sand. Right now, the Russians were operating *in this country* within the nuclear freeze movement, while laughter echoed down the corridors of the Kremlin at the Americans' incredible naiveté.

"I *was* talking about survivalism," Creed said to Greaves. "I still am."

Greaves stared back at him, and Creed startled him by laughing. You did not survive by turning your back on reality. In fact, unless you tried to change the situation, you did not deserve to survive. Patriots did not watch the evening news and shake their heads sadly. Patriots got out of the chair and picked up arms and did something for their country.

If you did nothing, you were no patriot. If you were no patriot, you deserved to die.

There was a war coming; anyone could see that. Already it had begun, and already some had died. Many more would die in days and weeks and months to come. Creed knew that and was not bothered by it. You did not make an omelet without breaking some eggs.

There was only one way to change things, permanently and for the good, and that was through radical surgery on the body politic. The weak men in Washington and the half-baked generals, and even the cops, were not up to the job.

So they had to be eliminated.

"I'll tell you where this is leading, Captain Greaves," Creed said calmly. "We are going to make ourselves a brave new world."

Greaves leaned forward and put both hands on the edge of the desk. "How much is this world going to cost?"

"We've got enough for the down payment already," Creed said. "Which is why things are, as you say, coming down. We're going to take over, captain—starting today."

Creed did not like the look in Greaves's eyes, nor had he liked the man's attitude lately. Yet he felt the need to talk this out, and he was genuinely curious what the man's reaction would be—not that it mattered. . . .

"The money—from the Fisk job, from our current operations—is going to buy us some preliminary power, captain. When we have enough of it, we are going to take control."

"With that band of mobsters outside?" Greaves snorted.

"We tried the military angle, as you know," Creed said coldly. "It didn't work—*as you know.*" His patience was growing thinner. "Those men happen to be useful for now, and time is a factor. It happens to be more efficient to buy killers than to train them at this moment. When they are no longer useful—"

"They're dead," Greaves finished.

Creed smiled. This country had to change—quickly, before it was too late, and the Russians had to see that change, and believe it. There was only one path to true freedom for men who truly merited freedom, and that was by showing the Commies that we did not fear them, or their missiles, or their bombs. If they wanted a fight, Creed was ready to give them one hell of one.

Creed shrugged meaninglessly. "How about you, captain? Do you believe nuclear war can be survived?"

Greaves straightened. "I wouldn't be here otherwise."

"That's fine," Creed said, almost casually. He rose from behind the desk and went to the window and stood motionless for almost a minute, staring down at the compound below.

Finally, he turned. "Because you see, captain, I believe we're going to have to start one."

Chapter Twenty-eight

The Hughes 500C shot west at one hundred sixty-five miles per hour, fleeing the Saturday sunrise at its back. Chris estimated they had been airborne about an hour. Sacramento was coming up off the right runner, the dome of the Capitol building reflecting the first long rays of dawn. The home office of Stern Associates was about fifteen minutes away.

Bressio had briefed them just before they left. According to his intelligence, security at Stern Associates was no greater than was typical these days at any corporate office building. On a Saturday morning there would be a door guard, another stationed outside Stern's private quarters, and two or three rovers. They would be private cops who had likely never drawn their sidearms in duty's line. Chris was skeptical, in light of Stern's known involvement in top secret matters.

Bressio had laughed. "Nobody likes to live or work surrounded by armed men," he said. "Besides, this is the United States of America in the twentieth century. This is real life. And in real life kidnap squads do not descend upon pastoral think tanks on quiet spring Saturday mornings."

Until now, Chris thought.

She sat in the middle pair of the chopper's seats, next to Helena. As Sacramento drifted off to their rear, Helena looped the intercom phone over her ears and gestured for Chris to do the same.

"Change of plans, Little Sister." Helena's voice was harsh and scratchy in the tiny speaker. "There are a couple of things we kind of forgot to tell you."

There was no point in rising to that kind of mindless baiting. Chris waited for Helena to get to the point.

"For starters," Helena said, "you and I are going in alone."

"What about George?"

"George was never in on this job. He's got another assignment. We happen to be going his way, so he caught a lift."

In the seat in front of her, George half-turned, sensing he was the topic. He was rubbing furiously but unconsciously at the scars on his wrists, like a relief pitcher working a rabbit's foot.

"Do you have any problem with that, Little Sister?" Helena pressed.

"If I do," Chris said, "you'll be the first to know."

The chopper slewed to the right and into a steep descent. A road switchbacked twice and came out into an almost level clearing near the ridge line, and as the chopper came closer Chris saw a car parked where the road came in, a Pinto station wagon, four or five years old. The chopper pulled to a hover a few feet above the grass. Chris saw the orange-on-black of California license plates below the Pinto's tailgate.

"Go!" Helena barked.

George Dial smiled at Chris, and she mouthed, "Good luck." His smile widened. He pushed open the door, ducked onto the runner, then dropped to the ground. Helena climbed up into the vacant seat and relatched the door. The chopper was already ascending.

Dial used a key on the rear door of the Pinto, swung it up, and took out a small suitcase. That was all Chris saw before the chopper veered sharply west again.

Three minutes later they overflew the inverted V of the Briones Reservoir and the longer finger of the San Pablo, and then the chopper crested a ridge and the Stern Associates building was off the left runner. Chris recognized it from television newscasts; it often appeared as a backdrop to the reports of correspondents who could get no closer to Stern than his parking lot. The building was a cube of steel framing and huge, tinted glass panels, perhaps a hundred yards to a side, set amid a neat lawn surrounded by forest. A gravel drive opened into a parking lot at the building's front, empty except for four cars, a VW bus, and a pickup truck.

The drive ran about a half-mile to a paved road, empty of traffic at this hour. The chopper followed the road north a mile to a state picnic ground. Dirt and the leaves of the previous autumn skittered across the clearing under the rotor's prop-wash. Helena Frome hit the ground simultaneously with the runners, and Chris ducked and dove out on her heels. Behind them the chopper lifted off into the brightening dawn.

The morning was crisp and cool. Helena set a fast pace, her wiry legs pumping in a steady hard jog, though Chris had no trouble keeping up. They turned into the woods about twenty-five yards before the drive and threaded a path parallel to it, moving in a half crouch, slowing only enough to avoid low-hanging branches.

At the edge of the lawn Helena stopped and held up one

hand, like the lead scout of a wagon train. They had come out on the building's side.

"You be sure to play it just the way we laid out," Helena panted. "You fuck up and you can kiss your ass goodbye, Little Sister."

Chris didn't waste breath replying. She unbuckled the strap of her fanny-pack, unzipped the compartment, and took out a nylon shell, shaking out the wrinkles before slipping it on. With the zipper pulled up a few inches, the gun on her right hip was concealed.

"Move out, Little Sister," Helena ordered.

Chris edged through the woods to the gravel drive, then sraightened and walked along its curve toward the building's front door, not overly casual, but not hurrying either. From the corner of her eye she caught the movement of Helena sprinting toward the cover of the side. Chris began to whistle tunelessly.

Through the tinted glass of the front door Chris saw a high-ceilinged lobby, wide as the building was long. In front of the far wall was a modernistic receptionist's desk, and mounted behind it were framed pictures, plaques, and citations. There were a couple of chairs and coffee tables, a few potted plants: the usual waiting room paraphernalia. A little farther down was a bank of four elevators, and beside them a little three-sided countertop enclosure. A security man in a blue peaked cap sat inside it.

Chris rapped on the door's glass with the heel of her hand. The guard looked up, a little startled. When he came across the lobby Chris could see the thatch of gray hair sticking out from under his cap. He had a comfortable rolling gait, as if he had learned long ago that hurrying was rarely worth the effort. His face was deep-lined and leathery, with soft kindly eyes; he looked like somebody's grandfather. Chris imagined he might be an excop from Oakland, collecting his twenty-year pension but keeping his hand in, the habit of the uniform and badge and gun too ingrained to break because of retirement.

Chris felt ashamed at what she was about to do.

The guard looked her over and pressed a button next to the door. A speaker squawked a burst of electronic noise, and the guard said, "Can I help you, miss?"

"Geez, I hope so," Chris said. "Do you know anything about cars?"

"What's the problem, miss?"

"I don't know," Chris said into the speaker. "It just went dead. It's down on the road, near your drive." She pointed, the dither-headed female to whom auto mechanics were as obscure as quantum theory.

"I can't leave my post, miss." He really sounded sorry. Chris pictured him with small children in his lap, telling them tales of cops and robbers.

"Could I use the phone?" Chris appealed. "I'm a member of the Auto Club."

The kindly faced guard studied her. "I suppose it would be all right."

Chris flashed her most winning smile. The guard pulled a ring of keys from the spring-loaded reel attached to his belt, worked one and then another in the door locks, and pulled it open. Chris said, "I really appreciate this."

Helena Frome spun around behind her, her weapon out and leveled on the guard. Chris moved out of the line of fire, pulled open the nylon shell, and drew her own gun. The guard took a step back. "You tricked me, miss," he said reproachfully. Chris had trouble meeting his gaze.

"Right you are, Mac," Helena snapped. "Now you're taking us upstairs—fifth floor, the boss's suite. No questions, no quick moves."

"I don't think so," the guard said calmly.

He lunged at Helena, his hands crabbing for her gun hand.

Chris shot him in the stomach at a range of five feet.

The guard grunted at the impact. He stared unbelievingly at Chris, lurched in her direction, and crumpled to the polished hardwood floor.

Chris knelt and held his wrist. His breathing was regular, and his pulse was steady. There was no blood. In his abdomen, a few inches above the navel, was a needle dart. Chris plucked it out and dropped it in her pocket.

Bressio did not want to compromise their bargaining position by leaving corpses behind. The guns they were carrying were Beeman/Webley Hurricane air pistols in .22

caliber, modified to shoot tranquilizer darts. The guard would come around in about four hours, suffering only from a bad headache and some embarrassment.

The last elevator was open. A youngish, coffee-colored man was sitting on a three-legged stool in one corner, his head against the wall, his eyes closed, and his mouth open and emitting ragged snores. Chris tapped him on the shoulder with the barrel of the B/W. He did not react. Any elevator man working this shift would naturally become a past master at the art of napping.

Chris slapped his face twice and put the barrel of the pistol in front of him, so it was the first thing he saw.

"Fifth floor," Chris said. "Snap it up."

"Wha?"

Chris lay the barrel against the bridge of the guy's nose. "Fifth floor, or your brains are all over the wall." She hoped this was going over big with Helena.

The guy stood carefully, Chris tracking the gun on him as he sidestepped to the control panel. The elevator doors hissed shut and the car rose silently; numbers above the door counted from one to four. The elevator men took out a keyring like the guard's and reached for a control lock below the push buttons.

"What are you doing?" Helena demanded.

"The interlock has to be disabled before the car will go to the next floor." He indicated an LED and ten-number keypad; the display showed five zeroes in square red figures.

"How do we know it doesn't set off a signal upstairs?"

"It . . . it"—the guy stared at the two guns—"it does."

"Okay." Helena smiled wolfishly. "So do it, and don't waste any time afterward."

The operator twisted the key and punched out five quick digits, as if dialing a touch-tone phone. The LED cleared, and the word "Confirmed" appeared in the display. The operator jabbed the button marked "5," and the elevator rose again.

Helena flattened herself into one corner, and Chris pushed the operator roughly out of the way and took the opposite side. The operator sat down on his chair and tried to make himself small.

The car stopped, and the doors sighed and began to slide

open. Helena nodded a go-ahead, and they spun simultaneously and came out in a fast low crouch. They were in a small reception area. A young man in a suit was behind a desk with a guard standing beside him.

The guard fumbled at the flap of his holster, and Helena put a dart in his chest before he could undo the snap. The young man started to rise.

Chris shot him, and he moaned and flopped across the desk.

Behind him the door opened and another young man in a suit charged out, a cocked automatic pistol in his hand. He made the mistake of wasting a split-second gawking at the two fallen bodies, and Chris put a dart in his throat. The man swatted at it like he'd been bitten by a mosquito and fell like that, hand clamped to neck.

It occurred to Chris this was going awfully smoothly.

Helena led the way through the open door, down an entryway, and in a door to the left. That put them in a laboratory. Across the room a man in a white coat was bent over a microscope.

Helena barked, "Stern!"

A woman's voice said, "What is this? What do you want?"

Helena moved into the room, Chris beside her. The woman had been working at a bench to their left.

Across the room, the man straightened and turned reluctantly, as if whatever he had been studying was infinitely more interesting than women with guns. He regarded them with a faint, uncomfortable smile, like the guest of honor at a surprise party.

"I'm Charles Martin Stern," he said calmly. "What is it you want with me?"

Chris Amado stared from him to the woman.

Dennison and Miss Paradise stared back.

Chapter Twenty-nine

"That's them," the clerk said. He pointed past William Sterling Price out the front window of the Winnemucca Post Office. A Toyota Land Cruiser with an open top was pulling up to the curb. Both men in it wore jeans and flannel shirts, and one of them had a blue baseball cap. The clothing didn't seem quite right on them, like the brown suit, white shirt, and narrow tie of the plainclothesman who can't understand why everyone instantly makes him for a cop. The driver climbed out and stood beside the rig, looking up and down the street.

"Always the same men?" Price asked.

"Beats me," the clerk said. "They dress the same, they all look alike. Same rig, anyway."

"Thanks." Price spread a fifty-dollar bill on the counter. The clerk stared at it. "You already paid, mister."

"I paid for information. That's for forgetting I asked."

"Bribing an employee of the U.S. Postal Service is a federal offense." The bill disappeared in the clerk's fist. "Already," he said solemnly, "my memory is as foggy as valley dawn."

Price looked at him in surprise. The clerk nodded, then slammed down the accordion-pleat awning. On it was a poster featuring Mister Zip and a placard reading, "No Window Hours Saturday and Sunday."

The man in the baseball cap came in, shot Price an incurious glance, and went to the wall array of P.O. boxes. He removed a handful of mail, sorted through it, separated one letter, and dumped the rest in a trash can already overflowing with catalogs and advertising circulars.

"Can I talk to you for a second?" Price said.

The man looked up. "About what?"

"Colonel Creed."

"Never heard of him."

The door swung open again to admit an old man in dirty

bib coveralls, a slouch hat, and wispy white chin whiskers. He wore dusty work boots, and one of his cheeks was as fat as a chipmunk's with an enormous wad of chaw. He looked so much like the stereotype of the desert rat prospector that Price expected to see a pack-loaded burro tethered to the parking meter out front. Instead there was a Willys pickup that had to be thirty years old, covered with about a half inch of alkali dust.

The old-timer looked them over and went to the boxes.

"I'm not looking for trouble," Price said to the guy in denims. He indicated the letter. "I saw an ad that gave this address, but no one answered my letter. From what I hear, Creed has some right ideas about survival, and I thought if I came here I could talk to him."

"Think again," the guy said abruptly, and turned away.

God damn it, Price thought. The play could not have gone more wrong. He'd tipped his hand and learned nothing in return. He rummaged through the mail the guy had discarded and came up with a shopper's newspaper, a flyer from a real estate broker, and a packet of cents-off coupons, all addressed to Box Holder.

That was it, Price figured: they had run out their string. There was no way to tail the Toyota across open desert gravel roads without throwing up a telltale dust plume fifty yards high and a half mile long. They were back to square one, and the other players had the dice.

"Weird birds."

The old-timer was the only other person in the room. He was studiously reading the return addresses on his mail, his lips shaping out the words. For a moment Price had the feeling he had imagined the voice.

"Beg your pardon?"

The old-timer looked at him. "Them soldier boys is weird birds."

Price let his perplexity show.

"Don't let them dude clothes fool you," the old-timer cautioned. "That's just their Saturday come-to-town outfits. Back in the desert they like to dress up like they was about to storm the Argonne."

"You've run into them before?"

"You bet your ass I have, sonny."

"Did they give you trouble?" Price did his best to sound
sympathetic. He hadn't been called sonny for a long time.

"We ain't exactly asshole buddies," the old-timer said. "I
been prospecting that high desert country northwest of here for
going on forty-seven years. Maybe that don't mean I got claim
to the whole territory, but neither do they. I don't take kindly to
being threatened and pushed around and run off, that's for shit-
sure. Room for everyone to live in peace is what I say."

"That's right."

"Of course it's right." The old-timer worked his chaw
around and spit a brown stream of tobacco juice into the exact
center of the trash basket. It hit the side of a manila envelope
and streamed down in a viscous rope. "I got three-quarters of a
lifetime invested in that desert, sonny. They got maybe seven–
nine months. What right they got telling me where I can't go?"

"They've got a lot of nerve."

"Too goddamned much."

"Do you know where their place is? Have you seen it?"

The old-timer's gaze narrowed. "I know where every
goddamned rock in that goddamned desert is, too. So what?"

Price could not afford to lose the guy. The mission was
hanging by a thread now, and one more twist could part it.

"Maybe I could buy you a drink," Price said carefully,
"if it's not too early."

"Don't be a fool, sonny," the old-timer snapped.

Price's heart lurched.

"Stop gawking and start walking," the old-timer said.
"With a drink, there's no such thing as too early."

Chapter Thirty

Helena Frome jutted her bony chin at Miss Paradise and
said to Dennison, "Who's she?"

"My wife," Dennison said levelly. "What are you people
doing here?" He wiped his hands on the front of the white lab
coat and looked mildly bewildered.

Helena was glaring at Miss Paradise. Chris had suspected that Helena's antagonism was not reserved for her alone, that Helena had little use for any woman. When she encountered someone as stunning as Miss Paradise, it had to be a crushing reminder of how plain she was.

Helena reached in the pocket of her baggy fatigues and took out a snub-nosed .32 revolver. It was no air gun. She offered it to Chris and said, "Waste her."

Miss Paradise's face was set in a mask of contained fury.

"What are you talking about?" Chris demanded.

"You're the one who wanted in on this, Little Sister." Helena gestured with the gun. "Prove you're with us. Start earning your keep."

"Wait a minute—"

"We don't have a minute." Helena glanced at her wrist. "That chopper is setting down in the parking lot in exactly three minutes and twelve seconds. If we leave her here, she'll be on the phone to the cops before we reach the elevator. She's had time to look us over. The FBI has lots of pretty pictures of me, and they'd love to move them to a 'case closed' file."

Chris stared at the gun.

Helena laughed. "I had you pegged all along, didn't I, Little Sister?" she gloated.

She raised the revolver in both hands, sighted on Miss Paradise's torso, and thumbed back the hammer. Miss Paradise stared at the stubby tips of the bullets in the cylinder.

"It's been nice knowing you, Mrs. Stern," Helena Frome said.

Chapter Thirty-one

Above the Sparks warehouse, atop a slope that ended in a jagged scarp of wind-eroded granite, Matt Conte stared into the desert glare. His right foot was asleep, and he stretched and twisted his ankle in a three-hundred-sixty-degree circle until it tingled and began to regain feeling. It was ten-thirty in the morning, and he had been in position since before dawn, almost six hours in all.

He glanced over his shoulder to make sure the sun was still at his back before raising the high-powered binoculars; he did not want a telltale glare pinpointing his position. Within the fenced perimeter of the warehouse yard, one of the last two semitrailers rumbled to life and pulled away from the loading dock. It swung around in a long, clumsy arc, paused briefly at the gate, then turned north toward the interstate, gathering speed and raising dust as the driver jammed his way through the four-by-four gearbox.

Something was going down, but Conte was damned if he knew what. He had seen Chris board the helicopter, along with the two creeps they were after; that was four hours earlier, at daybreak. But Dennison had ordered him to stay clear; he'd promised to see to Stern's safety, and that was good enough for Conte. Conte tried to put his concern for Chris out of mind. She had accepted the same conditions as he and would have to watch out for her own neck.

A couple of hours after the chopper lifted off, a garage door went up and a caravan of three cars emerged, sleek dark sedans traveling in close formation. The first and third cars were each packed with six hard-looking guys, but the sandwich car held only the driver and two passengers in the back seat. As the convoy turned out the gate, Conte made out their faces.

One was Eddie Turin, the renegade Mafioso the Old Men were so unhappy with. Conte had never seen the other man in person, but he knew who he was. Rudy Marcoux's description of Frank Bressio had been detailed and specific.

Conte stifled the urge to scramble down to the rented Camaro Z28 parked below and put a tail on them. They were not going to lose Bressio; wherever he was going, Chris would have to hook with him after the Stern snatch. It would be up to her to figure a way to report in.

It was hard for Conte to adjust to notions of teamwork. He had always operated alone. But since signing on with Dennison, he was facing a lot of changes, and he was beginning to see they were maybe to the good.

At the warehouse's loading dock, the last truck's diesel engine growled and grumbled and began to idle.

Conte backed away from the edge of the scarp on knees and elbows until he was covered. As he moved down to the Z28 he took out the Colt automatic, fished a stubby black silencer from his jacket pocket, and threaded it over the muzzle.

The sullen guy on the gate had a familiar face. He was a bodyman for a Revere Beach, Massachusetts, *caporegime* named Granitola. Conte flipped through his mental card file and came up with a name.

" 'Lo, Jerry."

Jerry peered in the window. Conte raised his dark glasses to his forehead and brought up the gun. Jerry said, "Shit."

"In the back, Jerry."

"Hey, listen, Mr. Conte, all I know is—"

"In the back," Conte said.

Jerry opened the door and slid in behind Conte, who twisted to keep an eye on him. "Take a look out the back window, Jerry. Get a load of the view."

All the color drained from the guy's scowling face, but he had guts. "If you're gonna grease me, Conte, I'll take it face up."

"Turn around, Jerry."

Jerry turned white as paste, and his jaw began to tremble. He turned, and the sap swished through the air and into his temple. Jerry slumped to the seat, and Conte levered him to the floor.

No one else challenged Conte as he drove around to the door. It wasn't locked, and the corridor beyond was unoccupied. Through the view window, Conte saw that the warehouse was as empty as a chorus girl's promise. A forklift was easing a loaded pallet into the last trailer. Two more pallets waited nearby. Within five minutes the moving job would be completed.

Conte went down the corridor, quick-checking the rooms opening off it. In Bressio's office a cigar stub had been ground out on the floor; in one of the billets there was a copy of *Penthouse,* and in another two dimes and three pennies on the night stand. Chris's room was empty of everything but furniture.

As he came out of it, a toilet flushed two doors further on. Conte waited, holding the silenced .45 pointed at the floor.

A guy pushed into the hall. "Over here," Conte said softly. The guy looked up and his face clouded.

"I thought everyone was gone," the guy bluffed. He scratched at the top of his head with his left hand and grinned.

It was a nice piece of misdirection, but Conte had seen it before. The guy's right was creeping for his holster.

"Don't," Conte said.

The guy didn't listen. Some guys never did.

He got as far as touching his gunbutt before Conte shot him in the forehead. The soft wet whap of the impact was louder than the silenced report.

Across the warehouse, the forklift operator was driving the last pallet into the trailer. The driver was standing by looking impatient.

Conte glared down at the corpse and shook his head. If the guy had stayed in the shitter for three more minutes, he and the forklift operator both would have lived. Now he had to make sure the forklift man didn't contact Bressio about his dead buddy, and there was no time for finesse. The truck driver was swinging up into the cab; exhaust smoke billowed as he put it in low-low and pulled away. Conte's job here was finished; there was no longer a reason not to tail the truck.

Conte unscrewed the silencer as he moved down the corridor until he found a door that opened into the warehouse proper. The forklift guy was coming toward him, making checkmarks on a clipboard.

It was a long shot for a handgun, but Conte had made it before. He pushed open the door, sighted, drew breath and held—and made it again.

In the back seat of the car, Jerry was still out colder than a landlord's heart. Conte spun the Camaro around and headed for the gate. Across the flat scrub wasteland he could make out the semi entering the eastbound on-ramp of the interstate.

Conte stomped hard on the gas, and the Camaro leaped forward, gravel rooster-tailing into the air behind him. The big rig was Conte's last tie to this assignment, and he had no intention of being cut out before seeing it through to the bitter and bloody end.

Chapter Thirty-two

Chris Amado was still desperately trying to think of some way to stop Helena when Dennison made his move.

He shot across the room with incredible speed, covering the distance in three long, loping steps. Before Helena could get the gun on him his right hand flashed through the air, the hard edge of his palm chopping into her wrist. Helena yowled with pain, and the revolver dropped from her numbed fingers. Dennison kicked it under the lab bench.

"That's enough!" Chris ordered. She leveled the Beemman/Webley on Dennison.

"Maybe we can act like adults from here on," Dennison said, with genuine heat.

Chris waved her gun. "Over with your wife, Stern." She edged around them and retrieved Helena's .32. When she looked up, Miss Paradise was holding Dennison's hand, and on her face was the purest glow of pride.

"Hand over that gun, Little Sister," Helena Frome demanded furiously. Her forehead was greasy with sweat, and she glared at Dennison with vengeful loathing. "She is dead, mister. Your bitch is fucking dead."

"No she's not," Chris said coldly.

Helena gave her an incredulous look.

"Wake up, Helena," Chris said. "He saved you from doing something very stupid."

"What are you—"

"Shut up, Helena." Chris had an edge, and she meant to press it. "What we need from you is more brains and less bullshit. Do you expect Stern to cooperate after we kill his woman in cold blood? Maybe we should blow them both away, right now. How do you think the boss would like that?"

Dennison looked from one to the other.

"What do we do with her?" Helena asked sullenly.

"We take her with us. We've got no choice. Let the boss

decide. Alive, she might be worth money, but dead she is only bad news."

Chris didn't give her a chance to argue. "Time's up Helena. Let's get out of here." She turned to Dennison and Miss Paradise. "Smooth and easy, and no funny moves. We're interested in keeping you alive, but only as long as it isn't a lot of trouble. Keep that in mind."

The grandfatherly guard was still down and out in the lobby. As they went through the front door into the parking lot, the chopper came into view over the treeline. As it descended, the propwash whipped hair across Chris' face.

Helena grabbed Miss Paradise by the arm, but the tall woman yanked free and stared a challenge to try it again. Helena decided not to; so far it had not been her best day.

"All aboard," Chris said, and dog-trotted for the helicopter.

The Hughes bubblefront followed the line of Interstate 80 for about an hour. When the azure of Lake Tahoe, the landmark indicating the California–Nevada line, came into view, the chopper swung abruptly north. Within a few minutes the conifer forest thinned into high plains scrub brush, which gave way to desert. Helena Frome rubbed at her wrist and divided dark looks among Dennison, Miss Paradise, and Chris.

The chopper dropped to five hundred feet. The barren country racing past underneath was empty of any sign of civilization beyond a few faint lines of gravel road or Jeep trail. They passed over a hardpan alkali playa that had been a lake eons before and a cutbank creek bed that flowed maybe a total of four or five days, in a wet year. Flat-topped buttes stood sentinel over plains as level as griddles, chased with cracks like dried leather.

Twenty minutes north of Tahoe the chopper threaded a course between two table mesas and swept up and over a ridge. On the other side the ridge dropped off abruptly into a deep bowl about a hundred yards in diameter. The sides fell away vertically, then eased to a slope near the floor, a good two hundred feet below. The only apparent access was to their right, a defile no wider than a two-lane road that formed a fifty-foot crack in the dish's side. Someone had spent a lot of money, effort, and dynamite in its construction.

In return he had gained a perfectly defensible natural fortress.

The chopper arced around and began to descend in a tight quick circle. Chris saw armed men patrolling the upper rim as they dropped past it. Below on the canyon floor, a compound had been laid out with some care. At the mouth of the cut was a guardhouse. Opposite, on a ledge carved into the wall thirty feet above the floor—where the slope became vertical cliff— was a one-story frame structure reached by a railed wooden staircase with one switchback. Chris guessed this was the headquarters.

To this building's left was a long, low barracks with a smaller billet beyond and a little behind it. As they dropped lower, she saw its windows were barred. On the other side of the command building there was a large, prefab Quonset hut, its curved, corrugated tin roof sparkling in the noonday sun. It had double garage doors and two armed guards posted in front; it probably warehoused the equipment and weaponry that had been moving out of the Sparks warehouse.

At first Chris thought the darker place in the canyon wall beside the Quonset hut was only shadow, but as they touched down she realized it was some kind of cave or tunnel; in the sharp desert sun she could not see inside. An insulated black cable ran from it to the Quonset hut and then to a smaller building beside it; other cables ran from the generator hut to the barracks and the command building. A lighter cable was threaded through screw eyes up the side of the canyon face to a dish antenna on the rim.

Besides the guards up there, Chris counted eleven men. Some were helping unload the semi parked between the Quonset hut and the cave's mouth; others were working on a couple of the 4WD rigs parked at the end of the barracks; a few were lounging in the sunshine. Each was dressed in the same unmarked fatigues that the men had been wearing in the Sparks warehouse.

"Very impressive," Dennison murmured.

"Put a lid on it, Stern," Helena ordered.

Dennison gave her his benign smile.

The chopper came to rest on the canyon floor, and the pilot began to shut down the engines. "Eyes straight ahead, and do what you're told," Helena ordered. Dennison looked stiff and awkward when he got out, as if his startling speed and agility in Stern's lab had been an illusion. As Chris started after him, Helena laid a heavy hand on her shoulder. "The same goes for you, Little Sister," she said in a low voice. "Don't start thinking this field trip automatically makes you one of the girls."

Chris shook loose. Eddie Turin and Skelton were waiting at the foot of the wooden stairs. Helena walked the prisoners toward them, and men stopped what they were doing to stare. Miss Paradise had doffed the white lab coat to reveal a dark green nylon jumpsuit cut to accent her sweeping curves, the sleek material shining wetly.

When they were out of the turbulence of the feathering chopper blades, Helena grabbed Chris again. "You keep pushing, Little Sister, and I'm gonna push back. You could find yourself pushed over the edge—and believe me, it's a long way down."

"What's that supposed to mean?"

"You keep your mouth shut about what happened back there. We've got Stern and his whore; that's all that matters. And stay away from George. You can't give him anything but pain."

Chris smiled. "There's one thing I can give him that you can't, Helena." She leaned closer and whispered in Helena's ear.

Helena jerked back and tried to slap Chris's face. Chris caught her by the wrist and squeezed. It was the same wrist Dennison had struck, and tears glazed Helena's eyes. Chris squeezed harder and twisted, and Helena went down on one knee like a supplicant.

The men were drifting closer, trying to keep one eye on Miss Paradise and the other on the cat fight.

"Thanks for the friendly advice," Chris said. She gave the wrist another wrench and tossed it away like a candy wrapper. She turned on her heel and followed Dennison and Miss Paradise, deliberately showing her back to Helena.

"Trouble?" Turin asked sardonically.

"Not a bit," Chris said briskly. The scarecrow was grinning; he liked to see girls beating on each other. "Missed me, huh, Skelton?"

"He's waiting," Turin said.

He led the way up the stairs. Chris and Skelton brought up the rear, and behind them she heard Helena scrambling to catch up.

The command building was a two-bedroom kit house, utilitarian and undistinctive. The front room was an office, with the same furniture that had been in the warehouse. Bressio was no longer hiding in shadows. He sat behind the scarred desk dressed in fatigues starched stiff as cardboard. He looked them all over with vast satisfaction, like a regent addressing his loyal populace from the balcony of his palace.

"So," he said expansively, "everything went well?"

"Well enough," Helena replied sullenly.

Bressio regarded her with the fond smile of an indulgent father. He was having a fine time.

"You both did an excellent job." He studied Dennison, looking him over from head to foot and back again. "There's only one problem."

Bressio stabbed a forefinger in Dennison's direction. "This man," he said, "is not Charles Martin Stern."

Chapter Thirty-three

George Dial parked the rented Pinto station wagon in a fifteen-minute loading zone on the Sixth Street side of the Greyhound Bus Terminal, not far from the San Francisco–Oakland Bay Bridge off-ramp. He took a leather satchel from the seat beside him, locked the keys in the car, and went inside. It was Saturday, approaching noon, and the big open room was bustling. Three of the tiers of molded plastic seats in the waiting area were filled with a troop of Girl Scouts fidgeting with the effort of behaving themselves, all green berets and matching knee socks and colored badges and scrawny legs peeking out from under green felt skirts. Three saffron-robed Hare Krishnas, their heads shaved to the skin except for topknots, were making atonal noise on tabla, finger cymbals, and a thighbone trumpet.

On the far side of the room, next to a lunch counter, there was a bank of coin lockers. Dial inserted a plastic-tabbed key in one, pulled it open, and removed a parcel wrapped in brown paper about the size of a carton of cigarettes. He put it in the leather satchel, rebuckled the top, and crossed back toward the door that opened on Mission. A skinny kid wearing jeans with frayed bottoms, sandals, a leather vest with no shirt, and a beaded headband had stationed himself by the door. He had hair halfway down his back and a Fu Manchu mustache; he looked like he had just arrived via time warp from 1969. As Dial approached he bopped out and said, "Spare change, man?"

"Get fucked," Dial snapped, and pushed through the door.

"Peace, man." The kid showed a two-fingered V to Dial's back.

Dial got into the back seat of the first cab in line and said, "The Seaspray, on Beach Street."

"Tourist?" the driver said into the rear-view mirror as he pulled the yellow Checker from the curb. He was a middle-aged man in an old-style, soft-crown cabbie hat over tightly curled dark hair. He had chubby cherub cheeks and a mouth made for kissing babies.

"Hey, listen," the driver said, "you want, I can take you by the scenic route, give you the grand tour—Telegraph Hill, Golden Gate Bridge, the cable cars, all that shit. I been driving in this town for twenty-seven years. I been around."

"I'm in a hurry," Dial said.

The cab turned onto Third and headed north, past the Moscone Center. The cabbie downshifted and said, "Hey, that's the trouble with people nowadays. Everyone is in a hurry. People jump in the cab, all they want—"

"The Seaspray," Dial interrupted. "On Beach. Shortest way you know."

"Hey, right," the cabbie said. "So people jump in the

cab, they got to be there ten minutes ago. I say, what's the hurry? You gotta take life one step at a time. Hey, I say, take time to smell the goddamned roses."

The cabbie leaned on the horn and ran the light at Market. Third jogged right and became Kearney. Somewhere behind them there was the sound of tires leaving rubber on pavement. The cabbie didn't seem to notice. "Hey, I've had some famous people in this cab. You know what'sername, the one used to be on *Dallas*. You know the one with the tits. She was sitting right there where you are."

"Yeah," Dial said. "I think I can still smell a whiff of her."

"Hey, right, you want anything, you gimme a call. Ask for me special." The cabbie poked a business card through the connecting window. It was wrinkled, and there was an arc of coffee-cup stain across it. It read "Nick Constantinas, King of the Cabbies," and below, in smaller italic print, *"With Nick, You're Along for More than the Ride!!!"*

"Hey, there's folks all the time ask for Nick," the cabbie babbled on. On the other side of Broadway, the office buildings started to give way to sidewalk cafes, small shops, porno theaters, and twenty-four-hour topless bars. The light changed at Powell, and this time, for some reason, the cabbie decided to stop. Dial watched a sidewalk barker try to talk a sailor into a bar advertising "Live Sex on Stage—This Is the Real Thing!" "I ain't shittin' you, Admiral," the barker was telling him. "We got a octopus in here makin' it wid a bagpipes!"

"They come from all over," the cabbie said, above the wrenching noise of grinding gears. "The big cities of the industrial East and the villages of Middle America. From the factories and the farms."

"What," Dial said despite himself, "are you talking about?"

"Hey, my regulars," the cabbie said. "They call me 'cause they know Nick can get 'em what they want. You want girls, I got girls. I got boys, you swing that way. Hey, no Greek jokes now," the cabbie cautioned with great good humor.

The cab swung sharp right on Beach. "Hey, I don't make this kind of offer to everyone, know what I mean? But you look like a right kind of guy."

"I'm not."

"Hey, a kidder. I love a kidder. Listen, you like a good time, I can fix you up." The cabbie pinched an imaginary roach between thumb and forefinger, put it to his lips, and inhaled with great gusto. "What you need," he repeated, and laying a finger beside his nose like old Saint Nick, gave a noisy snort. "Hey, best stuff in town."

The cab pulled over and the driver turned off the meter at $4.70. The Seaspray Hotel had reached the stage where outright shabbiness was still a few years away but as inevitable as fate. It was five stories high, and from the upper two you could see the bay a couple of blocks north.

Dial took the satchel and slid out on the driver's side. The cabbie rolled down his window and showed Dial his saintly smile. Dial handed him a five-dollar bill. The driver turned it over and studied it, like an artifact from a lost continent.

"Hey," he said, "here in San Francisco we got this custom called the tip. Ever hear of it?"

"Yeah."

"So what are you waiting for?"

"My change."

The cabbie stared up at Dial. Without dimming his smile, he extended his hand over the windowsill and dropped three dimes into the gutter, one at a time.

"Thanks," Dial said. "Here's your tip." He flipped the business card in the cabbie's face.

"Hey," the cabbie said genially, "you're a cheap motherfucking cocksucker, you know that?" He dropped the transmission into gear and pulled carefully back into traffic.

The desk clerk was a very pretty man in his early twenties, with rings on each of his eight fingers. Dial gave his name as Geoffrey Davis, and the clerk made a production of checking a list. "Oh yes, Mr. Davis, I have your reservation right here." He flashed Dial a smile as impersonal as a whore's kiss. Dial gave the clerk three twenty-dollar bills for two nights and told him he'd find the room himself.

It was on the top floor and faced north. Dial put the satchel on the bed, and the springs creaked in futile protest. He pulled the chair around to the window and sat staring out. To his right were the commercial piers, to his left Aquatic Park, and directly ahead the cluttered length of Fisherman's Wharf. The day was bright and fog free. Above the slope of Russian Hill the north tower of the Golden Gate Bridge was visible, and beyond the bay the rolling hills of Marin County, green with the spring rains.

After a few minutes, a dreamy smile crept over Dial's features, and he began touching at the insides of his wrists, his fingertips barely contacting scarred flesh.

It was early afternoon when he left the Seaspray, carrying the leather satchel. He wore gray slacks, a fresh shirt under a light jacket, dark glasses. Though it was still a couple of weeks to Memorial Day, the sidewalks were crowded on this Saturday with tourists and locals alike; Fisherman's Wharf was among the required stops on a San Francisco visit. Along the Embarcadero the sidewalks were thick with milling masses, but Dial was in no great hurry. He moved with the crowd's flow, feeling better than he had in some time. Part of it was being away from Helena after so long together; part of it was the promise that Chris represented; part of it was the power he knew he commanded, and the pleasure it would provide later on this day. He looked around at the vacant-faced, gawking pedestrians with curiosity and a touch of pity.

He could pick any one of them and stub out his life like a cigarette butt.

Dial stopped at the railing of a bumper car ride and watched the squealing children furiously spinning the little steering wheels in desperate attempts to slam into someone, anyone. The cars' contact heads ratcheted back and forth across the overhead electrified grid, trailing shooting sparks. In the far corner from Dial, a small boy, too short to see over the car's cowling, had pulled over out of the melee. Suddenly another kid spotted him; he twisted the wheel hard, veered, and bore down on the boy at full speed. The boy paled and opened his mouth and tried to get out of the car, all at the same time. He was half-standing when the other car plowed into his side, and the impact tossed him out and into the retaining wall. There was a blood-chilling scream, and the ride operator, who had been deep in conversation with a girl in toreador pants, lunged for the controls. Above the cars the sparks died, and they slowly coasted to a stop; their arms stopped clicking against the metal grid, and the only noise was the boy's scream. The ride operator weaved between the stalled cars, looking stricken. Other adults followed, so within moments there was a knot of people hiding the screaming kid, saying the things people always said: "Give him air." "Keep him warm." "Call an ambulance." On the sidewalk behind Dial there was a popcorn cart, abandoned when its proprietor joined the throng around the kid. Dial helped himself to a bag and left a dollar bill under the salt shaker. When he got back to the railing of the bumper-car ride, a heavily muscled man in a sweatshirt held the boy, doll-like, in his arms. Blood from a deep gash in his forehead was streaming over his face, but he was still half-conscious and whimpering like a whipped puppy.

That's how it goes in real life, kid, Dial thought. If you try to hide in a corner, they find you every time, and when they do they kick the shit out of you. If you were smart, you got them before they even thought of getting you.

Farther down the sidewalk was a brassy-looking cocktail lounge. Dial peered in the window; all the waitresses were blond and wore hot pants. When he moved on, Dial realized that the place was divided in half, with separate entrances. One was marked "His and Hers"; the second was marked "His and His." Dial looked in the other window. This room was the mirror image of the other, except that on this side the ones in the blond wigs and hot pants were the waiters.

Across the street, a biker in a denim jacket and colors was trying to knock over a pyramid of three plastic milk bottles with a softball. The woman next to him was wearing high-cut satin shorts and a T-shirt tight enough to show the contour of her bra, had she been wearing a bra. She kept saying, "Come on, Dicky. I wanna goddamned stuffed dog." The biker reared and threw. Two bottles toppled, and the third teetered tantalizingly before righting itself. The woman said, "Come on, Dicky." The biker pushed the two remaining softballs into her hands and snarled, "Let's see you do better, Doris." The woman peered at the balls, trying to focus so there were only two of them. She cocked her arm, lost her balance, tried it again, and threw. Her momentum carried her over the counter, but the ball fell six feet short of the bottles. Dial stared at her butt; her shorts had ridden up into the crack of her ass, and she wasn't wearing underwear. Dial had thought he'd lost interest in that sort of thing, but since Chris . . .

"What the fuck are you staring at?" the biker said. The woman threw and failed to reach the bottles again. Dial looked reluctantly away from her butt and muttered, "Nothing."

"Come on, Dicky," the woman said. When she tugged at his arm her breasts jiggled. "I'm bored. Let's go somewhere."

"You didn't do so good, did you, Doris?" The biker seemed considerably cheered by her failure. "You know what, Doris? The only thing bigger 'n your tits is your mouth."

The woman steadied herself against the counter. "Is that so?" she said, with something like dignity. "Well, Dicky, the only thing smaller than your brain is your cock."

They glared at each other, and Dial felt a little thrill at the anticipation of violence. Instead, they burst into laughter. *Morons,* Dial thought.

He tilted back his head and poured the last kernels of popcorn from the bag into his mouth. At the end of the street he ducked under a neon sign that read "Spaced Out-dyssey" into a dimly lit place he thought was a bar. It turned out to be a video game arcade.

The only illumination came from a strip of hidden, low-wattage bulbs along the perimeter of the ceiling and from the game screens. They were lined up against opposite walls of the long, narrow room, and a child stood in front of nearly every one. The average age looked to be about ten, and almost all were boys. Each stared into his machine with total absorption, like a chicken watching the sun. The machine stared back, throwing its unnatural glow into the child's face, so in the eerie lighting each one's complexion took on a ghastly greenish pallor. The children looked like they had fallen under the mesmeric influence of zombies from outer space and were about to turn on their elders and eat their flesh. Dial stopped to watch over the shoulder of a child playing a game called "Berzerk!" Dial wasn't sure what the object was, but the child seemed to be accomplishing it with admirable dexterity; in one corner of the screen the score was running up like the stock exchange volume after an assassination. But then the entire screen exploded in a mind-searing flash, an unctuous mechanical voice made a sarcastic crack, and the screen went blank.

The child kicked the front of the machine and wheeled away; his fists were clenched, and a vein pulsed in the side of his neck.

"You'll get 'em next time," Dial said, in what he imagined to be a sympathetic tone.

"Get the fuck out of my way, asshole," the child snapped.

From where Dial stood the arcade seemed to bore endlessly into the building's bowels, like a portal to hell, but as Dial moved more deeply into it he made out the last of the machines and three doors labeled "Boys," "Girls," and "Manager."

He went into the boys' bathroom, squinting against the sudden glare of normal incandescent lighting. A child was peering into the mirror and forcing a comb through greasy hair, pulling it straight back so the sides of his head looked like the tail fins of a 1962 Cadillac.

"Hi," Dial said.

The child met his eyes in the mirror and gave Dial a dark, hard look. The child hawked, then broke the gaze and spit in the sink.

Dial went into one of the two stalls and latched the door. He unbuckled the satchel and removed a molded plastic box about four by four by six inches, white with green and yellow flowers in relief on the front. The case had come from a popular brand of air freshener. Dial peeled paper backing from two adhesive strips on the back and fixed the box to the wall above the toilet tank, out of reach of children. He flushed the toilet, rattled his belt buckle, and went back into the arcade's gloom. When he came onto the sidewalk he was whistling cheerfully.

That would fix the little shits.

In a restaurant at the far end of the Wharf, George Dial ate a grilled filet of red snapper, a side of wild rice, and a green salad. At this hour of the afternoon the place was almost empty, but by evening it would enjoy a large Saturday crowd. The waitress was a psychology major at San Francisco State, she said. The food was good and the service excellent. Dial left a good tip, and another of the plastic boxes in the men's room.

He hoped the waitress was off duty that evening; he'd kind of liked her.

At the shore end of the Wharf there was a gift shop whose stock ran to brightly painted plaster of Paris marlins mounted on bases with the exuberant legend, "I Visited Fisherman's Wharf!" Dial politely talked the owner into allowing him to use her restroom; it was an emergency, he said winningly. He left the third box there.

The last box found a home in the men's room of a cocktail lounge at the other end of Beach from the video arcade. It was called the Jolly Roger; the waitresses wore hip boots, black vinyl miniskirts, and eye patches, and the customers wore enough leather to shoe the populace of an emerging nation. Dial left by the back door. He removed the brown paper-wrapped parcel from the satchel and stuffed it inside his jacket, then discarded the satchel in a trash dumpster at the end of an alley.

In his room on the fifth floor of the Seaspray, Dial stripped the wrapping from the parcel. Inside was a cardboard carton, and inside it, cushioned in curls of styrofoam excelsior, was a metal box painted dull black, about the same size as the boxes he'd scattered around the Wharf district. On the front were two rows of two black snap-covers and a fifth below them, enameled red. Below the four black caps were push-to-make button switches; below the red cap was a toggle, a red pilot light, and a raised-letter tape label reading "enable." From the top of the box Dial extended a four-section whip antenna.

Dial aimed the antenna toward the ceiling and flipped the toggle. The pilot light blinked faintly. Dial slowly lowered the antenna, aiming it at the Wharf, and the light began to blink more brightly.

He pointed the antenna at the seafood restaurant at the far end of the pier, and the pilot light glowed blood red.

George Dial laughed with the heady pleasure of it. In his hands he held power. He placed the black box tenderly on the bed and took his seat by the window. On the street people streamed past in their endless flow.

Dial imagined them screaming and bleeding and torn, saw pieces of their arms and legs and heads flying through the air.

He thought of Chris Amado, and the life they were

destined to make together. He thought of Helena, and the humiliation she had heaped on him all those years he had believed she cared for him. The afternoon meandered on, and Dial did not note the passage of time, lost as he was in his drifting fantasies.

Chapter Thirty-four

Matt Conte's kidneys were taking a hell of a beating. The roadbed of the desert track was washboard gravel that hadn't seen a grader's blade since Prohibition, and the big semi rig was as hard sprung as a tank. Hanging on to the wheel and keeping the tractor-trailer combo on the rough road was a constant struggle.

After leaving the warehouse, the truck had remained on the interstate for about twenty-five miles before taking the Wadsworth exit and heading north on State Route 34. Here the road was two lane blacktop, but it was too isolated and the terrain too flat for effective tailing.

The alternative was to take the truck. So Conte took the truck.

Jerry, the gateman from the warehouse, was either still in the back seat of the Camaro or beginning a long hike back to civilization. The truck driver was curled up in an inert lump on the floor of the cab in front of the passenger seat dressed in jockey shorts and a dingy gray T-shirt stained with blood. Conte wore the guy's fatigues and web gunbelt, into which he had transferred his .45.

On the seat beside him was a hand-sketched map. He hoped the driver had been scared enough to draw it accurately.

Conte was worried. It was an unfamiliar emotion, and it came from tying in with other people. He did not like the way worry felt, but for all his rationalization about Chris looking out for herself, he could not shake his concern. She was in a hell of a lot deeper than he, and she was his partner.

His attention had drifted from his driving, and too late

Conte realized the curve was sharper than he'd figured. He eased off on the gas and fought the impulse to jab at the brakes as the trailer began to drift. He wrestled the wheel one-handed, took a chance and dropped the transmission two gears. The trailer teetered on the edge of lost control. Conte tapped at the gas, holding his breath.

Slowly, reluctantly, the trailer began to track again.

Conte worked down through the rest of the gears and pulled the rig to a shaky stop. He let out breath, unaware he had been holding it in. From the blouse of his fatigues he fished out a cigarette and the Zippo. He got the butt lit on the third try.

"Both hands on the wheel."

Conte coughed out smoke. Framed in the passenger-side window was the business end of a broad-shouldered man with close-cropped salt-and-pepper hair. His hand was just outside the window, and there was a gun in it, aimed at Conte's right temple. The man's eyes darted to the body on the floorboards.

"What the hell?" Conte protested.

The man stepped off the running board and swung the door open so he could keep a clean line on Conte. "Slide across and get out. Take all the time you need, but don't let me lose sight of the hands."

Conte had to raise his feet and shinny them along the dashboard to get past the body on the floor. He stepped down and leaned agaist the side of the trailer in the classic four-point stance. The .45 ceased to make weight on his hip.

"Where are you going?"

Conte started to turn.

"Uh-uh," the broad-shouldered man cautioned. "Second and last time: where are you going?"

"Houston," Conte said over his shoulder. "I must have taken a wrong turn at Denver."

There was a gunmetal click behind him. Conte knew the sound intimately.

"Hey, ease up, buddy," Conte protested. "I'm a working guy on a run."

"I don't think so."

"Listen, pal, unless they passed a law against driving a

truck since the last time I was in Nevada, one of us is in big trouble."

"Yeah," the other guy said. "Guess who. You always pack a pistol on a run?"

"I'm a nervous guy."

"What about the fellow bleeding on your floormats? Was he a nervous guy too?"

"I didn't get a chance to ask."

Behind Conte the broad-shouldered man sighed. "Let's start with something simple: who are you?"

"His name is Matthew Conte."

No one seemed to have anything to add to that, so Conte chanced turning around, moving cautiously and keeping his hands over his head.

The big man still had the gun out, but it was pointed at the ground somewhere between them. Next to him was another guy in fatigues. He was a head shorter, almost boyishly slim-waisted, and he wore very dark sunglasses.

"He isn't a threat to us," the short man said. His partner uncocked the pistol and holstered it.

"Don't be so sure," Conte said. "Having guns pointed my way always gets my back hair up. Who are you guys?"

The short one removed his sunglasses, and Conte said, "Well, son of a bitch."

Vang responded with a polite nod.

Conte lowered his hands and looked from one man to the other. "Will one of you please tell me what the fuck is going on?"

"Sorry." The big man offered Conte his gun, butt out.

"Thanks," Conte said dryly. He reholstered the weapon. "I always feel naked without it."

The big man's hand was extended. "I'm Bill Price," he said. "It looks like we're all on the same side."

Conte stared at the proffered hand, then clasped it. "Wonderful," he said with weary resignation. "Now if anyone can tell me what side that is, I'll die a happy man."

Chapter Thirty-five

Dennison laughed and said, "If I'm not Charles Martin Stern, you've gone to a lot of trouble for nothing."

Chris Amado tensed, ready to back her boss's play if the charade went to hell.

Bressio regarded Dennison with faint superior amusement. He opened a folder on his desk, glanced at the top sheet of typescript, and said, "Where were you born?"

"This is absurd," Dennison said.

"Where were you born?"

Dennison sighed. "Potsdam, New York. A lovely place."

"Your mother's maiden name?"

"Now there's a good question." Dennison seemed to be having a good time. "I included it in the first interrogation model Stern Associates produced, in 1961. It has all the qualities of a perfect control query: simple, direct, the correct answer can be confirmed independently, and as an indicator it is almost one hundred percent accurate." Dennison scanned his audience—Bressio, Turin, Helena Frome, Chris, Skelton, and Miss Paradise—like a professor counting the house at his first lecture of the semester. "Everyone knows his mother's maiden name."

Dennison looked back to Bressio. "My mother's maiden name is Bernhard."

But Bressio's amusement waxed. "Would you pull up your left pant leg, please?" The courtesy was sardonic.

Dennison was clearly disconcerted. He masked it with annoyance. "This has gone far enough," he protested. "You had me kidnapped. If you don't believe I'm who you wanted that's your problem. I don't see why I should help you confirm your success. I'm willing to agree that I'm not Charles Martin Stern, and my wife and I will be on our way."

"It doesn't work that way," Bressio said.

"Then what do you—"

"Memorizing quiz questions is one thing," Bressio said. "Bullet scars are another." He checked the typewritten sheet again. "At the age of fourteen, Charles Martin Stern and a schoolmate were taking target practice with a .22 short one-shot pistol in an abandoned quarry outside Potsdam. Stern was checking the holes in a tin can when his friend accidentally shot him in the left calf. The bullet lodged in muscle, did no real damage, and was never removed, so there is no exit wound.

"Just as everyone has a mother with a maiden name," Bressio said, "everyone has one or two identifying marks. May we see yours, Mr. . . . Stern?"

"You may not," Dennison said.

Bressio stood so he could see over the desk and nodded to Skelton.

The stickman pinned Dennison's arms behind him. Eddie Turin dropped to one knee and skinned up Dennison's trousers. A seam ripped.

Bressio stopped smiling.

In the meaty part of Dennison's calf, five inches below the knee, was a round, puckered ridge of scar, faded by time but still apparent, no bigger across than a dime.

"Even today I sometimes feel a twinge, an hour before a thunderstorm," Dennison said. "Your man is hurting my arms."

"Let him go," Bressio ordered.

Skelton reluctantly released Dennison. Dennison stretched the kinks out of his arms and massaged the elbow joints.

"I'm a cautious man, Stern," Bressio said.

"Good for you."

"Nobody knows what you really look like. I can't afford to make mistakes."

"May we get on with this?" Dennison said. "What do you want from me? Money, I suppose."

"Oh yes. Money is an excellent place to start. How does one million dollars sound?"

"Extravagant," Dennison said coolly.

Bressio took another page from the folder and pushed it toward Dennison. "This describes a location in the vicinity and gives instructions for finding it from the air. Between six-fifty-five and seven-oh-five this evening—not early, and definitely not later—the money is to be dropped at this site." Bressio checked his watch. "That is approximately four hours from now."

Bressio gestured at the phone on the desk. "This is tied to a radio in the back room, which transmits through the antenna you saw on the rim of the canyon. You will use it to contact the appropriate person in your organization, and you will read that person these instructions. You will say nothing else, and you will answer no questions."

"And if I don't," Dennison said, "or if the money is not delivered, I will of course be killed."

"You will of course *not* be killed. You are probably the more secure kidnap victim in the history of the crime." Bressio glanced speculatively at the tall, green-clad figure of Miss Paradise. "I suppose I could kill your lovely wife," he said contemplatively, as if the idea had just occurred. "But that would be a waste." He looked at Eddie Turin. "It's been some time since most of the boys have had R&R, hasn't it?"

"Yeah," Turin said. He gave Miss Paradise a long once-over. "I'll bet with this one you'd get plenty of recreation and not much rest."

Miss Paradise responded with a look of such searing disdain that Turin blanched.

"This is getting us nowhere," Dennison said.

"I agree," Bressio said briskly. "The facts are these, Stern: whether the money is delivered or not, you will be kept alive and in good health. I can't say the same for your wife, and I can't promise you complete freedom from pain; that all depends on your cooperation."

"In what?"

"In becoming a valuable member of my organization." Bressio aimed a forefinger at Dennison's chest. "You, Mr. Stern, are intimately familiar with some fascinating matters—such as national security, international relations including unpublicized agreements, top secret systems of weaponry, communications, intelligence—hi-tech defense systems in general. I'd be interested in knowing what has been developed, what is on the drawing board, and what is being contemplated.

"I suspect," Bressio continued, "that you are also intimate with what one might call gossip: the sort of information that could be extremely embarrassing to people in positions of power around the world. You're going to share that with me."

"That will be difficult," Dennison said, "if I'm dead."

"Your life is in no immediate danger. I thought I made that clear."

"If you don't plan to kill me and you don't plan to release me, why should I pay you one million dollars?"

"Because you are a humanitarian, Stern. If the money is not paid, there *will* be death. A great many people who have nothing to do with this will die without warning."

George, Chris thought.

"One of my men is in San Francisco," Bressio said. "By now he has planted four white phosphorus incendiary devices in strategic locations on Fisherman's Wharf and in the immediate vicinity. I understand it's a balmy, springlike Saturday in San Francisco today. Would you care to guess how many hundreds of people will be in range of those explosives by seven-thirty this evening?"

Bressio did not wait for an answer. "You are an amateur chemist, Stern. You are familiar with the properties of white phosphorus, and you know the destructive potential of an explosive device employing that element. First, the primary detonations will destroy most people and structures within the immediate vicinity; the exact range depends on the thickness and number of walls containing the explosions. Second, nonfatal injuries will be agonizingly painful; a tiny speck of white phosphorus will burn a hole in the flesh down to the bone. Finally, the flash temperature is several thousand degrees, so spontaneous combustion will occur in nearby structures, and the resultant fires will quickly spread.

"Picture the scene," Bressio said. "The Wharf is a cul-de-sac, so anyone whom the explosion doesn't kill or maim will be cut off. Some will jump into the bay, a fifty-foot drop in the dark. Those too old or young or disoriented or panicked to jump will face a wall of flame. It's possible a section of the Wharf might shear completely off.

"At the same time," Bressio said, "there will be two

more explosions at either end of Beach Street. Emergency personnel will converge on the scene, but not for long minutes. Meanwhile the terror will be unimaginable. People who might otherwise have survived will be trampled. Others will be overcome by the smoke or the heat. It will be unlike anything seen outside a combat zone."

"How?" Dennison asked calmly.

"I beg your pardon?"

"How is all of this going to happen?"

Bressio considered. "I don't see any harm in answering that. The incendiaries are self-contained in a package with a radio-triggered microprocessor detonator. The man who planted them has the remote. At seven-thirty this evening—it should be about full dark in San Francisco then—he will trigger the devices. Unless he receives my order to abort, via this phone, before that time."

"You sick son of a bitch," Miss Paradise said in a low icy voice. "Someone ought to gut you and hang you up to bleed." She advanced on Bressio, her fists balled.

Skelton got one claw around her wrist—and Miss Paradise turned and twisted and did something with her feet and Skelton was flipping over her in an awkward flailing arc that was all arms and legs. He hit the plank flooring along the length of his spine, hard enough to crack the planking. He stared upside down at Miss Paradise towering above him, with more surprise than pain. This wasn't the way it was supposed to go: he hurt woman, not the other way around. Finally his eyes fluttered and closed, as if his nerve system were so wire-thin it took a long time for it to register and transmit pain to his brain.

"That's all right, my dear," Dennison said mildly. He looked down at the man on the floor and shook his head, as if he might actually feel sorry for him. "How do I know," he said to Bressio, "that you won't detonate the incendiaries even if the ransom is paid?"

Bressio was staring curiously at Miss Paradise. On the floor, Skelton groaned and stirred and lay still again.

"You don't," Bressio said. "But you'll be the one gambling with the lives of several hundred people."

"In any case, neither I nor my wife will be released."

"Correct."

Dennison looked suddenly weary, worn down by responsibilities he had not asked for and for which he did not have the strength to cope. "What in God's name do you hope to accomplish?" Defeat rang in his tone.

"In the short term, a great deal. For one thing, it will prove it can be done. People will know that anywhere, anytime, a holocaust of this magnitude can be unleashed on a mass of innocent people in a major American city. The act will reveal in vivid detail how toothless this country's law enforcement really is—how a single man with a bomb can cause havoc, with the authorities powerless to stop him."

"They'll stop you," Miss Paradise said. She held Dennison's hand. "They'll come at you with everything they have, and they won't stop until they find you and crush you to dirt. You'll think you were hit by a train."

"That's where your husband comes in. With whom and what you know, Stern, my people will be able to breach security at every level, up to the very highest. I'll use the dirty little secrets you are going to reveal to me to throw the law enforcement community into a spate of such infighting among themselves they'll never be able to coordinate an effective effort against me. By the time they've sorted out their squabbles, it will be too late.

"Because in the meantime," Bressio said, "the citizens of this country will be helping me immensely—even if they are not aware of it. First, the terrorist attacks engineered by my people will inspire copycat acts. People who are already afraid to walk the streets will go from suspicion to paranoia. Those who can afford to will barricade themselves in their homes; those who cannot will attack those who can. Class and racial warfare are excellent possibilities. Civil liberties will finally be suspended; perhaps martial law will be invoked. In the attempt to restore order, many more people will die.

"As the system is undermined, democracy will turn into anarchy, and then into chaos. The only law in force will be the law of the jungle."

"Why?" Dennison's face was drawn. "How will this possibly benefit you?"

"I'll be in control."

"Over a wasteland."

"A wasteland can be rebuilt." Bressio placed both palms flat on the desk. "Mr. Stern, I am a patriot. I love this country, and I've watched it governed by compromise and concession and moderation. I've seen it become a second-rate nation in a second-rate world—because it is weak.

"Because our country is weak," Bressio said, "I believe it's in grave danger. We are at war, whether declared or not. Because as soon as the USSR perceives that our weakness is great enough to allow them to unleash a nuclear attack with impunity, they will. If we let that happen, this country will lose millions, not hundreds."

"Sometimes the cure is worse than the disease," Dennison said.

"That may be. But the patient comes out stronger. It is time for change, Mr. Stern. This time it will be done correctly."

On the floor, Skelton rolled over and dragged himself to a corner, like a coyote that had chewed its way out of a trap. No one seemed to notice.

"What's your plan to save the world?" Miss Paradise said.

Bressio looked at her. "Strike first. Hit them so hard they won't get back up for generations."

"With nuclear weapons?"

"Unless you know of something more effective."

There was something fascinating in Bressio's hypnotic monologue—and in a flash of horror, Chris Amado saw what it was.

"Go ahead," Bressio said to Dennison. "Tell me I'm insane."

"You're crazy as six waltzing mice," Miss Paradise said.

"All right," Bressio said amiably. "Now tell me it can't be done."

No one answered.

Bressio was crazy, but he was right: it *could* be done.

And Chris had less than four hours to figure a way to step between Bressio's horrific dream and an even more horrific reality.

Chapter Thirty-six

Above the desert, five miles across a bowl-shaped alkali sink, a turkey vulture spread its wings to their full five-foot span and wheeled into a kamikaze dive, tiny capped head extended, tail up and straight, muscle-motionless as it plummeted toward the barren, hardpack sand at a seventy-degree angle, its flight line as straight as a rifle shot. Too late the scavenger bird pulled out of the sash-weight drop—but then, in a violation of gravity and physics and nature, it was not too late after all, and the vulture came to a hovering stop inches above the track of the dirt road. Talons stabbed into the cold carrion body of some desert varmint—a gopher, or maybe a jack rabbit—that had been crushed into a mush of blood and fur under the wheels of some rig, possibly Matt Conte's semi. The vulture had no interest in the species of its prize nor in the way of its demise. As long as it was dead meat, the vulture was satisfied.

Conte watched the bird flap lazily west. There was a vague bilious taste in his mouth, but it didn't come from the vulture. Conte's acquired art of patience was being stretched to the limit. His partner was either nearby or there were people nearby who could—and would—tell him where she was.

People were going to die on the desert this day. Conte looked at the speck that was the retreating vulture and thought, *That's just an appetizer, pal. Stick around for the all-you-can-eat buffet.*

Twenty-five yards upslope, Vang and Price had taken cover behind a semicircle of square-sheared boulders about waist high, the shape of a kid's snow fort. Conte checked the terrain beyond, then crouched and dog-trotted in their direction, dropping into the enclosure next to Vang.

Another twenty-five yards farther on was the rim of the steep-sided bowl that contained the compound that the old-time prospector had described to Price in Winnemucca. The space between was an open no man's land of rocky rubble and a few stunted, gray-purple sagebrush, roots clawed into the sterile ground and holding on for dear life. It was coming on to mid-afternoon, and although it was not much over seventy degrees, the sky was absolutely clear and the sun sharp, stern, intrusive. There was no breeze.

"There," Vang said, and nodded toward the rim.

Conte uncapped the field glasses hanging from a thong around his neck and found the man in their frame. Conte adjusted the thumbscrew, and the blurry image resolved into a hard-jawed face.

"Terry Picard," he said in a low voice. "One of Bressio's bodymen in New York. No one knew where he came from, but somewhere along the line he learned some interesting ways to use a Buck knife." Picard had pasty Gallic features and a nose that had been broken so often it looked like the vulture's beak. His khaki fatigues were stained under the arms. He was carrying an M16 carbine by its folding handle, and he looked bored.

"How many others?" Price asked.

"Just him that I can see."

"Four in all," Vang said in his soft, toneless voice.

Conte lowered the glasses. "Are you sure?"

"He's sure," Price said.

"A moment, please," Vang said, and backed out of the enclosure.

Conte put the binocs on Picard again. The hard-faced sentry looked around self-consciously, like a schoolgirl contemplating shoplifting, then slipped his arm through the M16's web sling and shrugged it over his shoulder. He pulled a tin of Copenhagen snoose from his blouse pocket, twisted off the top, dipped a pinch, and stuffed it between his cheek and gum. He was replacing the top when Vang appeared in Conte's field of vision.

Vang cupped Picard's chin in the palm of his left hand and jerked his head back. Picard's eyes bulged as Vang jabbed his knife between the two lowest back ribs into Picard's kidney. In what seemed like the same motion Vang pulled the blade free, and for a moment it flashed silver-red in the thin sunlight before Vang drew it across Picard's taut, exposed throat. The

248 *Dennison's War*

front of his neck peeled open, and blood flushed over the front of his blouse. Vang caught the limp corpse under the arms and pulled it behind a coffin-shaped boulder.

His back still to them, Vang raised two fingers of his hand and made a forward chopping motion. "Let's go," Price said.

They caught a glimpse of the next guard along the rim as they scrambled forward, but the man was sitting against a rock, his back to them and his head down, dozing and dreaming and fifty yards from death. Conte and Price dropped prone next to Vang in a little swale, the vestigial remnant of a long-dead creek. It afforded enough cover for the moment, and it gave them a panoramic view of the compound two hundred feet below, nestled within the protection of the high walls.

Conte used the glasses to scan the buildings. Several men were helping to unload a semi at one of the Quonset huts; another group was lounging around the front of the long barracks. In all there were about a dozen men in sight.

"I can put a name to seven or eight of them," Conte said softly. "Some of them came into New York with Bressio, and others jumped to Bressio from the Families. But none of those were missed much by the Old Men. They were punks, strongarm men who liked to push too hard, who got their kicks from breaking the arms of candy-store owners or running girls, because candy-store owners and girls can't push back."

On the edge of his field of vision Conte caught new movement. "There are a couple of West Coast and Nevada boys; I suppose they jumped, too. Bressio must be paying plenty." Conte got the wooden frame command structure in focus. "Dennison filled you in on Bressio and those two scumbag mercs we're after, right?"

"Right," Price said.

"Add in what you told me, and you can figure this Creed—however he and Bressio are tied in—he isn't running any kind of survivalist community. This is a summer camp for killers."

A tall, slim figure came onto the porch below. "Eddie Turin," Conte said. "Looking real pleased with himself." There was movement behind him; Conte fine-tuned the binocs focus.

"God damn," he swore, too loudly.

The sound of bootheels scraping rock cut the crisp air. Conte raised up and got sight of the guard who had been dozing. He was looking around, wondering if he had heard a voice or dreamed it.

"Sorry," Conte muttered. "I'm not used to the great outdoors."

"Excuse me," Vang said, and slipped away.

Conte looked back to the porch and swore again, more quietly. Eddie Turin was leading a parade down the switchback staircase. Dennison and Miss Paradise were behind him, with Chris Amado and a chisel-faced woman who had to be Helena Frome next in line. A tall and impossibly skinny guy brought up the rear.

Conte offered the glasses to Price, who shook his head and said, "Thanks, I get the picture." He was following Conte's line of sight, and there was a hard set to his mouth. Conte tracked the little formation across the flat floor of the compound to the small billet with the barred windows.

"We've seen enough," Price murmured.

Vang materialized as they backed out of the shallow swale and turned downslope. Conte noticed a smear of red on the sleeve of Vang's blouse; on the otherwise immaculate garment, the blood was as jarringly out of place as an overcoat in a nudist colony.

They ducked past the semicircular enclosure, circled behind the lip of the rise running up to the rim, then trotted across the flat toward the butte behind which they had left the semi, along with the Land Rover Price had rented in Winnemucca. Conte was breathing harder than he should have been when they reached it. He chalked it up to the thin air and dug out a cigarette.

Price got a canteen from the back of the Rover. He took three shallow gulps of water, then passed it to Vang. Both were breathing normally.

"The guy Hammond you're after," Conte said when he was able. "For an innocent lamb, he's sure fallen in with wolves."

"Hammond isn't our main concern," Price said, "although I'd like to get him out of there in one piece if possible.

He did serve under Creed in Nam, and I think Creed may have tried to exploit his one-time loyalty."

"And subvert it." Vang passed the canteen to Conte.

"Apparently," Price agreed. "But even if Hammond is a sort of innocent bystander, that doesn't go for the rest of those men down there. Conte's identified enough of them so there is no question we're up against a well-trained army of professional killers. Does anyone doubt that?"

Conte shook his head and drank. Some of the water went down the wrong way, and he coughed and drank more slowly. Price seemed to have appropriated the position of leader, but so far Conte had no quarrel with that. The guy sure as hell seemed to know what he was about.

"Our original assignment—to liberate Sergeant Hammond—is on standby," Price said, "as is yours, Conte—the execution of Frome and Dial. The primary mission now is to find out how Bressio and Creed are tied together, and in what."

"We've already got a good idea," Conte said. "Creed's running an army and training them for jobs like popping that North Dakota bank. Bressio has taken those two creeps Frome and Dial into his roost and is running the flash stuff—the kidnappings, the extortion."

"I agree," Vang said, "to a point. But I suspect there's more to it."

"There probably is." The cigarette tasted lousy, and Conte flicked it away, half-smoked. "But there's no point in playing high school debate club over this. Those people down there are bad trouble. I say we plow them under—right here, right now."

"What are Dennison and Miss Paradise doing in that compound?"

"Playacting." Conte filled them in on Chris's tip-off about the Stern kidnapping. "Dennison took Stern's place." He took another sip from the canteen. "I don't understand what Miss P. is doing there, though."

"She is with him," Vang said.

"How's that?"

"She never allows him out of her sight," Price explained. "That's one of her rules."

"I thought Dennison made the rules."

Price allowed himself a faint grin. "Not all of them."

Conte recapped the canteen. "All right, we've agreed that the butler did it. How are we going in?"

"We're not," Price said. "Not yet."

"Three of our people are down there."

"I know that, Conte," Price said without anger. "That's my point. Substituting for Stern wasn't some wild-ass, last-minute idea of Dennison's. He has a plan."

"He must have whipped it up goddamned quick."

"Over the years," Vang said, "Dennison has had some experience in contigency planning."

"All right," Conte conceded. "So he went in with a plan. But Bressio is one ruthless son of a bitch, and from what you tell me, Creed didn't get through 'Nam without learning a few things—like him living and the enemy dying. How do we know Dennison's plan is working? What if his Stern cover didn't hold?"

"And there is Chris," Vang suggested.

"I'll admit I'm worried about her, too," Conte said.

"She is a professional."

"She hasn't walked the same streets we have."

"She appeared to be secure when we observed her from the rim."

"That doesn't mean anything," Conte pressed. "She's . . ."

"A woman?" Vang suggested. "Yes, I noticed that the first time I saw her."

"All of us are concerned, Conte," Price said. "About all three of them. Concern comes with the territory. We're going to do everything we can to assure they get out of there whole. But if we charge in now, we may screw up more than we accomplish. Maybe the three of us can take that camp—we'd better figure we can, anyway—but for now we hold off and give Dennison a chance to run with the ball."

"You're playing God."

"I'm not playing at all, and neither is Dennison. We're serious as all hell. That's why we are sitting tight."

Conte turned abruptly away. He suddenly did not want either man to see through the transparency of his anger to the fear he felt for Chris Amado, thinking somehow it would make him less strong in their eyes. He got out a cigarette, stared at it sourly, and was replacing it unlit when he felt a touch on his shoulder, light as a snowflake.

"Have faith."

Vang's emotionless mask was intact, but there was compassion and reassurance in his tone.

Conte looked at him. "Sure," he said cynically. "Faith in the Almighty?"

"Faith in Dennison," Vang said.

Chapter Thirty-seven

The man in the next cell wore a pair of skivvy shorts, white wool socks, and nothing else. He lay on the bare mattress, his back to the bars, knees drawn up to his chin in the fetal position. There was a livid bruise above the waistband of the skivvies, over his right kidney. The man was moaning, but the sound was instinctive, without expression or emotion, a monotonic reaffirmation that he remained alive.

Miss Paradise had climbed up on one of the metal crosspieces that braced the cell's bars. She ran her fingers around their tops, then got down and checked the crease where the bars were bolted to the wooden outer wall of the building, and the edge of the floor. She stood, dusted at the knees of the green jumpsuit, and said to Dennison, "I don't think we're wired."

"Thank you, my dear." Dennison was staring at the back of the man in the adjacent cell. "Albert," Dennison said softly.

The man stopped moaning, but did not move.

"We're friends, Albert." He remembered what Price had said about delayed stress syndrome. "We're Americans."

Albert Hammond unfolded his body one joint at a time, moving as stiffly as an octogenarian. He managed to turn his head toward Dennison.

He did not look badly hurt physically, but his eyes were haunted, hollow, the pupils as big as silver dollars. The effect was so disconcerting that Dennison had to study the man for several seconds before he was sure this was the person in Elaine Hammond's photo.

"Are you all right, Albert?"

Hammond stared back out of his otherworldly eyes, then began to laugh. His laughter was a demonic, cacophonous noise having nothing to do with joy; it sounded like a canvas bag of chains rolling down a staircase. After a time it degenerated into the same toneless moan. Hammond turned away and curled back into a ball.

Miss Paradise was watching this pathetic scene with a drawn expression. Dennison took her hand in both of his and said, "Are you all right?"

Miss Paradise pulled away. "Yeah," she said tightly. "But some other people aren't going to be so good." She squared her shoulders. "What's the poor bastard doing here anyway? What does Creed get out of turning the guy into a vegetable?"

If she had a weakness, Dennison thought, it was compassion. She could not keep from becoming involved, and he worried that some day involvement would warp her judgment in a fatal way. Dennison knew that you could not let the tiniest fraction of your attention wander once the fight was made. A hairline fracture in your mental armor could widen into a chasm.

Yet she always had taken care of herself, and Dennison knew from experience that she was the equal of any of his People, as a warrior and as a survivor.

"Originally," Dennison said, "the advertisement in the survivalist magazine was probably an attempt to legitimize this operation. My guess is that at one time Creed actually considered the idea of recruiting men like Hammond here, men who had come under his influence in Nam and could still be manipulated."

"Or driven over the brink."

"Creed should have figured on it." Dennison looked at Hammond again. "Anyone who'd still fall for his crap ten years later would have to be unstable to begin with."

Miss Paradise sat on the bunk. "All right, boss dear. What now?"

It was a damned good question. Two hours earlier, Dennison had made the call demanded by Bressio. He read Bressio's instructions to one of Stern's people, the Young Man named Paul. Since Bressio would obviously monitor the call, Dennison had briefed Paul on how to answer: for Bressio's benefit, Paul was to say his instructions would be followed.

In fact, Dennison had ordered him to ignore the call. Paul was not to arrange for any ransom delivery, nor was he to attempt to help Dennison. Most importantly, he was not to contact the authorities.

Dennison knew the caliber of young man Stern employed. Paul would follow orders.

Which meant Dennison and Miss Paradise were on their own.

Dennison did not fear death. He had lived intimately with its lurking presence all his adult life, so by now it was only an annoyance, constantly with him but basically inconsequential, like an amputee's phantom itch.

But there were other fears he could never conquer, and did not wish to. He feared for the country to which he had dedicated his life, and the good people who lived within and made its system work. And he feared for those few who fought at his command, the lives that he brokered like some kind of cosmic chessmaster.

The antidote to fear was action.

"Five o'clock," Miss Paradise said, sensing his thoughts. "Two and a half hours before . . ." There was no point to finishing.

Dennison lowered himself stiffly to the bunk, and Miss Paradise rested her cheek on his shoulder. Dennison stroked her golden hair.

"For now it's up to Chris," he said.

"I hope she's as good as you think, boss."

"We'll give her the chance." Dennison ran one finger along the smooth skin of her forehead. "If it turns out she can't handle it, we've always got the old fallbacks."

"Oh no," Miss Paradise protested. "I've sworn off showing my tits to save your ass."

She was kidding. She had an extraordinary sense of Dennison's mood, knew when he needed to be pushed and when he needed to be propped up, an arcane and dear intuition comprised of instinct, affection, and savvy.

In the next cell the pitch of Albert Hammond's desperate moan rose sharply. Dennison pulled away and went to the bars.

Hammond might be beyond their help, but several hundred people in San Francisco were not—at least not yet.

Hammond wailed on. *The clangor of hell's bell*, Dennison thought. *It tolls for thee*.

"Take the girl with you."

"The Frome bitch?"

"We'll see to her when this is over. I mean the Amado woman."

Eddie Turin grinned. "My pleasure."

Bressio glanced at the digital watch on his left wrist. "Leave in twenty minutes. That will get you to the drop site by six-forty-five. Give them until seven-ten at the outside, and then get back here immediately whether the money is delivered or not."

"Why the girl?" Turin asked. "I mean why in the first place? That story of hers—"

"—happened to be true," Bressio finished. "As far as we could follow it, the details jibed all the way down the line."

"All right. So why do we need her?"

"We don't." Bressio studied Turin; it occurred that the ex-Mafioso needed some cutting down to size as well. "But she came in handy on the Stern assignment and did an adequately convincing job."

"So," Turin said, "are you convinced?"

"That's irrelevant," Bressio said. "I don't trust her because I don't need to. She's been useful, but now that we have Stern there will be no difficulty recruiting useful allies. Before too long they'll be beating down our door. Which is why I want her to accompany you to the drop.

"Be certain," Bressio said, "that you return alone."

Chapter Thirty-eight

Across the alkali sink to the west was a jagged ridge. It looked to be ten miles away and was probably three times as far; distances were deceptive in the desert, and the punishment for underestimating them was harsh. Except for nomad tribes, prospectors addled by heat and thirst as much as gold lust, and the odd outlaw on the run, no one in history had ever come into this country voluntarily. The desert was a place for passing through on the way to somewhere—anywhere—else. On the faraway ridge, the vulture Conte had seen a few hours earlier would lay its egg on a bare rock ledge and abandon it immediately for the sun to incubate. From the moment it breathed air, the hatchling would be on its own, to survive or die.

Which was the name of the game, Conte thought.

Somewhere on that ridge, the vulture was finishing its carrion meal. Not far from where Conte, Vang, and Price had set up their base, a band of human vultures was preparing to do the same.

The sun sat a few degrees above the ridge, red-yellow and twice as big as it appeared from the canyons of New York's streets. Conte's Rolex read six-thirty-two. Within twenty minutes the sun would touch the horizon; full dark would come quickly after that.

Conte crushed out his tenth cigarette in the last three hours and turned to Price. They had played the waiting game long enough, dammit. But Price beat him to the punch.

"Vang will go in alone at twilight," he said, "primarily to make contact with Dennison. You may also be able to liberate him and Miss Paradise, but you'll have to play that part by ear." Price turned to Conte. "I understand you're a pretty fair shot."

"I am." It was a statement of fact.

"Good," Price said. "You take the ridge, and I'll stand

by in the Rover, outside the defile that leads into the compound. If Vang is blown and needs help, I'll listen for your shots before going in. Questions?"

"Yeah," Conte said. "What do we have for firepower?"

Price swung open the back door of the Rover and folded up the benches that ran perpendicular to the front seat, fastening them up against the side walls by their web straps. Under each was two long, metal boxes with padlocked hasps. Price spun the combination dials, undid the latches, and stepped back to give Conte a look.

In the first box were three Armalite AR-15 automatic rifles and a dozen speedloader magazines, two thirty-round boxes welded end to end in an L shape; when the first was empty, it took only a couple of seconds to drop it out, flip the assembly, recharge, and fire. The extra forward weight also helped compensate against muzzle climb.

From the other box Vang took an AK-47 assault rifle. He caught Conte's look.

"I had a chance to field-test both your M16 and the Communists' Kalashnikov," Vang explained. He seated a banana clip and pulled back the operating handle, and Conte heard the click of the bolt carrier chambering the first cartridge. "The Americans were more reliable allies, but the Communists made more reliable guns."

Conte shrugged. "I knew guys who carried AKs when they could get the ammo, but something about depending on a Red gun rubbed me the wrong way."

"Depending on a weapon that jammed at the most unpleasant moments had the same effect on me," Vang murmured.

But Conte was no longer paying attention. In the bottom of the second box, under several coils of rope, another long gun was wrapped in a scrap of cloth. Conte threw back the flaps and smiled. The rifle was a Winchester Model 70 bolt-action chambered for .458 Magnum. It had the kick of grain alcohol and enough muzzle energy to drill a neat half-inch hole through a yard of white pine. Mounted above the receiver was a variable-power Leatherwood scope. Conte raised the gun to his shoulder, sighted, and sighed with satisfaction. "It'll do," he murmured. "I can't wait to see what's in the other boxes."

"Mostly explosives," Price said. "Do you have any experience with HE grenades?"

Conte frowned at him. "Yeah," he said. "My experience is that they're real nice for getting out of a jam."

"Good," Price said, "because it looks like—"

Behind them Vang interrupted, "Vehicle motor, small rig. Coming this way."

Conte strained his ears. Ten seconds passed before he made out the faint mechanical rumble.

"Check it out," Price told him.

"On my way."

The butte was about thirty feet high at its flat top, just long enough to hide the semi rig. By the time Conte got up on it, the sound of the motor cut clearly through the thin air. He moved to the leading edge of the plateau, braced his knees and elbows in a prone firing position, and laid his eye socket against the rubber gasket of the scope.

The rig was an open-top Jeep CJ-7, five hundred yards distant and closing. Conte clicked the Leatherwood up to 4X magnification.

Above the steering wheel, Eddie Turin's face came into focus. There was a cigarette dangling from the corner of his mouth, and he blinked smoke out of one eye. Conte moved the rifle a fraction of an inch to the left.

Chris Amado appeared to be staring directly at him, as if they were facing each other across a dining room table.

Conte worked the action of the Winchester and framed Eddie Turin's forehead at the intersection of the scope's crosshairs. The Jeep had closed to four hundred yards. Conte picked a point on the road about half the distance and waited for the rig to reach it.

Just before it would have, the Jeep veered sharply toward the sunset, downslope toward the alkali flat.

Conte swore. Now the Jeep was moving perpendicular to his position, so Chris was behind Turin and in the firing line. Conte kept his head as the range began to increase. It had become three hundred yards before Conte had an angle he was willing to risk.

He rested his cheek against the rifle's polished walnut stock, tender as a lover, the barrel steady as if it were resting on a sandbag. The back of Turin's head filled the scope. Where the hairline met the neck there was black stubble; Turin had had a bad haircut recently.

The Jeep jounced over a rut, and Conte compensated automatically, presciently.

He drew breath and held, then squeezed the trigger.

The Winchester's stock dug into Conte's shoulder. In the scope the back of Turin's skull imploded and drew into itself. His forehead crashed into the windshield, which dissolved into a glaze of cracks but did not shatter.

Chris lunged across the front seat and grabbed the wheel. The Jeep swerved wildly, nearly tilting up on two tires before beginning to slow.

Vang had the Rover running when Conte scrambled down from the butte. Price was in the passenger seat. Conte dove in the back, and the heavy-sprung rig lurched toward the Jeep.

Chris Amado stumbled out as they pulled up. Her left hand and the whole left side of her face was covered with blood. She was trying to wipe it out of her eyes with her shirtsleeve.

"Jesus." Conte's voice broke. "Chris . . ."

"I'm all right." She gestured toward the mess in the Jeep, and Conte saw where the blood had come from.

Eddie Turin was slumped over the wheel. The bullet had entered in the middle of the back of his head, about two inches above where Conte had aimed, going in at an angle so the disintegrating fragments had taken out most of his jaw. There was a ragged crack in his forehead, and more blood had poured out of it to commingle with the great sluice of blood that still dribbled from where his mouth had been.

There was an acrid smell. Turin's cigarette had fallen into his lap and by some miracle lay on his thigh surrounded but untouched by the puddles of gore. It had burned through Turin's pants and scorched a one-inch line in the flesh of his thigh.

"Nice shooting," Price murmured.

"Right." The sight of blood all over Chris still shook him. He shrugged out of his blouse and tossed it to her. "You're a mess," he said roughly. "Clean yourself up." He wanted to tell her more but didn't know how, not in front of the others. Instead he snapped to Price, "What now? We're wasting time."

Chris was toweling off her hands. "We don't have any to waste, either." She grabbed Conte's wrist and twisted it so she could see the dial of the Rolex. "In forty-six minutes, Bressio is going to blow three acres of prime San Francisco real estate, along with a couple of hundred people, into the bay."

"Tell it," Price ordered.

No one interrupted while she did, and no one spoke for a moment when she was finished. Then Vang went to work while Price outlined the plan.

Vang used the butt of the AK-47 to knock the glass out of the Jeep's windshield, then brushed the shards off the seat. He dumped Turin's corpse in a gully and used a tarp from the rear deck to cover the mess left behind. When Vang cranked the ignition, the motor sputtered and caught. Price took the wheel of the Rover, and Chris and Conte climbed in the rear. When Price slewed the rig around, the centrifugal force tossed Conte against Chris.

He mumbled an apology and added, "Nice job."

"It's not over."

Conte shot her a glance. "It is for you."

"I was in on the overture, and I'll be in on the final curtain."

Price said over his shoulder, "She's right. We're all in the same boat, and everyone has to pull an oar."

Conte scowled and said nothing. But as the Rover came to a stop next to the semi-tractor rig and he started to pile out, Chris lay a hand on his arm.

"Hey," she said softly. "Thanks."

"For what?"

"For caring enough to worry."

Conte snorted.

Chris leaned forward and kissed him lightly on the lips. "Tough guy," she murmured, and jumped lightly, almost gaily to the ground.

Chapter Thirty-nine

The first of the remaining guards on the rim wasn't nearly as incompetent as his two dead buddies. He caught movement, or the flash of sunlight on knife blade as Vang drew it from his belt sheath, and the guy was turning and bringing up his M16 as Vang came on. Vang stiff-armed the gun barrel with his left and jabbed underhand with his right, and the eight-inch, double-edged blade sliced into the guy's navel. Vang jerked up and out, and the guy stared down at the ropes of guts spilling out of the slit.

He managed to scream as he went down.

His partner, a hundred yards farther along the rim, heard the noise, and spun around, squinting for a moment into the sunset backlighting Vang, trying to identify the figure. Vang swung the Ak-47 from where it hung over his shoulder by strap leather, and the guy made up his mind and tried to fire.

He didn't make it.

Vang stroked the trigger of the Kalashnikov, and a three-round burst stitched across the sentry's chest. He threw up both arms, and the M16 clattered to the rocky ground and his body followed it.

In contrast to the twilight desert stillness, the report of autofire was too loud. But Vang was not concerned.

He had no need to be. No one else paid him any attention at all—because a heartbeat later, all hell broke loose in the compound below.

The guy in the guardhouse at the inside end of the defile that led into the fortress looked up uncertainly at Turin's Jeep as it came toward him. He saw the new girl behind the wheel, but there was no sign of Turin. He'd felt envious when they'd driven out together, figuring that Turin would for sure get a piece of that sweet ass somewhere along the line. Guys like Turin always got lucky that way.

Then the gateman saw the semi behind her nearly plugging the narrow canyon. The driver down-shifted. Shit, that rig was supposed to come in hours ago—and who was the guy in the cab with the driver? The Jeep was slowing, and the new girl was giving him a friendly smile.

He came out of the guardhouse as she pulled to a stop and started to say, "How you doing, babe?" when the girl jammed down on the gas and laid rubber away from him. Before he could figure out what to make of that, the semi drew up. The guard took a step back so he could look up to the driver's-side window.

The last thing he saw was the silencer on the muzzle of Matt Conte's .45, before a slug plowed into his brains.

Chris spun the wheel of the Jeep hard right, toward the barred billet at the near end of the barracks. A guy in khaki looked up at the rig barreling down at him and froze for a moment, like a mule deer caught in a spotlight, before diving clear as Chris raced past. The guy hollered something after her, but she couldn't make out the words and wasn't much interested.

Dust rose as she skidded to a stop at the near end of the barred billet, slewing around so the Jeep's nose was aimed back at the compound proper. On the floorboards below the dash, Conte had screwed down two wire loops. The one on the left had a longer wire attached, and Chris used it to hold down the clutch. When she punched down the gas pedal with the heel of her hand, the engine screamed; the second loop held the pedal in place. She jammed the stickshift into first, then unloaded two of the Armalites, slinging one over her left shoulder, holding the other in fire-ready position. The end of the loop wire was in her left hand.

The guy she had almost clipped had made his feet and was running toward her, screaming, "What the fuck do you—?"

Chris jerked on the wire, and the Jeep's clutch popped free. Tire rubber spewed twin rooster tails of gravel before traction took hold, and then the rig was careening forward. The sight of a driverless rig bearing down on him must have unnerved the guy, because this time he wasn't quite so quick. He tried to dive right, but as he did one of the front tires of the

The Pastori brothers were together as usual, half covered by a Jeep parked at the entrance to the tunnel. Chris threw a burst at them, and they ducked back down. The ass end of the Jeep was facing in her direction.

Chris flicked the fire selector to semiauto, sighted at the fat bulge of the gas tank hanging under the end of the rig's rear deck, and squeezed off a shot. For a split-second nothing happened.

Then the gas went with a massive whoosh, liquid flame spewing everywhere. One of the Pastori boys came shooting out of it, completely encased in a suit of fire, screaming like a gut-shot rhino. He managed to run maybe a half dozen steps before he went down, and by then he was only a vaguely man-shaped lump of black.

Chris started to stand, and a line of searing pain slashed across her right side. She stumbled and went down on the bottom step.

She had been shot before, but it was not something you got used to.

She raised her head. Helena Frome looked down on her from the top of the stairs. Her sharp-featured face glowed with triumph. In her hand was the little .32.

"Conte!" Chris tried to shout it, but raising her voice hurt.

"He's in there," Helena said. She came down a few steps. "But he's busy with Bressio. I had a gun on Bressio too, Little Sister. I was ready to off him myself unless your buddy-boy let me go. He didn't have much choice."

Chris touched at her side. An inch above the waist her shirt was torn, and the ragged edges were scorched above a long shallow groove in her flesh. Her fingers came away stippled with blood, and she could feel the warm wetness spreading.

"Help me, Helena." She let her voice crack with pain and helplessness.

"You bitch," Helena Frome exploded. She took another step. "You incredible fucking bitch. You turned me and George. I knew I should have killed you the minute I saw you again. I told them, but they wouldn't listen." She was five risers away. "But there's still time to do the job."

Helena Frome raised the .32 and sighted down the barrel, no more than ten feet from Chris's skull.

The gun roared, and the little slug plinked into wood where Chris had been a millisecond before. She ducked and rolled, slid under the railing, and hit the slope of the wall on her stomach as she brought up the Armalite.

Helena Frome screamed and fired again, and Chris Amado emptied the rest of her magazine into Helena's bony trunk.

The impact carried her back and over the railing. Her head hit the rocks with a sickening thump, and then she began to roll, arms and legs limp as wet wash. Chris regained the stairs as Helena's body tumbled past.

Chris stared for a moment at the crumpled sack that had been Helena. She used the rail to pull herself to her feet and moved on up toward the headquarters building. Each step cost her a spasm of fresh pain in her side.

"Is everyone all right?" Dennison rapped. He looked from Vang to Price to Miss Paradise. Behind them, on what was left of the porch of the barracks, corpses littered the floor and were draped awkwardly over the railing, and blood soaked darkly into the planking.

"There is some kind of tunnel on the other side of the compound," Vang said.

"I spotted it when we came in," Price said. "Storehouse of some kind?"

"That would be my guess," Vang said.

There was the sudden sound of a motor, and a Jeep came shooting around the end of the barracks, carrying two men. Miss Paradise brought up her M16, but before she could get a shot off the semi rig blocked her line of fire. "One of them was Greaves, I think," she said, lowering the rifle. "I got hold of a file photo before we left."

Price was at the end of the trailer. "They tried to make the exit and saw it blocked. They're heading for that tunnel mouth." He gave them a tight grin. "I was just about to look into it anyway."

"Fine, Bill," Dennison said, already moving out. "Meanwhile, we'd better look into Bressio."

* * *

Chris hit the porch of the command house and rasped, "It's me, Conte."

"Everything okay?" Conte's voice called.

"So far."

"Get in here."

Bressio was behind his desk, the telephone at his elbow. He looked calm. Conte stood against the wall, where he could watch his prisoner and the door at the same time. He darted a look at Chris and then back to Bressio.

"Don't look so pleased," Bressio told Chris. He checked his watch. "In four minutes you'll have very little to be pleased about."

"Is that your blood, Chris?" Conte said, watching Bressio.

"This time it is, but it'll wait."

Bressio smiled at them both.

"You are picking up that phone, Bressio," Conte said. "You are calling off your dog."

"I don't think so." For a man with a gun on him, Bressio looked quite pleased. "The only leverage you have is to kill me—but the only way you can stop those bombs is with me alive. I'm the safest man in this camp."

"Do it, Bressio."

"You'd like to kill me, wouldn't you, Conte? It's what you do, isn't it? I imagine you'd also like to settle the score over your friend DeChristi."

There was nothing to that, but Conte did not waste time and breath saying so.

Footsteps sounded on the stairs. Chris dropped the empty magazine from the Armalite's receiver, flipped the speedloader, and slammed the full magazine home. She moved to a corner where she could cover the door and Bressio. But the voice that called out was Dennison's.

"We've taken them," he announced as he came through the door, Miss Paradise behind him. "Vang is standing sentry on the porch, and Bill is mopping up."

Miss Paradise saw the blood soaking the side of Chris's blouse. She took her arm and guided her to a chair in the corner. "I'm okay," Chris protested. "We've got to stop Dial." But she sank into the chair.

"She's right, Dennison said.

"I'm handling it," Conte said. His eyes never left Bressio.

Dennison gave Conte a shrewd evaluating look. "It's up you, Matt," he said calmly.

Conte smiled—and Bressio saw something in that smile, and his own ceased to exist.

"In three minutes," Bressio blustered, "George Dial will detonate those four bombs. You are going to tell me that if I don't make the call that stops him, I'm a dead man."

"That's right," Conte said.

"But I'm a dead man anyway."

"That's right."

Conte's voice was mechanical as a phone company recording, and as frightening a sound as Chris Amado had ever heard, utterly inhuman, the voice of brutality. She knew what he had been, yet seeing this side of Conte laid out so baldly made her skin crawl like fingernails on a blackboard.

"You've heard of the Surgeons," Conte said to Bressio.

Bressio did not reply, but color drained from his face. He had heard of the Surgeons all right.

"The Old Men don't call on the Surgeons too often," Conte said in his icy voice of nothingness. "They don't have to; just knowing the Surgeons exist keeps most folks walking the straight and narrow. Maybe once every couple of years the Surgeons actually go to work. When someone has done something very bad, like to one of the Old Men. When the Old Men have to know something and the person who can tell them this thing is stubborn and tough and stupid. When a made Mafioso breaks *omerta* in a major and dangerous way. Then the Old Men call the Surgeons."

Conte smiled his rictus smile. "Few people have seen the Surgeons in action. I'm one of the lucky ones. You do not forget, believe me. If you don't make that call in the next two minutes, we'll see how much I remember."

Bressio looked away.

"You'll be a dead man sure—but not for two, maybe three days. You'll be alive and awake until then because the pain will never let you retreat into sleep. You'll watch it all, and you won't be able to close your eyes because you'll have no eyelids. You'll see parts of your body come off, and you'll smell your skin burning. You'll swallow pieces of your own flesh. After a while you won't have a nose or lips or fingers or toes, and then you won't have balls or a cock. You won't be able to smell or taste or touch, and then your tongue will come out so you won't be able to scream, and finally wires will go into your eyes and ears, so you won't hear or see. You'll be locked up inside your body, but right up to the end you will feel. You will feel like you have never felt before."

No one moved.

"What time is it?" Conte's eyes drilled into Bressio.

"Seven-twenty-nine," Miss Paradise said.

"Vang!"

Vang came in from the porch. Conte put his hand behind him and said, "Knife," and Vang slapped the haft into his hand.

"Put out your hand," Conte said softly. "Flat on the desk, palm down."

Bressio shook his head, as if denying the devil.

"Put out your fucking hand!" Conte screamed, beyond the point where anyone could stop him.

Bressio saw the madness glowing in Conte's eyes.

Conte hacked the knife blade into the wood of the desk, and Bresso jumped in his seat.

"The hand," Conte hissed.

Bressio moved it, slowly, carefully. It hovered over the table for a moment, then moved on.

Bressio picked up the radiophone headset, waited a few seconds, and began to speak.

William Sterling Price stepped over the drainage ditches cut into the rock floor of the main tunnel and proceeded on to the level section. He was wearing a backpack he had retrieved from the cab of the semi. He stayed close to the wall, but he did not try to keep cover; the tunnel ran straight, and any ambush would come at whatever lay at its end, he figured.

As it turned out, he figured wrong.

He saw the bulk of the Jeep before he heard it, about

thirty yards farther on, where the tunnel flared into some kind of cavern. It looked like a GI rig, but it was virtually noiseless, and it had closed another ten yards when Price realized it must have been refitted with batteries for underground operation. Greaves was in the passenger seat, and the other man was driving.

He was bearing down directly on Price.

The options clicked through Price's mind. The walls were sheer and offered nothing except a place to get pinned. On foot he'd never beat them back to the surface.

The only edge he had was maneuverability—and firepower.

Price brought up the Armalite and put a burst over the rig's hood. As he fired he saw both men duck down behind the dash.

Price stood his ground.

The rig was traveling at a good thirty miles per hour by now, at five yards and closing. He could see the driver peering over the spoke of the steering wheel.

Price feinted left, saw the front wheels turn, and dove right. The Jeep's front bumper missed his ankle by a few inches, and rough rock scraped at his knees and hands as he half went down.

The Jeep skidded into a turn, but Price was up and running for the main cavern, dodging like a running back. A swarm of slugs ricocheted off rock and screamed past on his right.

He made the cavern fifteen yards in front of the accelerating Jeep. What happened next was a product of pure instinct—along with twenty-five years of warrior experience.

Price cut left as he hit the big room, and for a moment the array of six fuel tanks flanking the tunnel cut him off from the Jeep's line of sight. In the same motion he flipped the Armalite over his shoulder by its strap, grabbed the bars of the tank-array's framework, and swung up like a gymnast mounting the uneven bars.

He let the momentum carry him over as the Jeep swerved by below.

"What the fuck?" Greaves screamed, as Price dropped onto the rig's rear deck.

Maybe the driver was a little cooler, or maybe he was expecting something like this—whichever, he was already twisting around with a cocked revolver in his left hand.

Price swung the Armalite free and slammed the butt into the side of the guy's head. The guy's eyes went opaque, and blood squirted out of his ear.

Greaves dove for Price's leg as the driver fell across the steering wheel, and the Jeep swerved wildly. Price stumbled, grabbed the side of the open rear deck as Greaves howled and pitched out of his seat. The Jeep careened on, heading for the rock wall. Price steadied himself, then crawled forward until he could grab a fistful of the dead guy's khakis. Price pulled hard, and the corpse rolled to one side.

The dead man's foot would not come unwedged from the accelerator.

Price dropped the Armalite and bailed out.

He hit on his feet, stumbled, rolled, and came up with his back to the wall.

Greaves was on hands and knees in the middle of the vast cavern. His rifle lay ten feet away, in Price's direction. Greaves looked at the weapon, then at Price. He dragged himself to his feet, and Price took a step toward him.

Greaves turned and half-stumbled, half-ran toward the smaller tunnel on the far side of the massive room. Price dove for his Armalite, but by the time he'd gotten his hands on it he'd lost the guy to the maw of the dark passage.

For a moment there was silence. Then Price heard a dull rumble, like some very large animal's threatening gnar, and immediately after Greaves's terrified scream.

Rock dust billowed from the opening. Price stared, then ran toward it.

The pile of jagged granite rocks was ten feet inside the shaft, and blocked it completely. One of Greaves's hands stuck out from under it.

For a few moments, back in the main cavern, Price looked around, frankly impressed. Not only was it quite a little bag of tricks, but it was also a rather incredible engineering feat.

Price unslung the backpack and began to unload what

he'd need. It was a shame no one else would ever get a chance to admire it.

The man who called himself Frank Bressio had seen the devil come for his soul—or Matt Conte, which right now amounted to the same thing.

He turned the latch of his safe and pulled open the door. Vang took a fistful of his shoulder and jerked him out of the way. Bressio lost his balance and sat down hard on the floor, as Vang began to remove currency and stuff it into a satchel.

At the desk, Dennison hung up the phone and said, "All set."

"You've got what you wanted," Bressio said from the floor. His voice was thin, shaky.

"That's right," Dennison said. Miss Paradise turned away suddenly and went out to the porch, as if Bressio had become pitiful beyond her endurance.

Conte was slumped in a chair in the corner. He looked at Vang's knife in his hands, as if he had forgotten he was holding it, then stood abruptly and offered it to the Hmong.

Vang took it and resheathed it on his belt. The satchel was full enough so he had to tug to fasten its flap. "I think we are done in this place."

"I'm sure we are," Dennison said firmly. He reached down and grabbed Bressio's elbow, pulling him to his feet.

Bressio looked at him. His eyes were wide and haunted. "You don't know," he said. "None of you know."

Dennison transferred his grip to Bressio's wrist and twisted his arm up behind him, then walked him out the door. He waited on the front porch while the People filed out behind him.

Below them, Price emerged from the tunnel and flashed a thumbs-up.

"What are you going to do with me?" Bressio bleated pathetically.

In response, Dennison let go of Bressio's wrist, planted his palm on the man's back, and shoved. Bressio stumbled, tripped over the top step, and went rolling down the first leg of the switchback, his limbs flailing. He tried to stop himself and could not, shooting off the landing and sliding down through the loose rocks of the slope to land in a heap at the bottom.

For a moment Bressio lay without moving. Then he climbed to hands and knees, and then, unsteadily, to his feet. There was blood on his forehead, but a twisted grin below it, as if he had outsmarted them after all. Conte shot a sideways glance at Dennison, but the boss's face was expressionless.

Bressio looked at them and laughed. The sound had nothing to do with mirth, nor with reason or sanity.

Bressio spun on his heel and raced for the tunnel.

Conte took a step toward the stairs, but Dennison put out a restraining arm and shook his head. "It's all right, Matt. It's over for him." He started down the steps.

Below, Conte saw Price step aside as Bressio, oblivious, ran past him into the mouth of the rock-walled passage. Conte started to voice a protest, then decided against it.

By the time Conte reached the Hughes bubblefront parked in the center of the compound, Vang had the rotors turning and the others, except Price, were fastening their safety belts. Conte took the right front seat and strapped himself in.

"I assume he has some kind of back door out of there," Vang said above the mounting engine noise.

"You're probably right," Dennison said calmly.

"Now wait a minute . . ." Conte began.

"Easy," Miss Paradise said. "It's okay."

"But—"

She leaned forward and put her hand over his mouth, very gently. Her fingers were warm against his lips. "Trust me," she said.

The man who had once been Benjamin Creed raced along the tunnel entrance. He was in good physical condition, and his heart pounded more from the adrenaline rush of his brilliant escape than from exertion. From the surface came the faint sound of the copter taking off, and he was vaguely disappointed. They were giving up too easily.

He made the cavern proper, dog-trotting past the body of Greaves's driver, noting the man's smashed face but unmoved by it. He called Greaves's name, without much expectation of a response. He'd seen Price come out of the tunnel and recalled that the man had had something of a reputation in Nam. If Price came out alive, it figured that Greaves was dead. That didn't move Creed either.

The cave-in gave him something of a jolt, however.

He was cut off from the escape shaft, and he swore under his breath—then stopped himself in mid-curse. It made little difference. He could dig through the mess in a couple of hours at most—and besides, it looked like the raiding party had already given up on him.

Benjamin Creed turned and stepped back out into the cavern, and the world came to an end.

It seemed to take a long time. He heard the very beginning of the explosion, but the rest of it happened for him in silence, because the first wave of concussion blew great rending tears in the membrane of both of his eardrums. Above his head, two crisscross fissures etched across the domed ceiling, then grew and gaped to release a cascade of rock slabs big as flatbed trucks. Before they could hit the floor, on the other side of the Big Room the fuel tanks disappeared like a conjurer's illusion, replaced by an angry red flame animal that fed on itself and shot toward him below the falling rock with such speed that he saw his hands and fingers char and turn instantly black.

At the same time the heat seared his eyeballs, so he could neither see nor hear the rock that crushed the life from him like juice from an orange.

William Sterling Price came out of the barred billet leading Albert Hammond by the elbow. Hammond stared around through shocked, uncomprehending eyes, stumbling as Price gently but insistently hurried him along. Conte helped pull the guy into the chopper and dumped him in one of the back seats. Conte saw Miss Paradise pull up his shirt and put a hypodermic needle into a vein at the inside of Hammond's elbow. The crazed eyes dropped shut.

The chopper engine's pitch changed, and it lifted off and circled up out of the canyon's deep-cut bowl. It passed the rim, then hovered. The floor of the canyon was at least five hundred feet below him. Conte stared down into it.

Something came out of the mouth of the tunnel far below,

and Conte saw the giant roiling ball of screaming flame a moment before he heard the roar of the explosion, muffled by the thousands of tons of rock that enclosed it. Next to the rim of the canyon, at a spot above where the cavern would have been, a huge sinkhole opened and swallowed the ground into it, and then the whole cliffside was sliding away into the deep dish that had housed the compound, in a massive avalanche of dirt and brush and granite. Shock waves buffeted the little chopper, and then a mushroom cloud of dust rose from the hole toward them, and Vang pulled up and away and into the western sky.

Dennison looked around the chopper and gave them all his most pleasant smile. "It's over, People," he said softly. "Let's go home."

Dennison's Compound
The 15th of May

"You scared hell out of me." Chris Amado tilted back the can of Miller and finished off the last couple of swallows.

"I scared hell out of myself," Matthew Conte said.

"I thought you'd lost your mind. I was worried."

"That I'd turn on you."

"No," Chris said. "That's not what I was worried about."

He had deliberately ignored the idea that she might have been concerned about him, too. There was an idea that would take getting used to. "I had to convince you," Conte said carefully. "I had to convince everyone in that room. The guy was a pro, Chris. He'd been on the other side of interrogations enough times to know the game the way the big boys play it. He had to believe I was going to start by chopping off his hand at the wrist, and I had to believe it too."

"You would have done it."

"That's right," Conte said, a little hotly. "I'm capable of it, if that's what you mean. If you're afraid that someday I might get so convinced I forget to separate the good guys from the bad, then try not to stand too close."

Chris only shook her head.

From the west came the faint whup-a-whup of rotor blades slapping air, and then Dennison's Bell Executive cleared the ponderosa pines on the far ridge. It skimmed the intervening valley and lowered into the grassy clearing in front of Dennison's headquarters building. Conte and Chris moved to the end of the surrounding forest, out of the propwash. Chris held lightly to his arm, and her hand felt smooth and very warm. The chopper settled past the limp windsock and touched ground, gently as a leaf in autumn. Vang cut the engines, and two passengers ducked out and started toward Dennison, who stood on the front porch with a welcoming smile on his face and Miss Paradise at his right hand. Samuel Stanhope wore a summer-weight charcoal suit, and Elaine Hammond wore a subdued flower-print dress and dark glasses that failed to completely conceal the haggard, strained look on her face.

"How's your side?" Conte asked.

"It was just a flesh wound, as John Wayne used to say." Chris smiled. "It's already mostly healed. It didn't even crack a rib."

Conte watched the two newcomers climb up to the porch. "I learned a lot in the last couple of weeks," he said suddenly. "Dennison opened my eyes—or maybe he just helped me look around. For a long time I haven't given a shit about anything that didn't directly touch me. I thought I had a good reason for being that way. Maybe I did, but there's no point in kicking it around now. The point is . . ."

"What is the point, Matt?"

"I'm confused, and I don't like it. I'm not used to it, and I think it scares me. Look," he went on quickly, as if he had to get it out before he lost his nerve. "There are a lot of creeps walking around out there. I knew that; maybe I was one of them, in a way. But Dennison showed me that a few people can do something about the creeps, and if you're one of the few, you have to try. It has to do with duty and responsibility and caring, and God damn it, Chris, I don't know much about those feelings."

"Don't, Matt, please. It's okay."

"You and Price and Vang have something to believe in. I know what you're going to do with your money from this assignment." Conte smiled ruefully. "You know what I'm going to do with mine? I'm going to spend it, like always."

"You earned it."

"Yeah," Conte said glumly.

Chris touched his arm again, and he felt the same electric warmth. "Give it time, Matt. Nothing comes all at once. But you've already gone through the door, and it's locked behind you. The only way back is straight ahead."

Dennison called to them.

"If you want to talk . . ."

"I don't," Conte said. "I like to keep my mouth shut."

Chris smiled. "The strong silent type."

"Not so strong."

"I like to talk, too," Chris said, "but I also like to listen. Maybe we can work something out."

Conte looked at her for a time before replying. "Maybe we can," he finally said.

The rest of them were already on the porch. The days were lengthening toward summer, and only Stanhope wore a jacket. Miss Paradise was in a full-cut peasant skirt over a shimmering, skintight leotard. Her pale golden hair was wrapped in a bandana, gypsy-style. She looked, as always, magnificent.

More of the tacky lawn furniture had materialized from somewhere to accommodate Vang and Price and the two visitors. Chris dug a fresh beer from a Coleman cooler and flopped into a vacant chaise. Conte chose a canvas-backed director's chair.

"You all know," Dennison began, "how Mrs. Hammond and Mr. Stanhope were involved in our recent case. I felt they deserved a full explanation." He showed his smile to the two guests. "Excuse me for not introducing my four friends by name."

"Get on with it, Dennison." Stanhope was scowling, and had been since his arrival.

Dennison stared at him for a moment, his eyes blank. "When Benjamin Creed volunteered for Vietnam, he was a brilliant, respected, idealistic young officer, totally devoted to his country," Dennison said finally. "When he got there, his idealism ran head on into reality. It's hard to say what makes a man become emotionally unstable, but we know now that for Creed his madness began at about that point. He was sent to help win a war, and he went about it totally and absolutely. He wasn't fighting for any purpose beyond victory; war became his universe.

"This was when the word 'charisma' began to come up in

reference to the man. It was partly deserved; he did have strong personality. But he was also using black market profits to buy his men's loyalty—and in the case of the Quang Hoi massacre, their silence.

"When the war was over," Dennison said, "Creed took the defeat personally. In his mind, everyone else was muddle-headed, completely screwed up—his superiors, the government, the people back home who had protested the war—or simply not served—and the system itself."

"A classic paranoid," Miss Paradise said. "Everyone was crazy except him."

"In any case, Creed really did believe that the system had to be changed, by any means possible, including any amount of necessary force. Creed was insane, sure, but he was also intelligent, tough, and a capable, even extraordinary officer."

"If Creed was such a patriot," Price asked, "how does the Bressio identity fit his ideals?"

"Bressio fit because Creed had no conscientious objection to anything that would help him to his goal. He'd already gone renegade to get money for his scheme—first on the Saigon black market, later with the late Frank Castelli. In that deal, he used his government contacts to expedite illegal arms shipments by providing end-user certificates, which are documents stating a certain legitimate order of armament is consigned to a nation with whom such trade is State Department-sanctioned. Once out of the country the shipments went astray, to whoever paid top dollar."

"What does this have to do with the murder of my children?" Stanhope demanded.

"I'm getting to that. Creed's involvement with Castelli put him in touch with a variety of international creeps, including Mafiosi. Creed figured he could play their game, only better. Even though he considered organized criminals the lowest form of dirt, he rationalized that a little more crime would make no difference. You've got to remember: Creed was morally certain that the threat was absolute and immediate. Unless he did something, and damned quickly, his country as he knew it and wanted to mold it was doomed."

"Why a second identity?" Price asked.

"Creed's name was in too many files; he needed a different one, without a history. It turned out to be a smart move because it allowed him to operate along two separate paths, which he was in the process of merging when we caught up with him. As Bressio, he bought himself a mob, using the money he made before the FBI busted up the gunrunning business. As Creed, he established a paramilitary unit. At first he thought the survivalist movement—he'd been peripherally involved with it—would be a source of recruits. His pitch was that nuclear war was imminent, which in a twisted way was true, since he planned to start one. Therefore any act, including bank robbery and murder, was defensible in the name of living through it. As it happened, the ad attracted only a couple of men who were emotionally disturbed, and it was dropped. The other two who had previously served under Creed were killed before we penetrated." Dennison turned to the woman. "How is your husband, Elaine?"

"The doctors say he may get better. I know he will." Elaine Hammond forced a smile. "For now, he's alive. I have you to thank for that, Mr. Dennison."

"I knew you wouldn't let anyone down, boss dear," Miss Paradise said.

"I'm glad everyone is so pleased," Stanhope snapped. "I wish I could number myself among the satisfied parties. Now I would like to know how this Creed or Bressio or whoever was involved in the murders of my son and daughter-in-law."

"He wasn't," Dennison said. "When that happened, Creed as Bressio had been in New York for several months. He'd recruited men, pulled off a couple of big-money jobs, and got downwind of the Old Men. After DeChristi was murdered and Matt retaliated by killing Bressio's lieutenant, Bressio realized it was time to pull out. The contract he put out on Matt was more smoke screen than anything else; the main thing was to get out of town, and fast. Eddie Turin and the rest of his thugs came along because he paid them a hell of a lot of money, which talks in that crowd.

"But as he was about to leave town, Bressio heard about the orphaned professional terrorists, George Dial and Helena Frome, and decided he could use them and their tactics—for a while anyway, since in his organization everyone was expendable. He offered them sanctuary and a job, and they accepted. Incidentally, using terrorist tactics for organized crime in this country is a damned good idea, which is why I've made certain that very few people will ever know about it."

Dennison looked around at his audience. "Meanwhile, Creed/Bressio was proceeding on several fronts. The Fisk bank job, run by his old partner in crime from Vietnam, George Greaves, was an experiment in using paramilitary tactics for crime and terror, which also turned a large profit. Likewise, taking the photos of the congressman was an experiment in blackmail; although Creed planned eventually to tear down and rearrange the political system, it didn't do him any harm to have a politician under his thumb for the time being. The idea of kidnapping Stern was a combination of the two: Creed planned to profit to the tune of one million dollars, then force Stern to contribute his international influence and top secret knowledge to the master plan.

"There is no doubt that Creed was willing to start a nuclear war, if it came to that," Dennison went on. "The desert compound in Nevada was his interim operations base, but it also served as a retreat, in the event he decided to bring on the holocaust, which he figured to wait out in his private, solid rock shelter."

Dennison leaned back and clasped his hands over his stomach. "How far he might have gotten with his scheme is a matter of speculation. For now, Bressio/Creed is out of the picture, along with the organization he built. It may not be a final solution, but it takes care of business for now."

"How nice," Stanhope said sarcastically. "For all mankind—except for me."

"Oh yes, Mr. Stanhope," Dennison murmured. "I almost forgot. There was a safe in Creed's headquarters. We got it open before we left, but it seems all the money belonged to the First Fisk Trust, so we had to give it back. I guess the ransom you paid has long since been spent."

"I'm not talking about money, Dennison, and you goddamned well know it. I'm talking about our deal: you guaranteed that both the Frome woman *and* Dial would die."

"Some places are beyond even my reach, Stanhope. George Dial is in custody of federal authorities in San Francisco. Once Creed called off Dial, I used his phone myself. Dial was arrested as he came out of the Seaspray Hotel on Beach Street. We'd all like to see him put away for a long time, but you know how it is." Dennison shrugged. "Anything can happen in a courtroom."

"Which is precisely why I never intended Dial to see the inside of one," Stanhope stormed. "I consider you in breach of contract, and I demand a refund."

"You knew the answer to that when you hired me."

Stanhope stood. "You'll hear from my lawyers, Dennison. You're out of business, mister; count on it." Stanhope made a big production out of shooting his cuffs. "I am now ready to leave this place."

"The chopper will take off in fifteen minutes."

"I'll wait inside it." Stanhope stomped down the porch steps.

"You left out a few things, Mr. Dennison," Chris said.

"Did I?" Dennison asked innocently.

"For starters, that scar on your leg."

Dennison shinned up his trouser leg to reveal the dime-sized puckered scar. "I'd forgotten about it." Dennison picked around its edge—and the scar tore off like a bandaid. "Miss Paradise's handiwork," Dennison said. "I think it would have held up under pretty close scrutiny."

"It fooled me," Chris said. "But how did you know Bressio would look for it?"

"I didn't, but it was Stern's only known identifying blemish—he'd discussed the childhood accident in interviews, before the lab accident made him a recluse. Duplicating it, in case Bressio did ask, was elementary tradecraft. Any other questions?" Dennison was enjoying himself.

"Just one," Chris said. "How the hell did you manage to replace Stern?"

"Oh yes," Dennison chuckled. "Good old Charlie."

"Charlie?"

"To his friends," Dennison said. "We go back a long time, Charlie and I."

"I don't care if you go back to Adam," Conte pressed.

"He hadn't left that place for twenty-five years. If the president of the United States had to see Stern, the president came to him. You make one phone call, and the guy clears out."

"I convinced him he had no choice. First, Charlie didn't feel like being kidnapped, but someone had to be. It was the only way to stop Creed, and I showed Charlie it was a matter of national security. He had no choice."

"That's all there was to it?"

"Not exactly." Dennison grinned. "Charlie is a brilliant man in most—but not all—ways. He can carry a model of the international political balance in his head, but it took Miss Paradise to figure out how he could go out in public and still protect the image he was worried would be compromised by the scars covering his neck."

"Which was?"

"I suggested," Miss Paradise said, "that he wear a scarf."

Conte stared at her incredulously.

"That was all there was to it," Dennison said. "What's really funny is that Charlie had a terrific time. It's been so long that no one came close to recognizing him. Now he has a new game: pretending to the public that he's a recluse, while sneaking around among them incognito. He's having a ball."

Dennison rose from his deck chair. "Thank you, my friends." He shook hands with Price, then Vang. He held Conte's a bit longer and seemed about to speak, but did not. He took Chris's hand in both of his, and there was moisture glistening in her eyes.

Price cleared his throat. "I'll be flying out with Vang," he announced. "If you need me, you know where to find me."

"I'll always need you, Bill," Dennison said warmly.

"I'll check out the Bell," Vang said. "I don't think Mr. Stanhope's blood pressure will stand much more of a wait."

Dennison turned his smile on Chris and Conte. "There are a few more things I have to clear up with Miss Paradise—if you have a moment, my dear."

"You're the boss, boss."

"Sometimes I wonder."

Chris took Conte's hand. "Come on, Al Capone. Let's take a stroll."

"What are you going to do now?" he asked as they entered the woods.

"I . . . I suppose I figured there would be more work with Mr. Dennison."

"Will you take it?"

"Of course." Chris paused. "I hadn't thought about it, but now that you bring it up, I guess I know my answer. What about you?"

Conte shrugged. "I've got money again. The only thing I ever knew money to be good for was spending."

"You'll be back?"

"Well sure," Conte said, surprised. "Didn't I just say so?"

"No." But Chris was amused.

"I was trying to."

"Keep trying, tough guy."

Conte looked her over. "Listen," he said. "That spending my money I was talking about—maybe we could do it together."

"Along with a little time?"

"Yeah." Conte put his hands on her shoulders and kissed her lightly on the lips. "I think that would be fine."

"Sorry to interrupt," Dennison said behind them.

Conte let her go. Dennison looked sheepish.

"Chris," he said, "I need Matt for a while."

"If you promise to give him back."

"I do," Dennison said solemnly. He put his arm around Conte's shoulders and walked him back toward the clearing, bending close to speak.

"Matt," Dennison said. "I wonder if I could impose on you for one more day."

San Francisco
The 16th of May

All things considered, George Dial was pleased with the way it had turned out in the heady two months since he had offed the Stanhope dude in the apartment on the via del Gladiatori.

For starters, Helena was dead; they'd told him all about that because they thought it might get to him, help break him down. It did the opposite; he felt relieved, and not much more. Sure, she had been his partner for a long time, but lately he had understood that all she really was was a first-class pain in the ass.

Now there was Chris Amado. Dial stroked the talisman scars. She was waiting for him. Dial knew she was waiting, sure as a priest knows God.

Dial sat in the rear seat of an unmarked black car. His hands were cuffed behind him, and two federal marshals sat on either side. They wore cheap suits and cheaper aftershave, and they had the chiseled, expressionless features of ventriloquist's dummies. They were shitheads.

There was a decent chance he would never go to trial. The evidence against him was circumstantial: he had been careful not to leave prints on the incendiaries, and he'd disposed of the detonator as soon as Bressio called, before they picked him up. If they tried to press the old fugitive charges, he had two of the top criminal lawyers on the West Coast, a couple of characters who wore blow-dried hair and gold chains and loved to see their names in *Time* and *Newsweek*. They were working for nothing, for the chance to be associated with George Dial, the famous old lefty and war protestor.

They were shitheads, too.

Dial laughed, and one of the marshals snapped, "What's so funny, asshole?"

American jurisprudence, Dial thought. *Liberty and justice for all. What a half-assed way to run a country.*

He would be free soon, one way or the other, and Chris Amado would be waiting. If she were not, he would find her. From here on life was going his way—and the first rule was that he was done taking shit, especially from women.

There would be money and power and love—or were power and love the same thing?

There would be more killing as well; that was another important part of it.

The black car pulled to the curb in front of a long, wide staircase leading up to a pillared portico. Four uniformed cops carrying pump shotguns were waiting. The two marshals hustled him out of the car, and the cops formed a flying wedge around him as they hustled him up the worn marble risers.

"I don't know what to say, guys," Dial crowed. "You shouldn't've gone to all this trouble."

"Move your ass," the marshal said.

Jesus, Dial thought, *these guys got great vocabularies.*

It was the last thing to pass through his mind before his head came off at the shoulders.

Blood and bone shards and gray pulp brain matter sluiced over the marshal on Dial's right flank. More splashed on the cop in front of him. All of them were shouting, and then a woman came out of the courthouse in time to see the gory mess that had been George Dial, and she began to scream hysterically. Instinctively the cops in the escort pulled away from the falling body, so that it rolled away from them, thumping down the steps inert as a log, leaving a smear of red behind it. Its momentum carried it across the sidewalk and into the gutter, where it came to rest atop a sewer. When the marshals reached it, the last of its fluids were plop-plopping between the grate.

In a sixth-floor hotel room a half mile away, Matt Conte lay the Winchester .458 on the carpet beneath the window and stood. He tossed his key on the unused bed and locked the door behind him as he went out. In the corridor he stripped off skintight leather gloves and stuffed them in his jacket pocket, and in front of the bank of elevators he pressed "Down."

A bellhop came bursting out of the first car that arrived.

"Someone reported a gunshot," he said. "You didn't hear nothing, did you?" he asked hopefully.

"Yeah," Conte said. "I think I did." He brushed past into the car, and the bellhop gaped at him as the doors shushed shut.

DENNISON'S WAR

We're in a war. We didn't start it and we probably won't finish it, but we're the ones who have to fight the battles.

The world is changing—and I'm doing what I can to change it for the better—but so far the world is going straight to hell. I just like to see the good guys win once in a while.

Most law officers are thwarted by the system. The bureaucracy has become as ponderous as a circus fat lady. The cops are wearing handcuffs now.

My people don't play by cop's rules. We don't deal in technicalities or legal loopholes or due process. We deal in action. The only method we're interested in is the one that works. The only result we're seeking is unconditional success—total victory.

And the battle rages on . . .

CONTE'S RUN

The explosive next adventure
by Adam Lassiter

Vancouver is a man of blood, a mercenary assassin who has blown away government witnesses, business leaders, generals, even heads of state. He's the most lethal killer-for-hire in the world, and he'll work for anyone—anyone willing to pay his half-million-dollar fee. Between assignments, Vancouver doesn't exist. There are no photographs of him, not even a verbal description—Vancouver simply materializes, and someone dies with a bullet in the brain.

Now Vancouver has raised the ante. His latest hit has yielded an unexpected bonus: Melinda Bannister, a voluptuous scientist whose knowledge of top-security U.S. defense systems is worth a fortune to the enemies of the free world. In less than twenty-four hours, Vancouver plans to auction her off to the highest bidder.

Someone has to liberate Melinda before some terrorist butcher gets a chance to pick her brains—and someone has to stop Vancouver for good. But when they call for volunteers, only Dennison's Warriors have the guts to step forward.

This time, Vancouver faces his match: one-time Mafia hit man Matt Conte, dispatched by Dennison to fight his way through a labyrinth of death to breach Vancouver's remote island hideaway. There, in the blistering heat of a tropical jungle, the two deadliest fighting machines on this globe will face off, with freedom riding on every blow.

Only one will walk away.

Cross your fingers that the good guy wins.

(CONTE'S RUN, *the new DENNISON'S WAR adventure hits the stores on February 15, 1985. Watch for it wherever Bantam Books are sold.*)